THE TREK

AN EPIC OF SURVIVAL

JACK L KNAPP

THE TREK

AN EPIC OF SURVIVAL

By Jack L Knapp

BY THE AUTHOR

By the Author:

The Wizards Series

Combat Wizard

Wizard at Work

Talent

Boxed Set, The Wizards Series

Veil of Time

Siberian Wizard

Concrete Angel, a short story in the Wizards Series

The Darwin's World Series

Darwin's World

The Trek

Home

Boxed Set One, the Darwin's World Series

The Return

Defending Eden

The New Frontiers Series

The Ship

NFI: New Frontiers, Inc

NEO: Near Earth Objects

The New Frontiers Series Boxed Set

BEMs: Bug Eyed Monsters

MARS: the Martian Autonomous Republic of Sol

Pirates (forthcoming, 2018)

Short Novel

Hands

Short Story

Ants

THE TREK: DARWIN'S WORLD, BOOK II

To Warren

For all the help

PREFACE

This is book two of a series, Darwin's World, Darwin's World II: The Trek, Darwin's World III: Home, Darwin's World IV: The Return, and Defending Eden.

Darwin's World introduces a number of concepts and characters.

The downtimers are from the future, perhaps the 22nd Century or even later. There may be one group of them or there may be several different groups, and it's not certain that they are working together. Some of the Futurists may have motives that differ from those of the others.

Human civilization of the future is dying. Science has advanced until there are no worlds left to explore or conquer. Human life spans have been extended indefinitely. Disease and planned cell death have been eradicated.

But this is no utopia. People have become bored. Lacking challenge, life has lost its meaning. Few children are being born. The population is shrinking not because of natural death but from boredom. Simply put, people become tired of living and end their life.

A few Futurists are visionary enough to understand that something has been lost from the human character. They hope to use technology to reintroduce what's been lost and save their civilization, their species, from extinction.

Crossing into parallel dimensions is a technology that has been known for some time. There are many dimensions, but all contain versions of Planet Earth. As well as crossing dimensional lines, the technology also allows travel in time. The futurists can visit the parallel Earths of the past but not the future.

One of the parallel timelines contains a version of Earth in which humans did not survive. Proto-humans in Asia died out before they could spread into Africa and begin the long evolutionary path that resulted in Cro-Magnon man.

The Earth of this dimension has been selected for an experiment.

It consists of harvesting humans from the past for transplanting to this parallel Earth. In order not to affect downtime history, only persons in the final stages of life are harvested. They are plucked from death's door in the final moments of life, then treated using modern medical science. A number of changes are made at the genetic level and the bodies are 'reconstituted' as healthy twenty-year-old specimens. They retain their memories and skills as well as a suite of implanted memories that will help them to survive after transplanting.

The transplants receive a young, healthy body but little else. Women are transplanted in groups of three and given shelter and a crossbow to better fit them for survival; men are transplanted singly with no one to rely on but themselves. They have a knife and camp-axe, slightly larger than a hatchet but smaller than a woodsman's axe. Those, and the clothing they wear, are the only advantages they have when they arrive. Their memories and implanted knowledge may eventually be of help, but the first task is to survive as best they can. They will receive no further assistance from the Futurists.

The Futurists hope the descendants of such transplants will have a highly-developed survival instinct, as well as the curiosity and ambition that mankind has lost.

The experimental subjects are made aware of what has happened to them. They understand that they are responsible for their own survival.

This is ultimate freedom; live or die, succeed or fail.

The transplanted persons are placed into a time that corresponds to the late Pleistocene of the Futurists. Transplants occur at selected spots around the planet, all within a zone lying between the 45th degree of north and south latitudes. The climate is temperate for the time, and transplants occur in late spring or early summer.

The late Pleistocene of Darwin's World resembles that of the Futurists' Earth in that the ice sheets have retreated. Glaciers still exist so temperatures tend to be cooler. Animals are plentiful and many are huge; mammoth, mastodon, giant ground sloth, and stag-moose are representative. Smaller animals similar to those existing downtime also flourish.

There are predators too, and some of them have evolved to prey primarily on the megafauna: saber-toothed cats, giant short-faced bears, dire wolves.

It is a harsh world, but humans had lived and flourished in such conditions uptime on the Earth of the Futurists. Armed principally with determination, those early humans had the ability to use stone, bone, and antler to fashion tools and weapons.

What nature had failed to give them they provided for themselves. Blades of flaked stone substituted for claws and teeth. Like wolves and lions, they organized and hunted in packs using numbers and organization to substitute for the speed and strength they lacked.

Tribes grew and populations spread. Humans soon lived in the

Americas, Eurasia, Africa, and Australia of this time, as well as on a number of islands.

Emulating nature, these are the locations selected by the Futurists for transplanting.

Some transplants failed and people died. Knowledge is often not enough; skill is also needed, and that is gained through experience. Determination counts. Experience grows, but learning comes from mistakes survived. An element of luck also enters the mix; life or death often happens by simple chance.

Transplants are soon spread across Darwin's World. They adapt and learn; some survive. Their descendants will become transplants into the overly-evolved world of the Futurists. They will be selected, extracted, educated, then released in the hope that they can revive a dying civilization. Such is the plan.

There are no laws on Darwin's World, other than what people make for themselves. There is no civilization, no culture. If they are to exist, the transplants must invent them. When children are born, the transplants must protect and educate them. They must choose from their memories which elements of downtime society they wish to retain and which they will discard.

They have among themselves the knowledge of history, written by humans who came before. They know of the great cultures of downtime Earth...but how many of these are useful in a world that's savage beyond anything known to humans of historic time?

Some of the predators on Darwin's World are human.

PROLOGUE

Pavel was waiting near the front of the column when Lee approached.

"Pavel, I want you guarding the left flank when we move out. Get food from the kitchen and move ahead where you can watch as we leave camp. Stay off to the left, keep a watch for danger and if you see tracks, let me know. We can send out hunting parties as soon as it looks worthwhile."

"Do it yourself, kid. I'm busy with my group this morning, and later on I plan on looking in on the group you've been with. I won't have time to wander around in the woods because you think it's a good idea."

Robert had come up while this was going on. He watched, waiting to see how Lee would handle this.

"Pavel, you were told before. Do what you're told, work for the group, or take your stuff and hit the trail. Go anywhere except where we are. That's still the only offer you've got; you're flank guard or you're out. We'll leave without you."

"Suppose we just keep up with the rest of you. We've been doing that and we can keep on doing it."

"Not you, Pavel. You've been a little slow to understand, so I'll lay it out in a way that even you can't mistake. We'll go on, you won't. If that means we leave you dead alongside the trail, so be it."

While speaking, Lee had unslung the heavy spear that always hung across his back. The long, sharp blade now pointed directly at Pavel's eyes from less than a foot away. He turned pale and took a step back.

"You would kill me because I won't pull your guard duty?"

"No. I'll kill you because you're eating our food and not doing your share of the work."

Robert asked, "Pavel, does this mean you're leaving?"

"No, Robert, I'll do the guard if that's what you want. But this kid has no right to be giving orders! I've been part of this tribe for a long time. Why is *he* giving commands?"

"He commands because I trust his judgment, Pavel. Matt and I delegated that authority to him. It's his until I decide it should go to someone better qualified. I don't know anyone better qualified." Robert looked squarely at Pavel, who simply turned and walked away.

* * *

ROBERT GOT the family groups moving. Travel would be slower; everything now moved by travois and backpack.

He missed Matt. It was not easily explained, but the man had exuded confidence. You simply knew that whatever came up, Matt would deal with it. It was hard to believe he was dead.

Briefly, Robert wondered how Gregor and Vlad had found Matt and

Pavel. Coincidence? They were all traveling in the same direction, after all, so it was possible.

* * *

PAVEL CAME into camp late that afternoon and decided to look in on the women that had been part of Matt's group. They now cooked for themselves rather than sharing the communal kitchen. Did they have treats hidden away?

"Pavel, you should be over at the kitchen. They'll be shutting down soon and if you don't eat now, you won't get anything before morning," Lilia said.

"I came over to get to know you ladies better. We need to work together now, right? So I thought I'd have my dinner with you. What are you making?"

"Just enough for ourselves. We're family. We'll be cooking for ourselves and taking our meals with family members."

"Still, there are four of you women. You'll need men around to help you."

Pavel felt a sudden coldness beside his ear. He reached up absently to brush it away...a bit of snow, perhaps...but froze when he felt the sharp tip.

"I wouldn't turn my head just now if I were you. Sandra's pretty good with that spear. And if she's not, you might spare a glance for Millie."

Millie stood relaxed, spear across her body but ready to be used with no wasted effort.

"I'll go, I'll go! There's no need for threats! I was just trying to be helpful, like."

"We don't want your help. You might remember that; next time, the lesson will be more pointed. The kitchen is right over there," Lilia pointed. Her expression might have been amused.

After they finished the meal, she spoke to Lee.

"I'm not satisfied with Pavel's story. Matt slipped, but somehow lost his parka and weapons? What happened to his bow? He also had a backpack and a quiver of arrows. What happened to those? How could Matt lose his parka while he was wearing a belt and quiver strap over it? If he had taken them off, there was no reason Pavel shouldn't have brought them back. And why were Gregor and Vlad even there? They should have been a mile or two away across the river.

"Their story is just too pat. I think they ambushed Matt and killed him. I'm going to backtrack Pavel. The three of them have about as much regard for hiding a trail as a mammoth! Maybe they left evidence, maybe even his body.

"I'll look around for a while, but eventually I'll come back and catch up. I don't' like the thought of him just lying alongside the river and no one to even look for his body. Explain what I'm doing to Robert, but not until tomorrow. I don't have time to argue with him and I don't want Pavel to know. I'm leaving tonight after dark and I'll be back in about a week."

* * *

THE COLD WOKE HIM. He was lying on a sandbar where he'd been left behind as the water receded. He was wet, shivering, and his right eye was glued shut.

He pawed at it, trying to open the eyelid, then washed his face and in the process found a large bump over his eye. Where had that come from?

Washing removed the crusted blood and he got the eye open. Blearily, he closed it again for a moment; opening it, he saw two images of the small tree that leaned over the bank. He closed the eye again and felt better.

He had a severe headache and the lump was sore, but at least it wasn't bleeding.

Muddy, shivering, he crawled off the sand into a pile of grass. Blown flat during the winter, left ashore when the river's spring flood receded, it slowly decayed on the river's bank. He crawled into the drift and pulled the grass around him.

He needed fire, but that would have to wait until he could see better. He had lost his parka, but the grasses would help. He pulled handfuls and stuffed them inside his shirt. They prickled, but he added more. Presently the shivering abated.

He found the small pouch of materials at his waist and opened it. There was a roll of string, a small flint knife, and a scrap of steel. The tinder was wet, useless, but he could find more.

He pulled more e grass and made a pile of it. Judging finally that he had enough, he pulled off his wet clothes and wrung them out as best he could. Naked, he crawled into the grass and burrowed in until he began to feel warmer.

He was hungry, cold, and exhausted, but no longer shivering. It took only moments for him to fall asleep.

A man stood before him in his dream and said, "Your name is Matt."

1

L ilia walked slowly through the camp. Sleeping sites had been arranged in two parallel rows on each side of the row of sleds. The kitchen, now deserted, had been set up in the middle between the rows. Families with children occupied the sites immediately before and after the kitchen. Others had taken sites close to friends.

There had been little socializing this evening. Pavel's news had spread quickly and the tribe had discussed it briefly among themselves. After that, conversation lagged and everyone bedded down early. There was a lot of work to be done tomorrow and they would need to be rested. Friends died, the rest had to move on with their lives.

She waited at the edge of camp for the sentries to pass. They circled the small camp every half hour or so and she didn't want to attract attention. Lee and the others from her camp already knew she was going and the rest would find out soon enough. She intended to be well on her way before that happened.

Most of the snow had melted. The ground was slippery where the sleds had passed so she moved away from the tracks, remaining close to the trail but not walking on the disturbed ground.

Even so, the ground beside the tracks was also muddy and she slipped a number of times. Finally, she gave up and picked a tree to climb. She would spend the night in the tree and go on in the morning. It was unlikely that anyone would miss her immediately. Robert might ask, but since she routinely made the rounds from camp to guards to kitchen to help as needed, it would probably take some time before he noticed.

In any case, the rest of the tribe would be occupied packing and moving on. There would be travois to build and no one would have time to look for her.

She unstrung her bow and slung it across her back with the quiver as she climbed the tree. A large branch projected from the trunk some twenty feet up, and there were limbs extending from the branch that would provide a place for her to lie back in relative comfort.

A safety rope attached her loosely to the main branch and she settled down to sleep. She was wrapped in her parka against the chill and had pulled up the hood to cover her head. Her bow and quiver lay beside her across two of the limbs and the small pack she'd been carrying cushioned her head. If the tree wasn't as comfortable as her sleeping furs back at camp, well...she'd slept in more uncomfortable places. She ate a piece of jerky on a slice of bread and drank from her water gourd before falling asleep.

She woke up once during the night. Something moved through the forest below; the animals were moving back north. She thought it was a deer, but it might have been something else. She had nothing to fear from it, whatever it was, and she was soon asleep again.

* * *

MATT WOKE up thirsty and sore. He crawled out of the pile of drifted grasses he'd slept in and continued the few yards down to the river. The water level had gone down considerably. The bank remained muddy and he slipped near the water's edge, saving himself from a dunking only with difficulty. Had he walked instead of crawling, he would almost certainly have fallen into the water.

He drank, waited a moment, and drank again. The water was muddy but he washed his face and immediately felt better.

Matt crawled slowly away from the water after drinking. He was shaky but able to stand by holding onto a tree. Waiting until he felt secure, he took a few experimental steps before examining his surroundings.

Both eyes were clear and fortunately, he was no longer seeing double. Reflexively, he rubbed at the barely-swollen lump on his forehead. It was still sore, but that would pass.

He brushed off the sticky grasses that clung to his body. Shaking out his deerskins, he pulled them on. They were clammy and cold, but not as dripping-wet as when he took them off. The skins stretched and soon felt warmer as he moved around.

He needed food. Nearly equal in importance was the need for weapons. He hadn't seen animals before winding up in the river...he still had no idea how that had happened...but there might be something else to eat. Plants had just barely begun to green up, so there would be no fruit or even leaves from sprouting plants just yet. There might be roots from cattails growing in the river, but he wouldn't be able to get to those until the water level went down.

But there were always insects or larvae. There might be fish in the river too. He'd caught them before by using hooks and weirs for fish-traps. He could do so again.

The sky was clear and the sun was well up. He had no idea how long he'd slept, but the sleep had helped him recover from the injury and near-drowning.

Bits of grass still stuck to his deerskins and some of the grass rubbed and prickled at his skin. For the moment, he could tolerate the itching; he had no urge to expose himself to the cold by removing his clothing again. Perhaps it would warm enough later for him to strip and vigorously brush away the grasses that he'd missed earlier. He could shake the deerskins and get rid of most of the grass, then brush off the rest. Even dare a quick swim to get the mud and grass off?

But getting clean would have to wait; it was time to forage for something to eat. Grubs would serve for now and he could use the cord in his emergency pack for a fishing line. When he spotted the first signs of small animal activity, he could unwrap the rawhide handle of his small flint knife and put out snares.

He found a dead log, downed a year or more ago. Insects had been burrowing under the bark, so he used a stick to lever a section of the bark free. Under the bark he found a dozen white grubs. They might have been round-headed larvae of woodboring insects, the things that woodpeckers seek when they hammer at the bark of dead trees.

Hunger was a problem, but eating more insects than his gut couldn't tolerate would be much worse. He pinched off the black heads and ate a half-dozen of the grubs, then waited to see if they'd stay down. While waiting, he used his flint knife to make a gorge hook. One of the remaining grubs would serve as bait for a fishing line while he waited.

A short length of his precious cord was cut off to make a sinker-line. He tied this around a rock he'd found lying beside the riverbank. The other end of the line he knotted to the longer fishing-line made from the cord in his emergency kit.

One end of the longer line was tied around a circular groove he carved in the middle of the gorge hook. The other end he tied to a small tree on the bank.

The two ends of the gorge hook were sharpened, designed to catch in the stomach and turn sideways after a fish swallowed the bait. The ends would then catch in the stomach's walls and prevent the hook from coming out while he pulled the fish ashore.

Threading a large grub onto the gorge hook, he tossed the rock sinker into the river. The fishing line tightened and the bait sank beneath the surface.

While the grub enticed fish, it was time for Matt to see what weapons could be contrived. There was a large rock on the riverbank that had washed down in some past flood. After a short search, he found a solid branch, broken off by ice buildup and strong winds during the winter. It would do.

His strings and rope had been made from plaited fibers, extracted from leaves and grass stems. Neither source was available this early in the season, but flexible roots would do until he could begin making more cord.

He found several thin ones where the soil of the riverbank had been washed away in the flood. Being as careful of his flint knife as possible, he cut the roots, then used them as crude cord to bind the rock to the tree branch. He felt better immediately; he had a real weapon now! If a cat should try to climb a tree after him, it would get a facefull of rock!

He checked his fishing line but felt nothing tugging back. Had the bait wriggled free? He pulled in the line and the grub was there, but a fresh one might be better. He loosened more bark from the dead tree and selected the largest grub he could find. The newly-baited hook went back into the river to wait for a bite.

The club was good, but a spear would be better. Two methods occurred to Matt; he could bend a small tree over, then use the club to batter the trunk until it broke. The shattered end could be trimmed into shape, sharpened, and hardened in a fire. For that matter, he could use fire or coals to *cut* the tree.

He went back to the tree he'd been extracting grubs from. Should he eat more? He decided to wait; the physical activity had lessened his hunger. It was still there but now only a dull ache which he could easily tolerate. He'd known hunger pangs before.

Using his club, Matt crushed a section of bark that still remained on the dead tree. He carefully peeled this free and beneath the bark was the powdered cambium layer, mixed with a sawdust-like material left behind by the roundheaded borers. It would catch fire readily. The powder would serve as tinder and the splintered bark could be added as soon as the first flames appeared.

Holding the steel scrap from his emergency kit in his right hand and the flint knife in his left, he struck the heel of the flint with the steel. Glancing strokes released a few sparks and he waited impatiently for one to ignite the tinder.

A number of the sparks vanished into the tinder before Matt saw the first wisp of smoke. He carefully blew on the tiny coal and it grew brighter, then the first tiny flame appeared.

Matt gathered more wood and piled this near the fire, adding it to the small amount he'd gathered from the downed tree. Small branches fed the little fire and soon it had grown to respectable size.

Matt left the growing fire to check his fishing line. A tentative pull on the line was answered by a strong tug back so Matt carefully pulled his catch ashore. A large, thrashing catfish soon lay gasping on the muddy bank.

A quick tap from the stone club ended the gasping. Quick cuts of the flint knife removed the spikes from the dorsal and pectoral fins; Matt knew by experience how painful a wound those fin spikes could inflict! He gutted the fish and removed the head, an easy task using the sharp flint knife. Those ancient ancestors had clearly known a thing or two!

Using a pointed stick to the fish over the coals, Matt transferred some of the burning sticks to the base of a small tree. He added more sticks, arranging them around the tree. The small fire spread.

Keeping an eye on the fire, Matt removed his fish from the coals. The fish barely had time to cool before he began stripping flesh from the bones.

Gathering up the head and the bones, he threw these into the river. The guts he kept; they'd be good bait for his gorge hook. The rebaited hook, removed from the fish when he gutted it, soon went back into the river.

Matt tended the small fire around the tree, piling the coals as close as possible. He attempted to twist the trunk free, but decided it was too soon. Adding more wood, he settled down to wait.

His full belly, combined with exhaustion, made him drowsy. He fought off the feeling and waited for the tree to burn through. A large pile of fallen wood waited. The spear was a defensive weapon primarily, but fire was an excellent defense too. Tonight Matt would sleep in relative warmth and safety, with a fire in front and another behind.

A last check of the fishing line brought in another catfish, somewhat larger than the first. He gutted this one and left it hanging from a branch near his fire.

The tree finally burned through and Matt laid it near the fire. Safe and warm between his fires, breakfast assured, and with a tree that he could make into a weapon tomorrow, Matt slept.

* * *

ROBERT WOKE up early and roused the camp. Lee was already up, munching on bread and a chunk of dried meat as he checked on the guards. Breakfast was grab-and-go, mostly jerked meat and bread baked the previous night washed down by water.

Breaking down the sled loads into packs, then arranging straps to carry them took longer than expected. Robert fretted; he had hoped to get at least ten miles farther on before night, but soon revised that estimate. There was simply too much to do.

Finally, shortly before noon, the tribe abandoned the sleds and straggled on their way. Robert shook his head at the confusion, but realized there was nothing to be done. They'd soon settle into the new form of travel.

Lee took charge as they moved away. He had a scout ahead and two others flanking the group, watching for danger and for any animal they might add to their food supply.

Laz and Millie worked together, each pulling one branch of a heavily-laden travois. This contained their sleeping furs as well as a share of the tribe's food. Sandra and Cindy followed, backpacks filled with the rations they'd eat during the day.

Robert noticed the small group late in the afternoon and wondered where Lilia was, but he was too busy at the time to do more than wonder. But there was no sign of Lilia during the day.

He found Lee when the tribe stopped for the night.

"I didn't see your mother today. Is she all right?"

"She decided she didn't believe what Pavel and his two cronies said, so she took off to backtrack them. She thinks Pavel and his gang ambushed Matt and killed him. She'll find out; she's a good tracker, and if possible, she'll find Matt's body.

"If his death wasn't accidental...Robert, just keep out of my way. I'll settle Pavel once and for all, and if his little gang gets in the way I'll do them too. That's assuming my mother doesn't beat me to it. She's no pushover; I watched her stick swords into a short-faced bear after it clawed me and broke my arm."

Lee thought for a moment before continuing.

"You *don't* want her angry at you. I've acknowledged your authority as leader, but in this matter I'm not willing to defer. I'll do whatever seems right at the time."

"You won't be alone, Lee," said Robert. "I'll be there with you, and probably Marc and Philippe will too. Laz won't be hanging back either. He liked Matt a lot, we all did.

"Pavel has few friends outside his gang of five. I don't favor hanging. We'll use the closest thing to a firing squad we've got, execution by arrows or spears."

Lee nodded, not convinced, but willing to wait for now.

* * *

ROBERT WASN'T the only one who noticed Lilia's absence. Vlad realized that two different women now brought up the rear of the tribe as they moved. He remarked on this and Pavel took a walk past where her group was camped. Lee, Laz, Cindy, Millie, and Sandra were there, but no Lilia.

Pavel watched for some time, making sure. She wasn't with her own small group, so that meant she'd left the camp. Why would she leave, and where would she go?

He continued to muse on this and finally brought up the subject to the men of his group. The women were away, visiting other women in the camp. This made it easy for Pavel to tell the men what he'd found. The women might gossip; the men wouldn't.

"Lilia's gone," Pavel said. "She must have gone last night. I saw her yesterday, but she wasn't following behind us this morning and she's not in her camp now. Anyone see her today?"

He waited, but no one said anything.

"So she's left the camp and I can't think of any good reason why she would do that. There's only one place she'd have gone; I think she's gone back to look for Matt.

"She won't find his body, that's miles downstream by now. But she might find his bow and quiver. Maybe his spear too. I knew too many questions would be raised if we brought those back, but we probably should have thrown them in the river. Having his parka and his weapons belt was dangerous enough, but I thought it was worth taking the chance. After we dumped the body, I just wanted to get away so I didn't take time to pick up his gear and brush out our tracks. I never expected anyone to go back and look for the site!

"Robert and Lee may also be suspicious, but they don't have any witnesses. It's been a couple of days now, but there might still be signs where we dragged him to the river after I clubbed him. Anyway, if Lilia finds the bow and spear she'll know she found the right place. If she's good at reading sign, she'll know too much.

"We've got to go after her. We have to kill her before she can tell the others."

2

"Lee?"

"What's up, Philippe?"

"There's an animal up ahead. Keep your voice down."

Lee whispered, "What kind of animal?"

"It's one of those big ones. That stag-moose thing? But I can't be sure. It doesn't have any antlers, but the color's right. It's tan with pale spots."

"OK, I'll be right with you."

Lee grabbed his spear and bow where they leaned against his pack. The tribe had begun setting up evening camp, laying out sleeping furs and arranging the kitchen. Some of the women had headed into the forest to scavenge for downed firewood.

Whether they had weapons with them was questionable; despite his admonitions to always go fully armed, many 'forgot'.

He slung the spear across his back; it might not be needed, but he never left camp without it. Selecting one of his few steel-pointed arrows, he nocked it. Ready, he silently followed Philippe away from camp.

Philippe paused for a moment, then whispered, "Marc is keeping an eye on it. It's browsing and doesn't look alarmed at all. I don't know if it even spotted us. Anyway, he's ahead in that clump of brush. I think we might be able to get a shot if we sneak up. Maybe if all three of us shoot, we can bring it down and won't have to follow a blood trail. That thing is big!"

"Have your bow ready, Philippe. We may not have much time. If it sees three of us, it might run."

The animal, probably a stag-moose as Philippe had guessed, was engaged in biting off the new leaves that had begun sprouting from branches as the weather warmed.

Lee watched for a moment, then signaled Philippe and Marc. By gestures he indicated that he would take the first shot and they should launch as soon as he released his arrow. They nodded understanding and made ready.

He watched a moment longer. The browsing animal, a doe or a stag that had dropped its antlers during the winter, fed contentedly on the tender shoots.

Lee usually tried to put his arrow into the body; an area behind the forelegs was best. If the arrow struck a little high, it would pass through the lungs. If it struck low, it would penetrate the heart. Either wound brought death in moments. But this animal was almost face-on. The head blocked the only other good shot, between the shoulders into the body cavity. The shot would kill because of blood loss, rather than vital organ damage. An animal this large might run more than a mile with an arrow wound that missed the heart and lungs before finally bleeding out.

The only other shot that might result in an immediate kill was a brain shot.

But the head was moving as the animal browsed. Even if it stopped, the target area was small. The arrow would need to go in below the crown ridge at the top of the skull, the thick bony support for those magnificent antlers which grew late in spring. If the arrow went too low, it would strike the nasal bones. In either case, there was nothing lethal behind those bones.

But the tribe needed meat; he would have to try the brain shot. Taking a deep breath, he half drew the arrow back and slowly rose to his feet, partially turned away from the stag-moose. As soon as he had solid footing and balance, he drew the arrow back and anchored it to his cheek.

Marc and Philippe watched, ready, waiting until they had a target. The animal would move as soon as Lee launched his arrow.

The stag-moose might have seen Lee, but if so it showed no sign of alarm. It continued browsing as he set himself for the shot.

Lee had been holding his breath since he rose to his feet. Now, braced and ready, he released some of the air and loosed his arrow. His right hand automatically reached for his quiver and extracted a second arrow.

The shot went slightly higher than intended, but if it struck the bony crown ridge it was deflected downward. It now stuck, quivering, from the front of the animal's face. The stag moose staggered, then dropped. As it fell, two other arrows punched into the body, entering between the shoulders.

They were probably not needed, Lee thought, *but it was good for Marc and Philippe to share in the kill.*

"Marc, give me a hand field-dressing this fellow. Philippe, run back and get help. We'll let someone else do the skinning and butchering. Tell Robert to send up a couple of the travois. We'll take everything we can use, heart, lungs, liver, kidneys too. Roasting sections of the lungs will be a treat for the kids. And thanks, you two. You did great!"

The two smiled at the praise. Philippe turned and ran toward the camp while Lee and Marc slit the belly skin, preparing to open the body cavity so the carcass could cool.

* * *

PAVEL and his three companions knew nothing of this. They'd left the camp an hour before, slipping into the forest before the sentries were due to begin watch. Now, they trotted single-file along the drag marks, following the trail left by the travois. Each carried a bow with ready arrow and each had a spear slung across his back. A small fanny pack carried their water gourds and a supply of food.

With the excitement of the kill occupying the tribe's attention, no one noticed their absence.

* * *

ROBERT BROUGHT a travois to where Lee and Marc were working, now skinning the animal. Half the skin had already been peeled back to provide a clean place to lay the internal organs. The body cavity was empty, except for pooled blood that hadn't drained out. The intestines were gone, dragged away by Lee as Marc began skinning.

Colin, following Robert, had brought his cleaver along. Waving Marc aside, he took over the butchering task. An efficient chop split the pelvis, allowing the lower carcass to spread. He completed the job by chopping through the breastbone where the ribs joined. The cleaver made short work of quartering the splayed carcass and separating the neck from the head. Preliminary work finished, he began dividing the carcass into easily-managed cuts. Lee watched in awe. He'd butchered a number of animals, but Colin had a professional's skill.

A steady stream of people showed up and began carrying cuts of meat and organs back to camp. Colin followed the last load of meat; he needed to build a fire and begin preparing some of the fresh meat for supper. The tribe had been living on dried meat and vegetables for months now, and while those foods had kept them alive and healthy more was needed.

They would eat well tonight and tomorrow morning. If they were late taking the trail, so be it; a real breakfast would be cooked and eaten tomorrow morning before the tribe left camp.

* * *

PAVEL'S GROUP passed through shade and dappled sunlight as they trotted alongside the trail. The sun was setting, so they wouldn't be able to follow the trail much longer. Spotting a small hill south of the trail, he led them to the top where they would camp for the night. The ground would be dry up there and there should be plenty of downed wood. They would build a fire for safety and sleep until dawn.

"Gregor and Vlad, collect firewood. I'll build a fire and we'll overnight here. Tomorrow morning we head northeast until we reach the trail. With a bit of luck, we'll find Lilia's tracks by noon. We'll need to slow down after that and make sure we don't lose her trail. If we do, we know she's going to the river; we can pick up her tracks there and still catch up to her before dark.

"I'll take first watch. Vlad, you'll take second and Nikolai will have third shift. Gregor, you've got the dawn watch. Wake me as soon as you can see the ground. We'll eat on the way.

* * *

THEY ATE their scanty meal the next morning as they followed the tracks and drag marks.

"Pavel, none of us brought much to eat. We're going to have to find something or we'll be hungry by tonight."

"I couldn't bring much either, Gregor. I got all they'd give me yesterday morning, but it was supposed to be for a day only. If we don't catch up to Lilia by this afternoon, we'll have to hunt. It's warm enough now that the animals should be moving back. Maybe we can get a deer. If not, we can set out lines and catch fish when we get to the river.

"We'll add as much food as possible to what we brought, then go after her. It's going to take her at least one more day to find where we dumped the body, so I think we've got plenty of time.

"If she turns back before she gets to the river, we just let her go. She won't have found anything. We'll need to keep going though, just in case, and dump his bow and arrows in the river. The spear too, if we can find it. Brush out the tracks and drag marks, then catch up to the tribe.

"If anyone asks where we went, we just went hunting because the tribe was short of meat. Everyone got that?" He got three grunts in return, all the trotting men were able to spare. Pavel would have to call a break soon. If not, his poorly fed men wouldn't be able to keep going.

By midday, Pavel had slowed to a walk. His three followers showed signs of balking even at the slow pace, but at least the river was only a few hundred yards ahead. Something might have come down to drink, and anyway their water gourds needed refilling.

* * *

LILIA'S TRACKS had left the trail half a mile back; the exhausted men hadn't noticed.

She had recalled what Matt had said, that he and Pavel would go south. Pavel and his two followers would have come from that direction when they rejoined the tribe. She reasoned that she could save time by taking a more-direct path from the trail to the river, then pick up their tracks somewhere south of there.

As it happened, she crossed their trail only a short time later. Three men had traveled northwest together, their tracks overlapping in places; she realized that this didn't jibe with what Pavel had said, that Vlad had remained behind to look for Matt's body. The evidence simply didn't support that claim, meaning Pavel had lied.

Following the tracks, she found Matt's steel-bladed spear. There was no mistaking it; that spear had stood beside the cabin door for months and she'd watched Matt use it a number of times. If Matt had indeed fallen into the river, how had his spear come to be left here, leaning against a tree? Had Pavel's men ambushed him here? But there was no bloodstain on the ground and no sign of a struggle.

Curious; the tracks didn't make sense. Why carry a spear this far, only to abandon it beside the trail?

Lilia picked up the spear, absently stroking the smooth wood as she thought about her find. The river was some three hundred yards ahead. She slung the spear over her shoulder and followed the trail to the river.

She spotted a disturbed section of ground about thirty yards back from the river. Searching the ground carefully, she found where a small amount of blood had sunk into the dirt. Circling, examining the ground for more evidence, she found several arrows where they'd fallen out of Matt's quiver. A short time later she found his bow, still strung, lying beside the quiver containing the rest of his arrows.

She unstrung the bow...it took all her strength to bend the limbs enough to release the string...and slung it across her back with Matt's spear. Picking up the spilled arrows, she replaced them in the quiver before adding it to her growing load.

Lilia soon found a trail joining the one she'd been following. This had been made by two men coming south along the river. It hadn't made by Matt and Pavel; she knew Matt's tracks. Could this have been made when Vlad and Gregor joined Pavel?

A faint trail led to the river. Two men had made it, and their deep tracks showed they carried a heavy load. They had stopped briefly near the river; the tracks were muddled from their moving about. From here, the tracks walked beside drag marks to a spot well back from the water's edge.

She worked out the meaning of the tracks. The two had likely been carrying Matt's body, perhaps after he'd been shot from ambush. The small amount of spilled blood meant he'd probably died instantly.

She glanced at the bloodstain and felt a tear spill down her cheek. Angrily she wiped it away; there would be time enough to weep for Matt after she'd stuck her spear into Pavel. As for his accomplices, arrows would do just fine for them but she wanted to see Pavel's face when her spear went into his guts.

No tracks led downstream. She wondered briefly why the drag-marks had stopped where they were, then realized that the river had been much higher when they crossed it three days before.

Perhaps Matt's body had hung up on driftwood? Lilia looked downstream and decided she could spare a few days to look for his body. She had no means to give him a proper burial, but at least she would find closure from having seen his body.

But his weapons were heavy and would slow her down. Looking around, she found a projecting limb a hundred yards downstream from where the murder had occurred. She would keep the spear for now. Her own lighter spear had been left with Lee for safekeeping, so Matt's spear would be useful. She hung the bow and quiver over the limb, then headed south, following the river.

Not the same thing, of course, but having that heavy spear slung across her back made her feel as if Matt walked with her.

* * *

PAVEL and his small gang surprised a foraging raccoon near the river. Two of their three arrows struck the small animal and killed it. The third arrow missed and was lost in the river, while Nikolai never got a shot off.

They soon had the raccoon gutted and skinned. The skin and head were tossed into the river; the rest they broiled over a hastily-built fire before eating their fill. Leftovers got divided up and put into their fanny packs.

They were all tired and sleepy. Pavel wanted to push on, but he faced a near-mutiny and finally backed down. They gathered more wood before bedding down for the night. Pavel took the early shift again and sat by the fire as the others went to sleep.

* * *

LILIA SLEPT as she'd done the night before, stretched out on a live-oak limb. The tree had great limbs that spread more than twenty feet from the main trunk. Wrapped in her parka, weapons beside her, she listened to the murmur of the river as she fell asleep.

* * *

MATT HAD EATEN his fill of fish, then collected crayfish for an appetizer.

A few scraps of memory had returned, although he still had no idea what had made the knot on his head. Clouds were moving in from the north, so he looked about for shelter. Finding nothing he could use, he decided to build his own. He soon had the river to his front, a large tree to his back, and a fire for protection, but he needed a lean-to. It would shelter the fire in case of rain and reflected heat would keep him warm during the night.

He began collecting poles and limbs for the frame. Rootlets would serve to tie the crosspiece between trees, and the weight of the items he leaned against it would hold it in place. While collecting materials for the shelter, he brought in more downed wood for the fire. This he stacked at each end of the lean-to as a wind deflector.

During his scouting, he had found a number of cobbles along the river which he brought back to the lean-to. It wasn't yet dark when he finished and he had nothing to cook, so he began chipping the cobbles, fashioning weapons and tools.

The flakes of stone soon acquired an edge; he now had replacements should the flint knife in his emergency kit break. Recent memories were hazy, but the knowledge of working flint and building shelter was there. Matt wondered vaguely why that should be true, but the thought was fleeting. He still had work to do before it rained.

There might be another fish in the morning, or perhaps a few more crayfish. If all else failed he would resort to eating the grubs again. The flint cobbles he'd been working on could wait too. The fire sank low and Matt added a dry limb to keep it burning. He watched the flames for a moment, then curled up under his lean-to and went to sleep.

3

Each small herd of deer consisted of a buck and three or four pregnant does. The bucks began shedding their antlers as the winter ended, sometimes just one, sometimes both. Irritable, they abandoned their harems and wandered away. Most soon joined with other bucks in pairs and trios, then moved north toward their summer range.

The does remained together after the bucks left. They too began drifting north, driven by instinct and the promise of food. The deer browsed on fresh green leaves and succulent branch tips as they traveled slowly north, bedding down in a different place each night.

The doe sought privacy when her time came. Lying down, she delivered a fawn just before daybreak. The full moon lit the scene as she licked the small form. In a short time, it stood up on long shaky legs and driven by instinct, moved close to its mother.

The doe ate the afterbirth, one of several survival mechanisms that deer had adopted over millions of years. It contained elements and minerals that would help her recover from the birthing process and also removed much of the evidence that there had been a birth here.

Otherwise, coyotes and wolves would find the afterbirth and begin searching for her fawn.

The doe soon moved away from the fawn to feed. The tiny creature crouched in the cover of a clump of grass and froze in position, hidden and virtually scentless. A predator could pass close by and never realize a helpless young deer hid nearby.

She returned after a time and held still while the fawn nursed. The tiny head butted against her small udder and sucked at the teat until it had drunk its fill. The two then cuddled together under cover, waiting while their respective breakfasts digested.

Later in the afternoon, the doe got to her feet. Testing the air, she led the way down to the river to drink. The fawn nursed again. She waited patiently until it finished, then the two headed cautiously north toward the summerlands.

* * *

LILIA WOKE at daybreak and climbed down from the branch. She washed her face in the river, then ate the last of her meat and bread. Refilling her water gourd, she replaced the wooden stopper. Carrying Matt's heavy spear had been awkward, but she would not leave it behind. She slung it across her back, shifting her small pack to make room. When both hung as comfortably as she could manage, she picked up her bow, slung the quiver over her shoulder, and headed south.

She found no game, but saw a number of tracks; deer and other animals had passed not long before. She would need to find game soon or stop and set out a fishing line. There hadn't been enough food that morning to assuage her hunger; soon, she wouldn't have a choice. She would have to find food or starve. Already quiet, she slipped forward with renewed alertness.

Hunger was no stranger. Still, it would get worse and if she couldn't find food within a day she would begin to weaken. Like the rest of the tribe, she was already thin from short rations and long days of work. There was little spare flesh left on her body.

She listened, slipped forward a few paces, listened again. From time to time she approached the river, looking for any sign that Matt's body might have washed up on the bank.

Her pace was slow, but if there was an animal ahead she might see it before it discovered her presence. It was during one of her pauses to listen that she heard a distinct tapping. Cocking her head to the side, she listened carefully, but the tapping had stopped.

Well, there were woodpeckers around. She resumed her slow pace forward.

* * *

THE CLOUDS BEGAN DRIPPING rain just before dawn. The cold rain woke Pavel and he soon had his small group moving. Some grumbled, but in a short time they were on their way. They ate some of the raccoon meat while heading south in single file.

Pavel passed on instructions while they walked along the trail.

"We might come up on her at any time. Make sure you're ready and this time, don't fumble with your arrow. If we see her before she sees us, we might try to get closer. But if she tries to run, take the shot. Even if you don't kill with your first arrow, you might wound her. Just don't let her get away; if she sees us, she'll know why we came back.

"That place we dumped him can't be too much farther. We'll just stay close to the river and when we find the place, we'll dump his weapons and brush out our tracks. Look for her tracks before you go stomping through the area. If she hasn't found the place, we can head back right away. She can look all she wants after we get rid of the evidence."

"We should have done that before we left, Pavel."

"Yeah, well...you were just as glad to leave that place as I was, Gregor. Anyway, we get rid of the sign, brush out our tracks, and the rain will wash away what we don't get."

Half an hour later Pavel paused and looked around.

"Gregor, come up here. Doesn't this look like the place to you?"

Gregor looked around, then moved a few paces and looked again.

"It could be, Pavel. If we find his weapons, we'll know for sure."

"OK, everyone spread out and look. Find those weapons. The spear...I can't remember. It's on the ground or leaning against a tree, but we left the bow lying on the ground and some of the arrows had spilled. We'll need to find those too."

Vlad came back to Pavel fifteen minutes later. "Pavel, this is the place; I found a bloodstain. There are drag marks too, down by the river where we threw him in. But I haven't found those arrows. I know where they should be, but they aren't there now."

"Crap. Are there any tracks around that we didn't leave?"

"Maybe. Look over here." Vlad pointed to a spot on the ground.

Pavel studied the ground. "I think you're right, Vlad. That's from a moccasin, smaller than any track we left. She's been here; I'll bet she picked up the arrows and his other weapons too. She'll take them back to the tribe.

"Robert will know Matt wouldn't have taken his weapons off. They'd have gone in the river with him. If she gets back with those weapons, we'll have to leave the tribe. I don't want to leave if we don't have to, but if they find out we killed Matt we won't have a choice."

"Yeah. So do we follow her tracks?"

"No. She'll head back for the trail and follow the tribe. We know about where they'll be, so we cut across country and outrun her. We'll get in position before she catches up and ambush her before she knows we're anywhere around.

"As soon as we're back, I'll leave you three to watch the back trail. I can sneak up close enough to the camp to make sure she didn't get back before us. I'll watch Lee's camp for a while, make sure she's not there. If she's back, that's where she'll be.

"If she's not back, we'll spread out and watch. One of us will hide on the north side of the trail just to be sure, but she'll probably be coming from the south.

"I figure we're a couple of miles south of the trail right now. We dumped Matt's body here, we know she was here long enough to pick up his weapons. She'll head north and follow the tracks. There's no reason why she'd cross the trail. Whoever watches the north, keep alert anyway. As for where to set the ambush, she'll be following the drag marks so we wait a half-mile or so behind the tribe. I'll watch alongside the trail, Gregor and Vlad will be south of me. She'll be moving, we'll be hidden under cover. We put a couple of arrows into her, cut her throat, drag the body off into the brush and rejoin the tribe. If anyone mentions us being gone, remember, we tell them we went hunting."

With that, Pavel took a final regretful look around the clearing, then turned his back on the river. Jogging again, he led his small band northwest. They would intercept the drag marks left by the travois and follow them until they got close to the tribe.

* * *

MATT WOKE to the slow drip of cold water on his neck. The lean-to wasn't watertight, but at least it had protected the fire. It was the work of a minute to stir the coals and add wood from the stacks at the ends of his shelter.

He still had most of a fish, so he warmed that over the coals and ate. Finished, he took the bones down to the river and threw them in before washing his hands and face.

Moving upstream, he checked the line he'd left set out the night before. There was no tug on the line, so he pulled it in and looked for where he'd gutted the catfish the night before. The offal was gone; something had come up during the night, found the guts, and eaten them. There were tracks, blurred by the rain so that Matt couldn't identify the scavenger.

Sighing, he went to find a log he could raid for grubs. Just as well, since he hadn't really wanted to handle guts that had been left out overnight. Even if catfish probably loved them.

But it proved unnecessary to look for grubs. The rain had brought out nightcrawlers, large fat earthworms. Matt gathered several by simply picking them off the ground. He had thought of a way to improve his fishing line, meaning he would need more bait.

It was the work of half an hour to carve two more gorge-hooks. Two short lengths of cord attached these to the fishing line above the rock sinker. This left him with three gorge hooks attached at intervals above the weight. The earthworms had tried to crawl away, but they were easily recaptured. Threading the worms onto the gorge hooks, he let the ends of the worms dangle free to wiggle enticingly as he tossed the arrangement gently into the river.

The river appeared to have risen slightly; had there had been more rain upstream?

Washing his hands again, he left the setline and walked back to the lean-to. Matt had been near starvation when he first woke from his injury, but now he found himself tiring of the taste of fish. As soon as he had weapons, he would hunt.

He warmed himself for a time. Already planning ahead, he would collect rootlets as soon as the rain let up and weave them into a basket. He had already accumulated several things he intended to carry when he moved away from the river.

He picked up the two rocks he'd been working with the night before and began tapping, using the smaller one as a hammerstone to knock long pieces from the core. He needed a second, longer, knife and a spearhead, plus the flakes could be made into arrowheads. He collected them as he worked and piled them beside the fire.

The name for the rocks, a form of chert, was somewhere deep in his memory. A fine-grained rock, it was a suitable raw material for tools.

He held up the core and examined it, then went back to his steady tap-tap-tapping. The slow rain continued to fall as he worked. Finally it stopped and Matt stirred up the coals of his fire. He laid the pieces of chert down and walked to the river to see what he'd caught.

* * *

LILIA CONTINUED her slow journey south. Slip a few paces forward; pause, listen; move forward again. The breeze blew from her right at first, then changed until it blew across the river.

She froze in mid step; she'd heard something. Her eyes scanned around before she saw movement. A deer was browsing, just beyond a forked tree; the motion she'd spotted was the deer raising its head to look around. Cautiously, arrow nocked on her bowstring, she crept forward seeking a better vantage point. Finally she had enough clear space for shooting.

There was a slight movement by the browsing deer. Behind the deer she saw a tiny form, a newborn fawn. The deer, a doe, turned around to lick at the fawn. Lilia watched regretfully. There really was only one thing to do. She lifted the bow.

The doe ran away as soon as she shot. The fawn dropped, kicked once, and died. She ran forward, but the only thing left to do was dress and butcher the fawn. The doe could survive without the fawn, but the fawn would have starved to death without the doe.

Darwin's World was as merciless to animals as it was to humans.

She had just finished skinning the small deer when she heard the tapping noise again.

4

_____

Robert took care of his own needs, then visited the small family areas to see how others were faring. It took less time than usual; Pavel's group was down to three, a man and two women.

"Where's Pavel, Monika?"

"I don't know, Robert. Vlad mentioned hunting, but no one said for sure. They were just gone when we woke up."

"Are you going to be able to keep up when we move out? I don't have a lot of help to offer; everyone has their own work to do and things to carry. Some are caring for kids as well as hauling tools and kitchen supplies. You may have to abandon Pavel's gear if you can't carry it, or stay behind."

"I know, Robert. We're already hauling a shovel and an axe, plus some of the tribe's dried food. Staying behind is out of the question; we'll stay with the tribe. Pavel's furs and sleeping pad will just have to be left behind. The things that belong to the men who went with him too. They were carrying some of the kitchen pots, so we'll add those to our loads but that's all. We've got our own things to carry. He should have made arrangements."

"Right, then; just leave their gear behind. If you need help deciding what to keep, let me know. Somebody will be following behind to provide rear security. I'll talk with them, and if they can help you folks they will. One thing we can do, we can slow down a little now that we've got more meat. That might help you keep up. But we're losing people. First Matt, then Lilia, now Pavel and three others. René died. That's almost a quarter of the tribe."

Monika nodded her understanding and Robert went on his way. He soon found Lee, now back with the tribe after posting the new security shift.

"Lee, we've got problems. Pavel and three of his people have decided to go hunting, At least, I think that's what they've done. Maybe they just decided to leave the tribe, but they didn't take much with them if that's what they did.

"Look at the numbers. We've lost seven people. You're using three for security, plus there's one more coming behind. Your guards have packs, as heavy as they can carry considering that they have to range out ahead and to the flanks, but the rest of the tribe has to carry everything else. The travois are heavy and people are getting weaker.

"No question, we're going to need to abandon some things. I'm hoping we can get along without the furs and sleeping pads, if not right away then at least soon. We'll just have to replace what we leave behind when we get where we're going. We won't leave food or cooking pots, but the grindstones and heavy furs have to go. It's too bad, but..."

"Robert, we're already seeing tracks. A few animals are back, so I think we could start hunting. How would you feel about camping here? Or maybe where we stop for the night? I'll take a hunting party out, see what we can find. I think the Wise Woman and a few others would also like to gather plants. There are already a few things greened-up that we can add to our diet. Fresh stewed greens, a salad, roots and stems that are fresh-sprouted...people need those. As for animals, I don't think it will be a problem. Based on the sign, this country looks to be rich in game. Or it will be when the herds migrate back north."

"We could do that. If you can handle the hunting and security, I've got a few ideas of my own I'd like to explore. Maybe we won't have to abandon things after all. Some of my people know about trades, not just building houses but making wheels. We've got the tools. We can try building carts too, even if it takes time; we can make up the time later on by covering more ground in a day. If we convert the travois-loads to cartloads, we can carry at least twice as much without adding to the workload and also move a lot faster.

"But this isn't a good campsite; what say we keep going and look for a stream or at least a large spring? If the land is suitable, we camp there. Plan to stay at least a week, let the people rest, hunt and cure meat, gather plants, and let the workers try making wheels and axles."

Lee nodded agreement and went off to see about his own workers.

* * *

NEXT MORNING, a mound of furs and personal belongings marked where the three people remaining from Pavel's group had left what they couldn't carry. If Pavel returned, he'd find his possessions by the track along with the two travois he and his men had used. The three joined in at the end of the long procession. If anyone noticed the pile they'd left behind, no one said anything.

The tribe stopped when the sun was directly overhead. They were still engaged in eating a meager lunch when the Michel returned. "Lee, there's a stream up ahead. I'd say it's a mile and a half, maybe two miles from here. Ground's pretty good. No bogs, no quicksand. There are a few rocks in the stream, but they won't be a problem when we're ready to ford it. The bottom is mostly sand, there are several springs that feed the stream, and the water's clear.

"There are trees along the banks," he continued. "There's a grove of bigger trees where the stream bends west. We can easily build shelters; there are plenty of willows along the stream, some of them pretty large. Big stands of cattails downstream, maybe five hundred yards, and I saw swirls in the water. I'm sure we can catch fish and I also saw lots of animal tracks around."

"What about firewood?" asked Lee.

"Plenty of dead limbs and there's at least two fallen trees. I'm guessing they blew down during the winter and we can cut those up if they're dry enough. We won't run out of firewood for a day or two and there's plenty of fallen branches farther away. We might have to drag them half a mile, maybe."

"Thanks, Michel. I'll talk to Robert, but it sounds good. I think he'll agree.

"Why don't you collect the two flankers and head for that bend? Gather firewood and lay out a campsite, pick sites for temporary shelters, and look for a central place where we can put the kitchen. If the ground's not too hard, you might scoop out a fire-pit for the cooks.

"Find a sanitation area too, someplace back from the water. Maybe think about a willow screen for privacy. If we're going to be camped there for a week or two, we don't want people just crapping where the urge strikes them."

Michel nodded. "We'll take a shovel and an axe. I know what to do."

"We'll follow as soon as the tribe's finished lunch," replied Lee.

"We've been moving slow, maybe too slow," he continued. "People are tired and we haven't had enough food. Everyone's hungry, and lately it's been almost all meat. They need different things. But we'll get to the grove as soon as we can, and whatever you three can do before we arrive will help a lot."

* * *

THE EARLY TREKKERS began arriving by mid-afternoon; Robert had remained behind with the slower ones to help where he could. Tired people put their loads down and slowly began setting up camp.

Michel and his small party directed them to campsites, collected willows to weave into shelters, and finished digging the kitchen firepit. Michel was as tired as anyone, but he dragged in enough dry wood for the first night and left it by the firepit.

Colin looked appreciatively at the stack of wood when he arrived and immediately began building a fire. Pots and food appeared as others came into camp. Colin put everything where it would be convenient and started supper. Assisted by Sal, he shortly had snacks of jerky and bread waiting. The main meal, consisting of stag-moose stew with dried vegetables, would be ready in about an hour.

Callie, Colin's daughter, gathered green needles from a pine tree she found in the grove. Colin heated water in the smaller pot and as Callie brought in the pine needles, he added them to the bubbling water; the needles would be dumped after the liquid was poured into gourds. A spoonful of honey made the tea, useful in preventing scurvy, more palatable.

Whenever he could take a break, Colin watched his wife as she worked around their personal camp.

The trip had been very hard on Margrette. Colin had often been busy with the Tribe's kitchen, so setting up camp and transporting an unusual share of kitchen supplies had fallen to her. Callie had helped, but as the trip progressed Margrette had lost weight, more even than the rest of the tribe. They were thin; she was gaunt.

As she lost weight, her mental state declined as well.

She often spent long minutes just gazing off into the distance. Colin suspected it was a left-over effect from the rapes she'd endured, but he knew of nothing he could do to make things better.

Colin had been rationing salt but even so, what remained would likely be gone within two weeks. He prepared Margrette a gourd of tea with an extra spoonful of honey, all he could do. He would have added more, but the tribe's supply of honey was also limited.

"Why don't you drink this and lie down for a while? I'll bring your food when it's ready. You need the rest."

"Colin, all of us need rest. I'll be all right, but if you don't need me in the kitchen..."

"I've got plenty of help. You drink your tea and relax. I'll send Callie with food when it's ready."

"Thank you, Colin. I'll try to eat more this time."

Colin resolved to speak to the Wise Woman. There might be something she could do. Robert, too; he would need to know about Margrette.

But Robert already knew. He'd considered Margrette's condition as well as the condition of the others when he'd accepted Lee's suggestion.

Like Colin, he'd become increasingly worried as food stocks dwindled and people became thinner. The trek was consuming their inner reserves. They were often withdrawn now, not even taking the time to converse with others in the evening.

"Colin, we're going to stay here for at least week. If the hunters bring in game and the foragers can find vegetables, we'll stay longer. We want to get to the western lands, but not at the cost of leaving our people dead along the way.

"Pavel and his followers...even if they do find game, they've left it up to the rest of us to pick up the load they should have been carrying. We can't depend on any of them as long as they listen to Pavel.

"Something strange about that, too. Pavel never told me he was leaving. I'd think he had just abandoned the rest of us and left the tribe, but he didn't take his camp gear. None of them did; they just slipped off and never bothered to explain what they were up to. I'm going to talk to Lee. If he agrees, I'm considering banishing Pavel. I hate to lose people, but he's more problem than help. If his group goes with him, so be it. I'll take people I can depend on rather than people who will fail us when we need them most."

"I agree, Robert. Just don't do it alone. Lee will back you and so will I. Marc, Michel, and Philippe are reliable too; they'll stand. They've been doing the scouting and hunting, they're well armed, and they know how to use those arms. If Pavel doesn't take the hint and leave on his own...well, we'll just leave him. After salvaging the arrows, of course."

Robert and Colin shared a thin-lipped smile. Hard choices are easier made when there are no others.

* * *

LATE IN THE AFTERNOON, Pavel's small band found the drag marks, but it was too late to go farther. They would camp near the trail and be careful not to blunder into the tribe the next day. He wanted to ambush Lilia behind the tribe, but not too far. Judging from the tracks, the tribe might be a day or more ahead. Still, they hadn't been moving fast; they might be closer than expected.

They made a cold camp that night, Pavel cautioning his men to be extra watchful; animals were more likely to approach with no fire to keep them away.

Three bedded down, weapons in hand, while Pavel took the first guard shift.

He kept watch until nearly midnight, considering and rejecting alternatives, thinking over his plans for the morrow. Finally he woke Vlad and turned in.

They ate the last of their food the next morning while following the drag marks left by the travois.

Two hours later Pavel stopped. There was a pile of equipment ahead, but no one was around. Puzzled, he led his men up and found the travois beside their bedding and personal gear.

"Pavel, they've dumped our sleeping equipment. Have they thrown us out of the tribe? You didn't say anything about that when we went after Lilia," said Gregor.

"I don't know what happened, but I'll find out when I catch up, you can count on that! Sort out what you want to take, leave the rest here. The furs are heavy and the weather is warm enough that I doubt we'll need them before fall. We can get new ones by then.

"They can't be far ahead. I'd like to just rejoin the tribe, but with Lilia maybe still out there we can't do that. You three look around here, see if you can kill something. Gather greens too, anything we can eat. I'll scout ahead and see if the tribe's close. Meet me here in two hours. But keep your eyes peeled; we *have* to kill her.

"If she gets back, we'll have to run for it and maybe join up with the mine guards. I've been thinking about that. We won't have much chance of surviving, just four of us alone. The guards won't welcome us, but if we tell them where Robert and the tribe are I think they'll let us join up. They're mad at Robert and Colin anyway, so maybe they'll want to raid the tribe. Anyway, it's only a thought. I don't owe the tribe anything. I wouldn't mind teaching them a lesson, especially that little bunch that lived with Matt."

"How long do we wait, Pavel?"

"That depends on what you three find to eat, Gregor. If we've got food, we can afford to trail the tribe a few more days and make sure

Lilia doesn't get by us. If she's not here within a day or two, well...maybe she got killed. Lions, wolves...she's only a lone woman, so they'd snap her up quick. As long as she doesn't get past us, we can wait.

"Anyway, go find us something to eat. I'll meet you back here in two hours."

5

The faint pecking sound was somehow familiar. Lilia cocked her head to the side and listened. Curious...she knew the sound, but couldn't identify it.

Not a woodpecker after all; but unknown things were dangerous. She stole forward, arrow on the string, slightly drawn back, and ready for a fast shot should that be needed. Ahead was a small clump of willows, the sound appearing to come from just beyond.

Careful to make no sound, Lilia eased through the willows. And froze for a moment. It couldn't be...but it was...

"Matt! You're alive!"

Her fingers involuntarily relaxed and the arrow plopped into the dirt a few feet in front of her. She didn't notice. Matt stood up in shock, dropping the rocks he'd been chipping.

He saw a woman, holding a bow and dressed in leathers. She carried a bundled parka tied to a small backpack. A spear was slung across her back. The bow looked familiar, the recognition felt by a craftsman for the things he's made.

"Who are you? Do I know you?"

Lilia had crossed the small clearing where Matt worked. Experienced eyes took in the crude lean-to and the small fire that smoldered beside where Matt had been working. She looked at the dirty, stretched-out and baggy deerskins. No question, this was Matt; he looked different, but she knew every stitch that had gone into making those deerskins. She also saw the bump and partially-healed cut, all that remained of the injury he'd suffered.

"Matt, it's Lilia. What happened to you?"

"Lilia? Uh, I don't know. I woke up on a sandbar. I was wet and cold."

Matt stopped for a moment, then resumed his halting speech.

"I got dried off and warm. I don't know how I got there. I've been..."

He paused for a longer time.

"I've been eating fish. I've still got some. Are you hungry?"

"No, I killed a deer, a fawn." Lilia paused in turn. "If I'd known you were here and had fish I wouldn't have shot the fawn," she said ruefully.

"Just let me stir up the fire. We can cook part of your fawn. I'm hungry enough to eat the whole thing! But you called me Matt; do I know you?"

"Oh, Matt. I'm Lilia. You don't remember me? Or Lee? Sandra and Millie and Cindy? Laszlo? You worked with Laszlo, Laz, a lot. Laz and René helped you cut wood and build things."

"I don't remember. The first thing I remember is crawling out of the river. I was cold. I remember that, shivering and being wet. Since then, I've been building weapons and just staying alive. I guess I should have been doing other things, shouldn't I?"

"Matt, you're alive. That's all that matters. As for weapons, I've got your spear. And I picked up your bow and arrows. They're almost a day's travel behind me, but we can go back and get them."

"My spear? Let me see it."

Lilia handed over the spear and Matt hefted it appraisingly. There was a deep scratch just behind where the point joined the heavy shaft.

"I think I remember this. There was a bear. I remember a bear."

"That's right, there was a bear. We killed it. All of us, you, me, Lee, Sandra and Millie, all of us."

"Lee...I remember Lee. He had a broken arm. The bear broke his arm."

"Yes. Lee almost died, but he recovered. He's been helping you."

"Helping me? Helping me do what?"

"Matt, you were...you are...the trek leader. You are in charge of the tribe when we're moving. Lee takes care of security, he's got several helpers to do that. He has scouts, and I'm sure he'll be in charge of the hunting parties when we start sending them out."

"We're part of a tribe? How long...how long has it been? How long have I been here?"

Lilia thought for a moment.

"Matt, it's been almost a week. We thought you were dead. Pavel said you drowned. He said you slipped and fell into the river, but I didn't believe him. He had two of his men with him when he got to camp. I thought they'd killed you."

Matt reached up reflexively and rubbed at the bump.

"Maybe I hit my head when I slipped."

"No. I found a bloodstain well back from the river. That probably came from your head. Was it worse when you left the river?"

Matt nodded. "There was blood on my face too."

"Scalp wounds, cuts to the forehead where that one is, they bleed a lot. Pavel must have hit you with something before his men dragged you down to the river. I saw drag marks where they threw you in."

Matt thought about Lilia's statement. His fingers gripped the spear tightly.

"I think I'll want to ask Pavel about that. Saying I fell into the river. I want to see where they threw me in. You're sure?"

"I saw the tracks. Your bow and arrows are still there, hanging in a tree to keep animals from chewing on them. I can show you the tracks and the bloodstain when we get there."

Matt looked around at his small camp. Well, he'd been thinking it was time to leave the river. He would need to pick up the fishing line and carry the chipped stones with him, the ones he'd been working on. They'd be useful.

He had known his name because of the dream, and now he knew a lot more, though some of the memories were still just bits and pieces.

"We can cook some of the venison if that's OK with you. I'll put out the fire after that and we can go. Bow and arrows?"

"Yes, and a quiver for the arrows too. I made the quiver, you made the bow and arrows. You made your spear, and you also made a spear for me but it's back at camp. I left it with Lee."

"Lee's back where the tribe is camped? I wonder if Pavel's there too?"

"I'm sure he is. He's got a small group, four men counting himself, and two women."

"We should get my bow and arrows and go to the camp. I have a few questions to ask Pavel."

* * *

Lee found Robert leaning back against a tree. He was eating a bowl of Colin's stew and a second gourd held some of the sweetened pine-needle tea. Lee sat down cross-legged and waited.

"Did you already eat, Lee?"

"I did. Pretty good stew; I'm glad you brought Colin back. I doubt we'd have been eating nearly as well without him."

"I agree. Did you have something special you wanted to talk to me about?"

"Yeah, I did. I've been thinking."

"Uh, oh. What about?" Robert smiled as he asked the question.

"You know I've had scouts out ahead of us, but they haven't had a chance to really see what we're facing. We know there are going to be rivers to cross, maybe other dangerous things ahead of us. I was wondering what you'd think if I went on a scout? Maybe go out two or three days before I come back?"

"Getting a little tired of camp life, Lee?"

Lee smiled. "I am. It's okay, but it's the same old thing every day. I'm itchy; I want to know what's ahead of us."

"Tell you what, Lee, we need food more than we need to know what's ahead. You take a hunting party out tomorrow morning and see what you can find; if we have food, we can stay here for a week or two. It's worth taking the time. People are getting really worn down and we've still got a long way to go.

"Get us enough food for two or three weeks, then you can go. That'll give us extra rations when we move on. We'll be sending our foraging parties every day, but some days we may not find much. Rain, too much wind, maybe the country won't have as many animals. There might not be enough plants. We need a reserve. Who did you plan to take with you?"

"I thought I'd go alone, Robert."

"I'd rather you didn't, Lee. Take one of the scouts with you. Maybe Laz or Marc or Philippe."

"Not Laz. He's spending a lot of time with Cindy and I don't think he'll want to leave. I could take Marc or Philippe."

"You've done this before, with Matt. I'd suggest both; it would be good experience for them. But I'll leave the decision to you. I agree about leaving Laz, I will need an experienced hunter to help around the camp. So pick one or both of the others to take with you."

"OK, but first I'll want to take all three of them hunting; that way, we've got a better chance to do what you said, bring in a supply that will last for two or three weeks. We'll leave tomorrow. I can talk to Marc and Philippe about the scouting trip while we're hunting. I'll decide then which one goes with me."

Robert nodded and the two separated to do what needed doing, improving the camp for an extended stay.

* * *

LEE LED his three hunters southwest the next morning. He planned to repeat what he had done when he'd gone scouting with Matt, hunt southwest, bend northwest after a day, then turn back toward camp by heading northeast, then east. When they reached the stream, it would lead them back to the tribe's camp.

* * *

LILIA HELD out her hand to caution Matt while she looked over the clearing. Seeing no danger, she slipped up to the tree and found Matt's bow and quiver of arrows hanging where she'd left them. She slipped the quiver's strap off the stub, handed it to Matt, then took down his heavy bow. He already had the quiver and his spear slung when she turned around with the bow.

Taking the bow, Matt examined it for a moment. He braced a limb against his instep, then stepped across with the other leg. The practiced moves came easily. He flexed the heavy bow and slid the string into its notch. With the bow in his hand, he drew an arrow and examined it before nocking it to the bowstring.

His expression was nothing like that of the man she'd found only a few hours before. He might not have full recall of his memories as yet, but now his expression showed grim purpose. Lilia looked at him and shivered. Matt would ask questions. Pavel would need very good answers...if indeed he could answer at all.

"Is this where they threw me in the river?" asked Matt.

"No. That happened ahead of us, a hundred yards or so."

"Why don't we have a look?"

She led off, still cautious, but somehow the presence of Matt behind her was very reassuring.

"It happened here. I found your arrows and the quiver over there, and the bow was a little nearer to the river."

"I don't see any tracks. You're sure this is the place?"

"I'm sure. Look, here's the bloodstain I found., but the tracks are gone. There were tracks before, three men left them. And there were drag marks down by the river."

"We've had a little rain."

"Not enough to wipe out the sign, not as many marks as I saw. I think someone's been here. Maybe swept the tracks away with a branch or something."

"Tracks are easy enough to hide, but blood sinks into the dirt. Who would hide the tracks?"

"It had to be Pavel; he's been here. No one else would have a reason to hide the tracks. But this is the place, it's where I found your bow and quiver and hung them in the tree. That was a day ago, yesterday about noon. It's afternoon now, so Pavel was a full day behind me. I followed the river south and killed that fawn just before I found you. Pavel must have wiped out the tracks while I was hunting."

"Lilia, I wonder if he's still around? Could he have been tracking you?"

"Matt, it's possible. I didn't tell anyone, but our little family group would know where I was going. Others might have guessed. There aren't many people in the tribe and any absence would be noticed. Now that I think about it, Pavel would have realized I was gone when I didn't show up for rear guard. That's what I had been doing, follow along so I could help stragglers and make sure nothing dangerous caught us from behind."

"Would Pavel come alone? You said there were three of them before. Maybe he brought the other two with him."

Lilia thought for a moment.

"Probably. He's part of a group, the one they look to for answers. Two of the group are women and there are four men plus Pavel. He could have brought all four of the men, but not the women. They have friends among the tribe; he wouldn't have told them what he was planning for fear they'd tell someone else."

"So; maybe five of them. Well, we'll just keep our eyes peeled. How far ahead do you think the tribe is?"

Lilia thought for a moment.

"They'd have been going west while I looked for your body," she said. "But they weren't moving very fast, so I think we can catch them in two days, maybe three at the most. We can cut across country until we pick up the drag marks."

Matt nodded. "We'll need to be careful. If Pavel's out there waiting, we don't want him to see us before we see him."

"You're quiet, so am I. Pavel's bunch are like mammoths, they just blunder along. Unless they're hiding and waiting, we'll see them before they see us."

"OK. We'll stop early just to make sure we see them before they see us. We don't have much to eat, though. If we see a deer or maybe a pig we should stock up on food."

"Let's go ahead, Matt. We'll stop after lunch, eat the last of the fawn, then you hunt while I pick a few greens. I've seen dandelions, wild onions too, I'm sure there are other things."

"Sounds good." Matt glanced at the sun to orient himself, then looked where the wind was blowing. He adjusted his course slightly to move across the northeast breeze which barely stirred the new leaves on the trees. Moving with his usual caution, Matt led, Lilia following two steps behind and slightly to his right side.

* * *

PAVEL FOUND the tribe where they camped by the stream. He slipped closer, then watched as the tribespeople ate and went about preparing the camp for a long stay. He remained for two hours, but saw no sign of Lilia. Taking care to remain well concealed, he slipped away from the camp and went to find his men.

"They're having supper. It looks like they've decided to camp here; some are already putting up shelters."

"You think they've had trouble, Pavel? Or maybe they're waiting for us?"

"I don't know, Gregor, but Lilia's not with them."

"Maybe a lion or something got her?"

"No telling, Nik. We'll watch the back trail for a day; we've got enough to eat now, so we just wait and watch. If Lilia's not here by tomorrow, she probably won't be coming at all. But I think we'll wait for at least two days to make sure."

* * *

MATT SPOTTED a small horse late that afternoon. Slipping closer, he tried to approach for a killing shot. He was still some fifty yards away when the horse raised its head and sniffed the wind.

The nervous horse was across a clearing where only a few brushy plants grew. Matt decided he was unlikely to get a better chance for a shot. He drew back smoothly and launched the arrow.

The arrow hit, but not where he'd aimed. He might have flinched slightly, or perhaps the arrow had glanced off a branch; whatever the reason, it struck the horse too far back for an immediate kill. The wounded animal jumped when the arrow struck and bolted northward.

Matt realized immediately that he shouldn't have tried the shot...but he had. He searched the area where he'd seen the horse and found dark blood splashed on the ground. Not an artery hit, then; oxygenated blood would have been bright red.

It might run for a few yards or it might run a mile. Matt didn't like the thought of leaving an animal to die in agony. Darwin's World did enough of that already; he didn't need to add more.

He went back, found Lilia, and brought her to where the horse had been standing. The sun was already low but maybe they could follow the flecks of blood and find the horse before dark.

Together they set off north, following the tracks and splotches of blood left by the wounded animal.

6
___

L az had decided to skip the hunting trip. Lee had simply shrugged; if he didn't want to go, he likely wouldn't be much help. Marc and Philippe joined Lee and the three inspected their weapons, then stoned the steel points of their spears. Little things like sharpness might be the difference between meat and no meat. Or life instead of death.

Colin brought them enough dried meat to last the hunting party for two days. Lee took a third, then divided the remainder. Marc and Philippe added their share to what they already carried in their small packs. Water bottles would be refilled at the stream before departing in the morning.

Lee ate a last gourd of stew with a little of the dry bread, all that was left now, and was soon asleep.

He woke up well before daybreak and roused Marc and Philippe. A few minutes later the small party moved out, walking in single file and heading southwest.

They crossed the stream a mile below the camp, then spread out. Tall trees, sustained by the running water, lined the stream on both sides.

Beyond the treeline scrubby bushes and briars gave way to a grassy plain. Maintaining rough alignment across their front, they slipped through the trees and watched for an animal.

Lee hoped to avoid the plain, at least for now. His previous experience hunting in the tall grass had produced a lot of meat, but it had also cost René his life.

Life and death decisions; hunt where it was easier to find game, but also more dangerous. Or hunt where the hunters were safer but had less chance for a kill? He might not have a choice; if the tribe faced starvation, risks would have to be taken. But if he could bag a few deer, perhaps a woodland bison or a stag-moose, the tribe would have meat and they could be choosy about where to hunt.

The tribe had already lost René and Matt. Pavel and his men were gone, who could say where or whether they might ever return. Lilia had gone too; she would return, but there was no way to know when. Few other tribespeople had hunting skills, meaning that risking a hunter when not absolutely necessary could potentially endanger the tribe. Lee mulled decisions and kept his eyes searching as he slipped along.

As for danger, forest predators, the jaguars and lesser cats, hunted alone. It was necessary to be alert, of course, but a man with a spear could defend himself against a cat. Solitary cats were unlikely to attack a group of three, preferring to ambush prey. But the open-plains predators were more numerous and more mobile, and there was no refuge out in the grasslands for hunters who became the hunted. Superior weapons and numbers helped, but even so three men might easily find themselves overwhelmed. Lions hunted in prides of as many as a dozen, sabertooths hunted in pairs or trios, and a wolfpack might have even greater numbers.

The predators had not learned to be wary of people. Until they did, the transplanted humans were just another source of meat. In any case, more animals were migrating north as the snow retreated.

There would soon be game enough even in the forest as the spring progressed, if the tribe could avoid starving in the meantime.

Lee decided they couldn't afford to move beyond the trees, at least not unless they became desperate. Signaling Mark and Philippe, he adjusted his course to follow the stream for a while longer.

Noon came and the three rested briefly as they munched on dried jerky. They'd seen tracks, droppings, but no animals. They were already more than five miles from the camp, meaning transport of meat back would be a problem. Unless they had better luck soon, they would have to try the grassy plain.

The first rule of any hunt is to hunt where the animals are. If the open plain was dangerous, starvation was dangerous too. People would soon begin to succumb to hunger; the youngsters were especially vulnerable. Adults had eaten less so that the children could have more, but that strategy could only work for a short time.

The three discussed whether to sleep in a tree or set up on the ground and keep watch during the night. The decision was unanimous, get as much sleep as possible. That meant sleeping in a tree, preferably one near the grasslands. Wake at dawn, see what was stirring out on the plain, now green with new grass.

At least the grass wasn't tall enough yet to provide cover for predators. Maybe hunting the plains wouldn't be as dangerous as it had been last year.

Lee ate more of his dwindling stock of jerky that evening, then got as comfortable in the crotch of a large tree as he could. The tree, a walnut or perhaps a pecan, had produced nuts last year and something had cracked the thick shells to get at the nutmeat inside. Whatever it was, he was more danger to it than the animal was to him. He soon dropped off to sleep.

Waking the next morning, he ate more of his jerky. There was only a little left. They'd be hungry by nightfall if they didn't kill something today.

Lee led west, slipping cautiously through the sparse trees. They reached the edge of the treeline as the sun rose behind them; there were briars and brushy plants here, a transition zone between the trees and the treeless plain ahead.

They saw a gently rolling landscape and a low rise about a hundred yards ahead. Nothing moved between them and the rise, and there was no way to see beyond that point.

Bushes and low thickets of blackberry dotted the landscape to their front. The berry vines were growing and new green leaves sprouted thick on the thorny stems. It would be a month at least before the blackberries began producing fruit, but rabbits loved blackberry patches. They would feed on the fresh leaves of the berry plants as well as the new grasses and the thorns provided a refuge from predators.

"Marc, climb that tree and have a look over the rise. You might see something big that's not too far away. Philippe, let's you and me see if we can bag a rabbit or two around those berry vines. That'll be enough for our supper, even if it won't be enough to feed everyone back at camp. If we do, we can stay out until we find something bigger.

* * *

MARC SLIPPED the ready arrow into his quiver, slung his bow, and jumped to catch a tree branch. He spotted Lee as he cautiously moved around a large briar-patch; Philippe had already disappeared, likely gone around the other side.

Marc kept climbing until he'd reached thirty feet up where he had a relatively-unobstructed view. The tree continued another fifteen feet above, but the limbs were unlikely to bear his weight; his current position would have to do.

A quick scan revealed nothing moving. A second, slower, examination was unproductive at first, but then Marc noticed moving shadows. He realized that he was looking at a small herd of bison feeding their way northward.

Marc looked carefully near the small hill that had blocked their view from the ground but now saw only grass and scrubby bushes beyond the slope. He mapped out a possible route of approach they could follow should Lee decide to stalk the bison. He saw no predators, but there was also no protection if he had missed one.

Recon finished, he descended from limb to lower limb until he'd reached the ground. Glancing at landmarks, Marc fixed the location of the bison herd in memory and headed for the briar-patch to report his find to Lee and Philippe.

* * *

"No predators? Just the bison?"

"All I saw were bison, and I only found them by their shadows. There might be predators but I wouldn't have seen them. They wouldn't cast shadows if they were hiding behind bushes, maybe lying around or something. There weren't any moving, anyway."

"The bison were grazing north, you said? We can keep in the trees for a couple of hours while we try to get ahead of them, then head west. We should be in position for a shot within three hours at most, wherever we can find a place for an ambush.

"Besides, the herd is moving north and the tribe's up there."

Lee grinned. "If I knew they'd keep going the same way, I'd just set us up across from the tribe and kill as many as we can. But they're feeding upwind, so if the breeze changes they might go anywhere. I don't think we can afford to wait any longer than we have to. We get ahead of them, and as soon as they're close enough we'll pick three and take them down."

The others nodded understanding. Lee moved deeper into the trees and headed north, jogging now.

* * *

MATT AND LILIA tracked the horse until dark but were unable to catch the wounded animal. They finally found a tree and bedded down on branches. Lilia offered to share her parka, but that proved impossible. Finally, she wrapped herself in the parka and slept while Matt huddled to expose as little skin to the chill as possible.

He endured, slept for short spells during the night, and woke shivering. At least the temperature no longer dropped below freezing during the night!

He woke Lilia as soon as false dawn turned the eastern sky gray. They ate a little of the leftover fish, not particularly palatable now but it kept hunger at bay. The rest he discarded.

They soon crossed the tracks left by the travois. The horse's carcass lay a few hundred yards beyond that; the animal appeared to have lain down and died.

The two soon had the carcass open. Thick steaks and roasts filled Lilia's pack and Matt's small bag that he'd woven from rootlets. Regretfully, they decided they'd have to leave the rest. Final cuts gave them enough for a substantial meal and Matt built a fire. Lilia roasted the horsemeat while Matt dozed, catching up on the sleep he'd missed out on the night before.

"Should we go back and follow the drag marks, Matt?"

"It's just as easy to cut across. It's not as if there's a road or even a trail. We head west-by-southwest and we'll soon come to their tracks. We might even spot the people first. I suspect they'll be surprised to see me!"

"Pavel too, Matt. Surprised, but not pleasantly. It's not good when the fellow you reported drowned shows up in camp!"

Matt was holding the spear as she said this, ready to sling it over his shoulder when they were ready to leave. He hefted the spear, examined the tip for a moment. "I might have a few pointed questions for Mr. Pavel." He grinned and Lilia smiled in return.

"Fire's out. Ready to go?" She nodded assent and they set off.

* * *

THREE HOURS later they hadn't found the tracks but Matt decided they couldn't be far away. Just a little more to the south...

Lilia spotted the watcher first. A low hiss caught Matt's attention and he crouched, watching Lilia to see what she'd discovered.

She slipped up until she could whisper near his ear. "There's someone hiding ahead of us, maybe a hundred yards or so. He's behind that clump of brush over there, just left of the pine tree with the forked trunk. See him?"

Matt looked, then shook his head before whispering, "I don't see anything. Are you sure?"

Lilia replied, voice barely intelligible. "It's a man wearing buckskins. He's got a spear slung over his shoulder. That's what I saw first, a flash when the spearpoint caught the sun. But he's also got a bow and there's an arrow on the string. But you can still see the spear point. Look just above that bush; see the black spot?"

Matt looked carefully where Lilia indicated. Finally he saw the black object. It moved slightly while he watched.

Matt nodded. Lilia had sharp eyes!

"If he's from the tribe, he could be hunting. Poor technique, though; he should have laid that spear aside while he was waiting."

"Matt, would someone be hunting where the tribe has already passed? Wouldn't that scare off any game?"

"It might. If I were doing it, I'd want to be ahead where no one has disturbed the animals. Even so, this one doesn't look like he knows what he's doing. Maybe we should ask him."

"Matt, what if they're waiting for me to return? If they knew I'd gone to look for you..."

"One way to be sure. There are enough bushes between here and where he's hiding. We need to get closer and make sure he's alone before doing anything. How would you feel about drawing fire? Just stand up for a second, then drop and crawl under cover. If he's friendly, he'll say something. If he draws that bow you mentioned, well, I'll know what to do. If you don't hesitate, he'll see you but won't have time to shoot."

Lilia nodded.

Matt led, Lilia followed. Crawling slowly, they approached the clump of bushes where Lilia had seen the man. Finally Matt judged they were close enough. He looked at Lilia and pointed to a downed log. When he had her attention, he mouthed, "Stand up, then duck behind the log. I'll see what he does."

Lilia looked dubious for a moment, then decided she was safe as long as Matt watched. The spear point was now obvious, projecting above the bush where the man crouched. He would have to stand up to launch an arrow, and if he did, Matt would have a clear shot.

Carefully she thought through her actions; stand up, wait briefly, then drop behind the downed tree-trunk. Crawl a few yards to a large beech tree while concealed, then she could stand. By then Matt would have decided what to do and the watcher wouldn't know where she'd gone.

Taking a deep breath, Lilia stood up. The clump of brush she watched was only thirty yards away...and Nikolai suddenly saw her.

His eyes opened wide in surprise and he sprang up, fumbling with the bow and arrow. The arrow had come loose and it took a second for him to replace the nock on the string. He glanced down as he did this and when he raised his eyes to where he'd seen Lilia, she had disappeared.

Well, she couldn't be far. But Pavel would need to be warned.

He drew back the bowstring and called "Pavel! She's here!"

He never felt the arrow punch through his temple.

Matt had immediately nocked a second arrow, but it wouldn't be needed. He watched as Nikolai collapsed bonelessly behind the bush he'd used for concealment.

Matt had heard Nikolai call out, as had Lilia. He slipped over to the log and the two sought better cover.

"There are more of them. You said Pavel has...had...as many as four men. He's only got three now. He looked south before he called, so they're probably over there."

"Matt, we're outnumbered."

Matt nodded. "For now, we wait," he murmured. "See what they do. An hour from now, if they haven't gotten here, you see if you can reach Lee. Pavel's bunch won't have come far from the camp. Get Lee and as many others as possible and bring them back here. I'll wait, make sure they don't try following you."

* * *

TWO HOURS later Lilia returned with Robert and Laz. She'd found Lee gone but had taken the time to pick up her spear. That was now slung over her shoulder. She'd left her pack with the horsemeat in camp; by now, Colin probably had started cooking.

The three spread out as they approached where Lilia had left Matt, waiting. But he had disappeared. While they were wondering where he might have gone, Matt waved, then approached from the south.

"Pavel took off. I saw him, but couldn't get a shot. He had two others with him."

"Welcome back, Matt. I've never been more pleasantly surprised than I was when Lilia told me she'd found you alive," said Robert. "Pavel only had three men with him. He left one with the two women in his group. What used to be his group, anyway. The three you saw are all there were. Lilia said you lost your memory, at least some of it?"

"It's been returning in bits and pieces, Robert. Anyway, I'm glad to be back. Lee's not with you?"

"No, he took Marc and Philippe hunting. We've been getting pretty hungry over the last few days. We needed meat."

"Lilia and I brought some. Probably not enough for everyone, but every little bit helps."

"You said Pavel took off?"

"Yeah. They were running at the time, probably close to half a mile away and I didn't think they were worth chasing."

"Good thinking. If they try to come back, we'll get to use that firing squad I thought about. If they're gone, good riddance. Maybe a sabertooth will get them.

"Let's head back to camp; people are going to want to see you. I imagine you're tired, too. It's noon, so Colin will probably have food ready. How about a salad and a nice slice of horse steak?"

7

Lilia, along with several of the women, headed downstream to look for wild vegetables. Another group, led by the Wise Woman, went north; Sandra and Millie went with the second group. Accomplished archers, they were along more to protect the gatherers than to search for food. Cindy could help Lilia guard the other group. Behind them, the camp resounded with saws and axes. Some of the men cut firewood, others cut tree sections for wheels.

Matt collected the weapons belt his group had kept for him. It felt very natural when he buckled it around his waist and settled the knife and camp-axe on his hips. Walking through the camp, he soon met Robert. After exchanging greetings, they discussed losing Pavel and his men.

Nikolai's body had been left for the forest's animals to dispose of. Pavel, Gregor, and Vlad were gone, fled to who-knew-where. The tribe was now down to twenty-six members, consisting of fifteen women and eleven men.

Seven camped in Matt's group, five including Colin had come from the mine and camped around the kitchen where they worked, the rest were from Robert's original tribe. Of these, three were easterners who had come to the tribe with Pavel.

"What do we do with the people from Pavel's group, Robert?"

"Matt, I think they will need to be put in with you or me. I can't see them fitting in with Colin. I could take the two women; they've already got friends among my group. I think the Wise Woman would like their help. Can you take the man?"

"I guess so, Robert. I'll give him a chance. He can work for Lee when he gets back. Maybe I'll take him hunting, see what he's like."

"You're going hunting too, Matt? Lee's already out."

"I know. But I want to see what my new member is made of before I consider him one of my group. I can do that better out in the bush."

"Well, you know best. I think he's been mostly a maker of things, arrows and sleds and travois and such. He's good with his hands."

"We can always use someone with those skills, Robert. But he's going to need to know more. Does he have weapons?

"Flint-tipped spear and bow. I don't know how good he is, but he's got the weapons. I think he made the weapons himself, but he used your chipped points and a bowstring made by Lilia."

"Yeah, she's handy. Knows a lot of stuff. OK, it's settled. I'll take him with me and we'll leave at dawn tomorrow. What's his name?"

"Piotr. I get the feeling Pavel never trusted him."

"A point in his favor, Robert. Well, I'll soon know."

Matt got up and went off to find his new man.

He wandered through the camp, observing, greeting and being greeted. He stopped for a time at the tribe's communal kitchen.

"How are we doing on food, Colin?"

"I'm worried, Matt. I figure maybe a week if we don't get something. That stag-moose helped, and the horsemeat you and Lilia brought in is enough to add a little fresh meat to the dried meat I've been depending on.

"Meanwhile, I've got my helpers building a fish weir. They can bait it with grubs until we catch something. After I clean the fish, the guts will go in the weir for bait. I plan on adding fish to our diet tomorrow; we know the fish are there, all we have to do is catch them.

Lilia and the Wise Woman are looking for plants. I've seen a few things I know are edible, so I expect they'll find things. I may put Sal to tending the fire and go looking myself; greens, maybe a few mushrooms too."

"You can identify mushrooms? You know which ones are safe?"

"Oh, sure. Nothing to it. I've been doing it all my life."

"OK, if you're sure. Maybe teach a few of your assistants too."

"I can do that. Was there anything else?"

"Now that you mention it, I've picked up a man who'll be camping with me. Name's Piotr, he camped with Pavel before. What do you know about him?"

"He's a willing worker. Quiet, never caused trouble. He helped me when I was learning how to set up a travel camp. I think he went back to working for Pavel after that."

"OK, thanks. Know where he's camped?"

"Sure, he's back near the end of the clearing. But I think he's down at the stream right now helping Sal set up the fish weir. Depending on how things go, we might put out several."

Matt nodded and left to see what was happening down by the stream.

Sal, a stocky olive-skinned man, was clearly in charge. Two younger men were cutting wrist-thick branches with axes and two others were working in the shallow water. Sal and the axemen had been in the water too; their buckskin trousers were wet to mid-thigh. It appeared that the work crew was taking turns in the cold water, work for a time, switch with someone else. Matt nodded; it was how he'd have done it.

"How's the job going, Sal?"

"We're making progress, Matt. I've got the opening all finished, and we should have the catch-basin done in less than an hour. Glad to see you're back."

"Glad to be back, Sal. Which one's Piotr?"

"He's holding the sticks while Dominick does the hammering. We're driving the sticks into the stream bottom, then lacing them together with green willow stems."

Matt nodded. "That should work fine. I see you're leaving a gap of what, inch and a half?"

"About that, yes. The little fish can escape; I don't want them anyway. Too much work, not enough meat. I could make fish soup with the bits of meat, but some don't like it and I don't have the spices to do it right, anyway."

"I've been hungry enough to eat it, but I can't say I like it. Anyway, send Piotr to me when you finish with him, OK?"

"You can take him now. We'll have this done in less than an hour and I've got a couple of boys hunting grubs and worms. I'll toss a couple of those in and keep the kids busy tossing in more every few minutes. I expect a catfish or two will follow the bait upstream as soon as they get the scent. We found a clay deposit and I've got a basket of damp clay waiting. I'll gut the fish, coat them with clay, and put them in the coals to bake. Just cook the whole fish that way, if it's not too big, and we'll have baked fish and fresh greens for supper!"

"OK, Sal. Thanks. Piotr!"

At the call, a sandy-haired man looked up from where he was weaving willow branches through the uprights they'd hammered into the streambed.

"Come on out, Piotr. You'll be staying with us, so grab your gear and bring it to my camp. We'll go hunting tomorrow morning early and I won't have to go looking for you when I get up."

"You're Matt; I saw you, but never got a chance to speak to you before. I'll be camping with you? What about Pavel?"

"Pavel's gone, and I doubt we'll see him again. I had something to discuss with him, but I guess it's not important. Good riddance. Is that going to be a problem for you?"

"No. I can't say we were ever close. He already had a group when I found them; they'd been together a month or two and Pavel was already the leader. I camped with them, but I wasn't really part of the group. I'd only been with Pavel and the rest for a week when we met Robert. What's going to happen to the women?"

"Robert said they had friends in his camp. They'll just join their friends and camp with Robert."

"All right. I'll just get my bedding; I don't have much."

"You know where my group's camped?"

"Sure, up near the front. I'll meet you there."

"Why don't you drop your gear by my camp and go over to the kitchen area. Colin might have some of that tea still hot and you can warm up by the fire. You look like you could use it."

"I wouldn't mind getting warm. That was my second time working in the water."

"Drop your gear by my area, warm up, and when you get back we can talk about what I've got in mind for tomorrow."

Second time working in the water and Piotr hadn't complained; he'd been matter-of-fact with his explanation as if it was normal to be working in water only a little above freezing. Matt had his own memories of just how cold the water was this time of year! It wouldn't begin to warm for another month or two, although people might brave the water long enough for a quick bath. A *very* quick bath.

* * *

LEE AND PHILIPPE removed the heads and feet before gutting the three rabbits. Lining their packs with a layer of fresh oak leaves, they put the rabbit carcasses in to wait until supper.

It was still early, only an hour or so after sunrise; they should have time to set an ambush, kill a bison or even two if the animals continued traveling in the same direction. Three experienced hunters could easily field-dress a carcass or carcasses. But dragging them to the treeline would take time, and the more time they spent away from the trees, the more danger they'd be exposed to.

If the herd was too far out...well, he'd either have to abandon the idea of hunting them or see if Marc and Philippe could drive them closer to the trees. For now, it was time to run; he could decide what to do after they got ahead of the herd.

Two hours later, Lee stopped. He could have continued, but Marc and Philippe were breathing heavily.

"We're making good time. You two wait here, I'll climb a tree and look for those bison. But if they're in sight, we'll need to go farther before we try to ambush them."

He got nods from the two winded men, both clearly glad of the chance to rest. Lee trotted over to an elm tree near the edge of the treeline and made quick work of climbing.

Like all elms, this one had a short trunk which separated less than six feet above the ground. The branches in turn formed other limbs and these branched still again, all pointing upward at a steep angle rather than spreading as did maples and oaks. The numerous branches made the tree easy to climb and there was almost always a crotch in that was suitable for sleeping.

Fifteen minutes later, Lee came back. Marc and Philippe were now breathing easier.

"They're still coming. They're quite a long way back, but when I looked north I could see a wide bend in the stream. I wonder if it's the same bend where the tribe is camped? If it is, the camp is closer than that herd is. Is it the camp, you think?"

Marc and Philippe shook their heads; they had no idea.

Lee continued, "The three of us can probably take three of those bison, but we'd have problems protecting the meat. Depending on where they fell, we might have to split up and I won't do that. It's too dangerous. Even together, if a pride of lions finds us we'll have to leave the meat and hope they go for the meat instead of us.

"But if Robert was to bring more men, we could take maybe a half dozen of them. Putting an arrow into the animals is easy, butchering and protecting the meat is what takes people. We really need as much meat as we can get.

"So here's what I'm thinking. Everyone's already camped, so Robert could leave a few people to watch the camp and bring everyone else to help with butchering and packing.

"With that much food, we could feed people well enough to recover from the trip and restock our supply of dried meat too. It's a chance, but I think it's worth a try.

"I'll stay here and watch the herd. How about you two go for that river bend and bring back as many people as Robert will let you have?"

"I'll do it, Lee. You keep Philippe with you. I can travel faster alone and I'll be back in four hours at the most, depending on how long it takes Robert to organize people."

Lee nodded his assent and Marc glanced at the sun long enough to orient himself, then trotted away through the trees.

If this worked out for Marc, Lee decided he'd found his traveling companion for the scouting trip.

* * *

LEE AND PHILIPPE perched in the elm tree Lee had climbed before. They watched for the herd and looked for other activity out on the plains, activity that might warn of predators. Lee also studied the terrain.

There was a slight rise ahead capped with small trees, none so large as those along the stream's flood plain but big enough to conceal waiting hunters...if the herd of bison continued to graze north.

The small rise was typical of the plains here, gently rolling, grassy, with occasional clumps of brush, berry vines, or small trees.

Two hours later, Lee left Philippe watching the herd and looked for a different climbing tree to see if there was activity in the direction Marc had gone. Three people were coming toward him, cutting directly across the area between where he waited and the stream's bend. They were still more than a mile away.

Lee watched for a moment. Disappointing...Robert had only sent two men back with Marc?

Strange...the tall man leading looked familiar. Lee searched his memory of the tribe members and couldn't come up with a name. Still, that gait was something he'd seen before.

8

"Matt! Pavel said you drowned!"

"Exaggerated, Lee. Pavel's men threw me in the river after someone whacked me over the head. If I ever see Pavel again, I plan on reasoning with him. An arrow or a spear makes a pretty good argument, and if I've got nothing better, I'll strangle the bastard with my bare hands."

"He's not with the tribe?"

"No. Looks like he took off after your mother and planned to ambush her after they couldn't catch her. I think finding me with her was a surprise. Anyway, one of them won't cause trouble. I killed Nikolai; missed Pavel, though. He took off running, and two others were with him. Lots of changes since you left. The two women who camped with Pavel have joined Robert's group and Piotr has joined us. I was planning to take him hunting, find out what he's like when we're out on the trail, but I can do that here. What have you found?"

"There's a small herd of bison, Matt. Small compared to some we saw before, anyway; I estimate maybe fifty or so animals. They're grazing their way toward us. I thought at first that we might set up an ambush and take one or maybe two, but since they were heading toward the camp I thought we might do better than that.

"The problem is preparing the carcasses and protecting them from predators. We haven't seen any yet, but they're out there somewhere. They'll take our kills away and maybe kill *us* if they get close enough before we see them."

"Good thinking, Lee. We've seen that behavior before, it's easier to steal dinner than to kill a bison that's part of a herd."

"Anyway, I think we've got at least two hours to get into position, Matt. There's a rise a couple of miles out with some small trees on top. They'll provide concealment and maybe protection if we need to climb. I was a bit worried about heading out on the plains with only three of us."

"Robert's sending more. It took a while for him to get people rounded up. I brought Piotr with me and Marc is bringing the rest. They'll be here in an hour or two. I think Robert wanted to bring a couple of the travois along to transport the meat, that's why they're slower.

"We've got four now, so why don't we head out and get into position? Marc knows where I intended to wait for the herd. He'll bring Robert and the crew up."

Matt nodded and Lee gestured to Piotr and Philippe. The four headed out into the open plains, Lee leading, Matt following behind Piotr and Philippe.

"I figure the herd is at least a mile to the south and they're traveling slow. If they begin to veer away, we'll need to decide what to do. I thought about trying to drive them toward the trees. What do you think?"

Matt thought about it, then said, "I could take Piotr with me. If the bison are beyond bowshot of that hill, we might be able them head your way. Let's wait a while. Plenty of time to decide when they get closer."

Lee nodded.

"Lee, have you thought of putting someone up in one of the trees? They could see a lot more than we can. Maybe your man Philippe?"

"Good idea, Matt. Why not Piotr?"

"Not yet; I don't know enough about him. If a predator or maybe several of them come our way, I want someone up there who'll for sure see them in time to warn us. Think Philippe can be relied on?"

"Maybe. He's got some experience, but I've got more. I think I need to be the one who goes up the tree."

"Go ahead. I'll put Piotr and Philippe in position. Time enough to take Piotr and head out if the herd starts to change direction. Wind's still pretty good, not very strong and it's coming from the northwest."

Lee nodded and began looking for a tree.

He returned after an hour.

"Matt, Robert's crew is coming this way and the bison are drifting in their direction. I think the herd will pass on the east side.

"We need to warn Robert to hold his position. If they stop pretty soon, they'll be able to push the critters toward us."

"I'll do it, Lee. You keep Piotr with you. I'll let Robert know what we intend. You OK with that?"

"Sure, Matt. That's probably best. We can take several animals and if they head your way, you can probably get one too."

Matt nodded and set off, slightly bent forward and trotting rapidly. Half an hour found him approaching Robert's group. He stood upright and waved his bow overhead in warning."

"Matt, did you find Lee?"

"They're on that little hill, Robert. Lee's got Piotr and Philippe with him and the bison herd looks like they'll pass between Lee and us.

We'll need to be careful, but if they try to pass too far from Lee, we might be able to kill some or push them toward him."

Robert nodded. "Bring up the carts. We'll put them out between us and the herd. If they decided to run over us, that might give us a little protection."

"You've got carts, Robert?"

"Sure do. We've got three ready and we'll have twelve or fifteen before we move on. Maybe more, or maybe we'll need to build spare wheels and axles. We're adapting the travois. Chop off the trailing ends of the main branches, tie them to the axle, and attach the wheels. It's easy to do. Making the wheels has been a little slow, but the biggest holdup is finding something we can use for grease. The wheels might last, but if we don't have grease we'll wear out axles fast."

"OK, we can talk about it later. Let's get everyone into position. Something else we can do, Robert. Get people gathering wood or dried brush, dried grass, anything. I'll build a small fire behind the carts. If the bison look like they're coming our way, toss brush or weeds on the fire. The animals will avoid that."

* * *

MATT PULLED DRIED grass stems and crushed them into a near powder. The carts, really just travois with wheels, were now lined up to form a barrier to the bison should they turn away when Lee began shooting. The first cart sat with the two branches resting on the ground. The other two had been lined up behind it and the branch ends laid across the axle of the one in front. Matt nodded; clever way of doing it. He dumped the grass stems he'd crushed behind the cart and began making a fire. He soon had a wisp of smoke and a tiny flame, enough for now. Fuel had been brought up by the other men.

Robert appointed a fire-tender in Matt's place and the two leaders moved up to watch the herd.

The older cow leading the herd fed placidly along and the rest followed. She had almost reached the watching men.

"Robert, I think we need to push them closer to Lee. We don't have time to move the barricade; I think we just move out, get as close as we can, and start shooting. The herd should move toward Lee and he can get one or two more. If they head for us, everyone retreats to the fire and build it up, fast as you can. You explain to the others. I'll take a couple of people with me and head for the herd. Join us when you're ready."

Robert nodded and turned away. Matt selected two men. "You're with me. Have your arrows ready. We'll get close, and when you think you're in range, take the shot. Try for yearlings. They're easier to kill and better eating. Less dangerous too if you don't kill right away. I'll back you up. I've got more range, but I haven't had time to replace the arrows I used."

The two men nodded and followed Matt, bent forward and trotting, toward the herd. Glancing to his left, Matt estimated where the outlying animals would pass. A gesture to the others caused them to slow. They stopped and made ready.

The old cow smelled something strange and stopped, raising her head sniffing the air. Matt and his two assistants were still downwind from the herd; she must have smelled the hunters waiting on the hill.

"We need to get her mind off Lee. Ready?"

The two men nodded, tense.

"Now!" Matt stood up and drew the arrow back, anchoring it with his hand tight to his jaw. Beside him, his two companions loosed, bowstrings thrumming. His concentration narrowed to the area he intended to place the arrow...just behind the shoulder, midway from the hump to the bottom of the ribs...

The arrow struck with a heavy thump. Dust and bits of hair puffed from the area he'd aimed at. The young bull fell to its knees. Matt immediately nocked another arrow; the young animal wouldn't need a follow-up shot, but he had time for one more before the herd fled...

His second arrow, longer range now, struck the only target he had, an older bull. The arrow hit, but Matt had little time to wonder how lethal the hit was.

The herd, veering away from Matt and his two companions, had moved into range of Lee's group which had arrowed several. They had turned again and were now coming toward Matt.

"Let's go! Back to the fire!"

Turning, he ran for the barricade, now facing the wrong way.

"Build up the fire, quick!" After that, he had no breath for anything but running. Behind him he heard hoofbeats. Gasping, he reached the fire, now flaring up as it consumed the dry grass and brush the fire-tender had placed on it.

Matt turned and pulled another arrow from his quiver. The two men who'd been with him were slower. Behind the last one, a big bull bison had seen the small creatures ahead.

A fast calculation and Matt moved away from the fire. He had one chance...

A fast draw, steady on the bull. Release. Reach for a final arrow, the last in his quiver. Nock the arrow and wait, judge the situation.

The bull was blowing blood from straining nostrils. The two men were nearing the fire as the animal paused, legs braced. Dust churned up by pounding hooves obscured the scene as they passed on, now two hundred yards distant and rapidly drawing away. Behind them, the bull collapsed, kicked, and died.

Behind Matt, two terrified hunters waited behind the fire.

Matt waited for the dust to settle. Several quiet lumps out on the prairie showed where bison had died. Two others waited, humped up, not dead but too badly wounded to flee.

Matt replaced his last arrow in the quiver and slung the bow across his shoulder. Spear in hand, he walked toward one of the downed animals.

"No need for that, Matt. Let me."

Robert paused briefly, string pulled back to his ear, and launched an arrow into the yearling bison's ribs. As it collapsed, Robert drew another arrow and trotted toward the remaining animal.

As it happened, Lee's group had had the same idea. The final wounded bison fell to Lee's arrow before Robert was in position.

"Tell Colin to bring up the carts and the rest of our people, Philippe. We can't carry all of them at once; we'll need to take three at a time and bring the carts back."

"Robert, I'll take over guarding these until the cart people get back."

"Good enough, Matt. We'll soon have the whole tribe here, except for two I assigned to guard the camp. I sent messengers off to find Lilia and the Wise Woman, so they'll be here too. I'm thinking we do most of the butchering here, then haul the meat back to camp and set up smoking racks there.

"But I think we'll use the fire to cook some meat right here while we're working. Chunks of liver and heart should cook fast and people will be glad to get the fresh meat."

Matt nodded wearily and went off to see if he could recover any of his arrows.

9

Killing the bison was, as expected, the easy part.

The tribe field-dressed them where they lay, working in two-person teams. They opened the body cavity, dragged out the entrails, and immediately salvaged the hearts, livers, and lungs. Colin and his helpers moved from site to site, collected most of the organs, and packed them back to camp. He remained in camp and immediately started a stew that would be ready as people straggled in. Lilia set up a secondary camp in the trees that lined the stream. She put her crew, almost all women, to constructing drying racks and building fires. Matt knew the smell of blood would attract predators, but leaving the offal where the bison had fallen might keep the predators away from the camps. In any case, he intended to keep guards posted.

Pairs of men loaded quarters of meat onto the carts and hauled them, axles squealing, to Lilia's temporary camp, but the carts proved less durable than Robert had hoped. The screech of crude wheels turning on equally-crude axles provided the first indication. The wheels had been 'greased' with beeswax, but the effort was futile; the first wheel broke while making its third trip to Lilia's drying camp.

Robert saw to unloading the broken cart and transporting the load via backpack to camp. A replacement wheel soon arrived, but the repairs took almost four hours start-to-finish.

Lee, Matt, Piotr and Mark kept watch over the butchering site. By agreement, Piotr paired with Matt while Marc stayed with Lee.

The two-man butchering teams worked on the most-distant animals first, field-dressing, skinning, then quartering the carcass for ease of transport. As the carts arrived, the two helped load the meat, then left to work on another carcass as the cart squealed away.

The bison had fallen within an area that was roughly oval and perhaps a quarter-mile long. The crews worked rapidly and the defensive perimeter shrank as the afternoon progressed. The four guards moved in closer, which was just as well; the first predator, a huge saber-toothed cat, arrived in midafternoon. He slunk up to a distant pile of intestines and began feeding. Others arrived and found their own pile of offal.

A second saber-tooth arrived, followed by three lions, then a bear. Matt watched, but couldn't tell the animal's species from his distant viewpoint.

The first to arrival often dragged a large section of intestine away to feed at leisure. As a result, guts and scavengers were soon strung out in an area a mile long and almost a mile wide. A number of fights broke out, but usually a series of thunderous growls sufficed to warn off would-be thieves. Even so, bold coyotes managed to get a share away from the larger animals.

Condors, vultures and ravens flew in and joined the impromptu feast. A fox and two bobcats sniffed around the edges and left, uneasy at being close to so many larger predators.

Lilia's crew had built the drying racks in a large circle. The smoldering fires would keep the predators at bay, and if that wasn't sufficient the women had their weapons if the predators followed the carts.

The butchering ended at dusk. Exhausted crews followed the carts and parked them near the drying racks. Finding a reasonably flat area, they lay down and were quickly asleep. Lilia's crew of women kept working and soon had most of the meat sliced into strips. Some they cooked directly over the fires, but most of the strips had already begun to dry in the smoke. Tired women lay down and slept when they could go no further.

Lee and Matt, still paired with their earlier companions, circled the drying racks and added more wood when the fires got low, but the stacks shrank as the evening progressed. Lee and Marc took a cart and collected a load of wood, dumping it near the center of the small camp before they too succumbed to sleep.

Piotr and Matt, nearly exhausted, remained awake. The two paused periodically to munch on fresh sections of lung, roasted over the fires. Matt understood that he might fall asleep if he stopped, so he walked the perimeter around the fires. Piotr never complained; he worked quietly, tending fires, cutting wood, and stacking it by the fires. Matt decided he'd make a fine addition to his small family group.

Lee woke up about four hours later and shook Marc awake. Piotr and Matt took their place among the sleepers.

Six hours later, the two woke and walked away into the woods for a necessary visit. Returning, Matt spoke to Lilia, now up and turning strips of meat drying in the smoke.

"I'm for the stream. It's only a couple of hundred yards away and I need a fast dip to wash off the stink."

"I would join you, but I can't take the time just yet. We'll wash off later, after everyone's up. I suspect your dip will be a quick one; that water is cold! I had gourds brought up and the small pot is boiling, so I'll make tea as soon as you two get back."

Piotr and Matt nodded and set off for the stream. The sun was just rising off to the east so there was enough light to see as the two approached the stream.

A small herd of deer, perhaps half a dozen, had been drinking. They spooked, bounding away as the two men approached the stream. Matt glanced at Piotr, who nodded back; the tribe had all the meat they could use for now. Still, it was a good sign; the animals had returned to their summer range. The tribe's hungry time was over.

The two took turns bathing, one always keeping watch, and they soon headed back to camp.

The tea Lilia had mentioned was...interesting, but at least it was hot. It could have used more honey. About a half-gallon of the stuff!

Matt and Piotr drank the tea, grabbed pieces of half-dried bison, and went off to relieve Lee and Marc. They took time to talk before the two headed back.

"Matt, I still think a scout is a good idea. I'm going to take Marc and head west as soon as people have recovered from yesterday. What do you think?"

"Good idea. How long do you expect to be gone?"

"I'm planning on a week. We'll head out a little south of west and try to hold that course for two days. After that, head north for a day. Plan on returning east and when we strike the stream, follow it downstream to Riverbend Camp."

"You'll be crossing the plains most of the time during the trip, Lee. Think you'll have a problem?"

"I hope not. If it looks too dangerous, we'll change direction or quit and come back. That's what we need to find out. If there are obstacles we can't cross, rivers or canyons or whatever, we'll come back and let you know. We're well past the mine by now, so I don't think that's a concern. All we've got to worry about is what's ahead of us.

We could go farther south or more toward the north if that way looks best."

"I might scout our back trail while you're exploring ahead. Pavel's back there somewhere, and I want to be sure he's really gone for good. He might be intending to raid the camp for all we know. He won't know that Piotr is with me now and the women have been adopted into Robert's group. Piotr's a good man. He pitches in and does his share of the work and more."

"I agree. We need to work on his weapons skills, maybe make him a heavier bow and a better spear as soon as there's time. He's a good worker, but we don't yet know if he's a warrior."

"You're right," agreed Matt. "I'll take him with me. I need to replenish my arrows first, but I'll be ready to go by the time you leave. We'll just be gone a day or two, and maybe I can check on his woods skills while we're out."

"Two people gone back to the east, two of us off to the west," mentioned Lee. "Does that leave enough security for Riverbend and Lilia's drying camp?"

"I think so. Lilia's got Sandra and Millie to help, and anyway nothing's going to approach the fires. I'll talk to Robert before we go, but the people at Riverbend are armed and they've learned to use their weapons. Plus Laz is there, and he'll have Philippe to help him. I think I'll leave Laz in charge. He can see Robert for more help if he needs it. Should be okay."

* * *

ONE OF THE women who'd been tending the fires was waiting when Matt returned to camp.

"Matt, can I talk to you?"

"Sure. You're Marja, right? You used to camp with Pavel?"

"Yes. Robert took us in; that's what I wanted to talk to you about. I've been working with Lilia or Colin, they're okay, but I would rather camp with you if that's acceptable."

Matt looked curiously at her.

"Did you have problems?"

"No, but I was more comfortable when Piotr was around. Since I'm working with Lilia now, I thought it would be better to camp with you. If that's all right."

"I don't see any problem, Marja. Let me talk to Lilia and Robert first, but I'll get back to you as soon as I can. For now, you can stay here with Lilia and we'll get it resolved before we leave for the west." Marja nodded and went back to work.

Matt found Lilia and brought up the subject.

"Marja wants to camp with us. I wanted your OK before I talk to Robert. What do you think?"

"Matt, I don't see any problem. If Robert agrees, she can move as soon as we get back to Riverbend Camp."

"I'll take Piotr and head over there now. I need to make new arrows, and all my tools and supplies are back at camp. I could send you Laz and Philippe to help Lee."

"We've got enough people, Matt. I've got Sandra and Millie, we've been watching, and we haven't seen any predators. I expect to be leaving in a day anyway, two at the most, as soon as the meat is dry. It'll be a lot easier to transport because it won't be as heavy. The only heavy thing we'll need to haul are the skins. We've been sleeping on them; they're smelly, but better than the ground. I'll take a few back to Riverbend and we can try tanning. I don't know if we'll have enough time...you can't hurry the tanning process...so if Robert decides to head west before the tanning's done, we'll just have to leave the raw skins behind. It will depend on how many carts he has by then."

"Spare parts too, Lilia. Wheels haven't lasted, and axles are going to wear out too."

"Rawhide will be useful, so I'll strip a few of the skins down into strings. We can splint axles and tied them on using rawhide laces. We didn't get a lot of fat from the bison, which is a shame. I think it's too early in the year. I'll talk to Colin and if he thinks we can spare it, we might try wrapping the axle spindles with fresh hide. There's some fat on that and it might help." Matt nodded and left.

He found Piotr at a fire, broiling a piece of fresh meat. Selecting a piece for himself, Matt joined him. As the meat cooked, Matt brought up Marja's name.

"Marja wants to join us, Piotr. What do you think?"

"Good idea. She's got friends in Robert's camp, but there are also a couple of women she avoids. I wondered about putting her in with them. I think she'll be happier with us."

"All right, Piotr. Why don't you let her know? As soon as we finish here, we'll head for Riverbend Camp. I'm going to be making arrows. How are you fixed for weapons?"

"My spear's good. I would like one of the steel points, but I know there aren't any extras. Anyway, the obsidian I'm using works pretty good. I could use a bow with a heavier draw, but that's it. I didn't have a good blank when I made that one."

"I'll take a look at what's in camp. There might be a better blank for your new bow. You can make your own if I get you a better piece of wood, can't you?"

"I can. My tools aren't good, so I have to work slow. But if you don't mind me using yours..."

"Not a problem; my tools are available to anyone in my camp. Just be careful with them, OK?

Piotr nodded. A few minutes later they were headed for Riverbend.

* * *

TWO DAYS LATER, Lee and Marc packed enough dried meat for a week and headed west-southwest. Matt and Piotr went northeast.

Piotr carried his new bow and a quiver filled with arrows. The bow was about the same draw weight as Lee's, slightly less powerful than Matt's.

Marja, with Robert's ready assent, had moved her bedding near Lilia's. The women were working together on improving their shelters as Matt and Piotr headed out.

"Keep an arrow nocked, Piotr. If we see Pavel, I plan to pin him to the nearest tree. Same with Gregor and Vlad. You know they tried to kill me, don't you? Lilia too."

Piotr nodded. "I heard. I won't have any problem with that. I'd just as soon not see them, but if it comes to a fight I know whose side I'm on."

"I can't ask more than that, Piotr. Not easy when someone you've been camping with turns on you. But we've all been members of one tribe and Pavel didn't let that stop him. Envy...it does funny things to people. Anyway, maybe they took off. If they aren't a danger to us, it's good riddance as far as I'm concerned."

10

"Woods skills are as important as being able to work with your hands, Piotr. We're going to need builders and craftsmen, but first we have to get there."

"I understand, Matt. I have learned other things, I can learn this too."

Matt nodded. "Why don't you take the lead? Head east-southeast for now and we'll swing north this afternoon. I don't expect to get back to Riverbend before tomorrow afternoon; just keep in mind that anyone you see is likely an enemy. Travel quiet and keep your eyes peeled."

Piotr nodded and led off. Matt watched critically as he adjusted to leading the way through unknown country.

Two hours later they paused atop a small hill, drank from their water gourds, and rested while looking over the country ahead of them.

"Couple of ideas, Piotr. Let's take a look at where we're going, then you can tell me which route is likely to be easiest for us to travel."

Piotr finished drinking and carefully fitted the plug into his water gourd before examining the land ahead.

"There's a lot of heavy timber a little south of us. It looks like part of a pattern, so I think it's part of that forest off to the south and east. Trees might mean there's a body of water there. I think we should probably stay to the north, swing past the heavy growth and stay near the edge of those smaller trees. They'll provide concealment, and if we run into lions or wolves, they're tall enough we can escape by climbing.

"Two or three more hours in this direction and I think we'll be ready to swing north. You're interested in looking over the area northeast of Riverbend Camp, right?"

"Right. We'll follow your route. I think if Pavel's still around, he'll have gone to the northeast. The mine's at least a week's travel in that direction for three men. They'll be able to travel faster. The tribe was slowed down by dragging the travois and stopping when the women and kids got tired. Still, Pavel would need to hunt and forage so they couldn't just keep moving. That means they might still be around. They may even be hoping to raid the tribe."

Piotr nodded and after a minute spent resting and looking around the countryside, he indicated he was ready to continue.

"See any animals, Piotr?"

"A fairly large herd of bison south and a little west of us, near that forest area. There's something a lot bigger behind them. Mammoths, maybe, or maybe ground sloths. I didn't see any predators, but they've got to be there somewhere?"

"They're there. Lions for sure, probably wolves too. Saber-tooth cats don't appear to be as numerous as I expected. Maybe there were more of them further west; that's where the biggest source of fossils was located. The animals had sunk in tar pits.

"Still, there are a few around. We saw them, and Lee and I killed one a few months ago. It was some kind of saber-tooth, even if the teeth weren't as long as I expected.

"Bears are around, but they won't follow the herds. They'll eat what-ever they find. If a lion kills something, the bear is perfectly happy to take it away from him. Until then, they'll eat grass and berries. They're omnivores; it means they could be anywhere. If we're going to have trouble with animals, I suspect it'll come from bears."

Matt paused to see whether Piotr understood, then continued.

"The true predators probably won't bother us unless we blunder into them. They're used to hunting plains game. Two humans aren't enough to tempt them to leave the herds. Not enough for a pack of wolves, either; they like to pick off the very young, the old and the injured or sick.

"Winter's different. Meat's in short supply then, so the predators will take what they can get. But it's springtime right now and there's plenty of game, so healthy predators won't be interested."

Piotr nodded. "There are also a few deer near the treeline. There were more a little while ago, but maybe they've started to bed down. Is there anything we need to watch out for when we get close?"

"Keep an eye on the trees," Matt advised. "Cougars, maybe a jaguar... they're around, but they'll avoid the lions and dire wolves and I doubt they'll attack us. Still, their usual prey is deer and I don't feel like rasslin' a cat, so keep a lookout.

"Maybe stay a little farther away from brush and briars. I could hear a swishing noise as you brushed past. Other than that, you're doing fine. I'm ready when you are."

Piotr settled his small pack and led off. Matt followed down the hill-side and the two were soon heading for where the deer had been grazing.

* * *

LEE AND MARC found an abandoned village, two days travel southwest of Riverbend Camp. A dozen huts surrounded a central area. The fire-pit had been used for several years, judging by the ashes scattered around. Well-worn trails led away to the north and south-west. Scrubby plants showed where someone had tried to develop farming.

Several huts revealed that the inhabitants had tried decorating. Wilted plants still survived near the doorways where someone had planted them. There were no blooms, but some had buds.

The two prowled around the deserted square and finally met after a few minutes.

"How long, you think?"

"Nobody's lived here for at least a year. Those ash dumps have been rained on. I doubt they would survive weathering more than two or three years. I think the people left at least a year ago, but not more than three."

"Sounds right to me, Marc. One of those huts belonged to a flint worker. There are chips around the outside. He had a stool, maybe a table to work from. I found the marks of legs, but the stool and table are gone. The people packed up and left or they got raided."

Marc nodded. "Could be either, but why would they leave? They had shelter. They had also started planting, meaning they knew some-thing about farming. They put a lot of work into this place just to go off and leave it."

"It takes time for a garden to begin producing. My mother had one and said she collected most of the harvest from the first two years to use as seed. The third season after she started, she finally began harvesting food as well as seed. I'm guessing the farming effort here hadn't been going on for more than a year, two at the most. They'd have needed to keep hunting and foraging until the plants produced enough to live on. If the game moved away, they might have had to leave."

"Maybe not. Take a look over here."

Marc led Lee to a hut east of the firepit. He pointed silently to a bit of shiny stone embedded in the wood framing.

"Busted spearhead or arrowhead, you think?"

"I can't tell which; it's the right width for an arrowhead. But if it was a spear, it broke before the point had penetrated very far."

Lee nodded. "Any idea which way they might have gone?"

"Couple of trails. They could have gone north or southwest, but any tracks have been washed away. They had a reason to be traveling along those trails. Maybe there's another village?"

"Maybe. Raiders would have taken the people captive. They'd also have taken whatever this village had in the way of wealth. That stool and table you mentioned, tools the flint-worker used, farming tools too. The captives would have carried everything."

Squatting, Lee felt the ground.

"I think we should follow this trail If there's a raiders' camp, we want to know about it. But we'll stay off the trail, maybe a hundred yards west. If that broken point is evidence of a raid, the raiders are people we want to avoid. Especially if there are more of them than us. So we stay off to the side of the trail, go slow and be careful."

Lee hesitated for a moment. "Something else. If they're raiders we can't chance leading them back to the tribe. It's better to avoid them, so I won't shoot if I can avoid it.

"Could you find your way back to camp from here?"

"Sure, no problem. Head east until I reach that stream...it's bigger than those two little creeks we crossed...and follow it north to camp. Are you thinking of sending me back?"

"Not yet. What I want you to do is stay at least a hundred yards behind me. If I run into something, I'll try to get away first, shoot my way out of trouble second. But either way, Robert and Matt need to know. You run for it and warn them."

"What about you?"

"You won't be able to come up in time to help me, so don't even try. I doubt anyone is setting an ambush, they've no way of knowing we're here, and I won't be on the trail. I don't expect to run into anything I can't handle, but just in case I'm wrong you hang back and watch what happens. Okay?"

Marc nodded. The two moved west together, then Lee headed south-west along a route roughly paralleling the trail. After he was a hundred yards ahead, Marc followed.

* * *

ROBERT WOKE up the next morning and made the rounds of River-bend Camp. He looked with disapproval at a number of sites where tribespeople had decided the dug latrines were too far away. Some sort of guide rope, so people could find the latrines in the dark? Maybe a fallen tree for a seat, something more comfortable than simply squatting over a trench? Colin and Sal might have suggestions.

Neither was in camp so he stopped at the kitchen fire and accepted a slab of meat served on a layer of dandelion leaves. There would be no more bread until the grasses began producing seeds. Stoically, he ate his breakfast and drank the gourd of hot tea.

At least they now had honey and wax. A worker had seen bees and followed them back to the tree where the hive was located. Pots that had once held grain now held honey. The wax combs had been melted down, broken into manageable sections, and wrapped in deerskin.

After eating and returning the gourd, Robert walked down to the primitive axle-and-wheel factory. A hundred yards beyond was the glue works, where unused bison skin and hair had been boiled down to make glue. Robert decided he didn't need to go that far; even from where he was, the smell was rank.

The wheelwrights were surrounded by thin slabs of wood sawn from large trees. A small fire burned in a pit; coals had been raked aside and a glue pot heated. A wooden paddle had been stuck into the liquid mass, ready for use.

The slabs were laminated to make a wheel, then carefully shaped using hatchets and knives. The wheelwrights pierced the wheel blanks with a chisel made from a piece of scrap steel. The final step was to add a kind of 'tire' made of rawhide stretched around the outer circumference, overlapping where the wet hide began. It would be laced into place while wet, then set aside to dry before trimming. The shrunken rawhide and glue held the wheels together. A stack of finished wheels, carefully sorted into pairs matched by size, waited off to the side, ready to be fitted to axles.

"Anyone seen Sal?"

"I think he's working down by the stream. The weir broke, either the stream flooded a or something went after our fish during the night. I think Colin's with him."

"Okay, thanks. You guys are doing good work; those wheels are going to make a big difference when we start moving again."

"Thanks. We'll have enough to convert every travois to a cart and have a few spares left over. It depends on how much trouble we have finding good, dry wood for the axles."

Robert nodded his understanding, then went on his way.

He found Sal knee-deep in the shallow stream, struggling to tie the stakes back together.

"What happened?"

Colin answered, "Some kind of cat, based on the tracks; guess he couldn't resist an easy meal. We had several catfish, big ones, some other kinds too. At least one was a buffalo-fish. We found the two mineral deposits that form above a buffalo's eyes."

"Any idea what to do, other than empty the trap every night? And make sure that people who come down for the fish are armed and bring a torch, something big enough to scare off a cat?"

"I don't want to post another guard, we're stretched thin as it is. I think I'll abandon the fish trap tonight. We'll take whatever we've caught, then break it apart. I don't like the idea of attracting a cat this close to the camp," said Colin.

"Good thinking. You're both busy but we need to talk. When you're finished, find me. I'll probably be near the kitchen fire someplace. How's your wife?"

"A lot better. The rest is just what Margrette needed. She's been eating well since we got here, and right now she's supervising food preparation. We're not ready to leave yet, right?"

Robert nodded. "I figure another week at least. By then, Lee will be back. I expected Matt yesterday."

"He'll get back when he's done what needed doing. Anyway, Margrette taking over the kitchen allows me to work with other people, the ones gathering plants and a couple I've trained to recognize edible mushrooms. Do you like the taste?"

"I do. Mushrooms cooked over the fire add to the flavor of the meat. Still, I'll be glad when we can start grinding grains and seeds. Nuts too. Animals got most of what was produced last fall. We'll probably find nuts by the time we get where we're going. They add to the flavor of the bread."

The conversation was interrupted by the arrival of Laz.

"Matt and Piotr are back, Robert. They brought three people with them and Matt asks if you can come to the kitchen."

Robert nodded a farewell to Colin and followed Laz.

Matt and Piotr were drinking tea and three other men were devouring slabs of the fresh-roasted meat. The strangers looked skinny to his experienced eyes. Each wore two of the short-swords that the mine operators had supplied to their guard force.

"You bring home some strays, Matt?"

Matt nodded, then motioned to Robert to follow him. When they were beyond earshot, he explained.

"They want to join us, Robert. I think we should take them, but I figured you should talk to them first. They used to be part of the mine guards. Pavel showed up there and he's now their leader. One of them didn't like the idea, so Pavel killed him; maybe there was more to him than I thought.

"They also had a fight with down-timers. The mine operators brought in their own labor force, security force too, and they have rifles. Those three picked up spare swords from the dead guards before they took off. Bad news, Robert. Pavel has a rifle. He only has one magazine and it probably isn't full, since the guy was killed toward the end of the fight, but even so a rifle puts Pavel in charge. And he's planning a raid. He's trying to recruit the original security force, but as soon as he gets that settled he'll be coming."

"You think they're telling the truth, Matt?"

"I do. They didn't have to tell us about Pavel or that he had a rifle, so that's a mark in their favor. Doesn't mean I'm going to trust them, at least for a while, but we can put them to work around camp and see how they fit in."

Robert nodded. "Looks like they've not been eating well."

"Next thing to starving, Robert. The former guards are hungry; they don't have bush skills or even hunting weapons. Pavel, Gregor, and Vlad have spears, one reason they didn't have problems taking over.

The rest are making spears with fire-hardened wood tips. They work, though; that's what killed that down-timer."

"I guess Pavel remembered what you taught him, Matt."

The two shared a grim smile. Their conversation was interrupted as Marc trotted into camp.

"Marc, where's Lee?"

"He's behind me, Matt. He ran into two men and I left; that's what he told me to do, leave and tell you. If they killed Lee, they'll be following my trail. We need to put people out for security in case they followed me."

Matt nodded. "Take time to catch your breath; you look pretty winded. Laz, you and Philippe follow me. Piotr, you able to go a little longer?"

Piotr nodded. "What about these three, Matt?"

"Bring them along. If they're going to be part of us, they'll have to fight. How about it, you three; are you up for a fight?"

One, a kind of spokesman for the trio, nodded. "We'll fight. Can we have more of that meat to take with us? We've been short on food for a couple of weeks now. We ate cattail roots and leaves from a couple of other plants, but if there's enough of that meat...?"

Margrette nodded and began slicing thick slabs from the roast, cooked by coating it with clay and putting it in a bed of coals. The broken shards lay near the firepit where she'd cracked them half an hour before. Other roasts waited in the coals; food was plentiful now.

* * *

AN HOUR later found Matt and his followers hidden in a hasty ambush. Matt kept Carlo, largest of the newcomers, with him. Piotr, low voiced, was instructing the man on how to use Matt's spear. The other two were split up, one with Laz and the other with Philippe. Like Carlo, they held spears they'd borrowed from their new partners, better weapons in a fight than their short swords. Laz and Philippe would watch to see how they reacted, as Matt would watch his two.

Unknown quantities, they would not be trusted members of the tribe until they showed what they were made of. And demonstrated, beyond question, where their loyalties lay.

Matt, Marc, Piotr, and Laz were armed with bows and knives. The bows would do most of the killing.

Matt spared a thought for Lee...the fact that he hadn't yet appeared was not a good sign. Wounded, perhaps dead?

How would he explain it to Lilia?

Matt worried as the ambushers settled in to wait and watch Marc's back trail.

11

Matt felt a touch on his arm and glanced at Carlo. The man nodded to the side where Laz waited; Laz was trying to tell him something.

Matt slowly held both hands out, palms up, to indicate lack of understanding. In response, Laz held up both hands, each with the forefinger extended. Matt nodded and repeated the gesture. Laz nodded and resumed his ready stance behind the concealing bush.

Piotr and Carlo were watching Matt when he glanced at them. Matt signaled with his fingers, two, then used his thumb to point to himself as a signal that he expected to act first. The others would remain ready in case they were needed. Piotr and Carlo both nodded understanding.

The two Laz had spotted were young girls.

Barely more than children, Matt guessed their ages at somewhere between ten and fourteen years. Best of all, Lee followed behind them. He stopped as Matt watched, stepping behind a tree to scan his back trail. Matt stood so that Lee would see him when he turned around.

The two girls stopped in confusion.

Matt signaled his companions to remain in place while he talked to Lee.

"I know. You found them and they followed you home," he murmured.

"Not exactly, Matt, but I'm glad to see you. Are you alone?"

"No, eight of us have been watching Marc's trail. The men are staying behind cover in case you picked up a tail."

"I may have, Matt. I hadn't planned on it, but there were two men chasing the girls. Slavers, Matt; they capture people, keep a few, and sell the others farther west. I've got a lot more to tell you when we have time."

"Take the girls on to Riverbend Camp and let Robert decide what to do. If he has no objection, turn them over to your mother; they can camp with us for now. Lilia will know what they need. After that, take a break, get some food, and if you think we'll need them bring some more men back here to help."

"I doubt anyone will be following close, but they'll find the two I left. They'll also wonder what happened to the girls. I tried to hide our tracks as much as I could, but I'm sure I missed some. They'll find the trail; slavers will know how to track people. How much longer is Robert planning to stay at Riverbend?"

"Long enough to finish the carts. Tell him what you told me, see if he can hurry things up."

"The farther away from those people we get, the better off we'll be. They've got more men, maybe fifty or sixty according to the girls."

"They won't bring all their warriors until they know what they're facing. If they've got other captives, they'll have to leave men behind. How far away is their camp?"

"I'm guessing about two days travel from here. The girls had already escaped when I found them, but they hadn't gotten far. They've got a story you'll want to hear; that escape took guts! Anyway, the two men I killed were following the girls. Maybe they expected a quick rape, but they got arrows instead."

"No problems, then?"

"No. They had spears and some kind of short whip. One was holding a whip, so I killed the other one. Whip-man was trying to figure out what happened when I shot him."

"Did you recover your arrows?"

"I did. Something else, neither man had a bow and I checked their hands and arms. Pulling a bowstring builds up a callus on the fingers and they didn't have them. They had small pouches with leather strings, but no thumb-ring or finger glove. Maybe they only have spears, but I don't think we can be certain yet. For what it's worth, I left wide cuts where I removed my arrows to make them think they were spear wounds."

"Easier for us if they don't realize we've got bows. Anyway, take the girls ahead. Figure on us keeping a guard closer to camp...I'll put Laz and Philippe to watch the trail, just in case. We'll need rotating shifts to replace them, say a new pair ever four hours. Four hours on watch, eight hours off, then four more. Half a dozen people should be enough. As for manpower, we've got some new people. I'll take a shift. The rest will be used too, after I've had a chance to assess their skill level. They'll need weapons, spears for now. Piotr should be able to handle that. The big guy is Carlo and he can use my spear until he gets one of his own."

Lee nodded and signaled the two girls to follow him. Matt noticed that one of the girls was limping and the other was helping her.

"Philippe, see if you can help that girl. They both look pretty tired, so do what you can."

Philippe nodded and put the ready arrow into his quiver, then slung the bow across his back. Hurrying, he caught the two girls and slid an arm around the limper. With his help, the group moved faster and soon disappeared into the woods.

Matt signaled the rest of his ambush crew to join him for a quick conference.

"We're pulling back closer to camp. I don't think anyone will be here right away, but we'll make up a two-man watch schedule just in case. Four hours on, eight hours off, then another shift. I'll talk to Robert and if he agrees, we'll pack our stuff, and head north. You need to know what to expect. According to Lee, there may be as many as sixty slavers about two days southwest of here.

"Lee doesn't think they have bows, so for now I'll leave Laz and Marc as first shift. I'll talk to Robert but I'll be ready to take second shift, maybe with Piotr or someone who's got a bow. You three new guys, we'll get you spears and start teaching you how to use them. Bows might have to wait a while. There are a couple of lightweight bows you can use for now. They're the ones we replaced with the heavier bows we're using now. They're easier to use while you're learning how to shoot, and we'll get you better ones when we have time. Questions?"

There were none, so Matt headed for camp, eyes scanning for a good ambush spot to post guards. Finally he found what he wanted, a thick bush on one side for concealment and another across the faint trail that would serve the same purpose. The camp was less than a mile away, far enough away to surprise any pursuers but close enough to send a man back with a warning.

"This will work. If there are more than you can kill, say three or more, arrow one to slow them down, then pull back and warn us. Don't try to be a hero. If you're sure there are only two or three of them and they can't get to cover before you shoot, then use your judgment. But the priority is make sure we know they're coming. Understood?"

Laz nodded, then gestured for Marc to move across the trail to the other bush. Satisfied, Matt led the others on to the camp.

* * *

SHOULD he take Piotr with him to watch the trail? He wasn't yet a proven warrior, nor the bowman that Laz, Marc, and Philippe were. Still, he *had* been the first to spot the three strangers and he had reacted well, calling Matt's attention to the movement he'd spotted. Piotr had clearly been ready to shoot, but he'd waited to see what Matt would do. Correct...but there had been no reason to actually shoot someone. Could he do that instantly when needed?

The men had been walking in single file at the time, moving cautiously but not expecting to encounter two men concealed in the brush. Matt and Piotr waited; thicker brush lined both sides of this partial clearing, so the strangers would be unlikely to change direction.

When they were about ten yards away, Matt stepped out and held up his hand. Piotr remained concealed, bow half-drawn.

"Going somewhere?"

The three stopped, confused.

"Maybe. Depends on who you are."

One of the others stepped up and tugged at the spokesman's sleeve. He murmured something too low for Matt to hear.

Matt half-drew his bow. If the three tried to attack or run away...

"He says your name's Matt?"

"Why do you want to know?"

"We're hoping we can join you. Willie saw you at the mine. We used to work there."

Because Piotr had reacted correctly, a possible conflict had been turned into an asset. No question, Piotr had unusually sharp eyes, but the only true test of combat ability is combat. Piotr had yet to prove himself, but he'd demonstrated good judgment, he would take a guard shift with Matt.

Robert was waiting when they arrived.

"Did you talk to Lee?"

"Yes. Lee said he was already suspicious, he'd seen a broken spear-point in a village and thought it might be left over from a slave raid. So when one of them reached for his whip, Lee killed both of them. He brought the girls with him, moving as fast as possible."

"One of the girls was limping."

"The Wise Woman thinks they're just tired and malnourished. Matt, they'd been whipped; they've got scars on their backs and arms."

"That's all we need, a camp of sixty slavers ahead of us and Pavel behind us."

"Maybe they'll kill each other off. We could do with a few less enemies."

"No such luck. Pavel will try to recruit them or join up. Our best chance is to get moving."

"We can be ready by tomorrow morning if we work late tonight," suggested Robert.

"Not a good idea. We'd need fires, maybe torches. They're visible from a long way off. Do what we can before dark, and tell Colin to have the kitchen fire out before dusk. Pass the word to everyone, no fires tonight, no noises. Keep the kids quiet too."

Robert nodded and went off to see Colin.

"Piotr, get some sleep. We'll be going out at dusk, so if you can't sleep at least try to rest. I'll come get you in about three hours."

Piotr nodded and headed wearily for his bed. He'd built the small wicker shelter himself. Unstringing his bow, he stacked his weapons by the entrance and was soon asleep.

* * *

MATT WOULD HAVE LIKED to rest too, but it wasn't to be. Not yet.

He found Lilia and told her what had happened. She'd seen Lee when he came in, but hadn't been able to talk to him yet. Seeing to the two girls had kept her busy.

"We'll be moving, probably first thing tomorrow morning. Cold camp tonight, so if you're going to cook, do it now. Get everything packed; we'll leave when Robert is ready. People have gotten used to the trek, so the only thing they'll need to do is switch from travois to cart. We can haul more stuff, do it faster, and leave less of a trail.

"Have everyone stack things on top they expect to need during the day. We won't unload the carts at night; it will save time breaking camp in the mornings."

"I understand, Matt. I'll see to it."

"Thanks, Lilia. Can you wake me in two hours, maybe a bit more? I'll need to get Piotr up and eat something. We're taking the next shift guarding the trail."

"I'll take care of it, Matt. Get some sleep."

Three hours later Lilia woke him and handed him a mug of hot tea.

"Where'd you get the mug?" Matt was muzzy from lack of sleep.

"Sandra made it. There's plenty of clay and she's been making things. Be careful, she fired it in the coals, but it may not last long. Hold your hand around the cup."

"Did you call Piotr?"

"He's waiting at the kitchen."

Matt ate on the way out to relieve Laz and Marc.

Piotr had a number of questions while they slipped along the trail.

"Matt, you said these people are slavers?" he murmured. "Why would they do that? It means to hold people against their will, correct?"

"It makes a kind of sense. There are no laws and no one to enforce them if there were." Matt's voice was equally quiet.

"There are a couple of reasons. If you want something, say a spear, how do you get it?"

"You make it yourself, Matt. I have made my own bow."

"And you did a good job; but suppose you don't have the skill or the tools? You can trade for it, or if you're strong enough you simply take it."

Piotr nodded thoughtfully. "I can understand that."

"But what do you trade? If you can't make things, you need something of value to offer the man who has the spear or bow."

Piotr nodded again. "You make arrowheads, I make shafts. We trade."

"Right. I suspect slavery didn't start that way, but something like that, trade, is what keeps it going."

"How would it start, Matt?"

"With a war, I think. Doesn't have to be a big war, just two groups of men who fight."

"Why they fight, Matt? There is plenty of room for all on this world."

"Not everyone sees it that way, Piotr. Say there's a water-hole and animals come there to drink. If two villages want the water hole for hunting, they might decide to fight over it. Or women. One village has women, the other doesn't. There will always be a reason to fight, whether it makes sense or not."

Piotr was quiet while he thought this over.

"So they fight, Matt?"

"Yes. Eventually one side wins. Do you kill everyone on the other side or capture them?"

"Well..."

"If you kill them, the story gets around. The next time you fight, the other side fights harder knowing they'll die if they lose. So the winner must capture as many as possible. What do you do with them after that, the ones you capture? If you find work for them, you've just invented slavery. And when you find yourself with more slaves than you've got work for, you look for someone to trade with."

"I guess this makes a kind of sense. But won't people fight harder knowing they'll be slaves if they lose?"

"Not always, Piotr. The people have to be willing to die first. Slavery starts in the minds of the losers before capture. People have to be fear death more than captivity.

"Anyway, we can talk after we get back to camp. Right now, we need to relieve the watch and be quiet."

12

Despite their best efforts, there had been too much to do. While the construction crews continued to work, others packed up and began dismantling the camp. There was no reason to leave more information for raiders than absolutely necessary. Robert circulated, assisting here, exhorting there, when he felt a tap on his shoulder.

"Robert, do you know where Lee is?" The speaker was the older of the two young girls Lee had rescued.

"You're Shani, right?"

The girl nodded.

"He and Laz left before daylight to scout the slavers' camp. They'll be back in a day or two. Did you need something?"

"No. But I don't know anyone else, just you and Lee and Lilia. I only met Matt for a few minutes."

"He's at his camp, Lilia too. He's probably asleep, but if you need help...?"

"No. I just wondered where Lee was."

"If you need anything, you can ask any of us. Why don't we walk over to where they're camped and talk to Lilia? I've got a question for you and I'm sure she will want to know the answer too."

"What question, Robert?"

"I'm wondering how you escaped."

"I'll tell you if you want. It wasn't easy; if they'd caught us, they'd have raped us again. Maybe they'd have killed us. They sometimes kill people who run away. The rest of the time they whip them and cut their leg just above the heel. They always limp after that."

"Not an easy thing for you to do, Shani. But the tribe needs to know what to expect if they're captured. And maybe they can escape the same way you did."

"They'd have killed us, or at least they'd have killed me. I killed the guard when we escaped. Bella, maybe not."

Robert nodded, but had nothing to say after her comment. The two soon arrived at Matt's camp. Matt was awake, drinking a mug of what was probably tea.

"Shani's about to tell us how she escaped from the slavers."

"Lee said she had a story to tell. I didn't want to press her until they had a chance to settle in."

Robert nodded. "Go ahead, Shani."

"The slavers tied us to a long rope at night. They string the rope between trees and use a shorter length of rawhide to tie us to the rope. Sometimes they tie the rawhide around our neck, sometimes it's around an arm, but usually they tie it around an ankle. They tie a knot in the rawhide that the slaves can't untie. The rawhide end is soaked and stretched first. They leave a loop in one end that's loose enough for the strap to slide along the rope. The rawhide is just long enough for us to reach the bushes if we have to go during the night.

"The other end had also been soaked and stretched before it was tied around our ankles. Rawhide shrinks as it dries, so we couldn't untie the knot. The slavers can't either, the have to cut it off. When they're ready for us to work, they just untie one end of the rope from the tree and slip the loop off. We wrap the rawhide strap around our waist while we're working. They put the loop back over the rope when they're finished with us. The rawhide chafes our legs, but they don't care.

"There's a guard who watches the rope at night to make sure no one unties it and slides the loop off. The guard sleeps, but he keeps his hand on the rope. He'll wake up if someone tries to untie it. I'd have escaped a long time ago if I could have gotten the strap off that rope, but I found a way to untie the knot around my leg."

"You said they soaked the rawhide and let it dry after they tied the knots? How did you manage to untie that?"

"I asked them for water just before we went to bed. I drank as much as I could and after they were asleep, I started soaking the knot around my ankle."

"Urine?"

"Yes. I could only pee a little at a time, because I didn't want to waste it. I caught it in my hand and held the knot in the pee. It was still tight, but I peed a little more and soaked it again. It didn't stretch very much but it finally got wet enough."

"If it didn't stretch, how did you pull the knot apart?"

"My fingernails were too short, the slavers keep them that way. I used my teeth."

Robert and Matt were astonished. Not Lilia; from her expression she'd have done the same thing.

"The knot was in a loop that was around your ankle? You must be very flexible."

"Yes. I'm still young enough to do that. Someone as old as you wouldn't be able to get at the knot with his teeth."

Robert winced and kept quiet. His respect for this girl was growing. Bending over until she could chew a knot free from around her ankle, a knot she had soaked in urine?

"I chewed on it and pulled with my teeth until it began to untie. After I got the loop off, I slipped over to the guard. He had the rope end in his hand so that he could feel it move if we tried to untie it. I yanked it out of his hand, then wrapped it tight around his neck while he was waking up. Then I took his knife. He never noticed, he was too busy trying to get the rope off his neck.

"The knife wasn't very long and he didn't keep it sharp, but it was sharp enough. I laid across him, cut his throat, and held him down until he died. After he was dead, I untied the rope and slipped as many loops off as I could so that the others could get away. Some might have been too frightened, but I think a few ran away.

"I brought my sister with me. The others may have been afraid they'd be blamed and woke up the slavers. Anyway, we hadn't gone very far when they caught us.

"They'd have found us sooner, but they couldn't follow our tracks until the sun came up. Anyway, they weren't in a hurry. No one ever escapes."

"You said Bella is your sister?" Shani nodded. "Well, you two escaped and we won't let them take you back."

* * *

LEE AND LAZ ghosted silently through the trees, approaching the spot where Lee had killed the two men.

The bodies had begun to stink.

Others had located the corpses. The two concealed themselves and watched. Two men quartered across the trail past the bodies. They kept their heads down, looking for tracks. After a low-voiced discussion, one of the trackers went back where the rest waited by the dead men. *Better them than me,* Lee thought.

Another conference; judging by arm gestures, the tracker wanted to follow the trail they'd found. The leader gestured at the bodies. Another slaver indicated the wounds where Lee had removed his arrows. but the tracker was insistent so finally the leader nodded. He spoke briefly to another man, who left the group and headed back in the direction the dead men had come from.

Lee slowly eased behind a large bush and gestured to Laz. Whispering, Lee said, "We need to go back. They've found our trail. They've sent for reinforcements and I'm guessing they'll be coming. Matt and Robert need to know."

Laz nodded and the two slipped away, using the bush for concealment. When they were far enough away for faint sounds to be unheard, Lee gestured and they began trotting.

"Shouldn't we stay away from your trail, Lee?"

"I'd rather leave them just enough sign to follow; I want them concentrating on the tracks when they walk into the ambush. As soon as we're about five miles from Riverbend, you take off as fast as you can. Bring Matt and as many fighters as he can round up.

"I'll shadow the slavers and stay out of sight. They won't expect an ambush. We can kill all of them before they know what happened. Even if we miss one or two, every one that we kill is one that won't be taking slaves. If we kill enough of them, maybe they'll decide to leave us alone. You tell Matt what I'm doing; he'll know what to do."

Laz nodded and the two resumed following the faint trail that Lee and the two girls had made.

* * *

Riverbend was still a few miles ahead when the sun sank behind the trees. They climbed a tree in the dusk before eating some of their dried meat. After a few careful sips of water, the exhausted pair slept.

Lee woke before daybreak and roused Laz.

"That bunch couldn't have tracked us after dark. I figure they're three, maybe four hours behind us, so I'll wait here. If you leave now Matt will have more time to get ready."

Laz nodded and looked back down their back trail. "How many did you see, Lee? Matt will want to know."

"I counted seven, including the trackers. There was one in charge, four others looking at the bodies. Is that what you saw?"

"I saw two more back by the trees. I guess they didn't want to get close to the bodies. That makes nine, and that fellow in charge sent one of them back to camp. He might have been asking for help, but he might have been reporting. They've got two dead men and two missing girls, so the rest of the slavers would want to know."

"Could be. Tell Matt how many you counted, less the one that went back. The others would have known two men went after the girls, but not that they'd been killed. It's going to be a real surprise when the messenger gets there. I just hope more don't decide to join this bunch, but let Matt know there could be more than we saw."

Laz nodded and loped away down the trail.

Lee looked after him for a moment, then resumed watching the trail.

His task now was to observe. It would make matters much more complicated if one of them spotted him. He'd have to run, and the slavers would be pursuing.

Far better if they continued following his tracks; the surprise would be that much more unpleasant when Matt triggered his ambush.

* * *

PAVEL LOVINGLY EXAMINED THE RIFLE. He had only a vague idea of how to use it, gathered during the fight; the weapon had features he'd never seen.

After a certain amount of fumbling, he discovered how to release the magazine.

There were a number of shiny brass objects in the box. With some nervousness, he managed to extract one and examine it. The pointed object...that was the bullet. He'd seen bullets downtime, before he was transplanted. But those bullets had been smaller, intended for use in target rifles, not this high-tech marvel.

Still, the rifle was worthless unless he learned to use it. Leaving the magazine out, at first fearful of damaging the rifle, he pulled back a T-shaped handle. Another bright cartridge popped free from an opening on the rifle's side that had been covered by a metal plate. He picked up the cartridge, wiped off the dust, and laid it beside the magazine.

He eventually worked out the functioning of the safety mechanism and tried the trigger a few times. With more confidence, Pavel inserted the magazine into its well until it clicked. Pulling back the T-shaped charging handle, he let it slide forward and push a cartridge into the chamber. Turning the safety to its 'S' position, he slung the rifle over his shoulder.

Unquestionably, Matt would be astonished. He would be surprised when he saw Pavel, but he'd have no way of anticipating that he now had a rifle. It would be the last shock Matt ever received.

* * *

MATT AND ROBERT were helping people get ready to leave. Little remained to do; they would need to pack their bedding and the kitchen supplies, but they could do that and be on the trail within an hour if Laz and Lee were back.

The time at Riverbend, resting and eating well, had made a lot of difference; the tribespeople had regained weight and strength. Even better, there was now ample dried meat, vegetables, and fruit, enough to last for the next few weeks. The weather was pleasantly warm and the game animals had returned. Plants were blooming, berries ripening on the canes, and numerous trees had fruit. It was too green at the moment, but there would be other trees farther west.

Laz found them at their work.

"Matt, there's a group of slavers headed our way. Two appeared to be trackers, so they'll be ahead of the rest. One's a leader. I counted nine, but the leader sent one back to their camp so there might be more."

"Lee's watching the rest?"

"Either that, or he's hiding and waiting for them to get closer. He didn't want to be seen, so he may have pulled back after I left. He thinks an ambush would be best. He said you would know what to do."

"I've got a few ideas. We'll round up as many people as possible and bushwhack them where the guards were posted. It's got plenty of cover for our people and no place they can run to. Can you come along and give us a hand? If they aren't on Lee's heels, you can rest there."

"Give me a minute. I need a drink first, but I do want in on the fight."

Matt nodded. "See what Colin's wife has available at the kitchen. You'll have a few minutes while I get people together, so get yourself something to eat and a drink. We'll leave from the kitchen when everyone's ready."

Laz ate a slab of jerky and drank a gourd of Margrette's tea. He managed half an hour of rest while Matt assembled his force.

Lilia, Sandra, and Millie were at the rear when Matt led off. Laz sighed wearily and joined the women.

At least he was walking now instead of running.

13

L ee concealed himself near the trail and settled in to wait.

He'd seen no sign of the raiders; perhaps they were having trouble following the trail? Still, they were slavers; they would know how to track someone. How else would they find escaped captives?

Matt should have the ambush party in position by now. Assuming that Laz had gotten through with the message, of course. Had something happened to Laz? Lee's situation might become very interesting if Matt hadn't set up the ambush!

But Laz was a skilled woodsman now. He would have gotten through with the warning and Matt was dependable; he'd be there.

Anyway, there was nothing Lee could do about it. He would act as if the ambush was waiting, but maybe have a backup plan.

The trackers wouldn't be far ahead of the rest, no more than forty yards, probably less than twenty. The main party would be close enough to provide support, but far enough back not to get in their way.

Lee decided that if necessary he would become bait for the ambush. He would reveal himself to the trackers and stay far enough ahead to keep them following, but not close enough to be endangered.

Another option; if necessary, he could slow the pursuit by putting an arrow into one or two. After what he'd interrupted when the slavers caught up to Shani and Bella, shooting a few others would be very satisfying! If the ambush wasn't ready, Lee would bleed them as much as possible.

He was a skilled archer; with luck, he might even wipe out their entire party. Did he carry enough arrows to kill all of them? A mistake could be fatal and the tribe wouldn't be warned. Some might be captured by the slavers before anyone knew they'd found River-bend Camp.

Better to lead the slavers into the ambush, let Matt and company kill them. But...

If the raiders decided to quit the chase, the situation would change. Lee could go back to camp for help or follow the retreating slavers and kill as many as possible by himself. He could try to salvage arrows; some inevitably became damaged and the slavers might break others. No, he could only count on the ones in his quiver. Lee had a dozen arrows, enough but only just. Shoot when he was certain of a hit, and make sure to not miss.

As for pursuing them, Lee knew where they would be going and there were numerous places where he could hide and wait. That would work even better, don't chase the slavers, pass around them while they watched their back trail. Ambush them somewhere ahead; launch one or two arrows, slip away.

He could do that until he ran out of arrows. Or targets.

If any of the slavers *did* manage to get back to their village, they'd be completely demoralized. Instead of chasing the tribe, they might be more inclined to run away!

Lee would wait a little longer. If the slavers didn't appear soon...

What if they had decided not to follow?

The tribe would then be left with two options, neither of them good: abandon Riverbend Camp and continue west, possibly while being pursued, or turn and attack the slavers.

Of course, the slavers might decide to simply ignore the escape of two captives and the death of three of their number, but that seemed unlikely. They survived by conquest and held their prisoners through fear. As soon as the other captives realized that Shani and Bella had escaped, they would try it too. The slavers might claim they had killed the escapees but sooner or later the remaining captives would find out the truth.

Slaves would die trying to escape, some might actually succeed, and others would have to be crippled. This would reduce their value. If more escaped, they would spread word of what the slavers were doing. Raiding would become more difficult.

No. The slavers would follow Shani and Bella. They would have to.

But for the tribe to attack a camp of sixty warriors, do it with only twenty bowmen? Say, a dozen shafts per bowman, two hundred forty arrows against sixty targets?

And some of the bowmen lacked the skills that Matt, Lee, and a few others had.

Suppose the raiders had used slaves to build a wall? What if there were traps along the trails to discourage captives from escaping?

No, attacking the raider's village was something to do only if they had no other choice. Lee's thoughts keep going, looking for the best option.

Fleeing and hoping to remain ahead of the raiders was dangerous too. Extra guards would be needed, which would take manpower away from other tasks. Even so, moving seemed less risky than attacking the raiders home village.

The raiders wouldn't want to leave. They had markets, villages that bought their captives and traded things the slavers couldn't make for themselves. They had discovered a system that worked, they wouldn't want to abandon it.

But what if the slavers decided to raid the tribe? Some would remain behind to guard the captives they already held. Perhaps half their number, say thirty of them, would be available for a raid.

Thirty raiders was a threat the tribe could handle, especially if they lacked bows. Better, the threat wouldn't last forever; after the tribe had gone two weeks on the trail with their new carts, they'd be too far away for this group to pursue. For another, attacking people who moved every day was not the same as raiding a fixed camp.

The raiding party had mobility and could choose when and where to strike. They could surprise the villagers, hit them when they were least ready. Defensive walls made a difference, but none of the villages Lee had seen had them. Building fortifications took time, materials, and labor, none of which were available to people barely managing to feed themselves. Their primary need would be food, followed by shelter, so raiding small villages was a simple matter.

But when the objective was moving, especially when it was a well-armed tribe, things changed. The travelers would be alert, so surprise was unlikely. Conclusion, a direct assault wouldn't succeed. The attack might fail.

How long could the raiders follow? Two weeks travel by the tribe meant twice that long for the slavers. The tribe would move faster and with less effort. Hauling supplies by cart instead of dragging them on a travois made a huge difference. The raiders would have to travel light in order to be more mobile than the tribe. The raiders would have to attack before they ran out of food.

Launch a quick frontal attack on people armed with bows? Suicide. The raiders' only chance would be to get far ahead and pick a spot to ambush the tribe.

His thoughts kept moving examining and discarding options. Already a warrior, Lee was learning to think like a leader. He would discuss his ideas with Matt when he got back to camp.

What if the tribe changed course every few hours? The raiders might lose the trail entirely, and in any case, they wouldn't be able to set an ambush. The mathematics of a chase actually favored the tribe, not the raiders.

As for supplies, the tribe had meat enough on their carts to keep moving. The raiders had no way of knowing that, but it would complicate their tactical problem when the tribe moved every day and the pursuers ran low on food. Even in a world that hadn't developed military science, logistics ruled.

When it became obvious that a raid was too risky, the slavers would turn back.

Lee ate some of his dried meat and decided he'd waited long enough.

Regretfully, he slipped away and headed for Riverbend.

* * *

LEE FOUND Matt late in the afternoon.

"I don't think they're coming."

"I agree. I'll leave Laz and Sandra to watch the trail just to be sure, everyone else can go back to camp. Lee, you and I can relieve them after midnight. It's always possible the slavers got smart and waited. We've based our plans on what we thought they'd do, but we've got to consider what they're capable of. If one of their scouts got past us, they'll know about our camp. Even so, it would take time to assemble people for a raid. They might be intending to attack tomorrow.

Attacks usually happen at dawn, so if you and I are watching we'll know about it before it happens.

"I'll keep Piotr with me, you take Marc with you and watch the other side. I'll talk to Robert; he can wake people up and get them moving at dawn. We'll catch up, watch behind the tribe for a while and when we're sure they aren't coming, catch up. How does that sound?"

"Sounds good, Matt. You feel sure of Piotr? I know you had concerns earlier."

"He's been steady. No way to tell for sure until he actually has to shoot someone or stick a spear in them, but I'm willing to give him the benefit of the doubt."

Lee nodded. He waited with Matt and watched as the rest of the ambush party assembled.

"Looks like we wasted our time, people. Laz, you and Sandra find a place closer to camp where you can watch the trail. Lee and I will relieve you at midnight. If you spot anything, we don't need heroes; I'm depending on you to get back and warn us. Questions?"

The two glanced at each other and shook their heads. "I understand, Matt," Laz said.

"Good enough. The rest of you, let's head for camp. Get some food, catch a little sleep, be ready to leave at dawn."

The group began to straggle as Matt led them toward camp. "Keep together, people. We don't know for certain the slavers didn't slip past us. Stay alert. We've got enemies and we don't know where they are."

The party closed up and they moved toward the camp as the sun slipped below the tree line. The weary party of would-be ambushers found little left to do at camp. They ate a cold supper and soon sought sleep.

Matt discussed his plans with Robert, then he too went to bed.

* * *

LILIA WOKE him at midnight and he got Lee and Marc up. They had food, kept out from the evening meal, and the two ate as they moved silently out to watch the camp's northeast side. Matt woke Piotr and the two ate as they slipped southwest out of camp in the darkness.

Laz and Sandra were nearly exhausted when Matt sent them back.

The night passed slowly before first light brightened the eastern sky. Matt decided to wait a few more minutes before heading back to camp. He had just joined Piotr when Lee approached.

"We've got movement. I can't tell how many yet, but they're not really skilled at moving in the dark. They're coming from the east. They might be following the drag marks."

"You left Marc watching them?"

Lee nodded.

"OK, I'll leave Piotr here and I'll go join Marc. Lee, slip into camp and wake up Robert. Try not to make any noise. We need everyone up, armed, and ready. If they don't realize they've been discovered, we can surprise them. How far out are they?"

Lee thought for a moment. "Half a mile at most. We were about five hundred yards out when we heard them moving. I didn't think anyone could cross the stream without us hearing, so we've been concentrating on the land approaches. I really didn't expect anyone would try an attack from that direction. Good thing we kept looking!"

"Yeah. I don't know if the people you saw are from the mine guards... it sounds like them, coming from the east, but I didn't expect them this soon. If it's the slavers, they found our drag marks and they're following them. I guess it doesn't matter; whoever it is, we're going to fight. Friends don't sneak up on a camp in the dark."

Lee nodded. "Any instructions for me?"

"Collect the people you know, the ones who were scouts before we got here. They're tired, but they'll just have to keep going. Keep them quiet and move out to the north, then head east for maybe five hundred yards. I'd like you to be about a hundred yards north of the trail and five hundred yards out of camp. I'll take charge of the rest of the tribe and we'll set up a defense east of the camp. If this is the guards, they'll have Pavel with them, Gregor and Vlad too. They'll know about how many of us there are, but they might not expect the three deserters we picked up. Anyway, they won't know how the camp is laid out and they won't expect us to be waiting. The new guys can stay with me."

Matt thought for a moment, then went on.

"If Pavel's with them, he has that rifle, so hiding behind a bush won't be enough; bullets will just go through it. You'll need to take cover behind large trees, something at least eighteen inches thick. Bigger is better. Be ready to hit them from the side As soon as we hit them from the front, you be ready to attack from the flank.

"I doubt they'll stand. The survivors will pull back as soon as the others start falling. But remember, we don't want to scare them, we want to kill as many as possible.

"A rifle is dangerous, but it's not that bad if you're careful. If you get a clean shot at Pavel, take it; I doubt anyone else knows how to use the rifle. But in any case, kill as many as you can. Don't worry about the ones who are down. We'll deal with them later.

"If they turn on you, try to counterattack. As soon as we know, we'll move out from where we're hiding. Either way, we'll have them between two forces.

"One last thing. Pass the word to your people. Kill them all."

Lee nodded, grim faced. "We'll do it. Be careful, Matt."

"You too, Lee. Good luck."

Matt caught up with Robert where he was waking the camp, remaining as quiet as possible.

"Send me people as soon as they're ready. I'll set up a defense line over there, to the east. We'll meet the raiders just beyond the edge of camp. Warn people to be quiet when they move up. Tell them to bring all their arrows and their spears. Have them find me when they get there and I'll guide them into position. I'll keep Carlo and the other new guys with me.

"If this is Pavel and the guardsmen, I plan to teach them a permanent lesson."

Robert nodded and moved away, silent in the darkness. Matt reached into his belt pouch took out a slab of the dried meat. He would eat now; he might not have time later.

As the tribespeople trickled into position, Matt pointed where he wanted them to wait. They moved silently, tense and some clearly fearful.

Matt took up his own position, spear on the ground by his right foot, quiver ready, arrow on the string.

Fearful or not, the tribespeople would have to fight. Once again, Darwin's World presented them with a stark choice.

14

M att settled in to wait, glad that he'd had time to eat. Wonder of wonders, none of his archers had the urge to talk; the only way to tell that two dozen people waited behind cover, all with bows and arrows except for the group waiting with Matt, was the absence of forest noise.

If Lee was right about the raiders and the noise they were creating, they wouldn't notice.

Matt had been waiting about an hour when he spotted movement across the clearing.

Very careless; the raiders hadn't even bothered with scouts. As nearly as he could tell, they had spread out slightly and followed the drag marks the tribe had left more than two weeks ago. If this was their idea of a combat formation, they were in for a rude lesson in tactics!

Matt couldn't yet recognize faces in the dimness, but it wouldn't be long. He spared a glance to the three spearmen who would guard him while he killed as many as possible before exhausting his arrow supply.

They were ready.

When his arrows were gone, Matt would look for a place where his group could enter the fight. Other tribesmen would be watching, and from that point on the fight would be mostly hand-to-hand. Absently, Matt let go the bowstring and touched his axe and knife.

The sky continued to lighten as the raiding party got closer.

Wasn't that Gregor near the center of the group? If so, Pavel would be nearby. Matt half-drew the bowstring; if he could get a shot at Pavel...

The raiders were less than forty yards away now, almost in range for the less-accurate among his bowmen. Matt waited; his conscious mind might wander, but the subconscious would be calculating distance, visibility...

Matt raised his bow and immediately launched his first arrow. Thirty yards away, Gregor fumbled at the feathers sprouting from his throat. Feebly clutching the shaft, he fell. Matt had another arrow ready before he hit the ground.

That other one, there...but the man dropped before Matt could shoot, two arrows sticking from his abdomen. The tribesmen had been waiting for Matt to take the first shot.

Matt waited, bowstring half-drawn and an arrow ready. Where was Pavel?

Somewhere behind the first row of raiders the rifle fired, two quick bap-bap popping sounds, then silence. Was Pavel that skilled, able to limit his fire to only two rounds? Or had he run out of ammunition?

Someone was down, wounded, possibly dying. There had been a choked scream after the shots and a thrashing in the brush where the tribe waited. No time to worry now, there was a target...the man Matt shot fell down. Matt reached for another arrow and searched for a fresh target.

No Pavel.

The raiders were milling about, beginning to back up. They bunched together momentarily and Matt put arrows into the mass without waiting to see what he'd hit.

Matt's searching hand came up empty. He glanced at the quiver; empty.

Matt dropped his bow, shrugged the quiver strap from his shoulder and let it drop. He stooped and picked up the spear, long steel blade glinting wickedly in the morning light.

"Time to get among them. You four, stay with me and make sure the one you stick isn't me!"

There was no time to look back; they would follow, or not. Matt, crouching slightly, charged toward the raiders.

Few of them were standing. Bodies littered the ground, one or two moving feebly. The arrows had done their work.

Matt spared a glance at Gregor...dead...as he ran past. Still no Pavel.

The group ahead was retreating. Not running yet, but if any of their leaders had survived it was not apparent.

More fell, this time to arrows from Lee's position. Confused, they hesitated just long enough for Matt to be in range of his spear.

They were still falling from Lee's flanking position! Matt saw his intended victim drop as an arrow suddenly appeared in his shoulder. Grabbing Piotr by a bloody sleeve, Matt yanked him back from the melee.

"Watch where you're shooting!"

The arrows stopped; Lee had heard.

Bushes rustled as Lee and his men filtered through to attack the remaining raiders from the side.

One by one, the raiders dropped their crude spears, those that still had them.

"Take off those swords. You won't be needing them." Clanks followed as the shocked men obeyed.

One of the raiders, recovering from his panic, stepped forward.

"Are you going to kill us?"

"I haven't decided," Matt answered. "Do what you're told, don't make my decision for me. Lee, take them around and see to the wounded. Leave Laz with me, I've got a job for him. Badly wounded raiders, have the captured ones finish them off. Not Pavel or Vlad, though. If you find them alive, put a guard on them and call me.

"For our wounded, send someone to find the Wise Woman. She can decide how best to care for them. Tell Sal to find help if she needs it. Piotr, ask Robert to join me here, Colin and Margrette too. I need to talk to them."

Margrette was the first to arrive, followed closely by Colin.

"Margrette, our people are going to need food. Round up some help, get the kitchen going. Hot meal for everyone quick as you can, OK? We'll need to sort all of this out first, but I want to leave the camp as soon as possible. We've still got those slavers to worry about.

"Colin, you're with me. When Robert gets here, we'll decide what to do with the live raiders."

Piotr came back and found Matt. Matt looked at his pale face and understood something was wrong. "What is it, Piotr? Are you hurt?"

"No, Matt. It's Robert. He's hurt bad. The Wise Woman is with him, but Robert..."

"All right. You stay with me. I'll see him as soon as I finish up here."

"Colin, we've got a mess on our hands. People aren't going to want to move, but we've got it to do. We have no way of disposing of the bodies. I don't have a count yet...I estimate at least twenty dead, about seven unwounded or only scratched. I haven't seen Pavel yet, but he was here. I heard two shots. Lee is seeing to the wounded. I told him to have the ones we captured execute their own seriously wounded, except for Vlad and Pavel. This is a lot of dead meat, and it's going to draw predators. Can you take charge of our people, get them ready to move as soon as we finish here?"

"Sure, Matt. I'll take care of it. What are you going to do with the other prisoners?"

"Turn them loose. No weapons, nothing but the emergency packets we all carry. I'll donate mine, can you round up six more?"

"Sure. You can have mine too. Didn't Pavel and his three have them?"

"You're right, they did. Collect Robert's packet too.

"I'll visit Robert and our other wounded. As soon as the Wise Woman has done as much as she can, we'll prepare a place on a cart for any who can't walk. Use lots of furs for padding, you'll know what's needed.

"Everyone's tired, but maybe we can travel for a couple of hours and quit early. But we've got to get as far away from here as possible before the scavengers arrive."

Colin nodded and left.

Matt, suddenly feeling the letdown, looked tiredly around the battle-field. Such a waste!

* * *

LEE RETURNED WITH THE PRISONERS, all of them pale and shaky.

"I've got one more job for you people," Matt told them. "After that, I'll turn you loose. What happens to you after that is your problem. The mine people didn't trust you, neither can I. If I ever see you again I'll kill you on sight.

"Lee, I've got instructions for you. But first, are you OK? You're pale."

"I'm fine, Matt. Not easy to order those men killed, but I understood why it had to be done. We couldn't help them and if we left them behind, wounded, some animal would have them within an hour. Killing them quick was the merciful thing to do."

Matt nodded. "I'd burn the bodies if we could, but we don't have the time. Our people have to get ready to move. Those slavers are still out there, we don't know where, but if we aren't careful they'll hit us when we least expect it.

"I've got a final job for your prisoners. I can't take the time to supervise them myself, you're going to have to do it. Take my three spearmen, Willie and Carlo and Karel...I'll keep Piotr with me ...and when the prisoners are done, give them one of our emergency packets. I'll send someone up with food, so feed them and turn them loose.

"Here's what I want them to do."

Lee looked at Matt in shock when he finished speaking.

"Matt, you're sure?"

"Yes. Did you find Vlad or Pavel?"

"Vlad's dead. Arrow in the chest, broken shaft; not yours or mine, someone else shot him. I salvaged the arrowhead. I put the prisoners to doing that as we went around, gathering up arrows. One of my scouts bundled them and they're back at camp. We found your bow and quiver, too. You can pick it up when we're back at camp...I couldn't be sure which arrows were yours.

"As for Pavel, he's alive. He's wounded, arm pinned to his chest by one of my arrows. I left it where it was."

"I forgot about my bow. All right, finish up, turn those people loose, then bring your scouts to camp. Robert's hurt bad, I'm going there as soon as I can, but first, where's Pavel?"

"He's right over there, by the two guards. The rifle...long black thing?"

"That's it."

"I moved it away so he couldn't reach it. But I didn't know what else to do with it."

"I'll take care of it."

Lee headed to where his guards waited. The cowed prisoners showed no signs of wanting to resume the fight.

Matt walked over to Pavel. The rifle was as Lee had described. Matt picked it up and looked at it...similar to what he'd seen before, but not the same. Well, he'd have time to figure it out later. He found the safety lever on the left side, noticed a similar one on the right, so the rifle was meant for left or right-handed users. He moved the lever to the S position and slung the rifle over his shoulder.

Despite the wound, Pavel was conscious and still full of hate. He glared up at Matt.

"That rifle wasn't much use, was it?"

"Fucking thing jammed after two shots. I would have..."

"You should have made sure of me, Pavel, back there on the river. We found the place later, bloody spot where I was laying after you hit me."

Pavel looked back at him and said nothing.

"Are you going to keep talking or get this arrow out of my arm?"

"Neither, Pavel. I've had enough grief from you."

Matt unslung his spear as Pavel's eyes opened wide. Stepping forward, Matt put the steel blade just below Pavel's rib cage. Leaning on the spear, Matt watched as the point slid into Pavel's chest. When half the long blade was in, Matt levered down on the spear to force the sharp blade to slice through lungs and up into the heart. Pavel's mouth sagged open and blood gouted. His eyelids drooped, then stopped moving as the blood flow slowed to a trickle.

"Tell Lee to collect his arrow and throw this body with the others."

Matt turned and walked away. Piotr looked pale...well, if he didn't know before, this world wasn't long on mercy.

* * *

Piotr led Matt to the Wise Woman. She was working on Robert, mercifully unconscious.

"How's he doing?"

She shook her head. "His arm is shattered. It will have to come off. It's just fortunate that he's not feeling it. I've never done major surgery. I know how, of course, but only from watching the surgeon do it. He had anesthetics and antibiotics, but I don't even have surgical tools."

"Do the best you can. You worked in a hospital downtime?"

"I was a medical assistant. I had some training and I've watched surgery, but except for basic anatomy and things like nutrition I'm not qualified."

"You're the most qualified person we have...Doctor. Get a couple to help, plan what you've got to do, get it done before Robert wakes up. You can use my knife, the axe too if you need it. We had classes on battlefield first aid and the history of combat medicine. One thing I remember about surgical procedures from the Civil War and the age of sailing ships, good surgery was fast surgery. The sooner it's done and the stump bandaged, the better." She nodded her understanding.

"I can't keep calling you Wise Woman; don't you have a name?"

"I do. But I preferred what Robert called me, the Wise Woman."

"So what's the name?"

"It's Bambi, all right? But if you laugh or call me Bambi, you'd better hope I never have to cut on you!"

"You don't like Bambi, I don't like Wise Woman. You can pick any name you want. No rule says we have to stick with what parents gave us. Any name you'd prefer?"

"Elizabeth. Call me Elizabeth, it's my middle name."

"Fine, Elizabeth. I'll let you get to work. Draft anyone except Lee or Colin or Margrette. They already have jobs."

"I'll take the new girl, Shani. Millie too. Millie's worked with me already and Shani's not afraid of blood."

"Done. Do the best you can for our people." She nodded and Matt walked away.

People were working and there was nothing that needed his immediate attention, so he headed back to camp. People would need help packing their bedding on the carts.

* * *

AN HOUR later four tribesmen brought Robert into camp, two with their arms slung under his torso, another who supported his head, and one carrying his feet.

"Bedding furs first. He'll need a thick pad. Lay him on the pad with his head up, feet down. Find Margrette and get something to eat, we'll be moving out soon.

"First, let me thank you for this morning. Not easy, but it had to be done. I wish we could stop to rest now, but we can't. The slavers are still out there somewhere and the dead will attract predators. Thanks again, and let's get to work."

Matt made the rounds and repeated the short speech whenever he found people together.

The tribe had been fortunate. Robert had fallen victim to the two gunshots Pavel had gotten off before the rifle jammed; the only other injuries were scrapes and a minor cut on a forearm.

Matt took a few minutes to examine the rifle. It needed cleaning, but the stoppage was a simple stovepipe jam where a brass case had failed to eject. Matt pulled back the charging handle and pried the stuck case out of the extractor. Apparently, Pavel hadn't known how to clean the weapon. It would probably fire if he needed it, but the bow was more reliable for now.

Leaving the rifle unloaded, magazine inserted and safety on, Matt laid it with his other gear on the cart. He recovered his bow, then picked his arrows out of the collection salvaged by Lee's crew. Two would need to be repaired, but the others were usable, if bloody. Matt put them in the quiver and slung it over his shoulder. Elizabeth showed up moments later and returned his knife and axe, newly cleaned of blood. Matt nodded his thanks.

Lee found him munching on a slab of the meat Margrette had prepared.

"All done?"

"Yes. I turned the captives loose. They weren't happy, but I showed them what had happened to Pavel and they understood. I had them pile the bodies across our trail. Animals will scatter the bones, but they'll be a warning as long as the drag marks are visible."

"The rest of it too?"

Lee nodded. "A couple of them vomited, but poking them with a spear got them over that!"

"Pick your freshest people, put two on point and two on flank security. We're moving out."

Half an hour later the tribe was gone, wheels creaking.

Behind them, a row of crude spears, collected from the raiders, stood across the trail that led toward the slavers' village.

Impaled on each spear was a slack-jawed head, chopped from a dead raider by his companions, watched silently. Matt had left a mute warning of what the slavers could expect should they follow.

Pavel got a final honor, although it was doubtful he'd have appreciated it.

His sightless eyes watched down the trail from the center of the line.

15

By Matt's rough estimate, the weary tribe had traveled perhaps ten miles by late afternoon, far enough to leave the carnage well behind. Scavengers would have found the bodies, but they'd have no reason to follow the tribe.

As for the slave raiders, if they followed Matt intended to be ready.

Lee had found a place where the stream widened and flowed over a sandy bottom. Matt consulted briefly with Colin, then decided to cross the stream before setting up camp.

Lee took charge of moving Robert, still unconscious, across the stream. He looked shrunken; being wounded, then undergoing a crude amputation had taken a lot from him. Matt touched his forehead...very warm, almost hot...but Robert didn't respond.

Matt found Margrette working by the kitchen fire, newly started.

"Robert's going to need broth when he wakes up. Maybe that willow bark tea you used before? Talk to the Wis...uh, Elizabeth...about that; she might know of other herbs you could include."

"I'll take care of it, Matt. As soon as I've got food cooking, that will be my next priority."

Matt nodded, then left to find Lee and Colin.

"Lee, guards out as soon as you can. Rotate them every hour tonight, say two people patrolling around camp until just before dawn, then add two more. Have them stay together and tell them to look sharp. The slavers have a lot more experience at raiding than the people we fought. That raid this morning might even have been their first attempt.

"People are going to be tired, but we can't just quit because we're tired. We got a little soft, living at Riverbend; it'll take a few days before we're able to do fifteen or twenty miles a day.

"Plus that fight took a lot out of people. Some are going to start remembering what they did. Killing people is never easy, even when you know it has to be done. If they're tired, they'll find it easier to sleep.

"Talk to your security people, make sure they're not having problems. I'll pass it on to Colin too; he's in charge of the camp until Robert recovers. Sal, too...he's responsible, so I'll give him a job. He built the kitchen firepit as soon as we stopped and put up a couple of forked sticks with a crosspiece for cooking. I'll talk to him about digging a latrine and putting up a shelter for Robert."

"Will do, Matt. Let me know if there's anything else you need, all right?"

"I will. I'm thinking we travel for a week or so, then take a break for a few days to get caught up. Find a stream or a spring for water, shelter from weather, and a place we can defend.

"While we're there, plan on sending someone reliable to scout our back trail. We don't know what those slavers will do. I'd like as much warning as possible if they decide to come after us. If they do, I've got a few ideas.

"Meantime, I found those lighter bows. Even the arrows were saved; we had to make new ones because with the new bows' stronger draw weights they flexed too much.

Everyone has a bow now, but we'll need arrows, a lot of them. I'll start teaching Piotr what I know about knapping flint points. Someone needs to take the short swords we captured and start removing the handles. We may even have enough to put steel blades on everyone's spear, maybe even make a few replacement spears.

"We've got more than enough blades, Matt. We ended up with more than thirty after the fight. The raiders had at least one and most had two."

"Good. Talk to Sal, tell him to leave handles on four or five swords. I want to make one into a saw, fine teeth with very little set to the teeth. Elizabeth had a hard time taking Robert's arm off. She needs a bone saw."

Lee nodded. "I'll take care of it, Matt. You need to rest too."

"I'll rest as much as I can. Who's your most reliable assistant?"

"Probably Laz, but Marc is good too."

"Which one is the better archer?"

"That's probably Marc. Laz has more power, but Marc rarely misses."

"OK. Put Marc in charge of teaching the new people. Have him set up a butts down by the stream. Use small branches with lots of leaves, tie them tight, start the new guys shooting from close range at first. I'd like them to shoot at least a hundred arrows each day until they're skilled."

"Uh, Matt...I don't think they can count. They didn't come from the future, they're like me. If it's more than what I can count on my fingers, I get lost. Shani, Bella, and Cindy too."

"Oh, my; I didn't think about that. All right, I'll work on it. Have them shoot as much as they can, then turn them loose after supper's ready. They can turn in after they eat."

* * *

MATT JOINED Lilia and the two ate supper in companionable silence. Matt spoke as they were finishing.

"I need a schoolteacher. If you were picking someone for the job, who would it be?"

"That's a tough one, Matt. Maybe Millie? Why?"

"Some of our people have never learned to do simple arithmetic. I'm guessing they can't read, either. Can she teach the basics, reading, writing, and arithmetic?"

"Matt, I don't know. But I'll find out. I'll look at other people too, see if there's someone better or at least someone who could assist her."

"Sounds good. How's Piotr settling in?"

"He's doing fine. He's a hard worker, helps everyone get their camp ready. He's staying next to our new woman, Marja; I don't know if you noticed."

"I hadn't, but I'm not surprised. I haven't had time to notice much of anything lately, what with the security problems and deserting guardsmen and escaping slaves!" The two shared a grin.

"Maybe it will get easier now that we're moving, Matt."

"Maybe. But I'm going to delegate, delegate, delegate. You're my contact with the other women, the one I turn to when I need answers; Lee's the general and chief cop. If we ever need one, that is. Marc's teaching archery, Millie's the education department, Colin will see to running the camp at night, Elizabeth is the medical corps, and I'm going to just sit back and let them solve all our problems!"

"Sure you are, Matt." The two laughed and Matt left to see how Robert was faring.

Elizabeth was clearly worried.

"He's not responding. I tried to slip a bit of that herb tea I made in his mouth, but it dribbled out. He's feverish. I just don't know..."

"Elizabeth, you've done all you can. Let Shani or Bella watch for a while. Take a break, get some of Margrette's tea with lots of honey, talk to other people. There's nothing you can do here that Bella can't do."

"You're right, Matt, I could use a break. Can you send Bella to me?"

Matt nodded and left.

He toured the camp. People were working, although showing the signs of the things they'd done. Finally Matt decided to call the various activities off.

"Start gathering at the cookfire, people. I've got a few things I need to say and it's better to say them there."

A few minutes later found most of the tribe around the fire, waiting.

"It's time to stop working and get some sleep. There are things to do, but there are always things to do. Guards are going to be out tonight, watching for animals and those slave raiders. It may be necessary to call you out during the night if you're needed. For now, everyone's had food and some of Margrette's excellent tea.

"We've had a long day. We're going to be stiff and sore tomorrow, all of us. I know you're worried about Robert, but there's nothing anyone can do. We'll do our best to care for him, but now it's up to him. I just wish we had medicines, even alcohol. But we don't. One day, when we get to our new home, we can set up a distillery and start developing better medicines. Better ways to care for our sick and wounded too.

"For now, the best thing we can do for Robert is let him recover on his own. I know you want to visit, but he won't realize you're there. He's getting the best care we can give him and Elizabeth or Bella will be there. He won't be unattended when he wakes up.

"We'll start archery practice tomorrow after we stop for the day. There's also going to be school for our youngest and anyone else who can help teach or who wants to learn. Education is a community effort and that's the way we'll begin. Defense, too. We're all responsible for defending our camp. Keep your weapons sharp and always nearby.

"If you have questions about supplies, talk to Margrette. Colin is the guy to ask about setting up camp. Sal will be working on our carts. The work is necessary, so if he needs you to help, give him a hand. Women, if you've got a problem, see Lilia. When Robert recovers, he may make other arrangements but let's do it this way for now.

"If we find a good spot to camp tomorrow, we'll stop early. Let everyone catch up on their rest, do what needs doing but also recover from what we've already had to do. If you've got ideas or suggestions, make them to me or one of my deputies. I'm going to be depending on you, all of you."

Matt stopped talking and the tired people headed for their beds. He went back to where his extended family was camped, found one of the folding chairs and sank into it. He intended to rest for a moment.

Lilia found him a little later.

"Matt, it's either more problems or a boon. Sandra's pregnant."

"Oh, my. I have no idea what to do about that."

"You don't have to do anything; women have been taking care of this forever. We'll take care of Sandra when she needs our help."

Matt nodded and leaned back. His eyes closed and he soon nodded off.

Lilia woke him a little later.

"Matt, come to bed. Tomorrow will come when it comes. You need rest too; we're all depending on you now."

Matt nodded and rose from the chair. He was asleep as soon as he lay down.

Sandra woke him the next morning. Matt stumbled off to take care of morning needs, stretching aching muscles over-used the day before. He'd felt this way before...but that had been downtime and he'd been quite elderly then, not to mention sick!

Margrette had a hot mug of tea waiting at the kitchen fire and Matt drank it gratefully. It helped. When had *she* gotten sleep? She would need an assistant or two. Someone...he would find someone. Maybe Colin could help.

Elizabeth and Bella found him there. Elizabeth's eyes were puffy, Bella was more solemn than Matt had seen her since she joined the tribe.

"Matt, Robert died. It happened during the night. Bella was with him. He never regained consciousness. She told me about it when I woke up."

Matt sighed.

"Elizabeth, Bella, thank you. You did the best you could. I'll tell the others when they wake up. We'll meet here, by the fire. If you could cover Robert's body for now...?"

Elizabeth nodded, and taking Bella by the arm went back to where Robert's body lay.

One more chore Matt would have to take care of. He wasn't certain what to do. This was the first time a death had occurred in camp. It likely wouldn't be the last. Robert...he'd been the tribal leader before Matt joined.

How should they dispose of the body?

On the plus side, there was a new life growing. He would let Sandra announce that in her own time. How far along was she?

He wondered for a moment. There had been opportunities on the trek and during that extended layover at Riverbend Camp...

Could Lee, maybe Laz, even himself...

Who was the father?

16

"Colin, I don't know what we should do about Robert. We don't have the time to dig a grave deep enough to protect the body, and it would take half a day with the few tools we have. Cremation is out; the smoke would be visible for miles! We've got enemies out there, some we know about and maybe some we don't. Plus people are still tired from yesterday. Got any ideas?"

"Matt, my people buried their dead at first. That got expensive, so cremation was becoming popular. Some started disposing of the bodies naturally on something called body farms. There was a place, away from people, that was used just for that. Put the body out, let nature take care of it."

"Would it bother people if we did it that way? Robert was the tribe's leader; I don't want people to think I didn't respect him."

"We've watched you two work together. It won't be a problem."

"Well, I'm not going to just dump Robert's body in the dirt. Find a couple of people and have them build a platform. Set up four posts and tie the platform to them, then lay crosspieces. The whole thing will need to be level and strong enough to support Robert, but that's it. Don't make it too tall, maybe four feet at the most. Lay Robert's sleeping fur over the crosspieces and put the body on that. When you're done, we'll have a short meeting and people can say something if they feel like it."

"What about his weapons? Early people left weapons and tools with their dead. Other stuff too, things the person loved."

"Robert's first love was the tribe and we need the weapons. We don't have enough spares as it is. I'll pass the bow and arrows on to whoever can handle them, same with his spear. Some are still using flint or obsidian points, waiting until we have new steel blades ready. Better, I'll have Lee decide who gets the weapons. Marc or Laz will probably have ideas too."

"You're serious about making people responsible, aren't you?"

"I am. Robert and I shared leadership and divided up our responsibilities. I plan to continue doing something similar. Lee will keep doing what he's been doing, I'll just give him more independence. But people may have their own ideas who they want as camp leader, so we'll need a meeting when we have more time. Let's get Robert's body taken care of, then get people moving. The faster we get back to work, the less time they have to brood.

"I want to make as many miles today as we can. We'll stop when we find a good spot this afternoon, set up camp and get people fed, then plan on holding a tribe meeting after supper. See what people want to do about the leadership."

"Matt, you're the leader. I think even Robert felt that way."

"Well...I suppose I can keep doing it, but we need to talk about it anyway. We'll do it today unless some kind of emergency happens."

"I'll see to it, Matt."

With that, Matt left Colin to his tasks and went to find Lee.

"Lee, I think we need a chance for people to remember Robert, say something before we leave. Colin is having a platform made, but we still need security. What do you have out now?"

"Two pairs out watching. One pair behind us, watching our back trail; the other is roaming, covering both sides and the front. I'll plan on taking a guard post while you're having your meeting. I'll use Millie and Sandra, team them up with Lilia and me. Let the ones from Robert's original tribe have a chance to say farewell."

"Good plan. Something else you need to know, I intend to make as many miles as we can today. We don't know whether those slavers are on our trail or if they found those heads and turned back, so we need to keep going.

"I want to stop an hour or two before dark, get camp set up and people fed, then hold a meeting to decide who leads. Your guards won't be able to be there, so talk to them and find out what they want. Everyone takes part. Any problems with that?"

"No. I'll change the guards, send the others back so they can be there when you talk about Robert. I'll talk to you later."

Matt nodded and headed for his own camp. Lilia and the others were packing the bedding already, so there was nothing for him to do. Well, he'd take a turn pulling a cart when the tribe moved out; Marja and Piotr could pull a cart and perhaps the two girls could pull the fourth one. Perhaps not; Bella was now spending most of her time with Elizabeth.

"Piotr, I'll be back after I'm finished seeing to Robert. Can you talk to Marja and the girls, Cindy and Shani? We've got four carts to pull and Lee will be on guard, Sandra, Lilia, and Millie too. Bella will be helping Elizabeth with hers. The others will come in after a while and take over as soon as we're moving, I don't want them to have to catch up. Our family will be leading when we move out. Colin will have the job of making sure the rest don't straggle."

"Sure, Matt. We can handle things here."

Matt nodded. The day had barely started and there were still so many things to do!

Colin had finished the platform and his workers had carefully laid Robert's body atop his sleeping fur, his thin leather 'blanket' covering the body. Matt wondered briefly if he had made the right decision about the fur and leather...the leather in particular was always useful...but decided that practical considerations would take second place to esthetics this time. The tribe would need to hunt soon anyway. Leather and furs would be found.

The meeting was short. Only Elizabeth wanted to speak, and she kept her comments short and to the point.

People took a last look at the covered body on its platform and drifted away. Soon only Matt was left.

He looked at Robert's body, misshapen now. The missing arm made it appear that the body couldn't be that of the vigorous, physical man Robert had been.

But there was nothing to do, nothing that remained to be said. Matt hadn't believed in religion before, and being transplanted and altered by futurists had done nothing to make him a believer. No religion he'd heard of envisioned humans being transported to a virgin world before death!

No, Robert was gone. He wouldn't hear what Matt said now.

Matt turned away; he had a cart to pull.

Behind him, the thin leather covering fluttered. Then the breeze subsided and all was still.

* * *

LEE WAS visible to the northwest, so Matt headed that way. The cart's wooden wheels squealed on axles never been properly lubricated. The load was far enough back so that the two shafts, formerly part of a travois, didn't feel heavy. Pulling it was bad enough without having sore arms or shoulders at the end of the day! Matt made a mental note to explore the idea of a strap system, something that crossed behind the neck before extending under the arms and attaching to the shafts. Perhaps with padding from rabbit skins...?

Lilia took over pulling the cart after the tribe took a short lunch break to eat and rest. An hour later found them moving again. Matt took Laz and relieved the two men serving as rear guard.

"We'll wait a while," he explained. "If anyone's following us, they'll be moving and we'll be hidden. I'm of no mind to permit being followed. Another head on a pole would suit me just fine, especially if the head belonged to one of those slavers."

Laz nodded. Bows ready, arrows nocked on the strings, they took up positions behind concealing cedar trees. The thick branches and abundant scalelike needles hid them very effectively, while allowing glimpses of their back trail.

Unlike the drag marks left by the travois, the wheels left comparatively little trace. The first heavy rain or strong wind would eliminate the trail completely.

Flies, including a persistent deerfly, found them and refused to be discouraged. Laz finally managed to kill it, but otherwise the afternoon passed without incident.

"Time to go, Laz. If they're following, they're far back. They may even have lost our trail. We're going to have to move fast if we intend to get back before supper."

Laz nodded and Matt led off, jogging until they were warmed up then picking up the pace. An hour later they stopped for a moment to listen. Ahead, the cart wheels creaked.

"Half an hour, maybe. We can slow down if you need to."

"I'm all right, Matt. We haven't really been pushing ourselves."

"I didn't think we needed to. We'll catch up before dark and we won't be too tired."

Laz nodded and fell in behind as Matt trotted toward the screeching.

"Laz, why don't you stop here? I'll have Lee send out a couple of people to relieve you. Shouldn't take more than half an hour. I'll see you at the kitchen. We'll be meeting there after supper anyway."

* * *

LEE HAD PICKED a spot just past a ridge for the tribe to camp. Scrubby trees on the crest would help conceal smoke and the ridge would hide the light from the flames. A sentry on the ridge would have a good view of the surrounding terrain.

The ridge provided enough elevation to give Matt an idea of the land they would cross tomorrow. He saw a succession of rolling ridges ahead, none very high, that extended as far as he could see.

Not good tactically, because someone could approach fairly close without being seen. But perhaps it could be turned to advantage; a watcher on the military crest, i.e. just past the top of a ridge, could detect anyone following.

The ridges were thick with grass, but Matt saw nothing moving. Well, animals often bedded down until late afternoon, then found a water source before they resumed feeding. There might be hundreds, even thousands of animals behind those ridges.

For the moment the tribe still had dried meat. Snares, set around camp in the evenings, would bring in small game, a welcome supplement to the dried meat. The women would find edible plants too.

Matt passed his comments to Lee as they ate, this time a stew Margrette had prepared from dried meat and roots she'd collected when the tribe crossed the stream.

"We need to have a meeting, just you and Laz and me. This one needs to be kept quiet; I don't want anyone to know what we talk about."

Lee looked at him questioningly, but nodded agreement.

The three walked away from camp while others were eating.

Ensuring that no one was close enough to hear, Matt told them what Lilia had said.

"Sandra's pregnant. It's her decision when she wants to tell people about it, but we three have our own decision to make. We don't know who the father is."

Laz simply looked at him. Lee looked at the ground and his ears grew pink.

"In practical terms, it could be any of us."

Matt paused and let that soak in.

"The women have decided all along who they sleep with. That's likely to continue. Whether they stay with one man or with a different one every night is their choice. We don't have anything to say about it, nor should we. Their bodies, their decision.

"Here's what I propose. I think it best if we *all* consider ourselves the baby's father. I heard of something downtime called a 'line marriage'; the benefit was that everyone accepted equal responsibility for raising the children. That has a lot of advantages for us. If someone's killed, the children will still have a family.

"I think this is the fairest way for us to handle the question of which man is the parent. There are going to be more pregnancies. We'll have to deal with the question, so I'd like the process in place before it's needed. Babies are babies, and raising them as a group is more important than who contributed the genes."

Lee didn't seem disposed to argue, although clearly, he had no idea what genes were and how they were contributed. Matt sighed. That would be one more thing to add to the educational curriculum. But later; they had their hands full for now.

"We keep adopting new people and now there are as many of us in the family as there were in Robert's original tribe. We accepted Piotr, Marja, and the two new girls, Shani and Bella. The three men, Karel, Willie, and Carlo, that warned us about Pavel have camped with us since they joined the tribe. I consider them full family members, because they fought with me.

"Whatever we decide is right for us regarding children and relationships, that's probably what the rest of the tribe will do. Not that I'll encourage them, but the women will talk to each other. If it works for us, they'll adopt the idea.

"We can't just abandon the others. I know we thought we might go our own way once, but that's not going to happen now. If the meeting tonight goes the way I think, we'll have responsibilities.

"Think about it and let me know if you have a problem with sharing the responsibility. Sandra's not the only one, you know; Millie's been visiting different men too. The women may not know which man's the father, and it doesn't really matter.

"As long as there's no problem, I'll stay out of the way and let the women decide. If people start having fights, I'll get involved; we simply can't afford to let that happen. We have to trust each other, not wonder if the man next to us will fail us when we need him.

"My mother has only been with you, Matt. At least since she found you and brought you back."

"I think you're right, Lee. I hadn't thought of it, but the other women have stayed away. Maybe she said something to them. I've been too busy to notice. Or care, really. I'm so tired by the end of the day that all I want to do is sleep!"

* * *

AN HOUR later the meeting went off roughly as expected. Matt was confirmed as tribal leader, Colin his principal deputy, and Lee was head of security.

Matt thanked the tribe for their confidence and sent them off to bed. Lee left to post a new shift of guards. Piotr would be on duty tonight; he would see that the guards were awake and that shifts changed periodically so Lee could get a full night's sleep.

Matt spoke to Lilia before bedding down.

"We're going to have to camp somewhere near the middle from now on. The tribe leader can't be camping away from his people."

"I understand, Matt. I'll see to it tomorrow. Marja may not like the idea, there's someone in the other group she doesn't like. If she prefers to keep her distance from them that's OK. I'm sure Piotr will stay with her.

"I'll have a talk with her. She's just going to have to ignore personal feelings for the good of the tribe. I'll find out who the person is she's avoiding and have a chat with that one too. I don't know about you, but I'm tired. What say we call it a day? I've got our sleeping pads set up over here, behind that screen of brush.

Matt nodded and the two headed off to bed.

Perhaps he wasn't too tired after all!

17

Five days later the members of the tribe crested a long ridge. They faced a steep slope, with a river at the bottom.

The ridge ran roughly north to south, paralleling the river's course. Across the river, the terrain looked much like what they'd experienced recently, rolling hills and grassy open areas broken by thickets of oak and patches of berry brambles.

Matt conferred with Lee and Colin.

"It looks like there are bigger trees down there, along that river bottom. I think we should camp here on the bluff tonight. It will be a dry camp, but we've got jugs and gourds of water. That should be enough for drinking and cooking. We can refill the containers tomorrow.

"We're getting low on dried meat. We're going to have to hunt soon and the carts are worn. Sal thinks we can reshape the axles, extend the taper back and cut off the worn ends, which will allow us to keep using the wheels a little longer. They're showing signs of wear too, so let's hope those trees can be used to make replacements.

"Lee, find us a good campsite by the river. We'll move there tomorrow. Send scouts out to look for game and watch our back trail. We haven't seen anything of the slave raiders, but that doesn't mean they're not there. Use two-person teams.

"Colin, it's going to take most of the day just getting the carts down to the river. We want a route that slants across the slope if we can find one. It's a lot easier, even if it takes longer than going straight downhill.

"We'll use as many people as necessary to get the carts down. It will take most of the day I expect, but that can't be helped. We'll also need a guard up here until everyone gets moved.

"Take the kitchen stuff down tomorrow morning right after breakfast, as soon as Margrette's ready. Her cooks can set up at the new campsite and have hot food waiting when people get the carts down.

"Lee, you'll need to use women for security; we'll need the men to handle the carts. Assign Millie or Cindy to take care of the little ones, but have the parents take them down the hill first. Whichever one you assign, she can take care of the kids while the parents help the rest of us.

"If a cart gets loose and heads downhill, it's dangerous. We don't want anyone in front. Another concern, some of our tools might end up in the river and we can't spare anything. Plan so it doesn't happen.

"We'll take the carts down one at a time, wheels first. Have the people hold onto the shafts to guides and ropes tied to the axles to control the speed. One or two men on each rope should be enough.

"No cart starts down until the one below is clear. If we use two teams, one can take a cart down, then climb straight back up the hill. The carts will stay in that gully, so have people climb straight up the slope. The next cart can be going down while they climb back and rest a bit. We can get everything done in half the time by doing it that way and no one will be looking uphill at a runaway cart.

"Be ready for mishaps. It's up to us to see they don't happen. If people are always above the carts, they can't be underneath if the rope breaks. Losing tools is bad, losing people is worse. Suggestions?"

"Matt, I think you covered it all. We might need a few changes after we get started, maybe the number of people needed to hold a cart back, but if it happens we'll cope," Colin said. Lee simply nodded.

"I want the camp to be something like we had at River Bend. We'll take a few days to rest and repair the carts while the hunting crews brings in meat. What do you think?"

"Sounds good, Matt. I'll get my security people out. I'll see you in camp when I get back."

"And I'll see to setting up the camp, Matt."

"Thanks, guys. I'm going to take a walk along this hilltop, see if I spot anything. Fresh venison would taste pretty good tonight."

Matt unslung his bow and nocked an arrow, then hunted south along the top of the long ridge. He walked slowly and swept his eyes from side to side.

In this way he found the abandoned campsite.

The site appeared to have not been used in the past week. Matt walked around and carefully worked out the evidence.

One person might have hunted during the day, then returned to the fire-pit in the evening. A large tree with low-hanging limbs stood nearby. The occupant had slept beneath the tree, judging by the crushed grasses and dried tips of branches left behind. The fire-pit was no more than five long paces away. A cautious person, then; the tree was available if danger threatened, the limbs would make it easy to climb, and the fire would keep most animals away.

Matt found a clear track in the dirt beneath the tree. The occupant had been a man, or possibly a woman with a very large foot. Woods-wise, whoever it was; Matt found an area that had been disturbed by digging. This had been a latrine or possibly a midden where bones and scraps had been buried. Wise people didn't toss food remains out for scavengers to find; the pit would have served to dispose of waste and scraps before the camper covered it with the excavated dirt.

The position of the track indicated he or she had climbed the tree, possibly to use it as a lookout. There were no tracks indicating a cat or bear had come by, so it was unlikely the tree had served as a refuge. As for wolves, likely they were following the bison herds, picking off the young or sick. No, he'd used it as a place to look over the countryside.

Matt wasn't curious enough to find out what had been buried; it was sufficient to know that something had. More significant, the man as Matt now thought of a man, had remained in this camp for several days and left little evidence of his presence other than the firepit and the crushed branch tippets where he'd slept. The bedding would be gone soon and the fire-pit would be covered by windblown grit. A person passing in the future would likely never realize a man had lived here.

When there was nothing more to find, Matt went on his way, now wary of human eyes as he searched for game.

He found a ravine leading down the slope at an angle. Apparently, a rock outcropping had diverted the course rain or snowmelt followed and over the years the depression had deepened and widened. This might possibly be a better route the tribe could follow when they left camp tomorrow.

The ravine opened up as Matt got closer to the river. The riverbanks were lined with growths of tall reeds and occasional patches of native cane, a kind of bamboo. The water wasn't flowing fast, but the river was broad and the water appeared deep. The tribe would be unable to ford this one; they'd have to find another way to cross.

Until then, the reeds would be useful and the grasses growing in the open were tall. They would be a good source of fibers for rope.

Perhaps Colin or Sal knew about crossing rivers. Matt would ask after the tribe got down the slope.

He surprised a group of pig-like animals, a little smaller than the domestic pigs of downtime but larger than peccaries. He put arrows into three of them before the others escaped.

Matt dragged the carcasses together after opening the body cavities and removing the entrails. He used willow branches to prop the body cavities open. This took less than an hour and he was soon following the ravine to the top on his way back to camp.

Colin and Sal accompanied Matt to collect the pig carcasses. Piotr came too, bringing Carlo, Willie, and Karel.

Matt showed them where he'd gathered the carcasses. Colin decided it didn't make sense to haul extra weight; using Matt's axe, he removed the heads and dumped them into the river. When Matt looked at him, Colin explained, "We don't yet know where we'll set up our river camp, but wherever it is I'd rather not have pig heads drawing scavengers. Let them float downstream." Matt nodded; smart.

The others took turns hauling the pigs. Two men teamed up by grasping a foreleg each and letting the lower body drag. The task was physically tiring but not otherwise difficult. Matt and Colin watched over the group during the trip.

Two hours later found them at the camp. Margrette and Colin took over then, butchering the carcasses and passing the cuts to assistants to cook.

"Just having fresh meat is good, Matt. It's too bad; we'll have to spit the meat and cook it over the coals. I'd have made a pork roast, but there's no clay up here.

I coated meat with clay at Riverbend and buried it in coals. It was a good substitute for an oven. Maybe later we can dig a pit and roast an entire pig. Lay hot rocks in the bottom, cover them with leaves and lay the pig on the leaves. Add another layer of leaves and pile more hot rocks on top. Cover it with dirt for a few hours while the pig cooks. Are there more of them?"

"A lot more, I think. They've been rooting all along the river. The group I surprised had at least a dozen animals. Another thing, we've been eating well since winter ended. I think we can afford to trim off the fat from these. If you'll save as much as you can, I'll appreciate it."

"Sure, Matt. What are you using it for?"

"I'm going to boil it first and skim impurities off before letting it cool. This makes it into lard, and that should work better than beeswax to grease cart axles. As soon as we trim the old ones down and refit the wheels, I'll slather on the grease with thick leather gaskets around the spindles to hold the goo in place. Maybe a squealing pig can stop the squealing of wooden wheels on wooden axles?"

Matt grinned and after a moment Margrette grinned back.

"We'll save as much as we can, Matt. Have you thought of mixing beeswax with the grease when you're boiling it down? The mix might be a better lubricant than either one by itself."

"I'll give it a try, Margrette. Any other ideas you come up with, just let me know.

"Sure, Matt. I'll tell the cooks too. Those three pigs will feed all of us, but only just. Don't expect a lot of leftovers."

"As long as people are well fed tonight, I don't care. We can get more day after tomorrow. Were you able to collect any vegetables?"

"I've got some greens. That river; does it have cattails or reeds?"

"It's got reeds, I don't know about cattails. I didn't see any, but I'd be surprised if there weren't some, maybe a little farther upstream or downstream. The tender shoots coming up from the roots are edible.

"Another thing, as soon as we're set up tomorrow, put out hooks. It'll be nice if we can have fish as well as pork to break the monotony of bison meat every meal."

"I'll see to it, Matt. Thanks for the pork."

Matt circulated through camp as people settled into evening routine. Some left for the cookfire after they finished arranging their beds, others looked for Elizabeth. Some had blistered feet, and she'd become adept at lancing blisters. There was no bandage, of course, but draining the fluid kept the blister from spreading.

Matt found Lee waiting for supper to cook.

"I found a campfire and a track from a large foot, probably a man and a careful one too. He bedded down under a tree he could climb in a hurry. His camp looked well set up. I guess he stayed here three or four days, judging by the ashes in the fire-pit. He may not have moved far and we don't know if he's friendly. But he's not one of the slavers; he'd have had no time to get here ahead of us. We also changed course a couple of times to get around brush and thickets of trees. He couldn't have known which direction we'd go after we did that. I think he's probably like I was, dropped here by the futurists, and he's been surviving on his own ever since. Warn your scouts, OK?"

"Thanks, Matt, I'll pass the word. They're watchful anyway, but warning them about the tracks won't hurt."

"We'll have our hands full tomorrow, getting everything down that hill. I'll work with Colin until the job's done. Unless someone comes up with a better place, I intend to follow the ravine down, the same one we came up while dragging the pigs. It's better than that small gully we saw.

"Find someone to scout the riverbank while we're taking the carts down. We want a place we can defend as well as a comfortable place to camp. I don't think it's worth looking for a crossing; that river's too wide and it looks deep. The little ones can't swim and maybe some of the adults can't either. Even with safety ropes, we'll lose people. A ferry would be better, if we can manage it.

"As for Sal, I'll want him to set up camp first, but after that I need him to work on the carts and see if any of his workers know a good way to cross the river.

"I'd rather have waited up here while you scouted for a good camping spot near the river, but if those raiders find us I didn't want to be trapped. We've got the high ground but no water except what we brought with us. Sending people down to fill our small jugs, then bringing water back...we can't supply the whole tribes that way. Another disadvantage, if we have to retreat we'll only have one way to go, downhill. If we can get among the trees, height advantage won't matter; their spears won't reach us.

"If raiders catch us while we're halfway down the slope, we're in real trouble. They'll have the high ground and there's no cover. If they throw spears downhill, we'll lose people, no way around it."

"If we can get across the river without being attacked, I think we're done with the slavers. It's just as well. I feel sorry for the people they captured, but I'm not risking our tribe to free people we don't know. If there were fewer of the raiders, I'd consider it; but for now I won't take the chance.

"The critical time will be while we're moving down that slope. Everyone is going to be busy and we won't be able to just drop what we're doing and fight. The women will be on guard, the cooks will be working on the kitchen, Millie or Cindy will have the children, and the men will have their hands full controlling the carts.

"I estimate the carts weigh about half a ton, loaded. We may even have to offload the heaviest ones before we can get them down the slope. If we do, the men will be packing heavy weights, dried meat, things like those steel blades, and the tools we stole from the mine, everything. There are also a few spare axles and wheels.

"I'll look at that slope again, Matt. Maybe I can put some of the women farther down the slope to watch. Is there any chance you could be up there with that rifle?"

"Good idea. I'll carry the rifle, but remember I've only got one magazine with twenty-three rounds." Matt held up his fingers, closed them and then opened them again to indicate twenty, then held up three fingers more. "I cleaned the rifle, but it might jam again. I won't know how reliable it is until I use it, and I can't practice because there's no replacement ammo.

"The bows are dependable. Make sure everyone's quivers are as full as possible. Collect any spare arrows, even the practice ones that are a little crooked. We can make more later, but we can't make anything if the slave raiders win."

18

Matt slept later than usual. Perhaps he was becoming accustomed to others sharing the responsibilities of leadership. Perhaps Lilia had influenced his behavior.

He found a bush east of camp that needed his attention. Refreshed, he looked for the kitchen and something to eat. Reflexively he looked for Robert as he approached the kitchen...but Robert was gone, his body abandoned miles behind the tribe.

In time, Matt would stop looking out of habit, but that time had not yet come.

Colin was there, assisting his wife with providing food. Lilia too; Lee had been there but had gone after eating. People were working and preparing for the day. Having nothing better to do, Matt went back to his bed and rolled up the furs, tying them in a long sausage-shaped bundle for easy packing.

Carrying his furs, he joined the group following Colin to the carts. All the rope in camp had been pressed into service this day, lighter ones braided together to provide three long pairs of heavy ropes to attach to the cart axles. A thoughtful person had tied a series of knots near one end of the rope to help the men hold on.

True to his word, Matt also carried the rifle, the unfamiliar weight slung over his right shoulder. His quiver rode at his hip and the unstrung bow slanted across his back, held in place by the bowstring. It would be the work of a moment to remove the bow and string it. But he missed the weight of his spear.

That spear held memories; it had never failed him. From first employment, killing the bear that mauled Lee to the execution of Pavel, the spear had been his go-to weapon for close work. It was now with his bedding on the cart. Hopefully he could reach it in time if it was needed.

Matt motioned to Laz and each grabbed a pole extending from the front of the cart. Leaning into the weight, they pulled south toward the ravine. Others lifted poles and followed. Soon all the carts had joined the familiar parade they'd established since converting their travois to carts.

* * *

LEE EXAMINED the weapons carried by the women who would provide security today. Sandra had been offered the job of caring for the children but declined.

"Use Cindy. I'll get enough of children later when we begin teaching. For now, I'll be more useful here."

"So be it. Mom...uh, Lilia...will you take charge of the left side of the defense? Take Marja and Shani with you. Sandra, you take the right side. Keep Millie with you and I'll distribute the rest of the women as they show up. I'll keep Elizabeth and Bella with me; if they're needed elsewhere, I'll release them.

"Set up the defense in a half circle, centered on the ridge above the ravine. I want the two ends about a half-bowshot north and south, the center of the circle a little farther out. As soon as you've got the line established, I'll take Elizabeth and Shani and move out a few paces in front. Keep everyone close enough to see a signal if you spot anything suspicious. I'd rather have to deal with a false alarm than not see danger before it got too close. Questions?"

Lee had adopted Matt's manner of ending a discussion. If the others noticed, none mentioned it.

There were no questions so Lee took his two charges and headed out to find a place they could watch from while remaining concealed.

His efforts were not good enough.

"You expecting company, boy?"

The words took Lee by surprise. Reflexively he started to raise his bow.

"You point that thing at me, boy, I'm gonna stick it up your ass sideways. If I wanted to hurt you I wouldn't have said nothin'. Use yore head if you expect to live long enough to learn better."

Lee lowered the bow, recognizing truth when he heard it.

"Who are you?"

"Call me Tex. We ain't got much time to jaw if them people over east of here ain't yore friends. I guesstimate they're an hour away at most."

"Okay, Tex. We don't have any friends in that direction; what did you see?"

"Maybe thirty people. About two dozen of 'em are packin' spears, rest are carrying packs."

"Nice bow, Tex. Where'd you get it?"

"Made it. Been with me a fair spell now. What're you gonna do about them people?"

"First, I'm gonna...going to talk to my mother. I'll leave her in charge here. I need to talk to Matt after that. Will you come with me?"

"I reckon. Matt's that tall drink o' water?"

"I reckon." Lee felt a flash of irritation...he was beginning to talk like this stranger!

Lilia was equally surprised. She hadn't seen Tex slip between her line and Lee's forward observation post. She understood that it was time to shorten the defensive line, assuming the strange man was correct; others could slip through as easily as he had.

The task had changed, from warning the tribe to holding off an attack until Matt could reinforce them.

"Howdy, Matt. This kid yours?"

"Next best thing. Consider him an adopted son. You the one been camping on the ridge north of here?"

"I'm the onliest one I know about, and I don't miss much as do say it myself. The kid says the people I spotted ain't friends of yore'n? You can call me Tex, by the way."

"Not friends. They might be slavers."

"That fits. Two dozen with spears, maybe half that many carrying packs. The ones with packs are roped together. Slaves, I reckon."

"We'll fight. You feel up to a scrap, Tex?"

"Wal, they chased off them camels I was huntin' east of here. That's how I spotted 'em, the camels took off, and I knowed I hadn't spooked 'em. So I looked, and here they came, bold as brass."

"Anybody every mention you've got an accent, Tex?"

"Nope. Not since I got here, anyway. Come to think on it, I ain't talked to anybody since that happened."

"We can talk later, then. I'll take the center and Lee will command the front. Feel like staying with me?"

"Nope. I'll get on up front with the kid. Lee, you said? Maybe I can shoot me one or two of them slavers. Never liked working for most bosses and I surely would hate to work for one if I couldn't up and leave. Nossir, I think it might feel purty good to stick an arrow from Ol' Slick here," he patted the bow he carried, a virtual twin of Matt's in thickness, "into a few of them people."

Matt nodded and went to find Colin as the two headed to where Lee had left Lilia and the women.

* * *

"Y'ALL LET your women do your fighting, Lee?"

"Nope. We all fight, men, women, for all I know the babies would bite if you got close enough. We've got a few women that can hold their own with anybody."

"You don't say! Well, this place is shore different, so maybe women warriors are natural-like here. They ever kill one of them saber-tooth things?"

"Maybe, but not since we joined the tribe. Matt and I did, once, but Matt said there were likely others with bigger fangs than the one we killed."

"Reckon he's prob'ly right. Once you see one with them long fangs, you won't wonder any more. It's plumb difficult for them to open their jaws wide enough to use them teeth."

"Tex, I've got to say, I never heard anyone talk like you. I never heard of anyone called Tex, either."

"Bunches of people with that name where I come from, back before Saint Peter picked me up and dropped me here."

"Saint Peter? Matt doesn't have a name for the one that brought him here. I was born on this world, what Matt calls Darwin's World."

"I figgered it had to be Saint Peter. Plumb magical, it was; he didn't make much sense when he talked to me, but I never talked to no angel before so I just let it slide. I was just glad I could walk ag'in! That hoss purely messed me up."

"We can talk later. If you're right, the raiders are maybe half a mile from here?"

"Might be a tad less. But you're right, no sense lettin' 'em know we're hidin' in the weeds. That woman you called Mom, she taken?"

"Matt thinks so." Tex shook his head in disappointment. "We're here, so let's get people ready."

Lee looked around and spotted Matt and Colin moving toward him, now about a hundred yards back. Matt was carrying the rifle. His bow had been strung, but still hung behind his back.

Matt left Colin to move the tribe's men where they would likely be needed and joined Lee and Tex.

"Any sign of them yet?"

"Not yet. Tex thinks they're half a mile or less. You leave anyone with the carts?"

"Just Cindy. She's got the kids and I didn't think a reserve would be worthwhile. We can't retreat, so we'll fight right here. Everyone's got a bow now. Colin will have them drop their spears by their feet. It'll be spear work after we run out of arrows.

"Colin will take the first shot at about fifty yards. Whoever gets past that, the women will be ready. They'll just about double our fire-power as soon as the raiders get closer.

"I've told Colin not to shoot before that, but not to wait either. At fifty yards, they're in range of our bows but we're not in range of thrown spears. I plan to give this bunch the same treatment I gave the others."

"Well, they'll definitely have a different view after it's over. You can see a long way from up here. We could see them already if it wasn't for those trees at the bottom of the hill."

"Better view, not that they'll appreciate it from atop a spear. If anyone spreads word about Robert's Tribe, I want them to tell people to stay far away if they're not friendly."

Tex was turning his head from one to the other as Matt spoke and Lee replied. Finally he too joined the conversation.

"That looks like one of them M-16 rifles. I tried one before, back before I met Saint Peter. You got any more of 'em?"

"Just this one, Tex. I've used an M-16 a lot. I'll keep this one."

"Too bad. Ol' Slick's handy, but she won't shoot near as far as that thing."

"I don't intend to shoot very far with this one either. If the bows are as effective as I expect, I may not shoot at all."

Conversation lapsed. The men now stood a couple of paces in front of the line.

Despite the natural tendency to remain close to others, Lilia and Colin had convinced the tribe to spread out; they now occupied a front almost fifty yards long and two yards deep. Here they would stand. Win or lose, it would happen atop this nameless ridge.

Lee looked around, appreciating the view. Would he meet his end here?

The sky was clear. There was no wind, just the long ridge stretching north and south. The land sloped gently to the east, scrubby brush giving way to low trees. The sun was now well up, behind where the raiders would appear. At least the tribe wouldn't be looking directly into the sun when the raiders appeared.

Would they attack immediately? They had figured out a way of overcoming the limitations that Lee and Matt had discussed, using slaves as porters to carry supplies. What would they do with the slaves when they realized their quarry was alert and facing them from the ridge?

Lee didn't have long to wait.

The trees at the bottom of the slope appeared to ripple briefly. The ripple spread to the left and right and Lee was looking at a line of armed men, lined up and looking upslope.

The slavers wore leather caps, some adorned with what appeared to be bone or tusks. They paused just long enough to bring up the slaves. While Lee watched, they took more leather from the packs carried by the slaves. The heavy leather formed an open-sided garment that each raider quickly tossed over his shoulders, half falling to the front and half to the back. They hastily tied leather thongs together at the sides. More leather came out of the packs and was quickly strapped on to protect their knees and lower legs.

Matt was standing by his shoulder when Lee glanced to the side.

"Some bright fellow has invented armor. It might even be cuir bouilli; if they boiled the leather in wax, it will turn a thrust from a flint spear. It won't stop an arrow, and if the rifle works the bullets will ruin their day.

"Pass the word along the line. We'll let them start uphill and leave them no place to go after we start shooting.

"Lee, you and Tex will get your chance when they're even with that bush. Let Colin take the first shot; I don't want to try making changes now." Matt pointed. "I'll see whether the rifle works after I see what the raiders do."

Lee nodded and resumed his tense wait.

After the raiders finished donning their armor, Lee found out what else they had planned.

"Matt, they're pushing those poor people out in front."

"I see it. Hold your fire for a moment. Each slave has a raider behind him. I wonder if one is the leader? Anyway, I'm about to find out how well this thing is zeroed. I'm going to start taking slavers out, the ones that think they're hiding. You two be ready. Call the slaves to come up and get behind us as soon as the ones behind them are down.

"Put one of the women in charge of them, Shani maybe. She might even know them and they're more likely to trust her. We can't have them running loose behind us.

"If I can't put those slavers down with the rifle, shoot the slaves. After they're down, kill the slavers. No quarter, no mercy. If they try to surrender don't bother. Just stick a spear in them and move on."

Lee nodded. Tex looked at Matt with respect.

"You'll do. I've seen bulls that weren't that mean."

Matt nodded and clicked the rifle's safety from safe to single-shot. Shooting slightly downhill, but at this short range he wouldn't need to hold low, the bullet's trajectory could be ignored...

Matt extended the rifle's butt forward until the weapon was upright, then placed the butt on the ground. He dropped into position immediately behind it and pulled the butt into the hollow of his shoulder. Wriggling about to get comfortable, Matt was soon lying with the rifle snugged into his right shoulder, left elbow under the forearm, sling brushed aside. At this range he wouldn't need the sling to stabilize the rifle. His opened left hand provided support as Matt lined up the sights.

His action had been seen; someone down there knew what a rifle was. A raider slid into position right behind the slave providing cover, only his eyes and leather helmet visible.

Almost close enough...and then they were.

Without conscious thought, long-ago training kicked in. Matt's finger squeezed the final millimeter and the rifle slammed. The recoil was slight, but enough to take Matt's view off his target. A tinkle to the side revealed the fall of the empty shell. Slight adjustment of the body, align the sights...another slam.

He smoothly switched from target to target. Below, the slavers hurriedly abandoned the slaves and ran back to their group. Four remained on the ground, motionless, victims of Matt's shooting.

Matt quickly removed the magazine and ejected the round in the chamber. Picking it up, he slid it into the magazine and stuffed that into his belt. He laid the rifle on the ground and slipped his bow from where it rested across his back. Drawing an arrow, he launched it toward the bunched raiders.

A virtual storm of arrows struck among the raiders. Many fell immediately while a few limped backward. In the rear, some saw what was happening and turned to run.

"Lee! Take your scouts after those people. Shoot them. No risks to our people, and I don't want any survivors!"

"I understand, Matt. Scouts! With me!"

Without being asked, Tex ran after Lee. He soon passed Lee, running as if he'd spent his whole life waiting for this moment.

Tex paused briefly to put an arrow through the throat of a raider who limped ahead of them. Pausing long enough to take the man's spear, Tex ran on. The pause allowed Lee to catch up and arrow a raider of his own.

They paused at the top of the next ridge to listen. Nothing moving, no noise...a slight breeze had come up during the fight. But no other sounds disturbed the quiet, only their breathing and the soft whisper of moving leaves.

Lilia found them. "I think they're all down. I counted ten running away and we've left that many on the ground behind us."

"OK, mom. Collect everyone and we'll start back. Nasty job ahead, but Matt wants it done."

Lee stopped long enough to behead the man he'd shot. Carrying the head by its long hair, he moved on to the next.

Lilia and Tex each had their own head now. As the scouts joined the small party, they soon acquired heads of their own.

Lee was happy to drop the head he carried by the mass of dead raiders. Three heads were already there.

Matt was supervising the task, jaw clenched. Clearly it was something he considered necessary but not something he enjoyed. He had done his share of the cutting; he held his axe in his right hand, blood dripping on the ground by his feet.

"Put the heads on spears, Matt?"

"Not this time; we'll stack them into a pyramid. I'll show you what I mean. I want their spears, as many as you can collect. We've just added nine new people, maybe. I'll talk to them and let Shani and Bella talk too. If they can be useful, we'll bring them into the tribe. If not, we can at least arm them before we turn them loose."

"I thought there were more, Matt."

"There were. The slavers speared two. When it became clear they weren't working as human shields, they just speared some to keep them from running. The rest were tied to the dead ones."

"Bad people. I'm glad they're dead."

"Me, too, but things have changed. I think we need to go back to their village and take out the rest. They only have maybe thirty people left and one of them is probably a recent addition, probably one we turned loose after the Riverbend fight. We can fix that mistake now. I had a chance to talk to one of the men we rescued. The village isn't fortified, something I was concerned about, and if we kill most of the slavers he says the captives will turn on them.

"We can leave day after tomorrow if you agree it's something we should do."

19

The discussion after the ridge battle had gone as Matt expected. Helped by input from the former slaves, the tribe had agreed that a raid was indicated.

The attack would have a dual objective, wipe out the remaining slavers and free their captives.

After their losses, the slavers would likely kill the other captives. They wouldn't want to leave anyone behind who might tell others. Grisly task done, the raiders would then move on.

The information came primarily from José, one of the men who had been used as shields.

The slavers, nomads back then, had surprised the villagers and moved in. A few of the original builders had been killed, others taken prisoner. The situation had remained that way for two weeks. Then the raiders learned the villagers feared being capture, taken by parties of three or four men that came up from the south every few years. Once taken, the people were never seen again.

The raiders contacted the capture parties and became their suppliers.

The village changed to a marketplace where slaves could be held until sold.

José's picture was incomplete, but it seemed likely that slave labor or peonage had taken hold in the territory that would be northern Mexico downtime. Trading parties came up in the spring and early summer to acquire new stock. Some of the slaves would farm, but there were also extensive mineral deposits. Primitive mining was dangerous and labor-intensive. Spanish invaders had used Indians in the same way, downtime.

Trade established, the nomads-cum-slavers scouted locations during the summer and raided during the fall after the intended victims had gathered food for the winter. The gatherers were added to the few slaves raiding parties brought along to pack their supplies. Burdened with food and their few possessions, the enlarged slave column made its way back to the village to wait until sold.

José might be wrong, Matt thought. *The slavers wouldn't abandon the life-style because they lost a battle. Like-minded replacements would be recruited to make up losses. They would keep the village until contact would be made with the traders. Slaving would begin again.*

* * *

AT THE MOMENT, everyone was resting. The tribesmen had spirit but not much stamina, at least when compared to Matt, Lee, and Tex.

"Tex, how long have you been here on Darwin's World?" Matt asked the question. The two were slightly apart from the group.

"I've been here...oh, must be ten years now. Ol' Saint Peter fixed me up better than new and seemed to think I'd have a hard time stayin' alive here. Shoot, I had it rougher in West Texas!

"It was a mite cold that first winter, but compared to Montana? Naw, I just built me a place to roost that kept the snow off. Scraped out a place for a fire, drug up a bunch of dry wood, crawled between a couple of buffalo hides at night and I was snug 'til the springtime. I reckon I was a little bit gamy by then, but nobody was around to sniff 'cept me, and I was used to it!

"Besides, you want stink, you oughta smell what it was like after I took a dump! I'd been eating buffalo mostly and sometimes I had to about rassle that crap before it would come out! But I got 'er done. No stranger to bein' like that, even if it was from a different cause back before I got here. Sittin' on a John Deere seat for ten or twelve hours, it sure-enough packs your gut tight!

"Saint Peter brought me here but this don't seem like any heaven I ever heard of. I expected maybe I'd meet somebody else if all them preachers was right. After I tried to kill myself, I figured I might not like where I ended up. But I wasn't gonna argue with the feller that dropped me off. I couldn't even walk before; I spent most of the time right after I got here running 'stead of walking just 'cause it felt so good."

"You tried to kill yourself, Tex?"

"Yep. Thought I'd finally managed it, too. Feedin' me through a pipe in my gut, tube in my mouth keepin' me breathin', that ain't no way to live. I could'a lasted for years that way. Druther just get 'er over with. Worst thing that could 'a' happened, I'd 'a' stopped breathing when I bit through that tube. I was already weak as a newborn calf, figured I'd be dead in a minute or two. So I bit down as hard as I could on that tube in my mouth, spit out what I could bite off, did it again and just waited to die.

"Next thing I knowed, Saint Peter woke me up and started stuffing my head with dumbshit ideas. But I could walk, and I prob'ly wore a hole in the floor walking around that little ol' room they had me in. You don't know how good it feels to just walk until you can't."

"You said something about a horse?"

"Yeah, danged ol' hoss stumbled. I was doing all right 'til he fell. Hell, I can ride 'most anything with hair, but he fell on me and broke m' neck. Worse than that bull that stomped me one time. The docs stapled me up after that wreck and I was back good as new in a few months. I already had almost enough points that year to get to the nationals. Hell, depending on the draw, I could'a' won. But then that ol' hoss got a burr under his tail and I woke up with more plumbing than one of them Vegas hotels, all of it sticking out here and there. Breathing tube, feedin' tube, tubes in m' arms, tube in m' dick, machine hummin' and clickin' off to the side.

"Maybe I could 'a' stood it longer, but the ol' gal that stuck that hose up m' dick, she was plumb ugly. Must 'a' been sixty if she was a day. More wrinkles than a fresh-plowed Arizona melon patch!

"I worked in one of them, late summer it was, after I got out of the hospital that first time. No life for a cowboy, ridin' a John Deere. Ranches weren't hiring and I wasn't in shape at the time to go back to rodeoin'.

"But soon as I was able, next spring it was, I quit farmin' and got my saddle back. I borrowed money from a feller and he held onto my saddle 'til I could pay him back, y' see. I saved my pay from punchin' that tractor and paid off the loan.

"Next thing you know, I was signed up for a rodeo in San Antonio. That was in early spring. Figured I'd make the circuit, take it easy for a while to make sure the staples didn't pull out No more than a rodeo every week, see how things were going. Maybe pick up the pace later on. I had enough entry-fee money to get in, but if I didn't start winnin' pretty quick I'd have to quit. I was hopin' one of the ranches would be takin' on help if that happened.

"Then that hoss fell on me. I was ridin' pickup at the time. Some old boy didn't show up and they needed another rider. I had a pretty good draw for the next day, a bull that was rank enough to get points if I could hang on for eight. But I never got to try him.

"I never figured on bein' stashed in a white room waitin' on th' angels!"

"No angels, Tex. No saint either; the man who picked you up came from the future."

"That's what he said, but I figured he was joshin' me. People think cowboys are dumb and rodeo cowboys worse than that, so they try all kinds of stuff on you. Make fun of you 'cause you don't dress like them or go to college."

"No, he meant it. You're here, live or die. I named it Darwin's World, not that Darwin ever heard of it. If you're not fit to survive after the Futurists drop you here, you won't. Mess up here, that hospital room might look pretty inviting."

"Nope, been there, didn't like it. Hell, I purely hated it. I'd rather just cash in and be done with it."

"It might happen yet. I guess we've waited long enough, let's get the rest of our weary warriors on their feet. José, that Spanish man we collected after the fight, figures we're at least a day, day and a half away from the slaver village."

"You've been pushin' these folks pretty hard, Matt. Some of 'em ain't lookin' too spry."

"They're not used to this much running, trotting most of the time really. I'm surprised they made it this far before I had to stop. You're doing pretty good, Tex."

"Like I said, I realized I had my legs back and even if I didn't have a hoss, I wanted to see some country. I run a lot, walked when I had to. I headed up north from where that feller dropped me, looked like northwest Texas. I got all the way to the mountains. They're not like the mountains I saw, back when I worked in Texas before. More like the Rockies, though they're not up to the Grand Tetons. I growed up in north Texas before and there were no mountains like that anywhere around. Everything else fit, though. Had to be Texas, but colder than I remember it bein' when I was a kid. You been to the mountains yet, Matt?"

"No, I was dropped off in the woods east of here. That's where I grew up, downtime. Headed north after a while, found some people and ended up trying to keep them fed and safe. That's about it."

"How'd you get that rifle? You mentioned it, but we were some busy at the time."

"I took it off a raider. I don't think the man who took it from the original owner knew how to take care of it. He got it by killing a man from the future. Anyhow, he got hurt in that fight with us and dead after that. He didn't need the rifle."

"I'll bet that pissed 'em off more'n somewhat, the people that had it first. They know you've got it, them future men?"

"Not that I know of. Anyway, there's Lee, coming back now. He's been having a look at the trail ahead of us."

Lee found the two and blurted out his news. "Matt, there's tracks up ahead. Not just the trail we've been following, but a man going the other way. We might have missed him when we went around looking for wounded. Maybe he hid, or maybe we just overlooked him. Bodies were scattered around, easy enough to miss one. But I'm guessing he's east of us by a few hours and following the same trail we are. He's heading back to the village. Soon as he gets there, they'll know their raiding party lost the fight. He might even have been watching us when we stacked the heads on that slope."

"Just one man. You're sure, Lee? If he saw us, it won't be good for the people they're holding. José said they wouldn't hesitate to kill the remaining captives and take off."

"I didn't find any other tracks. He's walking now, not running, but he might have been running before. I think he must have, to get as far ahead of us as he is. If he was only walking, we'd be on his heels by now."

"How far to their village?" Tex asked.

"Depends on how fast he can travel, Tex. If he's walking, sleeping at night, maybe two days. If he's running for a while, walking, then running again, maybe a day or a little more."

"Well, hell, if that's what he's doing, lazing along like that, I can catch him."

"Lot of running, Tex. You up to that?"

"Shore. Done a lot of it over the last ten years or so. I'll catch him."

"Tex, Lee's a pretty good runner too. So am I. For all we know, he might get to someplace he could warn them some other way. There might be more than one of them. Three of us are better than one."

"Think you can keep up, packin' that bow and the rifle and spear too?"

"I'll leave the spear with Colin. He can bring the rest along We kill that one ahead of us, scout the village until Colin gets there. Soon as our people are ready to fight, we hit them. What I mean is, if they're exhausted, we'll let them rest before we attack. Unless the slavers are warned and start killing prisoners, that is.

"Make sure you've got food and your water bottle is full. We don't know if we'll cross a creek or maybe find a spring on the way. The water we carry might be all we'll have until we catch that one ahead of us."

"Water's down a mite."

"We'll top off our bottles from what the others are carrying. Colin can find a spring."

"I doubt any of us will get thirsty, Matt. There are a lot of springs around, artesian ones, too. Water just comes shooting up out of the ground. It's good water."

"I hope you're right, Tex."

"Aw, I hunted all through here, must be seven years ago now. I killed a mammoth that fall and lived on him most of the winter."

"You killed a mammoth, Tex? You're not joking, are you?"

"Nope. Some of them big wolves was worrying at him, gnawing on his legs like. He'd killed a couple of 'em, I did for the rest. That was the bow I had before I made Ol' Slick here. Pretty good bow, as says so myself. Anyway, he was trying to limp off and I run around to the side and put an arrow right behind his eye. He just went down and I made sure he was dead, my last arrow right beside the first one but he never twitched. I knowed I couldn't move all that meat, so I built me a hut right there, close enough to keep the wolves and bears off. One of the bears didn't take the hint, so I got him too. It was already chilly and it got downright cold right after that, natural icebox like. I collected the hide off that bear, cut it down the middle of the back so I'd have some on the bottom and some on the top. It kept me warm all winter. I had a bunch of nuts too, took 'em off a passel o' thievin' squirrels. Pignuts and some other kinds, persimmons too. I could'a used some bread, but except for that, I lived pretty high that winter.

"Tell you this, though. If I never eat another mammoth steak it'll be too soon."

"Yeah, I can imagine. We're ready. Colin, you bring everyone up as fast as they can make it. I might need my spear, so don't lose it. We'll watch for you, somewhere before you get to the village. You worry about the rest, but Lee, Tex and me, we'll be all right." Colin nodded understanding.

Lee led off. Matt followed, Tex soon passing him and running alongside Lee. Matt tried to match their pace.

It was a struggle. He pushed on, weary legs maintaining the constant pace. One stride at a time, do it again. Remember the counting method he'd used downtime when he'd been a soldier.

Slow breathing in, controlled breathing out; Matt counted as he ran, each number a stride. The counting took some of his attention and kept exhaustion at bay. One-two-three-four while breathing out, five-six-seven-eight as he breathed in.

By the end of the first mile, Matt's was breathing on a count of three. One-two-three while sucking desperately for air, four-five-six as he slowly breathed out. Two miles later he was breathing on a two count, one-two then breathe out, do it again. He was able to maintain the pace, but it seemed as if the two ahead were breathing easier.

Tex said he'd spent a lot of time just running. Lee had done a lot of cross-country traveling too, being on the move most of every day. It was to be expected the two were very fit.

Matt wondered if he'd gotten a little soft; he hadn't done nearly as much running or hunting since becoming trek leader, then tribe leader. When this was over, Colin could handle things while Matt and maybe Laz went hunting. Someone with experience would be needed, so Lee could stay with the tribe this time!

It had taken a lot of effort and pain, getting himself into the shape he'd been in when he found the cabin. Wintering in the cabin had begun the process of losing that physical edge. Living as part of the tribe where someone else did most of the hunting and all of the daily work had clearly sapped his endurance.

His thoughts wandered as he kept up the pace.

All the tribespeople needed to be in better shape. Otherwise, they might not survive whatever challenges Darwin's World handed them; the stragglers and footsore people left behind with Colin made that obvious. Matt thought the problem through as he ran and counted off the strides, one two and three four. Concentrating on what he planned to do kept him from feeling the growing pain in his legs and feet.

Still, he was ready to stop when Lee finally held up his hand and slowed to a trot. Breathing heavily, Matt matched their pace.

Lee held up his hand again and they slowed to a walk. Despite his talk, Tex too was showing the strain.

"You run pretty good, boy." Tex panted.

"Don't call me boy. My name is Lee. I haven't been a boy since I fought that bear with a spear and killed a man later. Wolves and a cat, too. That good enough to get me off the boy list, or do I need to kick your butt first?"

"Wal, you're feisty, I'll give you that. All right, Lee. You run pretty good."

"You too, old man."

Tex grinned, still puffing a bit; but clearly, he relished the exchange and Lee's show of spirit.

"He don't look very old, but you've brung him up right, Matt."

"His mother and father did some of that before I ever met him. His father was killed by raiders, maybe from the first bunch we fought or maybe from the ones we fought at the ridge. I guess we can't rule out the idea of another bunch of raiders, but you'd expect that there wouldn't be three such groups operating in a region with only a few people. There are more people here than I saw when I lived in the woods east of here, but more doesn't mean a lot. One of the groups back there had been assembled by the future people, mostly to keep them from raiding, but also to keep animals away from their mine. Maybe that was why there were more people."

"What were they minin', Matt?"

"I don't know, Tex. I don't think anyone knows except the mine operators themselves. We've made guesses, but that's all they are, guesses."

"There's a spring over yonder, Matt. See that clump of trees? Artesian spring, cold pure water and it runs off to the southeast. Forms a little creek and usually there are deer and elk around the creek downstream. I killed a nice elk there, early winter maybe three or four years ago it was. Got an antler tip and made a tool for flaking arrowheads."

"You've been around, Tex. Let's go by that spring, get a drink and refill the bottles. We're gaining on that fellow. We'll catch him in an hour or two. Maybe less if he's not pushing it."

"Good to know. I'd hate to think all this runnin' was for nothin'!"

20

"Smoke up ahead, Matt."

"I see it, Lee. That fellow we've been trailing, I expect."

Ahead of them a knoll rose above the surrounding landscape. The slopes were grassy and a clump of brush crowned the summit thirty feet above. The smoke was rising from this point. As they watched, the smoke column stopped briefly, then resumed. Above the knoll two large, dark puffs of smoke rose into the air.

"Looks like the raiders know about smoke signals."

"Yeah, Matt. That's pretty simple. It won't mean anything to anyone except the raiders at the village."

"You're right, Lee, but he didn't do that by accident."

"Wal, we can jaw all day or go fix that feller's wagon for him. I'll just do that now. He can't be more than four or five miles away. You two can just wait here."

"We'll leave him for now, Tex. We can always find him later if Colin doesn't get him first. If he's warned the rest at the village, we need to push on or all we'll find is bodies and another trail to follow. We need to get there as fast as we can or we'll be too late."

Tex looked at Matt, clearly deciding whether to obey or go his own way. Finally he nodded and Matt led off, now running again. Lee followed and Tex fell in behind.

Matt hadn't missed the wavering. Something might need to be done about Tex. If he wasn't disposed to cooperate, he could go find another tribe.

How far ahead was the slaver village?

Not far, as it happened. An hour later found them crouching in shrubbery just beyond the outer edge of huts. The slavers had clearly interpreted the smoke signal as a warning. Now they had their captives packing goods and working at other tasks around the small town.

"They might not kill the captives after all, Matt. They could take them along to carry their stuff. If they have food enough, anyway."

"No way to know, Lee. Maybe they'll take all of them, but they might only want the strongest ones. We're in a good spot, so we'll just watch and see what happens.

The three settled in and tried to make themselves comfortable. Matt wondered if they were as footsore as he was. At least his breathing had returned to normal. He slipped some of the jerky from his pouch, avoiding any sudden movement that might attract attention.

His caution might not have been needed. The raiders obviously didn't expect anyone to be watching; they hadn't even posted guards. Only the increased activity revealed that something out of the ordinary was happening.

Matt chewed on the jerky, sipping water from time to time. Activity slowed as the captives completed the tasks set them by the slavers. One by one, they were collected into a group of about twenty.

Matt never saw a signal but suddenly three men gathered near the captives. Matt felt uneasy as he watched; this was different, not part of packing the slavers' possessions. The slaves appeared agitated too, moving around as far as the straps around their necks allowed.

Reaching a decision, Matt signaled Lee closer.

"I don't like this. Something's happening; I want you and Tex to slip in behind that briar patch over there to the right. If you have to start shooting, the briars will provide cover. They can't use those spears unless they're willing to bust through the briars. If they throw the spears, they'll be unarmed. You'll have easy targets if they get tangled in the briars.

"I'll watch from here. We'll wait for Colin unless that bunch starts the party, but if they do I'll use the rifle. I just wish I had more ammo."

Lee nodded, then signaled to Tex. Tex looked at Matt and seemed disposed to argue.

"Tex, get your ass over there and do what you're told! We'll settle this once and for all when this is over. If you won't work with us, there's a whole world out there waiting for you. Got it?"

"I got it. I don't cotton to little tin gods and we'll damn sure talk about it after this is over!"

The two vanished silently into the brush. Matt continued to watch, now with the rifle pointing into the village, lever moved slowly from safe to fire. There was a slight catch as the lever moved, but no betraying click. As ready as he was going to get, Matt resumed watching.

Three men against an estimated thirty-five slavers? He would wait for Colin unless the raiders began executing the prisoners. The three would need to intervene if that happened. despite the risks. How far behind was Colin?

A man slipped into camp and headed for the group of three. Was he the one who'd signaled from the knoll? There was as yet no sign of Colin and the others.

Whoever it was, he picked the largest man of the three and began talking rapidly. Matt couldn't hear the conversation, but the effect on the three was obvious. They looked around in agitation, then settled at a word from the big man. This one was probably the raiders' leader, Matt decided.

The new man disappeared in the direction of the piled packs of belongings. Selecting a spear, he returned to the group of three. The leader nodded and the four men walked purposefully toward the captives.

Matt tensed and had time for a brief thought, probably the same as every man throughout history has when faced with a sudden and unpleasant choice. Matt held the rifle sights on the leader but lost him as another man blocked his view. The men now held their spears pointing at the captives.

They were less than ten feet from the captives when Matt decided he couldn't wait. A gentle squeeze, loud crack and slight recoil, and the target dropped from view. The rifle cycled, ejecting a spent cartridge and chambering the next round. Matt looked for the leader but couldn't spot him. He shot another as the man hesitated, looking at the raider on the ground. That one wouldn't be spearing any slaves...not with that shattered head...and neither would the aston-ished one.

The leadership group left two of their number on the ground and the other two quickly melded into the rest. The suspected leader was somewhere among them, but Matt still couldn't get a shot. He got quick glimpses as the man began bringing order from the chaos Matt had caused.

The clumped raiders split into three parts, one running directly away. The other two went to Matt's left and right. Perhaps they thought they might circle and come at him from two sides...but then, Lee stood up behind the briars and launched his first arrow. Tex was right beside him, a loud yell announcing his presence as he reached for a second arrow. Two men writhed on the ground as the others froze in shock. Turning, they changed course and bolted toward Matt.

Standing up, he fired his next shot, using partial concealment from a tree. The rifle tracked briefly, cracked, and another raider dropped. The rest spread out, making it difficult for Mat to swing rapidly from one target to another. Finding the peep sight too restricting and the distance between the raiders and himself shrinking rapidly, Matt dropped the rifle and unslung his bow.

His first arrow took a raider in the leg. Matt hadn't aimed at him, but the group was milling around as they caught sight of him. Slavers they might be, but they were warriors too. Barely hesitating, the remainder split up around fallen comrades and came on.

Matt launched a second arrow that was more successful, spitting a raider low in the gut. Matt reached for another arrow. There were a few remaining, but not enough to kill all of them.

He risked a glance to where Lee and Tex were calmly shooting down the raiders who'd charged them. Several bodies lay on the ground, but the fight there wasn't over.

Last chance...Matt dropped the bow and picked up the rifle again. Turning the selector to B, he squeezed the trigger. The rifle fired three times, taking down another charging slaver less than ten yards away. A final twist of the selector put it to A and this time when Matt pulled the trigger, the rifle cycled through the remaining cartridges in the magazine. The raiders were at point-blank range as he pivoted his body, sweeping the rifle from right to left.

Two men still stood when the smoking rifle went silent, shocked and frozen by the burst of automatic fire and the carnage among them. Matt dropped the empty rifle and grabbed his belt weapons.

Axe cocked in his right hand, he leaped forward and swung at the foremost attacker. The man snapped out of his paralysis and tried to block the strike, but the axe chopped into his forearm and stuck. The man shrieked and finally remembered his spear, but too late. Matt released the axe handle and grabbed at the spear. Wresting it from the man's hand, Matt thrust hard at his belly and felt the momentary hesitation as the blade pierced through the skin.

The last man turned to flee, but an arrow punched into the right side of his chest. Lee and Tex, arrows now exhausted, abandoned their position behind the screening briars. Salvaging spears from raiders who no longer needed them, they prowled forward, efficiently spitting survivors. Matt turned his attention to his earlier opponent, weaponless, Matt's axe still stuck in the bones of his forearm, and trying to hold his entrails in. A final thrust with the spear ended the raider. He writhed, kicking briefly, before going still.

Matt recovered his axe by wrenching the handle back and forth until the blade came loose. Lee and Tex dispatched the final two living raiders as Matt watched.

The terrified slaves huddled together, held in place by the straps around their necks. Two of them had fallen during the fight; Matt saw blood spreading briefly before soaking into the ground.

The fight had not been one sided and their intervention had been none too soon.

The arrow that dropped the last raider facing Matt had come from Laz; he'd arrived at the village about five minutes ahead of Colin and the others.

"Good timing, Laz. Did we get all of them?"

"Some got past, Matt. I heard banging behind me, spears on spears maybe. They ran into Colin, I think."

"I don't hear anything now. I guess we should go see what happened."

Matt found two of his arrows that could be recovered without great effort and spent a few moments salvaging them. Picking up the bow and nocking an arrow, he glanced at the rifle where he'd dropped it. Empty now, it was no more than a poorly-designed club.

He caught up with Colin five minutes later. He and others knelt beside three people lying on the ground.

Two had clearly died of spear thrusts. The massive torso wounds had already ceased to bleed. The third man, gray faced with pain, still lived. He could move his head but Matt saw no movement of his arms and legs. They lay limply on the ground beside him. Colin wiped blood and sweat off the face and Matt recognized him. Matt glanced at Colin who minutely shook his head.

"Looks like you bloodied your spear, Philippe. Can you talk?"

Philippe's jaw moved but no sounds came out. Matt looked at Colin who mouthed "Broken back, we think."

Matt nodded.

"You need to see to the rest of your people, Colin. I'll stay here."

Colin nodded and turned away.

Matt looked into Philippe's eyes...bright blue, he'd never really noticed that. And now...

"Philippe, you're hurt bad. Are you in pain?"

The eyes blinked, the jaw wavered, but nothing else moved.

"There's only one thing I can do. I hope you understand; I know you'd do the same for me if our positions were reversed."

The eyes blinked. Matt patted the forehead and shook tears from his own eyes.

It wouldn't get any better for waiting.

He smoothly drew the big knife and placed it on Philippe's chest just beneath the breastbone. Blade angled to pierce the heart, Matt thrust hard and felt momentary resistance from the skin. Then the knife sliced in and blood welled. It pulsed twice, then stopped. The flow oozed across Philippe's chest and puddled the ground scarlet under his body. Matt reached to close the eyes, but they were already closed; perhaps Philippe had known. Matt hoped so. When his own time came, hopefully there would be a knowledgeable friend to administer mercy.

Wiping his knife on Philippe's breechclout...Philippe wouldn't mind, he knew...Matt sheathed it and rose to his feet.

The other two dead were Karel and Willie, former guardsmen who'd joined the tribe after deserting Pavel. Matt looked for their spears, but if they'd managed to injure a raider, their spears didn't show it. Training...Matt had wanted to do more, but there'd never been time to do all the things that needed doing. Perhaps they'd gotten more results from their shafts. The quivers now held fewer than four arrows in each.

Matt took the arrows. They weren't spined for his bow, but they were better than nothing until he could replace them with proper shafts. The slave-raiders appeared to be dead, but this world was never short of dangers. There were carnivores, and the noise and smell of blood would draw them here.

Tex came up as Matt was examining Karel's weapons.

"I think we got 'em all, by gum! That was a pretty good fight if I do say so myself."

"Yeah. I'll talk to you later, Tex. Right now I've got people to see to."

Matt turned and walked away. Eventually he would have to decide what to do about Tex, but not now.

"Colin, what shape are the others in?"

"Two people with minor wounds, nothing to worry about. The rest are tired and so am I. I'll give the bastards credit, once they ran into us they got to work with those spears. We were too close to use our bows effectively. If we'd run into them when we weren't expecting...well, it wouldn't have been good."

Matt nodded. "I guess they had a lot of practice. Good thing they never progressed beyond spears."

Colin nodded. "I expect the people they raided only had spears. Spears against spears, numbers, surprise...the slavers wouldn't have had a lot of trouble. Kill the ones that fought, capture the rest and tie them to that rope."

Matt nodded. "The two with flesh wounds, have they been bandaged?"

"Lilia's taking care of it."

"Lilia's here? I thought she stayed with the others."

"She caught up after you three went on ahead. I guess she didn't think you and Lee could handle it, even with Tex along to help."

Matt smiled for the first time since he'd taken the trail to the raiders' village.

"Yeah, she takes pretty good care of us."

"Same drill as before, Matt?"

"Almost, Colin. I figure the first thing is to cut the slaves loose and see if they can handle a spear. Give them a spear and knife from the dead raiders. Tell them we want the heads off and piled in the open space.

"We're going to burn this place before we leave. Leave a pile of heads, and if they're charred a little by the flames, so much the better. Anyone who knows what this place was can take warning."

Some of the slaves looked lost, but others went to work with a will. The pile of heads grew. Fluids leaked from severed necks and the smell was...well, not to put too fine a point on it, the village stank.

Perhaps it had done so before, but punctured human bodies added to the stench.

The fire might clear some of that up. Matt made a note which of the former captives took part in collecting heads. Those might make good tribe members. As for the rest, he would decide later. At worst, they would be alive, free, and with arms that had formerly been used to enslave themselves and others. Whether they considered Matt generous if he decided not to offer them membership in the tribe...well, hard decisions had to be made. Those who weren't an asset to the tribe would be turned away.

"Have them throw the bodies in one of the cabins. Plenty of room, but the heads stay outside. When we burn this place, the fire will clean up the mess. I want nothing left here but a bad memory."

"I'll see to it, Matt."

Two hours later, the war party retraced their way west, heading toward the ridge and the river.

Three of the simple racks had been built and the bodies of their comrades left. Matt had offered the freed captives the opportunity to care for the bodies of their fellows but they'd elected to lay them near the frames Colin's men had assembled. Well, the choice was theirs.

Behind them, flames crackled. Only a fading smoke trail showed where so much misery had been.

21

"Colin, we need to feed these folks for a few days and give them a chance to rest up. I'd like you to get with Lee and look them over. Some helped clean up after the village fight, but some just stood around looking lost. If they're not likely to pull their own weight, we'll have to turn them loose.

"I won't just turn them out, I intend to give them food and one of our emergency kits. They can have a spear, and if they can use it, a bow too. I won't accept them if they won't fight. They got captured but we don't know the circumstances. If they just gave up without a fight, they're a drag on the rest of us. They'll get some of our people killed. You understand what I'm talking about?"

"I'll talk to them, Lee can too. We'll let you know what we think. There might be a problem though; I don't know if they all speak English. They speak Spanish, but that's not good enough; they'll need to understand the rest of us. It goes back to what you said, if they can't pull their weight in a fight, we can't afford them. Better if they form their own tribe. Teaching them, arming them, I think we should do that. We might need allies. I'd rather make friends than enemies."

"You're right, but that's for later. We've already found out that our enemies outnumber us. If they're the kind of people we're looking for, people who will make the tribe stronger, we can teach them English. Anyway, you can look into that too."

Matt went on his way; Colin had work to do, let him get on with it.

José spoke passable English, so perhaps the others would too. Problems, problems; do something to help people and another can of worms opened up!

The augmented tribe had managed the descent from the ridge without incident. They'd set up camp in the flat area lining the riverbanks, waiting until Lee's scouts could find a better location. The former captives had pitched in to help; at least they weren't afraid of work!

Matt found Sal with a crew examining the trees along the river.

"How's it going, Sal?"

Sal shook his head. "Matt, I don't think these trees will work. They're not very big and most of them are twisted. I'm guessing this area floods every spring and the trees have taken a beating. The ones across the river look bigger. That bank opens out more and the trees look like they might be better than what's available here. The bank here is only about forty yards wide.

"Have you thought about moving across the river and camping there?"

"I hadn't got that far yet. We've got to cross eventually, so I don't suppose it matters if we cross before we start working on the carts. I've got some ideas about how we can get across. I wondered what you had in mind?"

"I intended to ask you what you thought first."

"I'd rather cross by ferry," Sal responded. "That means we have to build a ferry, but the trees are big enough. We might have to make a separate trip for each cart, but we can do that. We'll need more rope, but if someone else can make that my crew can have you a ferry in a day, two at the most."

"OK, Sal. Here's what I've got in mind. One thing, your ferry needs a keel along the middle. If you can't find a big tree, use smaller ones and make several keel boards we can lash between the logs."

"We can do that. But why put a keel on a ferry? I was thinking of something like a big raft."

"We don't know how deep that water is or what kind of bottom the river has. Mud would make for tough poling, pushing the raft across, and we'd drift downstream. You really can't steer a raft; I found that out a year ago when I crossed a river. Instead, we'll build a reaction ferry. But you've got to have a keel for it to work right."

"We can build it if you know what it's supposed to look like."

"I'm thinking two layers of logs, one straight ahead and a cross-layer over that. The ferry's got to be big enough for a few polemen. The current will carry the ferry over, but when it gets close to the far bank, we'll need polemen to push the last few feet. After that, we can tie a rope to a tree and use that to pull it the rest of the way to the bank. Put a fence around the sides, too; we'll be floating women and kids over, and some of them might not be able to swim."

Sal nodded. "More work than what I had in mind, but I take your point. We'll build your ferry." He motioned to his crew and gathering them, began drawing designs in the dirt.

Matt went on his way. Colin and Lee were talking to the rescued captives, so Matt passed on. Lilia was helping Margrette and her daughter Callie at the kitchen area; Matt motioned to her and she joined him.

"I'm going to need rope, a lot of it. The main one has to be strong and at least two hundred yards long. Can you organize that?"

"I'll need help from some of the men later on. That much rope is going to be heavy, but yes, I can do it. I'll see how many women are available; we can start by making smaller strands, then plait or twist them together, whichever works best. The long one is going to be too heavy for us to handle."

Matt nodded understanding. "You'll get the help. We'll use the former captives; I haven't decided whether they should be part of the tribe or if we should just give them arms and food and turn them loose."

"You don't plan to keep them?"

"I don't know yet. We can't have deadweight. They've got to be useful; we don't have enough resources as it is. More mouths to feed, more of everything. Al they've got now are some ragged breechclouts. Have you talked to the women?"

"Just for a short time, Matt. They had it rough; the slavers passed them around. One might be pregnant."

Matt shook his head. "We'll have to wait on that one, then. Maybe wait a month or two before we decide on the other women; I won't turn a pregnant woman out. If we're going to build a civilization that keeps us alive long-term, we need all the women we can get. Men too, but men can't bear children.

"Let me know what you find out, but first get the rope made."

"I'll take care of it, Matt."

Matt walked down to the river and looked at the brown water flowing slowly past. Could this be the Brazos, perhaps? Or at least what would become the Brazos a few thousand years hence.

He walked slowly upstream, moving away from the river when he came to an obstacle, returning to the bank when he'd passed.

About a mile upstream he found what he hoped for, a bend in the river. He kept going. One more thing would be needed to make the bend suitable for what he had in mind.

Turning, he retraced his steps. Soon he was back at the camp. He found Sal and his crew still studying the trees, deciding which ones would be suitable for building a ferry.

"Don't cut anything here, Sal. Bring your helpers and I'll show you the place I found."

Each man picked up a bow and quiver from where they'd laid them as they worked. Matt looked on approvingly as they slung the quivers and nocked an arrow; they'd learned. He led off, the men following. Half an hour later, he reached the spot.

"The bend we passed will help. We attach the long rope to this tree here. It should be big enough, but if necessary we can use more rope to tether it to others to relieve the strain. The other end of the long rope will be tied to the raft, the ferry. We'll use a separate rope, a kind of bridle, and tie it from the front of the ferry to the back. The long rope will have a loop that that can slide along the bridle. We want to be able to make it like the letter 'Y', but so we can shorten the front part when we cross the river, shorten the back part when we want to come back. That's where the keel comes in. The water pushes against the keel, and since it's not square to the current the ferry will be pushed across the river. Understand what I have in mind?"

"I think so. The flowing water is deflected and the ferry reacts by being pushed away. The rope, the long one that is, keeps it from drifting downstream, so the ferry is pushed across the river."

"That's it. It's called a reaction ferry, and it will save us work in the long run. That wide area on the other side, that's where we'll land. I'm going to put Lee and a couple of others over there first, for security. They can just push the ferry off and it will come back to this side."

"Matt, this is going to take a couple of days at least. Can we move the camp here while we're working? It will save time."

"I don't see why not. It makes sense; your tools will be here anyway, so you won't waste time going back and forth. I'll talk to Colin."

"You do that. We'll dig a latrine over by those trees and a firepit for the kitchen crew in that flat area over by the big maple."

Matt nodded agreement and headed back to find Colin.

* * *

THE MOVE WAS FINISHED by midafternoon. Margrette and Callie soon had the evening meal cooking over the new campfire. Their assistants were out scavenging downed wood for the fire. Others cut willows for shelter frames. Matt joined this group, along with many of the captives they'd rescued. For whatever reason, they seemed to prefer remaining near him. José was often only a few paces away.

Matt found Lee and Tex near their campsite that afternoon. He nodded to Tex, but addressed his comments to Lee.

"I'm needed here to oversee building the ferry, but we need meat. I saw tracks and droppings while we were moving camp. There are more pigs, probably quite a few of them, and the larger droppings were elk or a stag-moose. Feel like going hunting tomorrow? Take a day or so this time and don't go too far. After we get across, we'll take a real hunting party out and see if we can find bison, what Tex calls buffalo."

"Matt, what say I take one of them fellers of yours and go huntin' too? Never crossed the river, not that I remember, but I've hunted all through here. Shouldn't take long. Stag-moose, you said? Big rascal, dappled hide, got more antlers than anything I've ever seen?"

"Don't know what you've seen, Tex, but that's a pretty good description. Big palm-like antlers with long spikes coming off. They're dangerous, *really* dangerous. I saw one kill a lioness. She charged, he caught her with those spikes and tossed her. Then he finished her off with his hooves."

"That's the critter. Never saw one kill a lion, though. You saw this?"

"I did. And while he was celebrating, I put an arrow in him. We ate him. He tasted a lot like elk, like really lean beef from downtime."

"Yeah, I know what you mean. How about I take two men? One of the carts, maybe? We'll need it to bring back the meat."

"Sure, Tex; pick a cart, take Piotr and Marc. I think they'd like to hunt."

"I'll do that. We'll leave first thing in the morning."

Lee posted his sentries and announced who would relieve them during the night. Laz, now his deputy, would oversee the changes. Soon the camp grew quiet and people slept.

* * *

Tex, Piotr, and Marc were gone by the time Matt woke up. Lilia was at the campfire when he arrived for breakfast. Sal and his crew were eating together, off to one side. They finished eating a few moments later and moved away to start work.

"You sent Marc and Piotr with Tex, Matt?" Lilia asked.

"I did. Is there a problem?"

"I'm not sure." Lilia looked away. "It's just that Tex was talking to Marja. I got a funny feeling; I don't think she wanted to talk to him. Piotr was off helping Colin at the time. But she didn't say anything, so maybe it was nothing."

"Let's not borrow trouble, Lilia. It could be nothing. If there's a problem, she'll tell me about it."

"Well, she didn't mention it to me, but I hope she didn't say anything to Piotr."

"If it happens again, let me know. I'll talk to her."

"I will, Matt." Lilia went back to working at the fire.

* * *

THE HUNTING PARTY came back late that afternoon. The three had indeed found the stag-moose. They'd also found a large doe and two pigs. The animals had all been field-dressed and the heavily loaded cart groaned under the weight. Piotr and Marc pulled the cart, one to each pole. Tex followed behind, arrow nocked.

Matt looked on and approved. There were plenty of dangers around. The stag-moose was dangerous, but it appeared they'd had no problems bagging this large male.

Matt congratulated the three and helped push the cart to the kitchen fire. Colin was there and reached for his butcher tools. There would be fresh meat for tomorrow, enough to feed the entire tribe even with the new additions.

Matt found Lee. "What do you think about the people we picked up?"

"Matt, most are from Spain, wherever that is. They speak Spanish among themselves, but they all have some English. They learned it from the slavers...if they misunderstood, the slavers used those whips. They learned enough words to be understood. They're all from one village, the last one the slavers raided.

"They weren't fighters. The fighting men were all killed during the raid. But I think we need the rest; they're craftsmen, but not like Sal. They work with things like our spear points."

"They work with iron?"

"Right. They'd found a small deposit of some kind of mineral, they used a word I hadn't heard before, and they were using charcoal to heat it hot enough to get the iron out. I didn't understand everything they were talking about, but we could sure use more of that iron stuff."

"Will they fight if we teach them?"

"I'm sure they will, Matt. They don't know much, but once they learn I don't think they'll hang back. I'm willing to give it a try."

"I'll talk to Colin. If he agrees, offer them membership in the tribe. You'll be responsible for teaching them, I'll put Piotr in charge of making weapons. He'll need some help."

"Marc can help him. I've got some others in mind too."

"Not Tex, Lee? He made his bow and it's a good one."

"No. Not Tex. Matt, did you see the bruise on Piotr's cheekbone?"

"No; I pushed on the cart, but I didn't notice anything unusual. Did Piotr say how he got it?"

"He said he bumped into a limb in the dark this morning, right after they left camp."

"You think he's hiding something, Lee?"

"Matt, I just don't know. He's usually pretty careful. Walking into a limb...well, it's not like Piotr."

Matt nodded thoughtfully. One more possible issue to deal with.

22

"Anyone seen Tex this morning?"

"Not this morning. He talked to Lee last evening. Maybe he knows where Tex is."

"Thanks, Colin. Lee's out with his security guys right now, but I'll check with him when he gets back. How's Sal doing with the ferry?"

"He figures today or maybe tomorrow at the latest if the rope's ready. That's the drawback, having a rope cable that's long enough and heavy enough. We've only got one chance to test the cable, try it, and if it snaps we'll lose the ferry."

"It might be best if no one's on the ferry the first time we try the rope, Colin. We can push it out into the stream and attach a second rope to the bridle. Have people ready to pull the ferry back."

"Simpler to just tie both ropes directly to the ferry, Matt. Let it swing out, leave it there for a few minutes, then bring it back with the tether."

"You're right. Do it that way. The tether needs to be almost as big as the main rope but maybe only half as long. Say long enough to reach across the river with twenty feet to spare. Safer later on when we start crossing."

"We'll see to it, Matt."

"Thanks, Colin."

With Lee and Tex both gone, Matt decided to talk to Elizabeth. He found her camp south of the kitchen fire, but she was nowhere around. Perhaps she was off looking for herbs. Matt thought for a moment and realized that Lilia wasn't around either. Bella had gone with Elizabeth. Shani was helping Sandra with the little ones, not yet teaching, just getting to know them better. The oldest, Bear, looked like he'd be a handful. Sandra would deal with him, likely with a quick slap on the butt. If she had problems, she could get immediate help from the boy's mother.

It helped that people were rarely more than a few minutes away from each other.

Piotr was working, chipping at a flint core he'd found. This one came from an outcrop just down the ridge from where the tribe had fought the slave raiders. Matt wandered over to see how the project was going.

"You're making progress. Finished anything yet?"

"I've got a leather bag with arrowheads, Matt. They're not as nice as the ones you made, but they'll do. I'm still getting the hang of using that antler tip to flake the edges. I tried making a knife blade, but it broke. So I made it into another arrowhead."

"I did that a few times, Piotr. Knife blade, spear blade, if they broke I just converted them to the next smaller tool. They can always be scrapers or bits for boring holes. I didn't waste much after I learned how to flake instead of chip at the edges. Have you tried making a bow or spear yet?"

"Just my own, Matt. José is doing that, making weapons for his people. He'll do the wood part, I'll provide the flints, Marja is learning to make bowstrings. Lilia's teaching her."

"Good, the more people who know how to do things, the better. Eventually we'll have paper and can start writing things down. But for now, just spread the knowledge as wide as we can and hope for the best. Anyway, I'll stop interrupting you. I'm going to have a look at what everyone else is doing."

"See you later, Matt."

A larger group was working just up the river, so Matt went to see if they needed help. As he got closer, he realized that most of the tribe's women and a few of the men were working on the main rope for the ferry. Dominick and two other men had dragged the end into the woods and wrapped the heavy rope around a large tree. They now adjusted it, sliding more around the tree to take up slack as the women worked at the far end. The finished part was lying in a loose coil behind Dominick.

Lilia was overseeing several women as they joined smaller strands to make the larger cable. They plaited the smaller strands, and with each plait the heavy cable grew an inch or two. Other women waited to feed in replacements for the strands being plaited. When one grew short, another was fed in and the plaiting continued without a pause.

The cable was obviously heavy, but it would likely be very strong. At the moment, even with the tensioning going on at the far end, the cable was almost as thick as Matt's wrist. It would probably stretch in use; plaited items often did. Matt made a mental note to allow for that; the rope would probably have to be adjusted after the first few crossings.

Few noticed Matt's arrival. He watched quietly for a moment before spotting Millie in the shadows, bow in hand, arrow ready on the string. She had selected a position where she could protect the plaiting group as well as the ones tensioning the cable. Reminded,

Matt looked around and spotted weapons near each worker. He nodded his satisfaction, an unconscious gesture. The tribe understood the importance of security.

Matt found Lee at the cookfire when he walked back through camp. He was drinking a kind of tea made by Antonia, one of the women freed during the raid. Mixed with enough honey, the teas were tasty and according to knowledgeable women, good for various ailments.

Lee had found a bee tree upstream and thought there was another even farther upriver, so honey wasn't likely to be in short supply. The tribe could raid the bee trees after they established a better camp on the western bank; crossing the river would become simple as soon as the ferry began operating.

Someone was turning out pottery dishes too. Matt didn't know who, but new products had begun appearing and they didn't look like the ones made by Sandra and Millie. Matt picked up a pottery cup and filled it with tea.

"Lee, Colin said you talked to Tex and no one's seen him today. You didn't send him packing, did you?"

"Not yet, Matt; that's your decision. He's a good fighter, but he's not one to take orders. I asked him to work with the guards, but he said he was going scouting. I think he's across the river now."

"Well, at least he's doing something. Did he say what he was looking for?"

"I think he just wanted to see what was over there, Matt. I might be doing that too if I wasn't responsible for security."

"I know the feeling, Lee. Maybe you can train a couple of people to handle security and you and I can take off for a few days. Colin's running the camp most of the time and he's doing a good job; all he needs is more experience. We could turn things over to Colin and your assistants and go hunting for a few days."

"I'd like that, Matt. It's been too long. As for assistants, Laz and Marc are almost ready to take over. Each now runs a shift during the night and it gives me a break. If Colin keeps an eye on them, I'm sure they could handle security. Just you and me, or were you thinking of taking others too?"

"We can check with Sandra and Lilia, Lee. I don't know if they can drop what they're doing, but if they think they can be spared the four of us can go. I saw animals off to the west, but it was too far to make out what they were. I was looking from the top of the ridge and whatever I saw was a few miles away."

"Some of those mammoths, maybe?"

"Could be. But they might be bison, what Tex calls buffalo."

"I wouldn't mind a buffalo hunt, Matt. It's dangerous, hunting them on foot, but we could do it. We got a lot of meat last time."

"That's what I was thinking, Lee. When Tex gets back we can ask him what he saw. How'd he cross the river?"

"He said he would swim. I get the idea he's swum rivers before. I might try it if I were alone, but not with women and kids. And we've got the tools and things we've made. Tex only has Tex to worry about, so he can do things we can't."

"So he can. Well, if he's useful and not causing trouble, he can stay. Or he can go, if that's what he wants to do. We don't force anyone to stay."

"That's how I saw it, Matt. There was no reason to bother you with it. Anyway, he's being useful so far. About not causing trouble..."

"You know something I don't, Lee?"

"I don't know anything yet. It's just a feeling. I'm watching, but I haven't seen anything yet."

"Don't try to handle it yourself, Lee. If there's a problem, bring it to Colin and me. The three of us can decide what to do."

Lee nodded, and Matt left. Lee had a temper, but maybe this time he'd listen.

Continuing downriver, he found Sal and Miguel hip-deep in the river. Between them floated the ferry. A quick estimate put the length at thirty feet and the width somewhere around fifteen feet. Miguel was wrapping a rope of thin roots plaited together to secure one of the side rails. Another was finished, already standing above the ferry's cross-decking.

Matt inspected the lashings but found no faults. He congratulated Sal and while they were talking four men brought up the completed tether cable. A beaming Sal soon had it attached to the nearest end and gestured to Matt.

"Want the first ride, Matt?"

Matt grinned back and said, "Sure. Think this thing is safe?"

"Why don't we find out? A rope crew can control how far out we go, drag us back after we've reached the end. We'll need a couple of push-poles, just in case."

Matt nodded and went off to cut the poles. Half an hour later he returned, handing one to Sal.

"You understand that if the rope breaks, we're going to have a very interesting ride?"

Sal grinned back. "It's been interesting since I got here, Matt. But I think we can use the poles to take some of the strain off the rope. Just let me talk to the guys first. I want them to wrap the line around a tree and just let it pay it out as we push away from the shore, not try to hold the ferry by muscle power alone. I don't think we should try to cross the river yet."

"Not unless it's shallower than it looks, Sal. The current doesn't look fast, but it could be anywhere from six to sixty feet deep in the middle."

"I doubt it will be more than ten feet at the most. The poles you cut are twenty-five feet or so, plenty of reach and thick enough. Let's just see what the river looks like after we're away from the bank."

Matt nodded and jumped onto the raft, pole held overhead. The raft rocked slightly as Sal boarded behind him. Matt took up a post where he could best control the front of the raft, leaving Sal to control the rear. He would angle the pole to better resist the current when the ferry started to drift. Matt nodded readiness and Sal placed the butt end of his pole against the bank. He held the smaller end, arms wide apart for leverage and knees flexed to add power.

The small strip of water behind the raft widened slowly as Sal pushed. The ferry's progress was glacially slow, but it was definitely moving. Matt planted his pole and locked his hands tight, gripping the pole as Sal was doing. Leaning into his pole, Matt brought his weight to bear, pushing slightly upstream as the raft eased away from the bank.

There was a technique used by canoe paddlers, a kind of leverage stroke in which the paddler used the side of the canoe as a fulcrum, pushing the paddle deep into the water before pulling back on the grip. Would something similar work for poling the raft? Matt decided to give it a try.

Pushing the pole into the bottom, close to the edge of the raft, he pulled back and felt the raft move in response. Grinning, Matt looked back at Sal. Taking his hand off the pole, he flashed a 'thumbs up' to Sal.

The current caught the raft. Matt tried to pull against the pole where it was sticking up, but his moccasin-clad feet began to slip. The pole dragged him toward the edge of the raft.

Matt, approaching the side rail, released the pole, which whipped toward the water. The raft majestically drifted over it, leaving it to bob up behind them.

Sal was laughing, but Matt was too worried to find humor in the situation. Behind him, Sal pushed, driving the raft toward the center of the river.

The men on the bank saw the problem and quickly took an additional wrap around the tree. The tree shivered, but held.

The rope had sagged into the water as the raft swung downstream. The sag lifted behind them and the rope creaked as it took up the strain.

Water dripped, squeezed out from the rope as tons of raft pulled against the cable. Tension grew, squeezing more water out. The heavy rope stretched, becoming thinner. Matt heard a loud popping noise, then a bass thrum as the rope took the strain.

Would it hold?

The rope had been almost as thick as his wrist when Sal tied it to the raft. Now it was half that. The raft checked with a jerk as the rope finally reached full extension. The rope hummed. There was another popping noise.

"SAL! Over here by me, and get down low!"

"Matt, what are you talking about?"

"If that rope snaps, it can take your head off. Get down and stay out from in front in case it breaks. If it snaps...well, we can always jump and swim to shore, but not if the broken end whips across and kills us."

Sal's face grew suddenly white. He dropped this pole on the raft's deck, then scurried over by Matt.

Together they watched as the rope tightened and the raft slowly changed direction, now drifting across the current toward the river's eastern bank.

Matt anxiously watched the straining rope as it tightened. Water dripped, the patter audible over the popping noises.

23

The rope twanged every time a small surge in the current pushed the ferry. Slowly it drifted toward shore.

Matt and Sal remained flat on the deck, warily watching the tight rope. Ages later, the rope sagged as the craft reached slack water near the bank.

"Would you help your crew pull the raft back to where we launched it?" Matt asked. "I'll use your pole to keep it out of the current."

"Sure, Matt. I hope you do a better job of poling than you did before!"

Matt chuckled ruefully. "I learned my lesson, Sal; that mistake won't happen again. I'll figure out a *new* way to mess things up!"

Sal laughed and jumped for the bank, scrambling to get out of the muddy edge. The raft now floated quietly, parallel to the current. Matt positioned himself in the center. He would have to move back and forth, keeping the raft out of the current but also preventing it from hanging up on brush at the water's edge.

The drift downstream had lasted less than ten minutes. Pulling the heavy raft back, even with Sal helping, took a solid hour of work.

Matt was exhausted, as were the men hauling on the rope. But finally it was done, the raft floating quietly in an eddy near the bank.

"Lesson learned, Sal. We'll need four polemen to work the raft when we get near the banks. That raft is heavy!"

"I knew it was heavy, Matt, but I didn't expect this much trouble. We dragged every one of those logs down to the water, but once they were floating we could move them without much trouble. I didn't realize that it would be so hard to control when the current caught it."

"It should be a lot easier after we get the long rope on. Reaction ferries, which is what this is going to be, are easier to work than the kind where every foot the ferry moves requires muscle power."

"Sure hope so, Matt. But the first time we use it, I'll ride the ferry. I'll pick people who are good swimmers for polemen, in case the rope breaks."

"Take your weapons, too. You could end up miles down the river. It might take you a while to work your way back upstream."

"Will do. Lilia's crew should have the long rope ready by tomorrow. This rope worked just fine, although I was worried at first when I saw how much it stretched. We'll lay it out in the sun to dry, because I'm pretty sure we'll need it again. I'll let you know when we're ready to make the first ferry trip."

"Something else to watch out for, rising water. If there's a heavy rain upstream, the water will rise and the current will get stronger. If that happens, we'll have to drag the raft up on shore."

"Could be a problem if we strand people on the side away from camp."

"That's why we don't go anywhere without weapons. We know the dangers, and if we're careful and always have at least a spear handy we can survive until the ferry starts operating again."

Sal nodded and Matt headed wearily back to camp. Fix one problem, two more popped up.

Margrette and her daughter Callie were humming quietly as they knelt on a shaggy skin. Curious, Matt walked over and watched. The two deftly sliced steaks from a large hindquarter. Another lay waiting.

"Is that a bison?"

"Tex called it a buffalo, but it's the same animal. Fresh meat for tonight!"

"Tex brought it in?" At Margrette's nod, Matt continued, "Did you see which way he went?"

"Over toward the river, Matt. He left about an hour ago, maybe a little longer."

"Good to have fresh meat for supper. I'll go see if I can find Tex."

Monika was camped in that direction and Matt stopped for a moment. Her son, Bear, was playing with a bow suited to his five-year-old hands.

"Did Tex pass this way?"

"Sure did, Matt. He brought Bear that nice bow. It's a toy, but the sooner they begin learning, the better."

"Indeed. I hope he doesn't shoot any of us!"

"It's more toy than anything else, but I'll keep an eye on him. Tex went on toward the river, I think."

"OK, thanks. See you later, Bear." But the child had attention only for his new treasure.

Matt looked along the river but found no sign of Tex. Curious, he continued on until he found the group with Lilia. The long, heavy ferry cable appeared to be finished. The remaining few inches of cord were being wrapped around the end of the cable to secure it from unraveling.

"Looks good, Lilia. Did Tex come this way?"

"I didn't see him, Matt. But now that you're here, we need more men and a couple of carts. I'm thinking we coil as much of the cable on the first cart as it will hold, then coil the rest on the other one. We'll have to take it slow and keep the second cart right behind the first one, but with help we can have the cable delivered to Sal in an hour or so."

"Good job, Lilia. I'll find men to move the cable. Your crew has done a fine job."

"It was hard work, Matt. The longer the cable got, the heavier it was. We only had the men in the edge of the forest to pull it away and they're exhausted."

"I'll find others. Piotr can help, and Colin will know who else can be spared. The rope was work, but in the end using it will save work."

"Well, you know more about that than I do. We'll be waiting."

Matt gave up his search for Tex... he would turn up in his own good time... and went to find Colin. Collecting Piotr from his flint-working, Matt, Colin, Piotr, and Carlo picked the two sturdiest carts from where they were parked and pulled them to where Lilia waited.

The four began coiling the heavy cable onto the first cart, struggling to pull the heavy length toward the carts. Eventually almost half of the cable was arranged in two coiled layers on the first cart. Matt estimated the weight of the cable was all the cart could carry without risking a breakdown. Propping the shafts of the second cart on the bed of the first, the men continued coiling the remaining cable. Finally it was done.

"Piotr, bring some of the cord from my camp, please. We'll arrange this while you're gone."

Piotr nodded and left. Matt explained what he intended to the others.

"I'm going to tie the trailing cart to the first one. We can't allow them to separate, the cable is just too heavy. Tying the axles together is necessary, but it's likely to be tricky because we've got to be able to steer around trees. I'm thinking of something like horse-drawn wagons had, links from just inside the wheels of the rear axle to somewhere near the center of the front axle. Wagons used solid pieces, but ropes should work. We'll take it slow.

"We'll need two on the front shafts, they'll be hard to steer. As for pulling, ropes tied to the front axle will help. Put a couple of men on each, then all of us pull. We'll get it there in an hour or so."

"Matt, it would be easier if the weapons weren't banging on our legs," Colin objected.

"Lay them on the carts. Basic survival rule, never be more than a few feet from your weapons."

Piotr brought the ropes and Matt supervised lashing the carts together. The weight of the rear cart, transmitted through the shafts, lifted the shafts of the front cart clear of the ground. The completed arrangement did indeed look like a wagon.

"Matt, why don't we just try pushing on the rear cart? If that doesn't work, we can try your rope idea," Colin suggested.

"It might work. Just remember the front cart is the steering engine for this train."

Colin chuckled; he knew what a train was.

The carts creaked and groaned, but with Colin and three others pushing, Matt and Piotr managed to steer the front cart. They reached the tree upstream from the ferry site after an hour of hard work.

Sal and his crew had been resting. They joined the transport crew in tying the upper end of the cable to the tree, then began dragging the cable into the river. The first pair guided the floating cable, keeping in near the bank, while others fed in more.

"That bridle idea won't work, Matt. Too much strain against a single spot of a lighter rope. Tie the cable to the raft, say by feeding it through where the keel is attached. Tie it on, the raft should hold together."

"Okay. We'll still need other ropes to change direction." Sal nodded his understanding.

Matt supervised looping the cable and tying it securely. It might break, but the bowline knot wouldn't loosen. Sal also checked, before deciding it was satisfactory.

Matt called the men over to where he'd scraped a bare place on the ground and went over the plan again.

"A reaction ferry works because the current tries to push it downstream and the cable keeps that from happening." He sketched an arc across the two lines he'd drawn to represent the river. A longer straight line led straight up to a crude drawing of a tree. "We use shorter ropes, tied to the cable, to adjust the angle. When the current hits the raft's keel, it's deflected. Whichever end is more upstream, that's the direction the ferry will go. When we're ready to come back, we lengthen the bow rope and shorten the stern rope. We'll need four men to push, at least the first time. I think we can toss a rope from the ferry to a few men on shore and we won't need poles after we make the first crossing." Matt continued sketching to illustrate his points.

"But I think it's too late to cross today, and anyway we're tired. By the time we get the ropes arranged, it will be late afternoon. We'll tie everything on today, and tomorrow morning we try crossing. I want good swimmers on the first trip, understood? If something goes wrong, jump in and swim upstream. *Don't* get downstream from the raft. Don't fight the current. Swim with it and angle for the nearest bank. Any questions?"

The men nodded soberly. Sal took charge, sending men to do the different tasks. Matt watched for a moment, then headed back to camp.

Lee was at the kitchen, watching Callie and her mom prepare the steaks for broiling. Callie handed Lee a steak, already skewered on a green stick. He used one of the forked sticks around the fire to prop his steak over the coals. Matt's steak was soon cooking next to Lee's.

"Tex is a good hunter as well as a good fighter."

"That he is, Matt. I spoke to him for a few minutes. He said there's a herd of buffalo about two miles northwest of here. He said there was also a herd of mammoths, at least a dozen. He left after that."

"He's gone again?"

Lee nodded. "I think he wants to try for another buffalo."

"What did he do with the rest of the buffalo? I only saw two hindquarters."

"He said he couldn't drag more than that, so he ate some of the back-strap and left the rest. Coyotes and foxes gotta eat too, he said."

"I suppose; nothing's wasted here. What we don't eat, some other animal will. I wonder why he didn't stay in camp tonight?

"I don't think he's adjusted to living with people yet," Lee said. "He spent ten years alone. He'll come back when it suits him."

"I guess you're right. Maybe I'll get a chance to talk to him when he gets back. Time to turn the steaks, wouldn't you say?"

* * *

TEX CRAWLED FROM THE RIVER, picking up his bow, quiver, and spear from the lashed-together limbs he'd used as a float. He untied the thin ropes he'd used, coiling and slinging them over his shoulder. Finished, he pushed the limbs away from the bank and watched the slow current take them. Settling everything as comfortably as possible, he headed away.

Cresting a rise, he spotted the buffalo grazing about a mile away. There was no sign of the mammoths, but they'd be around; for such huge animals, they possessed an uncanny ability to disappear into the brush. Probably the gray skin and thin brown wool made it possible. But so long as they weren't a threat, Tex didn't care.

He passed upwind from the buffalo and watched as they alerted, heads up, the old bull taking position between Tex and the herd. Tex gave him a wide berth and continued on. Over the next rise...yes, there they were. Tex smiled and reached into his pack. The pot of honey he'd gotten from Callie was still there.

Tex had a plan for that honey.

24

Tex trotted across the grassy countryside, bow in hand but arrows in his quiver. The landscape was more open here and few trees or bushes existed to hide predators; he felt no need to restrict his speed by keeping an arrow on the string.

Despite the necessity of alternately climbing and descending the low hills and ridges west of the river, Tex was breathing easily. Ahead lay the location he'd discovered during the scout. He'd immediately seen the possibilities of the wide, shallow gully with steep sides that cut through the landscape. The half-acre pond at the lower end appeared to be seasonal, expanding or shrinking depending on rainfall.

A number of animals had been drinking at the pond. Tex identified the tracks of cats, dire wolves, and a number of hoofed animals. There were fewer buffalo tracks than expected, and for that matter the large cloven-hooved tracks might not be buffalo.

But the other hoofed tracks weren't cloven, and Tex had stiffened in excitement when he first saw them. The tracks were rounded. In his previous life Tex had seen thousands like them.

These were a little smaller, but there was no doubt; the tracks had been left by horses. Patiently he worked out the numbers before deciding this band had a larger stallion, perhaps a dozen mares and fillies, and a pair of foals from the spring birthing.

That seemed unusually low, but maybe the birth rate was different here, mares coming into season at irregular times. Or perhaps predators had killed the others.

It was something to consider, predators. They would go elsewhere or die. For now, it was enough to know that the horses were in the vicinity, they had good graze and water, hence unlikely to leave unless forced to do so.

As for the cats, there might be a use for them too. Tex had eaten cat a number of times and much preferred the taste of the saber-toothed variety to lion, which had an unpleasant, gamy taste. The skin was useful for making rawhide gear but not for garments; it tended to dry rough and stiff, and working it into leather was more trouble than the finished product was worth.

The rawhide carried a strong smell of cat. Tex intended to turn that liability into advantage.

Scattered trees on the plain offered concealment and protection. All in all, this area lacked only one thing, a woman or two for companionship. But that might be remedied after another visit or two to the tribe. The campsite was only about five or six miles back, and Callie had shown definite interest in him, maybe one or two others. He might even start his own tribe!

Selecting his campsite, he began collecting the things he'd need. He dragged in firewood, shaved off tinder to start the fire, chose branches for a shelter, then added a number of rocks he thought he could use. Finally deciding he had enough, he began constructing a simple shelter, cutting and stacking sod to make three low walls, then incorporating heavier beams and branches into a roof. It would leak, but he could fix that later.

The front he left open. Tex his firepit about five feet in front of his soddy, then lined it with rocks. He added more rocks in front to reflect heat into his shelter, then laid dried wood. Building a fire, he slept for a time.

Late in the afternoon, Tex picked up his bow and nocked an arrow. A shallow gully led down to the deeper cut. Tex followed the gully, looking for sign that animals had used it to access the pond. Finally he found what he wanted and hidden behind brush, settled in to wait. A few yards above, just past the edge, stood a tree he could climb rapidly if necessary.

There was a slight breeze and it was favorable, blowing across the trail to where Tex waited. He got as comfortable as possible and settled in to wait, only his eyes moving, ceaselessly scanning.

* * *

MATT CAREFULLY REEXAMINED the knot joining the raft to the long cable. Yanking on the cable, he felt no give. Hand on the cable, he followed it up through the shallows to a large oak. Sal's men had wrapped the cable twice around the tree, then secured the tie with a girth-hitch. Someone, perhaps inspired by the mishap the day before, had used smaller cord to secure the girth hitch against unwrapping. Careful was good; Matt looked, and approved.

A spring line had been added. It was firmly tied to the cable thirty feet above where it joined the raft, a loop tied in the spring line just below the knot. The remainder of the line had been passed around a log, then fed back through the loop before once again being tied to the raft. Clever...this would serve as an impromptu 'pulley' for use in adjusting the angle of the raft, now a true reaction ferry.

Assuming it worked, of course.

"I guess we're ready, Sal. Who's riding the first trip?"

"You and Lee are passengers, Matt. You'll get off when we reach the other side and keep watch. I'll work with a pole, pushing off, and I've got Dominick, José, Antonio and Manuel to pole from the sides. Good swimmers, and we worked with the poles before we quit yesterday so everyone's used to handling them. Hopefully we won't get in each other's way."

"If it works like I hope, we probably won't need that many polemen," said Matt. "Are you sure?"

"Better to have too many than too few. We don't know what we'll find over there, not the first time. We've got our bows if we need them, spears too. I think we're ready."

Matt nodded. "Let's do it."

Sal turned and nodded to his crew. The poles lay ready on the raft, and the men Sal had listed took their places at the stern of the heavy ferry. Matt and Lee laid their weapons on the raft, preparing to help push off.

"You two have a seat on the raft, Matt; we can handle this. Just leave me room in the bow. I'm going to handle the spring line myself. Unless somebody better shows up, I plan to be the ferryman." Sal grinned and Matt returned it. Sal had certainly looked more competent than Matt during the first accidental voyage yesterday!

Sal and the four polemen pushed the ferry away, and as soon as it began to move he grabbed the sturdy upstream rail and hauled himself aboard. The others followed immediately behind him, wet legs dripping on the raft.

Perhaps a small pier or jetty later...? But first, they needed to see how the ferry functioned.

Sal judged the current as his polemen took station at the aft end. Planting their poles, they pushed strongly. The raft responded and moved ahead. Sal began hauling on the free end of the spring line where it passed through the loop near the main cable. The raft slowly changed orientation, bow pointing upstream.

"Looks good, Sal. What happens if you don't get it right?"

"We just drift back where we started, Matt. It's pretty simple once you understand it. Being the ferryman is easy and it's a lot less work than setting up camp!"

Matt laughed. Sal was one of the hardest-working people he'd ever seen. Even in a tribe where everybody worked hard, Sal stood out. Always enthusiastic, always ready to help, he was a natural foreman. He might not be a candidate for tribal leader, but in his element he was outstanding.

"Poles in!" At Sal's command, the polemen lifted their poles and stood them upright, butts down and dripping on the deck. Matt moved closer to the center of the ferry to make room; the polemen might be needed on the downstream side as the ferry approached the far bank. For now, they simply waited. If the water was shallow enough, they could resume pushing from the stern.

The ferry drifted downstream, then began moving smoothly across the current. The course described an arc, crossing the center of the river, then slowing as it drifted toward the bank. Matt looked at the grinning polemen. They'd had a few minutes of gut-straining effort followed by a smooth ride, the kind of ride none had experienced since arriving on Darwin's World. Matt let a smile touch his lips; this could be something people would enjoy!

The long cable stretched as the safety rope had done the previous day. That rope now reached back to where they'd launched the ferry, but so far it hadn't been needed; the main cable had stretched, but being able to work with the current instead of fighting it lessened the strain.

Even so, there was danger; the rope might break after a few soakings. So the safety line would remain.

The polemen, responding to Sal's order, planted their poles and pushed. In the bow, Sal loosened the spring line and allowed the raft, now broadside to the river, to ease ahead. The ferry slid gently up on the sloping bottom, then stopped. Matt jumped and Lee followed.

Wading ashore, they found concealment near large trees, spears slung, bows in hand and arrows ready on the strings.

"Nice ride, Sal. Have Colin load the carts. We'll be watching, just throw us a rope when you get back and we'll pull you to shore."

Sal nodded. The pole crew pushed and the ferry drifted backward. As soon as the current caught it, Sal loosened the spring rope, allowing the former aft end that was now the bow to point upstream. Men hauled on the safety rope as the ferry approached the east bank. It would take at least an hour before it would return.

Matt and Lee scouted the woods west of the river. They shortly found a level spot, open, but with huge trees scattered about. Not far away were others that might serve as raw material for wheels. Their patrol took them half a mile downstream before Matt was satisfied. Retracing their course, they explored to the north. Finding no dangers, they headed back to the riverbank to wait for Sal's return.

* * *

TEX STUMBLED WEARILY into his camp. He'd carried the meat and skin more than two miles and had barely made it home before dark. The nights were cool at this elevation, so perhaps the meat wouldn't spoil before he could cure it into jerky.

The hide would need processing too, but it would have to wait for morning. He laid his tinder near the pile of wood and began striking sparks from the flint knife's hilt. Practice helped; barely a minute later the tinder was smoldering. Tex held it in his cupped hands and nursed the tiny spark, blowing carefully until flames appeared. Laying the burning tinder in the firepit, he added more until he was confident the fire was well started. Carefully, he fed small twigs into the growing flames. There was more than enough wood in the nearby stack to keep the fire going through the night.

Huddling close to the warmth, Tex sliced steaks from the backstraps wrapped in the skin. Good eating, none better; the meat had come from one of the big deerlike animals Matt had called a stag-moose. He placed a few vegetables near the edge of the fire, turning them occasionally so they'd cook evenly without burning. The steaks would need less time, so he waited for a good bed of coals to form.

Food, shelter, water close by...Tex settled in for a long stay. There was plenty of game and the horses wouldn't leave unless he chased them away.

* * *

HE'D WATCHED as the small band warily approached the pond. Wading a few feet into the water, they snuffled, then drank. The stallion watched while the mares drank, then drank himself. The mares and yearlings left the water and a mare, apparently older, watched for danger.

The horses grazed for a time near the pond's edge before drinking again. After the second watering, they walked away down the wide gully. Half a mile on, they found a trail, climbed up the steep side, and disappeared from sight.

Tex had discovered a possible pattern. The horses had come to water in mid-afternoon, arriving from the north and leaving to the south. If they were as habitual as downtime horses, they'd follow a predictable circuit. Graze at dawn, bed down for a short time, then graze again. Someone always stood watch while others snoozed.

Tex would watch again in a few days. Meantime, he expected to remain at least a month, possibly longer. Tex was patient.

* * *

WILLOW SEEMED to be the preferred building material; most of the tribe had built willow framed beehive-shaped dwellings about six feet tall. They had transferred their bedding and other possessions to the shelters, and short of a cloudburst, the tribe was ready to spend their first night in the new camp. The cookfire was going and tea was waiting; people began moving toward the fire as soon as they'd finished their temporary shelters.

Matt intended to remain in camp while Sal and his crew rebuilt the carts, but perhaps when that was done he could go hunting with Lee. If they found buffalo nearby, they could always come back and lead a larger party there. The carts could be used to haul meat, despite the need for repairs.

Margrette had already built a smoking rack. Matt or someone else would hunt; a good stock of preserved meat might last until late summer, even early fall. But first there was the task of killing animals, salting and smoking the meat, preparing the skins to replace what they'd lost or abandoned and to provide sleeping pads for the new members...

Two weeks or perhaps a bit more should see them back on the trek, Matt thought. Better carts, a new supply of food and skins, a chance to rest and eat better; the tribe should be able to travel faster when they resumed their long journey. They would *need* to move faster if they were to reach the mountains in time to prepare for winter.

Matt considered what they would have to do if there wasn't time to find that perfect location. Should they stay here, near the river? Perhaps build shelters on one of the ridges? Or maybe drag timbers into place to serve as a hasty barricade around the camp?

They were no longer threatened by the mine guards or the slavers. Even the predators had kept their distance, at least so far. How much food was in the vicinity? How hard would it be to build shelters that could protect them through the winter? But the river might flood, and there was no telling how severe the winter might be...

The tribe would be in much better shape next year. But after spending fall and winter near this river, would they want to go on? Would they choose to improve *this* location rather than look for something better?

It was preferable to the place they'd left, but still not easy to defend.

No; they wouldn't stay here, although stopping long enough to build winter quarters farther west might become necessary. They should be able to reach the location where the downtime city of Albuquerque stood if they resumed the journey within two or three weeks. The climate was not severe, not quite the warm winters of El Paso a few hundred miles to the south, but still rarely dipping as far as zero on the ancient Fahrenheit scale. Nights were cold, followed by cool days where the temperature rebounded to forty or fifty degrees. The nearby mountains would provide some shelter from prevailing winds if the tribe chose their location carefully. A river ran there just as it did here, and natives downtime had established farming and ranching long before the Spanish had invaded. The tribe could live there as they had.

And if that place couldn't be reached in time, there were other options. A reliable water source and a sheltered location were at the top of his list; if they found a place that provided those things, it might have to do. If timber wasn't available, the tribe could build durable shelters of stone or even earth. It wouldn't be that difficult if everyone pitched in. Regardless of where they stopped, they would have to collect food and furs for bedding, and store everything in case the winter should prove to be more severe than was the norm downtime.

The small West Texas town of Balmorhea was near the location of a huge spring that never failed. South of there lay the Big Bend country, desert downtime, but probably temperate and lightly-forested on Darwin's World. Either location could become a permanent home for the tribe.

Matt would talk to Colin tomorrow and see what he thought.

25

T ex had spent two weeks preparing. The steep-walled gully now had fences, made by dragging and piling trees and brush into place. Openings had been left, but more vegetation was piled nearby to close the gaps.

Best of all, he had spent late evenings by the fire braiding reatas, the leather ropes used by cowboys throughout the west. Mexicans had made the first ones, but American cowboys had adopted them soon after; incredibly strong, thin, and lightweight, they served a variety of uses.

Tex had begun reata-braiding by preparing the raw skins. An elk, two stag-moose, and a lion had provided the skins.

A string had served as his drawing aid, to produce the largest circle possible given the size of the skins. The circle told him how large to dig a shallow hole, necessary to prepare the raw skins for de-hairing. The skins themselves would serve as the waterproof liner. Placing the skins so that the center lay over the hole, he weighted the edges with large stones, then added water while leaving room for the next step.

Raking hot stones from the campfire, he added them to the water and let the skin soak in the warm water. Periodically replacing cooled stones with hot, the water soon approached boiling temperature. Half an hour later, the softened skin was ready and Tex began ripping away huge swaths of hair.

Spreading the damp and hairless skin on the ground, he sketched a circle and used his knife to carefully cut along the line. He soaked the leftover pieces in the next hide basin while hot water softened both.

Between hunting, preparing meals, and preparing the hides, Tex made a slicer using a scrap sliver of steel, a gift from Piotr. After shaping the steel by rubbing it on sandstone, he sharpened the edge using a variety of small, smooth stones he'd picked up nearby. Finally, he wedged the steel blade into a split at the end of a sturdy branch, leaving a slightly-hooked blade that was razor-sharp on the rear edge. Tying the split firmly closed, he decided the slicer was as good as he could make it.

Tex prepared the skin circles by soaking them again, this time in cool water until they were soft and pliable. Beginning at the edge, he carefully began pulling the rawhide into the slicer blade, trying to keep the thin strip between a quarter and three-eighths of an inch wide. Carefully pulling the skin, he continued. The cuts spiraled in toward the hide's center. He was patient and worked slowly; any mistake could shorten the thong.

Patience helped, but even so he made a number of mistakes until he mastered the technique. His mistakes, shorter strings from the first circle, made useful strings but they weren't long enough to be plaited into the strong rope he needed. The second attempt went much better.

The steel blade required sharpening from time to time. He trimmed the laces after the initial slicing when they were too wide, this time using his belt knife, a gift from the Futurist who had transplanted Tex.

Whenever he finished with a hide, he stretched the finished thongs between small trees to dry.

A simple four-strand plait would work. Downtime rawhide artists sometimes used six or even eight strands, but Tex had never learned their techniques. Still, the four-plait was simple; even a child could do it. The trick lay in pulling the strands tight before moving to the next plait. Lay one strand loosely across the end of the plait, secure it in place with the next strand, repeat using the third one, then do the same with the last strand, pulling it under the folded thong he'd started with. The final strand locked the previous one in position, and pulling all the elements tight into a square meant the plait wouldn't unravel. The square corners would stretch at first, becoming rounder. The corners would also become worn, increasing the roundness that was the mark of a true reata.

Finally he was ready. Two reatas hung from tree branches by grass cords, placed near the brush barriers that partially enclosed the gully.

Tex filled his small pack with jerky filled both water gourds, preparing for his ordeal. He had two choices; the one he preferred was the join-up method popularized by Monty Roberts, who had once been called the 'horse whisperer'. Tex had learned everything he could downtime from what Roberts had written. If it worked, Tex could corral the horses and take his time breaking them for riding.

The alternate method was a brute-force approach, simply drive the horses into the trap. This was more difficult and would likely be less successful.

Ready, he turned away from the sod house and trotted toward where the horses were grazing after their morning drink.

The oldest mare spotted him first and her shrill whistle alerted the others. The stallion responded by placing himself between the small band and Tex. They watched nervously as he trotted toward them, bow in his left hand and the third reata he'd made swinging in his right. The mare pealed her alarm and the herd pelted down the gully. As expected, they climbed rapidly up the side and vanished. Tex kept trotting.

He spotted the horses in the distance as soon as he topped the wall. He wouldn't catch them today and probably wouldn't do so tomorrow. But if he could make Roberts' method work, perhaps on the third day he could begin heading back for the small sod shelter.

* * *

MATT AND LEE started west at dawn and soon spread out to cover more ground. Slipping silently through the scattered trees, they watched for game.

Each knew where the other was. Occasional glimpses seen through the trees was enough to ensure their paths remained close, and either could help the other if needed. They'd hunted as a team before.

Lee pulled slightly ahead and bent his course to intercept Matt.

"Big hill to the northwest, Matt."

"Might be deer or elk up there. They like to bed down high up where they can keep watch."

"That's what I was thinking. Gets them away from the flies and they like the cool breezes this time of year. We could go up from two sides. That way, we'd catch anything that decided to leave."

Matt nodded. "How about you go in from the north, while I take the south slope?"

Nodding, Lee finished drinking from his gourd and replaced the stopper. He slipped away leaving Matt to work out his own approach to the hill.

* * *

He found Lee waiting halfway up the slope.

"See something?"

"Dozen or so stag-moose, Matt, bachelor bulls I think. They know I'm here, probably know you're here too by now. Our scent will be rising ahead of us."

"We'll stay together, then. We need to spot them before they see us, and a big tree is always better than a small one if they get antsy!"

Lee grinned, then led up the hill, slightly crouched in readiness. Matt moved a few yards to the left and followed. Experienced eyes spotted tracks amid the round pellets of dung. The stags hadn't yet split up to find females. The animals were always dangerous, but probably not as aggressive this time of year.

One animal would be enough; getting a carcass down the hill was a big task for two men. Lee had found them first, so he could have the first shot. Matt would try to put his arrow into the same animal if it didn't drop immediately.

The bulls were noisy. Immature antlers brushed against branches and the beasts snorted from time to time. There was a faint musky smell, not unpleasant, that indicated the animals were close ahead. Matt eased closer to Lee. Both were now poised, taking a slow step then pausing before moving ahead. Up ahead the noise suddenly stopped.

Matt felt a sudden uneasiness. "Lee! Tree!"

Following his own advice, he swarmed up the tree he'd selected. Stopping some twelve feet up, ready, he looked twenty feet over to the tree Lee had climbed. Lee had braced his feet on a pair of large branches and leaned slightly back against the trunk, waiting.

Below them the branches stirred and a huge bull prowled into the space they'd just vacated, head down to sniff, stubby antlers ready to lift and kill. Others followed closely behind the massive leader. Matt shook his head at Lee; let the big one pass, take one of the trailing animals.

Lee nodded. Below them the bulls milled around, sniffing the ground; they had little to fear from predators in the trees. Lee finally picked the animal he wanted and slowly drew back his bowstring.

Matt followed the direction the arrow pointed and selected a point of aim on the same animal. He waited for Lee's shot, concentrating only on the stag-moose. The animal was some thirty yards away from Lee, probably forty yards from Matt. The footing wasn't ideal, but it would do. Matt shot as soon as he heard Lee's bowstring twang.

The young bull staggered, then plunged ahead. The rest bolted when they smelled the fresh blood. Matt listened to the antlers cracking as they fled; the sounds soon died away in the forest.

Below them, the animal kicked and died. Matt waited. Lee would wait too, though he was less patient than Matt. The bull wasn't going anywhere.

Matt had an excellent view of the surrounding plains. Finding nothing of interest nearby, he looked farther out. The elevation allowed him to examine the plains off to the west. Grasses here were different, shorter, and more bunch-grass than the tall grasses of the east, rarely rising more than knee high. *Not tall enough to hide a predator, while still providing plenty of forage for grazers,* he thought; Matt much preferred this western type of grassland.

The dark-colored horses might have escaped his attention had they been grazing. But they were trotting and his eyes immediately picked up the movement. Curious, he looked behind them to see what had alarmed them.

"Lee...look over there, way out. See those horses?"

Lee looked where Matt was pointing. It took only moments before he called back, "I see them, Matt. But we've already got plenty of meat down."

"Not thinking of hunting, Lee. Look behind them, maybe a quarter mile or so."

Lee scanned the area finally spotting what Matt had seen. "Matt, that looks like Tex."

"That's what I think. But he's never going to catch those horses. I wonder what he's up to?"

"No idea. Are you ready to climb down and dress out that bull?"

"It should be safe enough. Let's do it."

Matt was thoughtful while they worked and several times he looked off to the west where they'd seen Tex. Maybe he wasn't looking for horsemeat after all.

* * *

SAL AND COLIN had found a huge tree only a few hundred yards northeast of the camp.

A small creek flowed past before joining the river a few hundred yards downstream. Beavers had constructed a low dam and built their lodges in the shallow pool behind; the large tree had been killed by the rodents, but they hadn't finished the task of gnawing through the trunk. Almost all of it was still intact.

There was no sign of the beavers and no recent tracks on the bank. Perhaps a predator had interrupted their dam construction.

In any case, this tree was ideal, even if felling it might prove dangerous.

"What do you think, Sal?" The two men looked at the tree and considered how they could bring it down in the most convenient location for working.

"I'm thinking we use axes to deepen the notch on this side, just chopping in where the beavers already started. As soon as we're about halfway in, leave off chopping and start cutting with the saw on the reverse side. Not deep, though. Take the cut in about a foot, leave a thick hinge for the trunk to pivot on. Then drive in wedges to finish the felling."

"Should work, Sal. But this job is more dangerous because of the beaver cuts on the back and sides. Use no more than two men at a time for cutting, and keep the rest well back until it's down. I wouldn't tackle it at all, but the wood's just what we're looking for. It's big, it's already dry so it won't be likely to crack, and we can probably get all the wheel blanks we want just from this one tree."

"Maybe so, Colin. Might need another tree, depending on knots and such. No way to tell until we start sawing."

"I'll leave you to it, Sal. I'll be back at camp if you need me. Laz said he might take a hunting party southwest and I want to make sure he leaves enough people to defend the camp."

"Makes sense. After we get the tree down we can cut wheel blanks in a day and then we can move them back to camp to finish the work. We'd be available if you needed us."

"Do that. Piotr is staying in camp, working on bows for the new people, but we need a couple more. Lilia's out foraging with some of the women. And Bear's what, about six now? He's staying in camp, fishing. Kid loves it, and we might get tired of fish before he gets bored with fishing!"

"Can he swim, Colin? In case he falls in, I mean."

"Monika taught him to swim. It's not a good idea to let him swim alone, but he's about half otter in the water. I think if we let him he'd go after some of those big catfish with that little spear!"

The two chuckled and Colin departed for the camp. On the way he saw Elizabeth and Bella. They had deerskin bags slung over their shoulders and were filling the bags with material picked from the short grasses that grew under the trees.

"Is that stuff edible, Elizabeth?"

"I'm not picking it to eat, Colin. This is fluffgrass. We've got a bunch of other fluff we've picked from the cattails downstream, but I wanted to try this too. See what's best at soaking up blood."

"Oh. That makes sense. People are going to get hurt, I suppose. Better to be prepared."

Elizabeth looked at him. "We've also got a lot of women in camp, Colin; we'll be using this for them. Deerskin pads help, but sometimes they just aren't enough. I think if we sew some of the fluff between soft deerskin, it will work a lot better."

"Oh. Well, you know best. I'll leave you to it."

The two women shared a smile as Colin walked away. Men! Clueless, and easily embarrassed by natural female functions!

26

T ex's legs burned. His lungs burned and his eyes tried to close, but he forced himself to trot ahead. His thick tongue licked dry, cracked lips.

A fleeting thought came and wouldn't go away. *In three days I made up for months in that hospital when my body wouldn't work.*

Ahead, the horses plodded across the land, strung out as the stronger kept going while the weaker hung back. It was time. Would Roberts' join-up work on these horses in the way the old trainer had claimed?

If not...well, it wouldn't be the first time Tex had invested work, sweat, effort, and gotten nothing in return. Some of the time he'd ridden the rough stock, some of the time he'd left with nothing but bruises and aches. And once a horse had put him into a hospital to stay, an experience that marked him even here.

Tex stopped, swaying. Ahead, the mare he'd decided was the alpha in this small band stood, head down and front legs braced. Tex drank the last of the water in his gourd and chewed the last piece of jerky, reclaimed from his pack, then he turned his back on the band of horses. He'd pursued for the last three days and nights; now he walked away, on his way back toward the shelter.

The mare turned her head and looked after him.

But he needed water and so did the horses. A bright patch of greenery announced the presence of a spring, so Tex headed that way. Footsore, he walked on, never looking back.

He took time to fill his water gourd and drink, then left the spring as soon as he finished. The mare was no more than a hundred yards behind.

Two hours later he crested a low hill and turned to look back. For the first time in three days, cracked lips lifted in a grin. Behind him straggled the small band of horses, following about a mile and a half behind.

It was a start. Just as Monty Roberts had written, the horses had identified with the strange creature that first pursued them, then turned away. Now they followed, taking time to graze and drink at the spring where Tex had refilled his gourd.

He deviated from his path long enough to arrow a young pig from a family group. That night he built a fire and ate, waking up around midnight and eating again. More of the pork, cut from a hindquarter, served for his breakfast the next morning and Tex walked on, refreshed. Behind him the horses came on, also refreshed by their drink and the chance to graze.

But they weren't back to his makeshift corral yet; an attack from a predator, any number of things could still cause the horses to turn away. Time would tell.

* * *

COLIN WAS PLEASED with the way things were going. Matt and Lee had come in with meat from the stag-moose and Laz had returned too, carts laden with buffalo meat. Margrette's smoking operations were well underway and the tribe was still feasting on fresh meat and vegetables foraged along the riverbank.

Sal's crew had reduced the large tree to sections cut across the trunk and then laminated them, ensuring the grain of the wood in one layer crossed the grain in another. The new wheels were three laminations thick and the necessary holes had been bored. One of the new tribesmen, a former slave, had shown Sal how to use a bow drill. It didn't do to force the drill to penetrate, lest the stone tip shatter, but if the drillman took his time the job could be completed without constant replacement of the tips. It required patience more than strength.

Rawhide laces held the wheels together, reinforcing the hide glue. The axle holes were more time consuming to cut, but another day should see replacement wheels ready to install on the carts.

Matt met Lee at the campfire and cadged a late breakfast from Margrette. The vegetables were especially welcome and even the tea seemed tastier. Perhaps it had to do with being away so long, eating mostly meat while they hunted.

The two found a place to sit and just rested, legs extended, backs against trees.

Matt's muscles had ached and even his knee joints had cracked when he got up. Crews worked on making more rope to replace what had been used up in making camp and in the myriad tasks that only rope could do. Matt mused for a moment as he watched. People might think bows and arrows were the difference, and certainly they were useful, but rope was the indispensable product of a thousand uses. Some of the ropes were thin, some thicker; some were made from grass, while others had been painstakingly separated from crushed leaves. The better ropes were made from the long fibers harvested after the plant stem itself was crushed, but all of them were useful.

And rawhide served a similar purpose, while possessing qualities that even rope and cord couldn't match.

Matt let his mind roam as he looked off to the north. Late summer...he'd seen lightning shimmer far to the north last night. But so far only a few wispy clouds indicated the possibility of bad weather.

We're going farther west. The American natives used portable dwellings made of leather called tepees. Could we do the same? They hauled theirs behind horses, but we have the wheels they never had. Our carts might be able to do the same thing, haul a shelter that could be set up without the need to gather local materials.

Some of the new-woven ropes would be used in remaking the carts, tying cross-members to stabilize the long poles the tribe used to pull the carts and securing replacement axles to the frames. The rebuilt carts would be better than new, because the wood members had dried and worked into a better fit with use. The new wheels would be heavier because of the extra laminations, but they'd be much more durable. Another new development also showed promise, a mix of beeswax dissolved in oils for greasing the axles.

Hot grease, collected during cooking, served as the primary base. Thin slivers of beeswax were added to the liquid and left to dissolve. Periodic stirring ensured the mix blended evenly and more wax thickened the goop. The final product could be spread with difficulty, but it wouldn't be thin enough to be runny. It would have to be renewed periodically, but probably would last a few days. Time would tell.

Thick leather gaskets kept most of the grease in place between the axle and the wheel. The loud squealing noise was much suppressed when they tried moving the first rebuilt cart.

Lilia had tried waterproofing a piece of deerskin using the grease-beeswax mixture but had given up in disgust; the coated deerskin was heavy, clammy, and smelly. She'd discarded it and gone back to making garments that had fringes along the sleeves and legs. The fringes helped keep the men dry by dripping water away. In any case, it looked better and was more comfortable to wear. Women now wore deerskin skirts with fringed bottoms. The older women wore sleeveless vests too; younger women frequently wore only the skirts.

Matt and Lee visited various parts of the camp and were well pleased. Laz, Piotr, Colin and Sal had performed well, and Lilia...well, Lilia was awesomely competent; the waterproofing attempt was one of her few failures. Margrette managed the kitchen and Elizabeth had amassed a collection of herbs and bandages in expectation of need. In truth, everyone had found a job they were suited for and went about doing it with no fuss or excitement.

The major complaint came from Bear, Monika's six-year-old son. He'd been forced to fish only part time after being dragged protesting all the way to Sandra and Millie's impromptu 'school'. He even found himself pressed into helping with the smaller children and he looked disgusted whenever that happened. None of the *other* warriors had to tend small children! And did he not have a spear and small bow of his own? But his protests went nowhere and his disgusted expression promised to become permanent.

No one mentioned Tex. If the tribe missed him at all, they didn't remark on it.

* * *

TEX HAD BUILT A FIRE, then crawled into his shelter. Waking long enough during the night to add wood and take a drink of water, he slept for a full ten hours. Finally the needs of his bladder forced him to crawl out of the shelter and find a convenient bush.

He slung the spear across his back, attached the quiver to his belt, and hung the reata behind that. The gully was a short distance ahead, now sealed at each end. The horses grazed in the lower end and only the stallion seemed restless. He too grazed, but from time to time he paced along the fence Tex had made from trees. Dragging them into place had been hard work, but if this worked it would all have been worthwhile.

Tex collected the jug of honey and a selection of dried grasses he'd cut before starting his epic run after the horses. He walked slowly down to the enclosure and pulled back one of the lightweight trees that closed the upper fence. Closing it behind him, Tex slowly walked into the enclosure.

The stallion showed signs of fight but Tex waved the bow at him and he backed away. Tex poured a small measure of honey over the dried grass and laid it carefully on a flat rock. Slowly backing away, he turned just before he reached the fence and looked at his shadow on the ground. Another, larger, shadow showed the stallion had followed for a short distance. Tex quietly left the corral as he'd entered it, closing the fence behind him. The horses watched as he slowly walked away.

Tex spent the afternoon scraping the scraps of rawhide left over after cutting the circles for reata thongs. The thongs he cut were shorter, but that didn't matter. They worked well for rudimentary horse tack, in this case a hackamore and a set of hobbles.

He needed softer leather for a saddle pad. He would use a girth strap woven from grasses for insurance, something similar to what he'd used when riding broncs bareback in rodeos. But the shallow pond provided the main advantage during the first ride; the horse would be fighting the water's resistance and slippery footing as well as trying to remove Tex.

A softened piece of rawhide, kept that way by beeswax, would keep the eventual girth strap from irritating the horse's barrel. He laced a piece of rabbit skin, with the fur left on, into a sleeve for the bottom of the girth strap. The cushion would soften as the horse sweated and would pad the strap. Eventually Tex planned to add loops of leather to the strap to serve as 'stirrups'.

Once he'd have scorned the aid, but Tex hadn't ridden a horse in ten years. He had been proud of his riding ability downtime. The skill would come back, he was sure of it...but there was no reason to be stupid. Meantime, he felt a momentary sense of loss for the comfortable working saddle and woven cotton pad he'd used during his ranch years. He would do what was necessary, "cowboy up" as the saying had it. Make do and not worry about the things he didn't have.

He would be riding essentially bareback and that ability might take a little longer to master. He would condition the horse to riding the same way the plains Indians had done, by making the first ride in water. Not quite the gentle-break method, not quite the more brutal breaking that had been common on the American frontier, but a procedure that fell midway between the two. Someday, he'd try the rest of Monty Roberts' method by using a real round pen, but for now, time was important. Roberts hadn't been alone when he broke horses.

The sweetened hay was gone the next day. He added honey to the bundle of grass he carried and laid it down in the same place. He repeated this process, gradually spending more time in the makeshift corral each day. The stallion now watched when Tex came to the corral and lipped the sweet hay from the flat rock even before Tex left. Another day, perhaps two, and he'd be ready.

Tex continued working on his tack that afternoon; it was almost ready. He rubbed the beeswax he'd retained into the rawhide hackamore as a preservative.

Tex added a new activity next morning. Laying his weapons aside, he uncoiled the reata and tossed the end away from him. Reeling it in, he repeated the process a dozen times.

The horses snorted and tried to bolt the first time he tried it. Paying them no attention, Tex worked on. Half an hour later he decided to stop. By now, the horses stood watching him from across the shrunken pond.

The shore showed signs where the horses had sunk a few inches into the mud and had slipped several times when they came to drink. It was almost time. Tex would make the attempt tomorrow, and if something happened...well, walking and running were better than being crippled, but nothing compared to the feel of a strong horse beneath a man. It was worth the gamble.

* * *

"How's that ferry doing, Colin?"

"It's working great, Matt. The rope worried me for a while, because it's only about half as thick as it was in the beginning. But there's no sign that it's failing."

"I expected it would do the job. Lilia's pretty careful."

"That she is, Matt. I'm glad she's with us."

Matt nodded his understanding. "Sal's wheels working as expected?"

"They're fine, Matt. He worked up a kind of sandpaper using river sand. Scraps of rawhide and warm hide glue on that, then pour sand over the mess and when it cures dump off the excess. He wrapped that around a stick and tied it tight at each end. That's what he uses to smooth the center hole where the axles go. The wheels are a little tight right now, but they'll work in during the first day and should fit a lot better than the old wheels did. As soon as all that meat has cured, we might be ready to move on. What do you think?"

"We've been here long enough. How much longer?"

"Maybe three days, Matt. I'll talk to people and get them thinking about the move. They'll need to pack and lash everything to the carts except kitchen stuff and bedding. What do you want to do about the ferry?"

"Leave it. Someone may find it useful and if no one finds it, the rope will eventually break. The ferry could end up in the Gulf of Mexico!"

The two shared a grin.

That night, thunder rumbled far away to the north. But when Matt woke up next morning and went to look, the river had risen only a little. The clouds overhead were thicker now, but there had been no rain. Only that thunder and the distant flashes of lightning showed that a series of storms had passed west-to-east beyond the horizon.

A breeze stirred the trees. The weather was changing. It was time for the tribe to move on while they still could.

27

The reata swung loose in Tex's left hand. The horses watched, heads up and ears forward. Much of the grass in the 'corral' had been eaten.

There was no more time to wait; today was the day.

He carefully stacked his weapons by the entrance after pulling the lightweight tree back into place. The knife still rode his hip, but other than that the reata was his only defense. With luck, it would be a tool, not a defensive weapon.

Tex had woven a loop into one end of the rawhide line. Not a proper hondo, but it would do. He shook out a loop and idly tossed it toward the horses. They watched but didn't attempt to bolt as they'd done a few days before, the first time he'd done this. The scary rope had become a familiar thing, nothing to be alarmed about.

Rebuilding his loop, Tex walked forward. His path wouldn't take him directly toward the horses, but was chosen to slowly close the distance between them. Ahead, the horses nervously moved on. The stallion remained between Tex and the others.

Tex ignored them and continued his slow pace, but now he held the loose coils of rawhide in his left hand while the loop swung ready in his right.

Gradually Tex worked closer to the horses. Every circuit of the small enclosure brought him nearer. The loop swung casually in his right hand. Finally, the stallion stopped and faced Tex, legs braced. Tex looked directly at him and swung the loose coils menacingly. The stallion bolted, but Tex kept up his slow, steady pace. The band of horses milled and snuffled before walking away.

Finally he was close enough and a final hard swing of his arm sent the loop sailing over the stallion's head. The horse reared and started for Tex, ears back, head held low. Tex had been waiting for this.

As soon as he'd launched the loop, he'd prepared for the coming fight by transferring several of the coils to his right hand. Only a few coils remained in his left hand. As the horse charged, Tex cocked his hand and stepped aside, slapping the enraged stallion across the nose with the hard coils of rawhide. The animal snorted in pain and tried to bolt, but the loop around his neck tightened and stopped him. Rearing, he hopped forward while Tex braced his feet and let the horse drag him. The smooth moccasin soles slid on the short grass, Tex hopping when necessary to remain upright.

The stallion finally stopped and faced Tex, panting. Tex slowly walked toward him and swung the loops again. The stallion turned and tried to bolt but again Tex restrained him. This time the horse stopped after a few seconds. Tex slowly pulled on the reata, as he walked closer.

With every plunge, every attempt to escape, the horse tired. Finally Tex was close enough to begin working on controlling the stallion. He slowly backed away, tugging gently on the reata. The horse took a step forward and Tex immediately slacked off slightly. He paused, then backed again. This time the horse stepped forward immediately and again Tex rewarded him by releasing the pressure.

By midafternoon the horse was responding readily to the lead rope. Tex had managed to get close enough to stroke his neck, loose coils ready if needed. But the tired animal allowed this indignity as he had to the other things Tex had done. The rest of the horses watched from across the small pond.

Getting the rawhide band around the nose and the crownpiece over the head also took time, but eventually the weary stallion submitted. Tex spent most of an hour leading him around the enclosure, finally allowing him to drink. While this occurred, Tex picked up an armload of dried grass he'd collected and placed near the entrance. He led the horse from the water's edge and dumped the grass in front where the horse could eat.

The preparations paid off. When Tex finally mounted, the stallion barely jumped. For a moment the years fell away; Tex was once again mounted on an animal that showed spirit and endurance. If this horse was considerably smaller than those he'd ridden downtime, that lack of size could be overcome by breaking the others to ride. Instead of riding one horse for a day, he might find it necessary to ride for three or four hours and change mounts.

There was no telling yet how the horses would adapt to being ridden. Icelandic horses were also small, but like Arabians they were very strong. Both breeds had found a niche downtime, Icelandics for their comfortable gait and Arabians for endurance. Perhaps these primitive horses would also have some special trait. In any case, selective breeding would yield improvements in a few generations.

But Tex was mounted now and that made it all worthwhile.

* * *

MATT WOKE up and finished his normal morning activities before heading for the cookfire. At least the rain had held off, although thunder had threatened and the lightning had flashed far to the north.

The smoke had irritated his eyes this morning...strange, because the light breeze was coming from the north and the kitchen area was west of his camp. It wasn't cold enough for anyone else to have their own campfire.

He accepted food and a mug of 'tea' from Margrette.

"Did the wind change direction? I wondered what you were burning in the fire this morning."

"I'm using the same dried wood as always, Matt. This is mostly oak, but I also had a few mesquite chunks that someone brought in."

"I wondered. I thought I smelled smoke when I woke up."

"You did, Matt; I smelled it too. There's not a lot of brush and even the trees aren't close together after you leave the river. There's some grass but I don't know if it will burn. You think that lightning started a fire?"

"I don't know, Margrette. I'll take one of the scouts and take a look to the north."

Piotr joined Matt when he left camp. The two climbed the slope west of the river and looked to the north. The faint smell of smoke had vanished.

Far off, there was a cloud of smoke or dust on the horizon. A few hundred yards away a herd of bison was grazing south, so perhaps it was only dust raised by their passing. With no immediate danger in sight, Matt and Piotr returned to the camp.

Matt knew the tribe needed meat and told Colin what he had in mind. If the animals were cooperative enough to approach this close, he would take advantage of it. A strong party of hunters and helpers followed Matt from the camp.

Hunting proved ridiculously easy compared to what they'd done before. He divided his hunters into pairs and issued instructions. An hour later, everyone in place, Matt killed the first beast half a mile north and perhaps five hundred yards away from the slope that led down to the river. As he and Piotr field-dressed the big animal, another pair of hunters positioned three hundred yards south downed a bison and began preparing the carcass.

The bison were soon loaded on the carts and the group took turns hauling them downslope to the camp. Lilia and Margrette helped Colin cut the meat into manageable sections, then cut them into something that could easily be cooked for dinner or sliced thin for drying. Matt helped for a while, then other tribespeople took his place. Matt climbed back up the western slope.

The plain was now dark with bison. In the time since Matt's party had killed those first five, more had drifted south. Worried, Matt looked north. Dust covered the plains. If there was a reason for the herd to head south, he couldn't see it.

He returned to camp and sought out Colin.

"You ought to take time to go up that rise and take a look. I've never seen this many bison in one place. I'm worried; it's too early for them to be moving south to get away from the snows. I wonder if there's a fire up there?"

"I doubt there's anything to worry about, Matt. The trees along here aren't likely to burn, and if they do they won't burn fast. Not much underbrush and we've picked up a lot of downed wood and burned it in the cookfire. But it won't hurt to take a look."

The two walked up the slope. As they neared the crest, the smell of dust grew stronger, as did a musky animal smell. The smell combined old sweat with traces of dung. The low, thumping mumble of hooves became audible too. The first bison came into view even before the two reached the top of the slope.

"Considering how hard we've worked for meat in the past, it's almost a shame to let that fellow go on by."

"We don't need more meat, Colin. If the bison stick around, we can preserve the ones we've got and collect one every day or so for fresh meat."

"There won't be anything left up here after they pass. I think Lilia has been gathering a few plants up here, but they'll be trampled into the ground after this."

"Yeah. Well, they're staying up here for now, so it's not a problem. I wouldn't want them to decide to head down this slope for a drink!"

"I know what you mean, Matt, but for now they're just moving."

"We might as well go on back. Once you've seen a million bison in a herd, you've seen 'em all."

Colin chuckled and the two returned to camp only to find an alarmed Lee standing guard. Laz and several other men stood with him, some looking north but most watching to the south.

"Matt, did you see that pride of sabertooths that came through camp?"

"They came through camp, Lee? How many?"

"I counted seven. They just walked through like they owned the place and kept going south."

"Colin, get the women packing. I want everything on carts and the carts parked as near as possible to the biggest trees you can find. That may help protect them. The steel tools are critical, lean them right against the tree so nothing will step on them. The bison are coming from the north, so I want the carts south of the trees. You've got half an hour, maybe. If the women can't finish packing in that time, drop it and get them to the raft as soon as possible. You may not even have half an hour, so be ready to move.

"Lee, get your scouts together. Put one or two south of camp, but use the rest to form a line to the north. If those bison get pushed over the slope they'll come through the camp. We won't be able to stop them. You won't be able to make the raft in time and there won't be room enough anyway. We'll be lucky if we can get the women and children on. Don't plan on using Sal for the defense line; he's the ferryman and he'll be responsible for the people on the raft. He can have enough men to push off, but then we need them to help form a defensive line. Brush, anything you can find, pile it in the way. If we can make it harder for those bison to come through, maybe they'll go around."

"What do we do if the bison do come, Matt?"

"Climb the biggest tree you can and hope for the best; there's no way we can outrun them. Right now they're walking but it won't take much to make them run. Get started, I need to find Sal."

Lee nodded and Matt trotted off, looking for Sal.

Colin had already found him and sent him to the ferry. "Sal, the rope is on the far bank so you should be all right. Take the ferry out to the middle as soon as all the women are on board with the kids. It will stay there if you adjust the rope bridle so the ferry is across the current. After this is over, I'll signal you to come back. The women will have to help push off...I can't spare the men."

"I understand, Matt. I'll take care of it."

"Good man. The women will begin heading this way soon. Be ready."

Matt ran back to the camp and found a beehive of activity. The first women, more alarmed for the safety of children, had already run toward the ferry. Others worked to pack their few belongings on the carts, already parked near huge trees. Lee's defense line was twenty yards north of the camp, the men positioned near trees they could climb at need.

A distant rumble became audible and Matt realized they had no more time.

"You women, head for the ferry! Run for your lives! Lee, get ready. Something's coming."

"We're ready, Matt. What about you?"

"I'm going to help you." Matt raised his voice to be audible over the distant noise.

"Shoot the first animal you can. Drop him so the others will change course. Maybe they won't come directly through camp, but don't wait too long. We can replace those shelters but we can't replace you!"

He heard a few faint chuckles from where the men waited.

"Matt! Those aren't bison! Get everyone up! Climb high, at least twenty feet!"

28

Matt glumly eyed the wreckage that was all that remained of their carts. Some cargo might still be salvaged, but the terrified mammoths had barely noticed the obstacles as they pushed their way through. The axles and cargo had been shielded, but the poles used to draw the carts projected past the protecting trees. As the animals stampeded through, they'd pushed the poles aside and the packed cargo portion had been dragged into the open. Some of the wheels had been broken and all the frames had been smashed as the huge animals passed through the camp.

At least none of the people had died, and the steel tools were usable even if some would require new handles. Carts could be replaced; the steel tools could not.

Matt had felt his tree quiver when a huge female brushed against it. He might have let the mammoths go through unmolested, but that contact had decided him; they were dangerous even to people who'd sought shelter in the trees.

Using one of his precious steel-headed arrows, his first shot struck a mammoth between the eyes but barely penetrated the thick skin.

Still, it was enough to cause the beast to turn aside. Matt's second shot had penetrated the skull just forward of her ear. She'd stumbled, then fallen broadside. The huge carcass checked the headlong rush of the trailing animals and forced them to divide, most passing between the camp and the river. Sal watched the great grayish-brown bodies pass. Awestruck, he counted twenty-two, then realized that there had to be many others he hadn't seen.

The bison herd was moving too. A minor stampede had sent most of the animals south, but the small fire died out as it ran out of ready fuel. The bison spread out and began to graze.

The predators had fled ahead of the herds, but they'd be back.

Sal brought the ferry back to shore as soon as the bison and mammoths had passed on. The tribespeople were soon engaged in salvage.

"We're not going anywhere right away, Sal. The carts will have to be rebuilt and some will need replacing. Save what you can. Leave the bedding in place, let the women decide what's still useable. Your job is building carts, Lee's job is securing the camp, Lilia can take charge of building shelters. They won't be great, but at least we can get the children under cover and if necessary we can roll up in our bedding and sleep on the ground. We can post someone to keep the fires going through the night.

"I'll need to talk to Colin and Margrette, but at least we won't go hungry. Some of the bison meat is gone, but we've got a mammoth down at the edge of camp and that will more than replace our food losses.

"Good job with the ferry, by the way. You managed to stuff all the women and children on that thing and you kept them safe."

"Nothing to it, Matt. You fellows had the dangerous job, facing up to those animals, not knowing when to climb out of danger. I doubt you'd have survived if you weren't ready to break off the defense and climb."

"Yeah, everyone did a good job and nobody panicked. Not easy to do when a big bull mammoth blunders into your tree!"

* * *

TEX RODE into camp late that afternoon. He whistled as he looked at the damage, then slid off the stallion and went to find Matt.

"Looks like you had some excitement."

"You could say that. Lightning set off a prairie fire. It didn't amount to much, but it spooked the bison and either the mammoths decided they needed a good run or they got alarmed when the bison headed for the horizon. Anyway, the bison were everywhere up that slope to the west, so the mammoths came down by the river and that took them right through camp. They busted every cart we had. We can salvage some of the wheels, but the carts will need new frames. There's a day's work just deciding what we can use and what goes into the kitchen fire."

"Guess you're right. I planned to surprise you by riding in, but I'm the one that's surprised."

"No surprise, Tex. Lee and I were hunting up on that knoll to the northwest and we saw you chasing the horses. I wondered if you'd ever manage to catch up."

"It was work and I ain't lookin' to try it again soon. But a man can run down a horse if he's determined enough. Or crazy enough."

The two shared a grin. "Are you moving back in with the tribe, Tex?"

Tex paused for a moment. "Tell you the truth, Matt, I ain't much on livin' with a lot of people around. I've been on my own for ten years now, maybe longer, and havin' people around makes me nervous. People are trouble. I reckon I could get along with two or three, but all these people you've got, well, they make me fidgety. I don't rightly see how you can stand it. You're livin' in a reg'lar town here!

"I've been building a place a little southwest of here. I think I might just winter over down there and train hosses. One thing, though, it's lonesome. It would do better if I had a woman there. I figured to talk to you about that."

Matt gave Tex a wry look. "I'm no woman, in case it escaped your notice."

Tex chuckled. "Not you, Matt. I been talkin' to a couple of women and I figured to see if one of them was interested in movin' in with me. But the friendly thing to do was talk to you first, so that's what I'm doin'."

"I don't have any objection, Tex, as long as the woman's willing. But let's make it clear up front, they get to choose. If they say no, it's over. Do we have an understanding?"

"Wouldn't have it any other way, Matt."

"Who were you wanting to talk to, Tex?"

"I've been friendly with Callie and... well, one other. No use mentioning which one right now. If Callie says no, I'll stick around camp for a day or two if that's all right with you and talk to the other one."

"I don't see any problem with that, Tex. But I don't want a misunderstanding so I'll lay it out. If one of them decides to go with you, you leave during the daylight so we can all see she's willing to go. You might want to clear it with Colin if Callie decides to go with you. He's her father and likely he'll want to know what you've got in mind."

"You're right. I hadn't thought about that, but I'll talk to him too."

"You said you're going to be breaking horses during the winter, Tex?"

"That's what I want to do, Matt. Plenty of hosses, plenty of graze, I doubt I'll have problems. You interested in swapping for some after I get them broke?"

"Might be. Depends on what you want for them."

"We can work something out. Right now, how's my credit?"

"Depends. What do you need?"

"I'd like a half-dozen jugs of that honey and some dried meat if you can spare it. I can hunt and dry it myself, but it takes a lot of time and now that I've got horses I can't afford to spend time in camp. I'll have to be around the horses or they'll be bait for a sabertooth. I started a place I could live in, but I'll likely have to rebuild. I'll find a canyon with water and graze, move the horses there, then build me some-place snug before winter sets in."

"The honey's shouldn't be a problem but I'll have to see how much we've got left. Some of the jugs probably got broken when the mammoths came through. But there are bee trees around so we can get more honey, and a couple of the women have started making pottery. If we don't have it now, we can get it in a week or two. Why not check with Margrette? If she's OK with swapping you honey, I am. It'll also give you a chance to talk to Callie while you're there. She's been working at the kitchen, but I'm sure we can find someone to replace her if she wants to go with you.

"But talk to Colin too. Dried meat, we've got quite a bit but we prob-ably lost some when the mammoths came through. We can get more meat, though. Might take a few days to cure it into jerky. Why not plan on sticking around for a day or two, maybe even a week?"

"Reckon I could do that. I'll see about fixin' up a corral downstream for the horses and I'll stay with them. The only one that's reasonably well-broke is that line-back dun. He's gonna be a good horse, once I break him of a few bad habits."

"Bad habits, Tex?"

"Bitin'. Kickin'. Little things like that. But I'm workin' on him. You might tell people not to get too close 'til I civilize him."

"Be glad to, Tex. I'll talk to Colin, too. You sure you don't want anyone else on your ranch?"

"Don't need much help right now, but maybe in a couple of weeks. Two of us could get more done if it was the right sort of feller."

"Safer for both of you, Tex. Safer for Callie too, or whichever one decides she wants to be a cowgirl."

"Hosses, Matt. No cows. Although I was thinkin'...you seen those llamas? There are quite a few of them just south of here. They ranch 'em down in South America and people up here were raisin' 'em too. Downtime, I mean, when this place was Texas."

"That might work, Tex. We've used their hair for fabric and the hides and meat are useful too, but you'll need fences to keep them from drifting. Camels might also work out. I don't know about riding one, but they can carry a lot of weight. Sure would make moving easier if you could break some to be pack animals."

"I'll think on it, Matt. Anyway, you've got work to do and I'll be hangin' around the kitchen fire for a spell. See you there, later on."

Matt nodded and Tex went on his way.

* * *

MATT FOUND Lee with the scouts. Piotr was there too; the hunt had depleted the arrow supply and Matt hadn't been the only one shooting when the mammoths burst through the camp. Piotr would be busy during the next few days.

Lee left his people with Piotr and joined Matt.

"Lot of work to do, Matt."

"You're right. One of the things I wanted to talk to you about. What do you think of building a fence across this low space where we're camped? I was thinking of trees dragged in to a line and tied in place. It might help if other animals decide this is the road they've just got to follow, make them change course."

"We could do that. Might take a few days since some of my boys will be keeping watch. I don't think we can afford to neglect that."

"I agree, Lee. Pick your spot and ask Sal about tools. He might be willing to loan you one or two of his crew to help."

"I'll do that, Matt. I saw you talking to Tex. What does he want?"

"Couple of things. He's planning on swapping horses when he gets them trained. I'll want him to show people how to handle them; your scouts might be naturals for that."

"I can see some advantages, Matt. I'll ask if any of my people know about horses. I'll let you know next time I see you."

"You do that, Lee. Think you might like to learn how to ride?"

"I might, Matt. I'll probably have to if my guys are going to be patrolling on horses."

"You might like it, Lee. Takes work, though."

"You know of anything that doesn't take work, Matt?"

Matt chuckled and went on his way.

He found Lilia working with Elizabeth and Bella. Racing through the woods to get on the ferry or to get up a tree while escaping the mammoths had taken a toll on the tribespeople, but none of the injuries were serious. Even so, several had sought assistance regarding scrapes and scratches. The women washed wounds with a tea made from herbs, then wrapped the abrasions with thin deerskin bandages. As one person left, another laid his tools aside and came in to have his injuries examined.

"Anything I should be concerned with, Elizabeth?"

"Just minor stuff, Matt. No one's going to need more than a wash and bandaging."

"How's the salvaging going, Lilia?"

"We lost some things, but nothing we can't replace. Some of the bedding is simply gone. One or two of those mammoths might be wearing a bison skin for a flag! Some of the meat can't be salvaged. You don't want to try eating anything that an animal weighing several tons has stepped on! It's more dirt than meat now. But we've got other food. Colin and Margrette are butchering the mammoth you shot."

"I suppose that needs to get done as soon as possible."

"We can use the fresh meat, and what we don't get will need to be dragged away. It'll stink us out of camp otherwise, and probably bring animals we don't want to have around camp."

"You're right. Dump everything we can't use in the river. "

"You're right. Remember how much trouble you'd have been in downtime if you'd done that?"

Matt chuckled. "I know. I think about that once in a while. But we do what we have to. It won't matter so long as there are only a few people on Darwin's World.

"Other people might do the same, use a river for a dump. That's why I prefer to get drinking water from a spring whenever I can. How much of our personal stuff is left?"

"We've got bedding. We'll need to share, though."

"Works for me, Lilia. Where are we set up?"

"Third campsite south of the cookfire. Lee is going to be in the camp next to us."

"Sounds good. I'll see you after supper. I'll go talk to Colin. Maybe he can use a hand butchering that mammoth."

* * *

MARGRETTE WAS quiet when Matt found them, Colin looked mad, Callie was downcast.

"Something bothering you, Colin?"

"Couple of things, Matt. Tex says he wants to take Callie off to some hole in the prairie to live. I tried to talk to him, but he handed me some lip and we didn't see eye to eye. He's a good fighter and hunter, and he mentioned he's got horses, but if he gives me any more lip I'm gonna take him down a peg or two!"

"Did he threaten you, Colin?"

"No. It's Callie's choice, anyway. But I tried to be friendly. I invited him to eat with us tonight but when I told him we were having fresh mammoth steaks, he got positively rude!"

29

Two days passed. Wreckage had been removed and salvage completed. The tribe had recovered some of the sense of normalcy that existed before the mammoth incursion.

Salvaged wheels and axles had been joined to new frames and nine carts now stood ready for use. Some were being used to transport meat; a hunting expedition went out every day and brought back a bison. Fresh meat was the rule for every meal, and what wasn't eaten was placed over the curing fires.

One hunting party had found a salt lick about ten miles to the southwest and two of the repaired carts had visited the site. Loading them with the cleanest salt they could find had taken the crews less than half a day and they'd returned to camp late in the afternoon. Margrette and Colin had developed a process whereby fresh meat was salted down overnight, then placed over the fires for final smoke curing. Cured meat was added to the tribe's reserve stores at the end of each day.

Sal's crews had found a large grove of old chestnut trees, some recently fallen. The workers soon developed a technique for splitting the huge chestnut trunks to produce boards. In additional to excellent lumber, the trees also produced large numbers of nuts. A few early nuts had been harvested and stored for later use.

Other boxes held salt, enough to see the tribe through the winter if used sparingly. Pegs joined boards to make boxes and the covers used thick leather hinges. The mammoth Matt shot had been useful in a number of ways.

Dried river mud was the source for new pots and the latest efforts were larger and better formed than the earlier ones had been. Some enterprising person had reinvented the pottery wheel and new pots, mugs, and jugs now appeared daily.

Matt wondered how they'd manage to haul all the things people were making and accumulating. Well, choices might have to be made, but for now an embarrassment of riches was certainly preferable to the mess the mammoths had created!

Tex had settled in, spending most of his time at his camp. The corral held the horse herd and Tex moved it every other day by simply building another fence south of the corral, then joining this to the first with a cross fence. When not engaged in that activity, he worked on training his other horses.

He'd built a collar, wood-framed and thickly padded, and had used it to train a mare to pull loads. A rudimentary system of straps around her barrel controlled positioning of the tug straps, while a wooden singletree attached the straps to the load. He'd not yet taught the horse to answer to reins, but he could control her by leading from the front. The breaking technique worked, but it required two men, one leading the horse and the other working with the load. Trees left behind in the first corral were hitched to the horse and dragged downstream to become part of the latest corral.

In this manner Tex found it relatively simple to move his corral every day so that the horses could have graze and water. Two men, José and Ernesto, took turns assisting Tex. They were learning techniques from Tex, but wouldn't be ready to take over caring for a horse anytime soon.

The two had joined the tribe after being rescued from the slave raiders. Matt wondered if they would leave with Tex when he eventually departed. Perhaps he would remain until the tribe was ready to move on; there had been no resolution regarding Tex's desire for woman to share his camp, at least not yet.

Callie had not yet left her parent's camp. She still worked every day at the kitchen fire, assisting Margrette.

Matt had remained aloof from the various interactions, feeling it was not his place to interfere in private matters that didn't affect the tribe.

* * *

MATT FOUND Colin in the afternoon and the two sought out Lee and Lilia for a discussion.

"I still think we need to move west. People are making stuff, we're almost back to where we were, but time is passing. Winter won't wait. We've got it easy right now, but those bison will move south when the snows come.

Plus we can't defend this place. We're near the river and it might freeze or flood, the same problems we had before. Whether from animals or people, we've still got to be ready to protect what we're building."

"Matt, it sure would be a lot easier if we had horses when we move."

"Yes and no, Colin. We'd move faster, but horses have to be cared for. You're going to need herders and night guards. If you plan on using half a dozen horses, you'll need at least double that number. Horses can't work every day, they've got to have a day to recover or you'll kill them. It doesn't matter whether they're being ridden or pulling a cart, they still have to rest. You can work them two days in a row if the work's not too heavy, but you can't plan on that. If heavy labor is necessary you can't work more than every other day and sometimes you have to give the horses time off after half a day. They're animals, not machines.

"Something else; we don't have the tack we'd need, and that will have to be made. Tex told me how much work and time it took to braid those reatas. We don't have the time, so I don't plan on using horses this year. If we work on building tack and other equipment during the winter, we can be ready to use horses next spring. But we still need to move west before then.

"I don't think we have time to build a winter camp, not where I wanted to go. The mammoth stampede put that out of reach. I think we need to start bending south as soon as we can if we're going to find a protected place we can defend."

"You have some place in mind, Matt?"

"I've got a couple of ideas, Lee. Tex and I talked; the country west of here's fairly dry downtime, but there are huge springs so clean water won't be a problem. I'm sure we can find a sheltered canyon with a spring-fed stream and a shallow cliff cave or overhang. There's a lot of limestone down there, left when this area was underwater a few million years ago. We can use limestone and build our shelters under the overhang, easy to do because the stone breaks along flat lines. The method is fireproof except for roofs, and depending where we build we might not need more than a basic roof anyway. Use ladders for access, just pull them up so animals or people can't attack. The country south of here will be warmer too. I think that's where the southern bison herd goes to winter, probably the mammoths and sloths too. We won't be left without game during the coming winter as happened last year."

"How long to reach there, Matt?"

"Three weeks, maybe four, using the carts. That means we've got to be moving soon, within another week at most if we want to get there before winter. We can do it if we don't wait too long. The farther south we go, the longer it takes for winter to set in and the sooner spring arrives. It shouldn't be nearly as hard this winter as the last one was if we're far enough south."

"Matt, I should take a few of my people and have a look. We don't want to get stuck somewhere worse than this place is. We're already quite a bit south of where we spent last winter."

"Good idea, Lee. Leave Laz with a couple of people for security and take three or four scouts with you. Pick up supplies from the kitchen, plan on making a fast trip. Make sure you've got arrows enough. When do you plan on leaving?"

"We've got plenty of arrows, Matt. Piotr has been busy, and all of us have a spare quiver with at least a dozen arrows. I'll pick my guys as soon as we finish here and we'll start getting ready. I'll leave tomorrow morning at daybreak.

"I'll plan on being back in five days. That will give us an idea of what's ahead and the scout mission won't hold you up if you intend to move on in a week."

"Do it that way, Lee. Colin, talk to Sal, see how much more time he'll need. I figure we should offer to swap a cart to Tex. If the people with him decide to go when he leaves, they can pull the cart. Has Callie decided whether she wants to go with them?"

"She hasn't said, Matt. Tex has been talking to Monika too, but whether he's just hanging around because he likes her kid or because he likes her, I don't know. That might be a problem, though."

"How so?"

"She's been staying with Dominick, or maybe he's staying with her. I don't know. But that's where he ends up every night."

"I guess we'll see. I told Tex that it was up to the woman to decide and that's still the way it is. If she wants to leave with Tex, that's between her and Tex. Dominick will just have to accept it."

Lee nodded. "Maybe. But I'm pretty sure Tex got in a fight with Marc before. They never made any noise about it, but Marc had a bruised face and Tex had a scratch over his cheekbone."

"Nobody told me anything about that!"

"Nothing to tell, Matt. It happened when they were on a hunt and it was over before they got back. I don't bother you with stuff unless you need to know about it."

"Well, maybe it will be OK. But if Tex can't accept that the woman decides, I'll have another chat with him."

"You think that will do any good?"

"I guess I'll just have to make it a little stronger. If Tex can't keep his hands to himself, he'll have to leave."

* * *

MATT WALKED AWAY and the others went about their business.

But Matt couldn't forget what Lee had told him. Was Tex someone who could be a hard worker one minute and a bully the next? If so, something would have to be done. This could destroy the trust that the tribespeople had built up.

Tex would be told to leave, and if that didn't work stronger measures would be necessary.

Lee was gone when Matt went to the cook fire for breakfast. Laz was getting his breakfast after posting two new guards. Sal was off to the side with his crew, getting ready to resume work on the carts. The new version had board sides and a flat board deck; the carts were balanced to put most of the weight slightly ahead of the axles for easy pulling. Instead of tying the cargo in place, much of it could be placed within the cargo boxes. Best of all, the new design could easily be adapted to use with horses someday if Tex could provide them.

Matt noticed that Sal was looking around. He appeared to be asking something of one of his crew and he left the others finishing their breakfast while he walked back into camp. Perhaps one of his crew hadn't gotten out of bed yet.

Whatever it was, Sal could sort it out. Matt considered himself fortunate to have found such a man to serve as foreman for the construction crews.

He headed for the latrine to deal with his usual morning business. Tribespeople disposed of ashes and bits of charcoal from the kitchen fire by spreading them in the trench, and Matt finished by shoveling in a thin layer of dirt. This kept the smell down, a necessity when the latrine was located near the camp.

The latrine now sported a shallow pottery bowl and a pitcher with water. Matt washed his hands and dried them on a long piece of deerskin.

The pitcher was almost empty, so Matt took the deerskin and pitcher with him. He walked down to the river, rinsed the deerskin and wrung as much water out as possible. He sloshed the pitcher and filled it with river water before returning the items to the latrine. Someone had been very thoughtful when they provided the basin and pitcher; it was only polite to keep them filled. Better sanitation would pay off in the long run by reducing disease.

Finished, Matt headed for where the carts were being made. Puzzled, he looked around but no one was working. It was very unlike Sal to be late. Matt headed back to camp.

No one was at the cook fire and that too was unusual. Matt heard noises coming from the south end of the camp so he walked that way.

The noise was coming from people, watching a fight between Tex and

Sal. Sal was clearly unused to fighting with his fists; he was getting the worst of it. Tex was smiling as he punched and as Matt watched, Sal dropped to the ground.

Matt pushed his way through the people gathered around the two.

"This stops *now*! Tex, step back or you'll be fighting me."

"By golly, I'm ready! I'm plumb tired of people telling me what to do, what not to do. This one," and he pointed at Sal where he was now sitting up, gingerly feeling of his jaw, "told me a bunch of crap about getting in a fight with that other feller. Hell, it was only a friendly fight, like. No knives, not even a head butt. Just settled it like men, that's what we done!"

"Who was the other man, Tex?"

"Hell, it ain't none of your business. Like I said, we settled it like men."

"Who was it, Tex? I won't ask again."

"Wal, it was that Dominick feller. I tried to talk sense to him but he wouldn't listen."

"So you got in a fight with Dominick, and then you got in a fight with Sal too?"

"Like I said, it was just a friendly kind of discussion. I've been in cow camps where the boys done worse than this to kind of settle their breakfast. It ain't nothin' special."

"Pack your stuff, Tex. I want you gone by noon."

"You still think you're some kind of God, and I've had about enough of it. If I don't leave, you gonna get the tribe to fill me with arrows?"

"Why no, Tex. I thought I'd just see whether you were all talk or if you still feel like a little more action. So what's it going to be, Tex? Are you leaving, or do I need to encourage you?"

Matt reached down to his belt and began untying the thongs that held his cased knife and camp axe. He handed them to Colin and turned around. Tex had watched this in surprise, but then a slow grin broke across his face.

"This is gonna be a pure pleasure!"

30

Tex was quick. A straight left rocked Matt, but he managed to take the punch on his shoulder instead of allowing it to thump into his ribs. Tex's follow-up right carried a lot more force, but by the time it arrived Matt had begun moving back so the punch lost most of its power.

But the hits brought a welcome surge of adrenaline. Training, mastered half a century earlier in Matt's downtime life, came roaring back. He felt a quick spike of joy; this enemy he could face and master without help from anyone.

Forced back by Tex's sudden attack, Matt quickly regained his footing. An open left hand brushed Tex's right fist, pressing it in the direction Tex had intended, but farther. Before he could recover, Matt launched a punishing strike with the heel of his right hand, delivered straight to Tex's forehead. He never got the chance to throw another punch.

Half stunned, Tex tried to stumble back and regain his footing. Matt gave him no chance. A fast step forward and Matt's left hand struck. He was able to change the strike from a modified spear hand, delivered with the fingers folded, into a punch that struck Tex's unprotected solar plexus. Suddenly unable to breathe, Tex started to fold. Matt's follow up cracked clean against Tex's jaw and he went down, unconscious.

Matt immediately realized that Tex was unable to breathe. Dropping to his knees, he pressed down on Tex's ribs, then did it again. Tex began to breathe normally and Matt stood up.

"Elizabeth, he might need a little more help, but I doubt he's hurt bad."

"Lilia, can you give me a hand?" The two women bent over Tex. He wasn't fully awake yet but was beginning to stir.

Matt was still feeling the effects of the adrenaline. He turned his anger on the circle of tribespeople who'd watched the fight.

"You people stood there and watched a responsible member of your community be attacked! And did *nothing* to help him! Suppose I hadn't been available? What would have happened? The next time it might be *you*, and it might not be a man but an animal. Suppose Sal decides to just watch while a dire wolf gnaws on your leg?

"Get your asses back to work, now!"

Cowed, the tribespeople headed back to the cookfire. Lee caught Matt's eye and winked. He understood; a valuable lesson had just been administered. The tribe would act next time instead of simply looking on.

Matt watched the two women working on Tex. Finally Elizabeth stood up.

"No real serious injuries. He might have a couple of loosened teeth, but there's nothing I can do. They'll reseat or he'll lose them. Maybe it might cause him to rethink the 'friendly fighting' he mentioned. You didn't spend a lot of time taking him down."

"Elizabeth, that's as friendly as I know how to fight. Two of those blows could have killed him if I'd changed them just a little. I don't know if he's aware of that."

"We'll point that out when he's fully awake. We'll get him back to the campfire, Matt. Do you really intend to force him to leave? He's probably not going to be in shape to defend himself for a day at least. He's got bruises already forming and he may have a concussion."

"Let him stick around until he's recovered. After that, it depends on his attitude. If he uses his fists on another member of the tribe, I won't take it easy on him. He'll remember the next lesson a long time...if he survives it."

"I'll tell him, Matt. Now let me take a look at your face."

"I'm all right, Elizabeth."

"I'm sure you are, but I've got a wash with some herbs in it to clean scratches and scrapes. You've got a good one on the jaw and cheek-bone. Looks like the skin is split over the cheekbone."

"OK, I might have a bruised shoulder too. Nothing much; wash the cut and I'll get back to work."

* * *

MATT LEFT the kitchen area with Sal's crew. They were soon at work, some sawing wheel disks and others splitting more boards from a log. Two men were whittling pegs from a dried oak branch.

The boxes would be needed. Some of the pottery being turned out resembled ancient Greek amphorae in shape, but these vaselike containers didn't have the ring-shaped handles. Another difference, they had larger flat bases that made for easier transport overland. Many already held dried fruits and vegetables, sealed against insect or rodent damage by a carved plug. The plug, in turn, used rawhide and beeswax for a gasket, keeping the contents of the jug dry and safe. This also kept the wooden plug from cracking the container by absorbing moisture and swelling. Usually.

Other dried material was already being used; breakfast now featured pancakes made from acorns.

The acorns were shelled, then placed in boiling water to remove tannins. The water was poured off...at some point, it would be used to tan leather...and the nut dried before being ground into flour. Served with honey, the pancakes made a welcome addition to breakfast.

Dried persimmons and mulberries filled other containers. Matt recalled the tasty hot drinks Lilia had prepared from dried berries and honey; they'd be very welcome during the winter!

But the accumulation of fruits and nuts came with a concern; summer was ending. The tribe needed to move as soon as Lee returned. Hopefully the carts would be finished by that time. The men were working as fast as possible; the real limit on cart manufacture was the lack of steel tools. The few they possessed needed frequent sharpening and were showing signs of wear.

Perhaps they could find iron ore, even coal? Some of the former captives professed to be knowledgeable of smelting and refining. Even if coal couldn't be found, it should be possible to create some form of iron using charcoal.

But for now, it would have to wait. The priority was getting to a place where they could build defensible structures, somewhere they could survive the winter. Shelter, food, and a dependable water supply were only the beginning. There was much still to do, and winter would be on them whether people were ready or not.

Lee arrived that afternoon and he brought a dozen people with him.

"What happened, Lee?"

"The slavers are back. Not the ones we fought, the ones they were selling to. They've gone back to sending out their own raiding parties since then, taking one or two people at a time, usually young ones. They sneak in and are gone before people can react.

"But they ran into a hunting party from a town south of here and there was a fight. Some of the people I brought in escaped during the fight, the others are the ones who fought the slavers. The escapees had joined the hunters and they were heading north when we found them. Some of the raiders were alive when they broke off contact and the ones who'd escaped just wanted to get away. They headed north to avoid leading the slavers to their village. According to them, it's southeast of here. I figure we passed it while we were trying to get away after the Riverbend fight.

"They know a lot more about the country south and west of here than I could have found out by scouting, so I brought them to you. They're pretty hungry; my scouts shared what food we had, but it didn't go far. I figured it was better to bring them here rather than hunt meat to feed them. There's also no telling where that capture party went after the fight. Only a few of these folks have spears, and the rest aren't armed at all."

"Why don't you see Margrette and get enough for them and your guys. I suspect you're hungry too, since you gave the refugees your food."

Lee nodded. "I could eat. They needed the food more than we did." Matt nodded and Lee led his group to the kitchen.

* * *

MATT VISITED PIOTR'S CAMP. He was there now, patiently crafting arrows. If he'd even been present during the fight, it hadn't taken him long to resume work.

Piotr had accumulated a stock of large feathers and several flint chunks for raw materials. He now spent his mornings finding suitable shafts, straightened them in the afternoon, then chipped the points. It was usually dusk before he finished assembling the arrows.

"Piotr, you need a couple of assistants."

"I like the work, Matt. I get out in the mornings and the arrows I'm building are good quality. Bows, too; I've built quite a few and I've got a supply of sinew now for bowstrings."

"Nothing wrong with your quality, Piotr, but we're going to need more than you can turn out working alone. Lee just brought some people into camp and they'll need weapons. I think we need a larger reserve, too. It looks like we're going to be in a fight. The raiders are gone, but the people they sold slaves to are back.

"The only way to stop them is to make it really expensive. If they lose a few raiders every time they come north, they'll understand it's not worth it. We're going to need a lot of arrows; maybe you could do the chipping and let someone else bring in raw materials, maybe assemble the arrows too. Could you do that?"

"I guess so, Matt. If you can find me a couple of people, I'll do what I can."

* * *

THE NEWCOMERS WAITED, standing around the cookfire.

Margrette and Colin sliced fresh steaks from a bison that had just been brought in. Callie and several other women were roasting the meat on skewers. Two loaves of fresh bread, the flour made by grinding ripe grain seeds and nuts, waited. More was being baked.

The first meal would be simple, meat and bread. The strangers wouldn't complain. Some had offered to help Margrette prepare the next meal. As for the rest, Matt would see where they could be most useful. Some might not fit in, but the people they'd rescued from the slave raiders had proved valuable additions to the tribe.

Hopefully, these would too. Eventually.

But for the moment, hunger was uppermost on their minds.

Matt quietly got the attention of Colin, Lee, and Lilia. Motioning, he walked away from the campfire. The others joined him in a few minutes, Colin wiping his hands on a ragged piece of deerskin.

"Didn't have time to wash, Matt. That soap works but it's pretty harsh. Maybe the next batch should have less lye, more fat."

"We can pass it on, Colin, but right now I wanted to talk about the people Lee brought in. We've had good luck with the others that joined us after that fight with the slave raiders. I think we should try the same approach with the new ones.

"I'll talk to them about the area they've come through. Lee, we need to work up a route to follow if they have enough information, otherwise you're going to have to send out scouts. We'll need information about camping spots, water, hazards, whatever we need to plan the day's travel. You're chief of scouts, so I want you in on the planning discussions. You'll also need to assess their weapons skills, if any. They'll need weapons and training as soon as we can find the time.

"Colin, see what jobs they can do. You'll know better than I will what needs doing. If any can help Piotr, he could use a couple of assistants for weapons making. I don't know if Sal needs help, but another pair of hands is always welcome. Ask him what he needs to get things moving faster. It may not be possible, but you can at least ask.

"Lilia, find a place they can camp and see if we can come up with bedding. Put up temporary shelters, but don't spend a lot of time on it; I want to be moving as soon as possible.

"Every trained bowman, and that includes the women, will be armed at all times now. Pass the word about what happened to the captives, tell everyone to be careful. If those capture parties travel up this far, I don't want them to grab any of our people."

"What happens if they do, Matt?"

"I don't know, Lee. My first instinct is to go after them. At the same time, my responsibility is to the majority. I can't leave the tribe undefended. It could take a week, two weeks even, to catch up to the snatch party. There's no guarantee of success either; we could waste a lot of time and never catch them."

Lee hesitated. "There's one other option, Matt."

"What's that? If you've thought of something I missed, let's hear it."

"I was thinking of Tex. He's got at least one, maybe two or three horses by now that are ready to ride. What about training a couple of people to ride, use them for mounted patrols or to go after anyone who's captured?"

Matt thought about it. "It's an idea, but could we depend on Tex? There's no telling about him right now. He might plan on leaving as soon as he can.

"Next year we can try the same method he did, chase down some horses and tame them ourselves. It will take us a lot more time, because we'd be learning how. Even so, it could be done. But we have a problem right now and I don't know if we can rely on Tex for a solution."

"I'll talk to him, Matt. It might be better coming from me."

"Go ahead, Lee. But meantime, pass the word to everyone. The best answer to this is not let people wander around without protection. Make sure they know about the capture parties; if people are out gathering vegetables, make sure there are at least two guards nearby."

The others nodded and the meeting broke up. Matt headed back to the fire. It was time to talk to the new people.

* * *

MATT FOUND much to think about after the conversations. This world was definitely different geologically from the Earth of downtime. The Rio Grande Rift and the river that flowed through it was likely shorter here. Instead, an arm of the sea now extended far into the area known downtime as the Big Bend. The Rio Grande was itself a formidable barrier, more than a mile wide just above where its waters met the sea. The broad river here flowed through a substantial delta, a haven for birds and transplanted people from downtime.

Across the seaway, a number of huge estates had grown up that used labor provided by slaves or peons, depending on how one defined the terms. Anyone within a week's travel north of the seaway was in danger of being taken; there was always a need for more labor on the estates, virtual plantations of the type once found in the old North American colonies.

What the owners lacked in technology they made up in brute human labor.

Lee found Matt two hours later.

"Matt, Tex is gone. He left Elizabeth and headed for his horses. The horses are here, but the only sign I found of Tex is a place where a scuffle happened. I think the capture parties followed us here and they've grabbed Tex."

31

"I've got half a mind to let them keep him!"

"You don't mean that, Matt."

"I guess not, Lee, but Tex would probably lead a revolution if they ever got him south of that seaway! Still, he helped us when we were fighting the slave raiders, so we owe him. Did you see any other tracks?"

"Laz is looking now. Piotr and Marc went with him. Piotr has sharp eyes; if there's anything to be found, he'll find it."

"I'll be going after Tex, Lee. Who do we leave in charge of security while we're gone?"

"Laz would be my choice, but he's been left behind a couple of times already. I think he wants to go this time, and I know I do."

"What about leaving Piotr in charge?"

"He could handle it. I don't think anything will upset him."

"Get people together. We'll head out as soon as Laz gets back. I'm about to see if I can ride Tex's stallion."

"You can ride that thing, Matt?"

"I've ridden before, but never bareback. And I never rode very far, maybe four or five miles once. I'm just hoping the skill will come back; maybe it's like riding a bicycle."

"What's a bicycle, Matt?"

"I'll explain some other time. What I've got in mind is loading up with my bow, spear, a couple of dozen arrows slung on the horse plus what I carry in my quiver. I'm going to loop ahead of the raiders and slow them down. I'll need a lot of arrows, because even if I can't get a good shot I'm going to drop an arrow in the middle to force them to scatter and take cover. You and the rest should be able to catch up that much faster."

"That should work. If you can ride the horse, that is."

"Time to find out, Lee. I'll be down at the corral. Tell Piotr he's going to be left in charge and he'll need to see that the horses are moved every day or so. I'll take Sal with me to the corral. I might need help, catching that stallion."

"I'll tell Piotr when he gets back from looking at the tracks. I'll see about finding extra arrows too."

Matt headed for the corral, Sal following. The horses were calm, grazing on the short grass. The stallion saw them and stood watching, head up, ears pointed forward.

"Matt, you know how to use a rope like Tex does?"

"No. What I have in mind is just open up a loop and walk up slowly. If the horses bolt, I might try that honey trick Tex mentioned. But if I use a big loop and get close, maybe I can catch that stallion."

"I'll watch, Matt, but if that horse decides to attack you we'll have horsemeat for supper!"

Matt grinned and picked up a reata from where Tex kept his equipment. There was also a square of leather and a wide band he thought was the girth strap. The hackamore appeared simple to use, even if it had only one rein; Matt's riding had been done with two reins. Still, if Tex had done it, Matt need only figure out what cues the horse responded to. Stopping the horse would be a universal signal, lean back slightly and tug on the rein.

Matt built a six-foot loop in the reata's end and held it ready as he walked toward the stallion. The horse watched alertly for a moment, then spun and bolted. The mares joined him, circling Matt where he stood in the middle of the corral.

Matt kept the loop ready and kept up with the horses. He needed to walk only a small circle while the horses ran the much wider circle, just inside the downed trees. Dust rose, churned up by the hooves. Matt sneezed and kept walking. The horses slowed, then stopped. Matt walked slowly toward them.

Half an hour later, he finally managed to toss the open loop over the stallion's head. The horse immediately stopped, understanding the feel of the reata. The loop drew tight as Matt pulled slowly on the rawhide. With the loop snugged tight around the horse's neck, Matt pulled on the reata and the horse followed him obediently.

A few onlookers had come down to see what Matt was doing. Among them were José and Ernesto, the two men who'd been assisting Tex. Matt noticed them as he led the stallion to where Tex's equipment lay.

"Either one of you know how Tex puts all this stuff on the horse? I could probably figure it out, but the horse will be more comfortable if I do it the same way Tex does."

The two men conferred briefly. "We know how it is done, Señor Matt. Would you like for us to tack up the horse for you?"

Clearly the two had been picking up Tex's speech pattern as well as learning his methods. Matt was happy to let them apply their knowledge. In two minutes the men were finished. The horse had submitted quietly while José fitted the hackamore and Ernesto fastened the saddle pad in place.

"No stirrups. Well, I'll just have to do the best I can."

"Señor Matt, Tex grabs the long hairs of the mane at the base. This is the withers, and that is where you hold the mane."

"I know what a withers is!"

"Yes, Señor Matt. Would you like me to hold my hands to help you mount? I do this for Ernesto."

"You and Ernesto have been riding, José?"

"Yes, Señor Matt. But Tex has not allowed us to ride outside the corral yet. We are permitted to ride in the old corral before we drag the trees away to make the new corral."

"Sure, hold your hands. Maybe I can learn how Tex mounts the horse another time."

"You will need to know if you get off the horse, won't you?"

"You're right. But let me try riding first; I'll stay in the corral until I'm sure I can stay on the horse. At least this one's not as big as what I rode downtime. I don't have as far to fall!"

"It is not so bad, Señor Matt. Ernesto and I have fallen many times. But we don't fall so often now, and soon we will not fall."

Matt accepted the boost and found himself astride the horse. Holding the rein in his right hand, he soon realized that it felt unnatural. Gingerly he leaned forward and passed the rein under the horse's neck. Sitting upright again, rein in his left hand and with the hank of mane hair in his right, he squeezed the horse's barrel with his knees. The stallion immediately walked forward.

Matt grinned and gripped tighter. A second, tighter squeeze that placed his heels slightly back from the centerline caused the horse to trot.

Matt jolted every time a hoof met the ground. Gently he pulled the rein away from the horse's neck and tugged on it. Obediently, the stallion turned left. Matt slipped momentarily but regained his balance. Bringing the hackamore rein into contact with the neck and pressing with his heel cause the horse to veer right. Old habits were coming back rapidly.

Matt rode the stallion around the corral, first going left, then right, then left again. Periodically he stopped the horse and started again. The horse patiently endured the heels and tugs. Finally he knew it was time. He thumped his heels into the horse's barrel and the horse lunged forward. Matt was ready and swayed backward. But when he reined the horse left, the turn was much faster than expected. Matt slipped and began falling. Reacting rapidly, he released the grip his legs had attempted to maintain and pushed away from the hooves. Sprawling on the churned corral, Matt shook his head and regained his feet.

The stallion had rejoined the mares.

Some adjustment would be required. Matt understood that turns would likely not be as rapid once the horse was outside the corral. He could probably stay on the horse's back during a canter, which was much smoother than a trot.

In any case, he could make a lot faster time than the raiding party could, trying to haul Tex with them.

A thought occurred. *Would Tex try to slow the raiders down? If he became too great an annoyance, would they simply kill him?*

Matt would have preferred more practice, much more practice, but time was critical. The sooner pursuit got underway, the better. Laz had joined the spectators so it was time to take a break and see what he'd learned. Lee was back too, now carrying two extra quivers filled with arrows.

"Pretty good, Matt. Except for that last dismount!"

"You'll get your chance after we get back, Lee. Laz, what did you find?"

"They were dragging Tex at first. I followed them for about a mile and Tex was walking by then. I can't tell if the people who were dragging Tex... his toes left a skid mark between two men... were part of the raiders or maybe other captives, but there are at least ten all told. Two of them came into camp and grabbed Tex, while the rest hid about a quarter mile down. They headed southeast, a little more south than southeast."

"That should be enough information. I'll take a swing due south for about five miles, then swing over east and see if I spot movement. Lee, you bring the rest and keep on their trail. Be careful; they might try to ambush you. They don't depend on speed to get away, they are prepared to fight. Far more prepared than the people they grab."

"Understood, Matt. We're leaving right now. Your weapons are here and we'll look for you down the trail."

"Are you taking food and water?"

"Water only. We shouldn't be gone more than a day at most. I expect to catch them in half a day or less."

"Understood. See you, Lee." With that, Lee led his group of seven men south. As soon as they left the camp, Lee broke into a jog. The rest followed, strung out at first as the men found their place in the column. In a moment only dust showed where they'd gone.

Matt decided he was loose enough, and the horse had become accustomed to his weight. Rein held in his left hand, both hands on the horse's neck and with the right hand grasping the same mane he'd held before, he swung his right leg over the horse as he jumped. His knees gripped the barrel as he settled, cushioning his descent. Matt would have grinned in delight had the occasion been less serious.

Sal handed Matt his weapons. He slung his quiver in its usual place, slung the bow across his back, and arranged the two spare quivers across the front of the pad. Finally, he understood he'd have to leave his spear behind. Even his faithful axe was problematic; the handle hung down and tended to rest against the horse. As soon as the horse began moving, that handle would thump against its ribs.

Matt handed the axe over to Sal. He put the axe and spear together and waved as Matt signaled José to pull one of the small barrier trees aside. Taking a deep breath, Matt rode out of the corral. José closed the gap behind him.

* * *

COLIN WATCHED HIM GO, then turned to Piotr.

"You take care of security. Organize whoever you've got left, but I'm going to talk to everyone. No foraging parties, no hunting parties until Lee and Matt get back. I want everyone in camp until this is settled. Have Lilia see what she can do using the women, they can help too. We've got plenty of food, there's water right here, we'll just wait until they get back."

Piotr nodded. "Sounds good, Colin. I would have been stretched pretty thin, trying to cover everyone. Even using the women, I'd have had to choose whether to provide guards for people gathering vegetables or keep enough here to protect the camp. Hunting wouldn't have needed security...the hunters can protect themselves...but having hunters away would mean there were fewer people in camp. I just don't have enough men to provide security for everyone. It will be a lot easier if everyone's together."

"We're not helpless. Everyone here, except for the new people, is well armed and has had at least a little training. They fought too, when

Pavel tried to raid us, so it's not their first time shooting at people. Do you have enough weapons for the people Lee brought in?"

"We already have extra spears, but we'll need a lot of arrows and more bows. I'll use the new people; Matt and I already talked about it. I don't feel comfortable putting the new people on security, but there's no reason we can't put spears in their hands. Not the steel-bladed ones, but ones with the flint points I made. I can also show them how to use a spear, let them practice half-speed with a shaft until they've got the hang of using a long weapon. By the time Matt gets back, the new people will be basic spearmen and I'll be working on bows and arrows for them."

"Sounds good, Piotr. You've come a long way since Pavel left."

"I had a long way to go, Colin, and I had a lot of help from Matt and Lee."

* * *

MATT RODE CAREFULLY, watching the horse's ears for any indication the animal might decide to change course. So far, the horse seemed docile, appearing to enjoy the freedom of being outside the corral.

Matt's confidence increased with every hundred yards he rode, but he understood that overconfidence might result in a fall. Worse, a mishap might allow the raiders to escape. His task was too important to take unnecessary chances; there would be opportunities for more riding after they struck the raiders and got Tex away safely.

Reining the horse gently, he guided it south. A few minutes later he decided the time was right. Lifting the rein and squeezing with his heels, he coaxed the stallion into a canter. Behind him, the camp faded into the distance.

32

T he tracks were easy to follow, enabling Lee to set a fast pace. Tex had apparently recovered enough to walk on his own. Still, the raiders had made no effort to conceal their tracks, depending instead on speed and knowledge that any chase would mean a fight. And there was no guarantee that the captives would survive the fight.

It had been enough, until now.

The band might have begun trotting, but the tracks were not clear. Tex's tracks had merged with the others. Likely he was ahead and some or most of the armed warriors followed behind him. Should there be any attempt to rescue the prisoners, the warriors would be in position to prevent that...or add more victims to the ones they already held.

But while the raiders were moving, they weren't setting ambushes. Lee pushed on as fast as he dared.

Two hours later he crested a small hill and came upon a confused mass of tracks. There had been a fight of some sort here. Two bloody splotches showed where men had been injured, but there were no bodies. The injured ones were still with the group.

If this had been Matt's doing, he was smart. Dead raiders might have been left behind, but wounded men would be taken along. The raiding party would be slowed helping their injured comrades.

"Spread out, but keep your eyes peeled. See if you can figure out what happened here."

At Lee's command, the men, bows ready, melted into the slight cover and vanished from sight. They returned moments later.

"Nothing, Lee. I think Matt shot a couple of them and took off, but they left as soon as he stopped shooting. I expect he'll hit them again, a mile or so south of here. Maybe he'll go two or three miles, knowing they'll have to go slow because he might hit them again. They'll be expecting another ambush, so they'll have to be careful."

"They don't know we're back here, Laz. If they think someone from our camp has gotten ahead of them, they'll be worried about their front, not what might be coming up behind."

"I'm glad Matt's on our side!"

Lee nodded and took a short drink from his gourd. Looking around, others were doing the same. Replacing the stopper, he put the gourd away and walked after the raiders. The others fell in behind him and soon he resumed trotting.

* * *

THE STALLION WAS GONE.

Matt had left him tied to a scrubby cedar when he ambushed the raiders. Returning, he had hurried to the stallion and the horse had sensed his excitement. It danced away and Matt tugged on the hackamore. The horse braced his front hooves and Matt yanked on the rein.

Alarmed, the stallion had reared and suddenly Matt was holding only the rein. The horse spun on its rear hooves and galloped away, taking Matt's two reserve quivers with him. Matt spared a glance at the rein...broken...then slipped into deeper cover. It was too late now to worry about the horse. Matt dropped the broken rein in disgust.

He was alone and he had only ten arrows remaining. Those arrows and his knife were his only weapons; would they be enough?

He could still ambush the raiding party, but this time he would need to shoot from a greater distance. Muscles sore and stiff from the unaccustomed exercise of riding might slow him.

He would be in serious trouble if the raiders understood that he was alone and decided to chase him instead of fleeing with their captives.

* * *

DON ALFONSO REALIZED his chances of taking more captives were slim.

The trip had not been profitable; the small villages, though widely separated, had devised means of warning others. There would be smoke signals when the weather permitted, and always there were the drums. They'd have carried word to the other villages by now and people would be hiding or forted up behind their defenses.

So he'd followed the ones who had escaped during that brief fight. If he failed to catch the escapees, he'd be forced to go home with little to show for this raid.

Raiders never intended to fight; it was much easier to lie in wait and pick up one or two, then get away before there could be pursuit...if anyone *did* decide to follow.

Now three of his men were dead. Two had died immediately, the other a day after the fight. The wounded man had slowed the raiders, and by the time Don Alfonso's men caught up, they'd joined another group camped along the river.

Don Alfonso and three of his men had sneaked in close. They waited while Don Alfonso decided what to do. And then Tex, still not recovered from his fight with Matt, had stumbled near to where they waited. He'd bent over and vomited.

As he straightened up, a hard-swung club sent him to his knees. While the leader and his second watched the camp, the other two lifted Tex by his arms and dragged him away.

The leader had walked behind them, watching over his shoulder, but he saw no one looking and soon he turned. Taking the place of one of the men carrying Tex, he slung his arm around Tex's waist and the small party made better time.

Tex was soon walking, stumbling from time to time but on his feet by the time they rejoined the raiding party. It had taken only a moment to attach Tex to the long strap they used to tie captives together.

And then had come those arrows. Two more men had been wounded, and now more of his men were helping the injured limp along.

Who could have done it? Had there been someone following *him* when they headed north after the hunters? Could anyone from the camp they'd just left have gotten far enough ahead in time to ambush the raiders?

No, it was not possible. True, they'd not made good time after picking up the injured man, but if someone had come from the camp they'd have had to circle wide to get in position without being seen. And manage to do this in less than half a day? No, impossible.

Impossible or not, someone was ahead of them. The raiders had seen no one. Just the two arrows they'd cut from the wounded men, only those; the arrows might have come from a ghost!

Not a ghost; but whoever it was, he was still out there somewhere. Having successfully attacked and gotten away, he would do it again.

The leader briefly considered whether he should simply abandon the captives. Already there was little enough profit to show for this trip. And there were the losses his group had suffered. Would others come with him when next he decided to raid north, or would they abandon him to follow more successful captains?

Don Alfonso's past successes would mean little; people would remember only this last trip, the disastrous one. So it was not yet time to quit; perhaps the unknown archer would be afraid. He might not try again, and if he did the men would be ready. The leader took a few moments to quietly pass on instructions to his men.

"He may have run away. But if he shoots again, look for where the arrow came from. Spread out and charge in that direction, but try to keep cover between you and his hiding place. There can only be one, or at least only one with a bow. If there were many they would have fought us instead of shooting and running away.

"How has he done this, when we've been unable to? Our bows are light, barely more than toys, but that man put arrows into two of my men and they're buried up to the nocks! Still, if he waits in hiding and tries it again, we'll be ready."

"We've only got three captures, Don Alfonso. I say we turn them loose. If he wants them that bad, he can have them. It's not worth dying over. What if the bowman is one of those headchoppers?"

The leader winced. He'd heard about the mysterious headchoppers too.

"Let's not panic. The headchoppers are far to the east of here. We're heading south and we're on a low ridge. If that bowman is going to hit us again, he must stay on the ridge too. We can surround him when the slopes get a little steeper, and either add him to the ones we've already taken or kill him. The only cover is on top of the ridge so he can't hide forever. If he descends the slope, we will see him."

"Sell the bastard to that miner, Don Alfonso. He won't last long in the lead mine!"

"First we've got to catch him. Then we can decide where to sell him!"

* * *

MATT TOO HAD NOTICED the ridgeline. It hadn't seemed important while he still had the horse, but now the ridge crest forced him to stay far ahead of the raiders while he looked for a way off the ridge, someplace where he could hit the raiders again and still manage to escape. Turning away, he ran south, dodging around trees, trying to make distance as fast as possible.

There would be a better place for an ambush. Meantime, the captives and the injured would slow the raiders. They could travel only as fast as the slowest member of their group, so the raiding party wasn't going anywhere. They were forced to stay on the ridge too. If they decided to head downhill, Matt would have the advantage of high ground *and* cover. He could hit them with impunity. They'd be slowed if they tried to attack uphill, essentially stationary targets he could pick off at his leisure.

For now, he had only to stay ahead of the raiders and look for a favorable terrain feature. Side ridges ran off from this one; perhaps he could find one that would work.

And he must not become too bold. There were other dangers, predatory animals or even another raiding party. A turned ankle, a foot placed wrong, the smallest thing could lead to disaster. Matt knew where one group of enemies was, but that wasn't the same as knowing where *all* the dangers lay!

* * *

TEX HAD UNDERSTOOD IMMEDIATELY when the two raiders had suddenly sprouted arrows. Somehow, Matt or Lee had gotten ahead of the snatch party. Not both; the two, if together, might simply have stood their ground, weakened the raiders, then come in to finish them off with spears. He considered whether one might have tried riding his horse and dismissed the idea. He would have done that, but no one else could have.

Still, just knowing that someone was out there was enough. His head throbbed from the combined effects of the fight and the club the raider had used to silence him, but at least his vision had cleared. Tex was thinking of ways he might slow the raiding party even more.

A rawhide band had been looped around his neck and attached to a thicker strap. This heavy strap led forward and the other captives had been attached to it in similar fashion. The strap was quite long, obviously intended for as many slaves as could be taken during a raid lasting a month or more. The length of the strap might be turned to advantage.

Tex kept walking, trying to go slow but still avoid a beating. The leather strap they used to encourage laggards left painful welts!

* * *

LEE ALSO UNDERSTOOD the tactical meaning of the ridgeline. He stopped briefly and divided his party, keeping three and assigning a pair to go left and another right.

"Matt's ahead of them, I'm going to be right on their heels, and if you guys can catch up on the left and right side we've got them surrounded. You'll be downhill from the raiders, so just be careful if they decide to leave the ridge.

"There's no way they can outrun us, not with Tex and two wounded men. They may have other captives too. Even if they turn Tex loose, we're going to keep following. I don't want them to think they can raid up north without paying a price. We'll kill this bunch, all of them. I know what Matt would do; he'd cut off the heads and leave them as a warning."

"You just want us to slow them down until you can bring your men up, Lee?"

"You've got it, Laz. Just don't let them escape. If they split up and it's one or two, kill them. If it's the whole group, slow them down and wait for us. Just hold them until we can get there. We won't be far behind, no more than half a mile. Don't shoot Tex, and if you see someone who's not armed, don't shoot them either."

* * *

DON ALFONSO TRIED to plan as they headed south along the ridgeline.

The ridge would eventually descend to the flats along the seaway. His men had left a pair of large canoes hidden along the shore. Once they reached the canoes, they'd be safe from pursuit.

It was a simple matter to paddle for a day until they reached the southern coastline, and then they'd be among friends. Sell the captives, recruit new warriors to replace the killed and wounded, then plan another raid for the following spring. Perhaps even try raiding the swamp people farther south in the delta where the seaway joined the Gulf, a dangerous business but raiding north had also become dangerous. It was something to think about.

But those were considerations for the future; for now, he had another ten miles or more of ridge crest to negotiate, all while avoiding that archer to his front and maintaining a pace that would leave any possible pursuit far behind. He nodded to the raider who followed close behind the captives and that man cracked his strap across Tex's back. Tex winced and increased his pace slightly.

The headache was gone now. Tex might yet find a chance to escape. The group was trotting, albeit slowly. Tex trotted along and waited for an opportunity.

He would not be a slave. He would die first.

33

Laz and Marc left as soon as Lee finished speaking. They headed west down the ridgeline and turned south as soon as the slope leveled out.

"I want to get a little ahead of Lee. They'll be pushing those people, and if we can be in position when Lee catches up we can take any that try to break away."

"Got it, Laz. The ground's not bad down here, not too many rocks and there are only a few trees. We can move faster than Lee's guys, and if they get into a heavy scrap we'll just move upslope to help. It's only about two or three hundred yards at most. We get within a hundred yards and we'll be in bowshot."

"That's what I was thinking. I'll lead off, you move maybe ten yards to my left. I don't think there will be anyone, but having a set of eyes looking from a different direction means we won't be surprised."

Marc nodded agreement and the two set off, running. After gaining a lead of some two hundred yards on the main body, Laz slowed to a trot.

"We'll keep this lead and just watch to make sure we're not too far ahead."

* * *

MATT WAS CONCERNED. He'd found no suitable cover for a second ambush that would also permit him to escape. A slight breeze was blowing from the south and the air smelled faintly of salt. The seaway couldn't be far. If the raiders got to the shoreline, there was unlikely to be enough cover for an ambush.

So be it. Matt found a bush that offered concealment and settled in to wait for the raiders.

Priorities had changed. With the coast behind him, slowing the raiders down was no longer enough. His arrow, launched from fifty yards ahead, thumped into the chest of the leading scout. The rest of the party paused in confusion, then began spreading out in response to shouted commands from someone. They charged in his direction. Matt reached for a second arrow and brought down a running man.

Tex had been waiting for an opportunity. In the confusion, he looped the long strap around the neck of the rearmost raider. Yanking back as hard as possible, he dragged the man to the ground. A fast stomp to the throat had left him gasping as Tex wrenched the spear from his hand.

Reversing the spear, he thumped the butt between the raider's eyes. Leaving the unconscious man, Tex used the spear's blade to slash through the leather strap. He pulled it through the loop in the cord that was knotted around his neck, then headed forward.

The line of raiders had slowed. None wanted to push ahead and be the next victim. A second, then a third man had fallen to arrows coming from a clump of brush ahead. The line wavered, despite shrieked commands from Don Alfonso.

Tex made a quick decision; the raiders had no idea he was loose behind them. Holding the spear low, he slipped in behind Don Alfonso. Gripping the spear tight, Tex lunged forward and thrust, the blade punching in below the ribs and left of the spine.

Don Alfonso arched backward in sudden agony. The other raiders heard his boots scrabble as Tex tried to pull the spear free. Realizing it was stuck, he finally abandoned it and stepped back, picking up a spear from a raider who'd fallen to Matt's arrow.

The raiders broke, some heading down the ridge to the east and others west. The remaining captives had slipped their neck straps free of the cord and one had found a dropped spear. The other went after the spear in Don Alfonso's kidney. Holding the body down with his moccasin, the former captive wrenched the spear left to right, cutting enough flesh to free the blade. Triumphantly he waved it overhead and ran to join Tex.

Lee raced up, attracted by the fighting and the shrieks of dying men. One of the former captives turned on him with the spear and backed slowly toward Tex.

"Friends! Put the spear down. If you want to do something, go after the rest of the raiders."

The man nodded, then trotted east down the slope.

Four raiders had taken the west slope off the ridge. Slowed by having to run downhill, Laz and Marc had found easy targets. None had gotten within fifty yards of Laz or Marc.

Matt, realizing the fight on the ridgeline was over, left his cover and approached Tex.

"Plumb glad to see you, Matt. I was getting worried. How'd you get ahead of us?"

"I rode your horse, Tex. But I lost him after the first ambush. The rein broke and he bolted."

"Lost my horse? Damn, I worked hard to catch him. Maybe I can get close enough to rope him, but I guess I can't complain. I'd have tried breaking loose at some point and they'd probably have killed me. I'm just glad you realized I was gone before they got clean away!"

"Yeah, I don't think they had you for more than half an hour when we realized you were gone. I thought you were more savvy than that!"

"I thought so too. I guess I had other things on my mind. You punch pretty good."

"You ready to play nice with the other people, Tex, or do you want to hit the trail?"

"I'll stick around for a while if that's all right. I'll leave soon enough, but I need to finish breaking one of the mares. I got used to riding. Having that bastard whup me with a strap so I'd run faster didn't change my mind."

"Is he one of these, Tex?"

Tex looked at the dead men littering the small clearing.

"Don't think so. I got the leader, though. That's him over there; called himself Don Alfonso. This wasn't his first trip north, not by any means."

"As soon as you're recovered, how about you and the other two start chopping the heads off this bunch? You'll want to get the rest of that strap off your neck first. Use my knife."

Tex nodded and accepted the knife. After slicing through the neck strap, he found the others who'd been captives and cut the straps from their necks too. The three soon had a growing stack of heads.

"Matt, they'd heard of you. I heard one of them say something about the headchoppers, but they thought all the chopping was being done by a tribe east of here. They didn't know we were moving."

"So much the better, Tex. We'll leave these along the shore. They must have canoes or boats somewhere. We can destroy them, or at least hide them where they won't be found without a lot of work."

"Sounds good, Matt. I think I'll just chop Don Alfonso first!"

* * *

LEE GATHERED the absent members of his party and they joined in the beheading. Soon everyone held at least one head, carried by gripping the hair. Matt leading, the party continued along the ridgeline to the shore.

Matt, Lee, and Tex stood with the rescued men, looking across the waterway. Far off, mountains showed to the southwest.

"I wonder where they left their boats?"

One of the men had overheard conversations between raiders. "They'll be more to the west. The raiding party planned a big sweep, loop northeast and then come back from the northwest. They didn't have time to complete the loop the way they wanted to. I figure the boats are maybe half a mile, a mile at most from here."

"Did they leave a guard?"

"I don't think so. They just pulled them on shore and hid them with brush. There are a lot of small coves and the people living north of the seaway don't use boats. People down in the delta southeast of here use canoes, but the raiders stay clear of them for the most part. The swamp people know every creek and pothole down there. Raiders have gone in, but few ever came out."

"Well, let's pile the heads above the high-water mark. Keep enough spears so that everyone is armed. Save me one too, I had to leave mine back at camp. Use the others to stick a head on, and leave the extra heads stacked on the ground. Make sure that Don Alfonso's head has a spear, OK?"

"Will do, Matt."

"Tex, let's you and me take a run down the beach. Lee, you come too. In case they did post a guard, three of us should be able to handle him."

"Matt, I could use more arrows. Your quiver is nearly empty too."

"You're right. See if you can gather up a few arrows. Tex, you'll have to make do with a spear."

"Been a while. I'll make out 'til I get back to camp. My bow and arrows are still there, far as I know."

"Should be, Tex. You did pretty good, grabbing that spear and sticking that Don fellow."

"I figured I owed him. He got the point."

Matt grinned and took the arrows Lee offered. The three ran down the beach, watching for any sign of the boats. Shortly they came to a cove and found two large canoes, dragged up on shore."

"Took them a lot of work, making these. The paddles too. Should we destroy them or just hide them better?"

"I've been thinking about that. We killed all the raiders, right?"

"Far as I know, that's right. I didn't count the heads.

"We got most of them anyway. If one gets here, he'll be hard pressed to drag this heavy canoe down to the water. And one man is bound to have a tough time, paddling it across to the other side. I can't see the coast at all, just those mountains. How far do you think they are?"

"I'm guessing at least twenty miles. Could be more."

"Waves, tides maybe, not easy."

"Not easy at all. And if he gets to the other side, what's he going to tell them? That he ran into a camp of the headchoppers? If that doesn't slow them down, the ones that find the heads will get the idea.

"We probably can't stop the raids. Still, if we make it expensive they'll have to send bigger parties, more boats too. If they figure to lose as many as they catch, they'll look for easier pickings. Raids won't be profitable, that's for sure. Bring twenty or thirty men in a raid to catch four or five? Not much profit to share around, even if they don't end up losing their heads.

"We'll just leave the boats. I think we'll be bending south as soon as we leave the river. We don't have time now to get where I wanted to go. If we end up close to this seaway, we can salvage the canoes. We'll need food and salt, and having a sea nearby can help. We could make nets. Catch fish, maybe clams or oysters? Lobster? I haven't had a lobster in a long time."

"Might be worth it. Tell you what, why don't we take one of these and paddle back to where the others are? We can send a few men to pick the other one up. Let's paddle a few miles northwest and find a place we can hide the canoes and when we do come back, the canoes will be there."

"Grab a canoe. Let's get it in the water."

Lee held the canoe while Matt climbed in the bow. Tex gingerly crawled over the side amidships and Lee pushed off. As the canoe floated, he slipped over the stern and picked up a paddle.

Paddling wasn't among their skills but soon the three were making headway. Turning parallel to the beach, they paddled northwest, soon picking up a natural rhythm.

* * *

THE RESCUERS WALKED into camp just after dark. Piotr, taking his turn at guard, saw them coming and came out to greet the weary men.

"You look beat, Matt."

"It's been a long day, that's for sure. But we got Tex back and a couple of others too. I'm going over to the fire, see if there's any food left. We're not in shape to help with guard duty tonight."

"We've got it covered, Matt. I expect Lilia will be glad to see you, Sandra too; she's been anxious ever since Lee headed out."

Matt nodded and led his party to the kitchen fire. Margrette and three other women had meat on skewers, broiling over the coals. Matt flopped down near the fire and Lilia handed him a mug of tea. Matt sipped the hot liquid...it had been liberally sweetened with honey...and felt better.

"Tex, you owe a few people an apology."

"Apology? What for?"

"Mainly for being an ass. We managed to get along with each other until you got here. If you're going to stick around, you need to get used to that. Get along with people, or get gone."

"Damn. Well, I reckon I can do it. Can I wait 'til morning? I'm fair beat."

"Tomorrow's fine, Tex. Get some food, find a place to sleep. We can talk more tomorrow."

"I'll do 'er, Matt. Say, is one of those chunks of meat about done? If it ain't still hollering, it's probably cooked enough."

34

"What do you think of the new people, Colin?"

"Mixed bag, Matt. A couple of them are very interesting. They were engineers of one type or another before being transplanted. I think we can use their knowledge."

"Are they going to be able to work without computers? If they're electrical engineers they're going to be useless until we invent electric things."

"No electrical engineers, although they probably understand quite a bit of the theory. I think one was a mechanical engineer and the other a civil engineer of some kind. I didn't ask what they did beyond establishing they designed and built things."

"They might be very useful. Are there any you want to send packing because they're likely to cause trouble?"

"Not so far. Like the others we took in, they're adopting our ways. We're building more carts, so they can haul their possessions and help with kitchen stuff. We've got a lot more than we had, so more hands are helpful. We'll have bows and arrows for them by the time we leave. We can get on the road as soon as the carts are done."

"It's late summer and we don't know when the first snow will arrive. Get the carts done, use enough people to help Piotr and if there's time Lee can use assistants to help with training. Maybe they can help with the daily hunt; that's a good way to build experience.

"Right now, I'm thinking we bend southward as soon as we're past the ridges. The land farther west is flat until we reach the mountains. That's where we'll find the canyons and undercut cliffsides I'm looking for. The Cliff Dwellers used that practice for centuries; we can too, and do it better."

"Having a couple of engineers, former engineers anyway, will probably be a real help."

"It will, but we could have done it. Most of us transplants know how to do things the ancients discovered by trial and error that took years. We've got the accumulated knowledge of centuries just from having lived in an advanced culture. We understand communications and transportation, food storage methods and the need for good sanitation, we know so many things we're using already. Experience will only add more. We'll be doing things in a few years that took centuries for humans to learn. Things like conservation of resources, about taking the older animals from a herd whenever possible, about breeding plants and animals. *Everyone* knows something we can use. Tex is founding ranching as an industry, even if he doesn't know it yet. The ones we rescued know about metals, and as soon as we find ore they'll start producing steel. That took centuries downtime."

Colin nodded. "I hadn't thought of it that way, but you're right. In a century, two at the most, we'll have highways and cars. Maybe telephones and computers; just knowing it's possible is half the battle. The resources are here and we'll be a long time using them up. Maybe we can skip some of the worst mistakes this time."

"Maybe. Or maybe we'll make new mistakes. For that matter, maybe we can find out things the downtime people never discovered. I won't do it, but my grandchildren might. And this time, the sloths and mammoths will still be around. Dire wolves too, even the giant bears. A viable ecosystem needs all of them. The futurist talked about humans losing their will to live, so maybe a little danger, enough but not too much, is the key to keeping a civilization alive."

"We need to pass as much of our knowledge along to the next generation as we can. That's why I intend to push papermaking, once we have shelters we can defend and food enough for winter. Winter is a good time to teach the young ones," Colin observed.

"Keeps 'em out of mischief too. That kid Bear is already a handful!"

* * *

DREADED jobs don't get easier for waiting. Tex made the rounds, apologizing and working to fit back into the tribe. But he soon tired of this and went back to his corral. The horses seemed glad to see him, or perhaps it was the hay he fed them.

The hay had been collected and stacked by his two assistants. Cutting the dry grasses was time-consuming, but it would become necessary if the horses were to be kept up in corrals.

One benefit to hand-cutting was that the grasses retained their seeds, making a richer mixture than downtime grass hay would have provided. The horses looked forward to their twice-daily feedings.

Tex spotted hoof tracks around the outside of the corral.

"Have you been riding outside the corral?" But both men assured him they'd done no more than move the corral in the same fashion Tex had done.

"That stallion's back. Let's leave the old corral in place after I move the horses onto the new graze. We'll open one side so he can get in and catch him up. Tie a reata to the side of the corral and when he's in, pull it tight to close off the opening."

The two men, José and Ernesto, nodded understanding. They rarely spoke other than between themselves. Perhaps they were less comfortable speaking English, or it might be that they simply preferred Spanish. Tex, rarely talkative himself, was happy with the arrangement.

The three worked with the mares, catching them up and teaching them to respond to being led. Tex left the first one he'd trained alone now, except when he needed her for dragging the timbers into place for a new corral.

The three caught the stallion that afternoon when he came sniffing after his herd. Tex repaired the hackamore rein and swung aboard for the first ride since he'd been captured. Matt's two quivers were still there, but the arrows had been lost. Tex stacked the quivers with his other equipment and spent a few minutes getting the stallion settled.

"José, time to take that mare out of the corral. Ernesto, help him get comfortable and when he's ready, open the side so he can join me outside. We'll ride around an hour or so, then he can turn his horse in with the others and you can ride outside for a while. The two of you should be ready for a longer ride in a day or two. We'll see how the afternoon goes."

The two nodded and soon Tex and José trotted the horses up the long ridge west of the river. Tex had tied his quiver of arrows and cased bow to the strap around the stallion's barrel, one on each side. He carried his spear slung across his back. José carried his spear in the same fashion as Tex, but had not taken the time to attach the bow and quiver. Both wore the knives that were part of everyone's dress.

Tex was in no hurry. Every hour on horseback was an hour of training for horse and rider. He kept the pace to a walk, turning around almost an hour later. The stallion seemed anxious, so Tex squeezed with his knees and the horse stretched into an extended canter. A glance over his shoulder showed José hanging on as his mare kept pace, even if he wasn't riding with Tex's easy grace. Where Tex sat upright and moved loosely with the stallion, José gripped a handful of mane that stuck up just forward of the mare's withers. His right hand held the rein, but at least he wasn't trying to hold his horse back.

He would learn. Practice for a day or two, get used to riding several different horses to pick up individual mannerisms, and they'd soon be riders. At the moment, all they lacked was experience.

* * *

LEE AND MARC watched Piotr and his helpers for a moment.

"Got a minute, Piotr?"

"Sure, Lee." Piotr laid aside the obsidian core he was breaking into long blanks and joined them.

"Thanks for handling security while we were trailing those raiders."

"No problem. I was glad to do something different. I'm spending too much time in camp; if you've got a place for me, I'd like to go on the next hunt."

"We can use you. Matt wants to get moving. I thought we could go on a couple of day scouts west of here. Matt wants to start turning more to the south as soon as the terrain is favorable. I know what he's looking for, mountains. How would you feel about taking someone and scouting for a day?"

"I'd like that. How many parties are you sending out?"

"I'm going, and Marc will go with me. Laz will want to go. Matt too, although he hasn't said so. He's not doing much in camp, just waiting for Sal's crew to finish.

"I hope we're not spending too much time on something that won't last. Matt wants almost everyone to have a cart. No question, we move faster, but I'm wondering how durable they'll be when we get into the mountains. The wheels will take a beating; there's no way we can avoid hitting rocks. If the carts break, we'll be back pulling travois. That will slow us down and it makes the work a lot harder too, meaning we'll need to rest more often."

"I could take one of the people who's working with me, Lee."

"Better not. The new people don't have bows yet and we should also have spares, not to mention arrows. Matt will want the weapons work to keep going."

"I'll be ready tomorrow. Take a day to hunt, then go exploring?"

Lee nodded, then left to find Matt.

Piotr resumed work on the obsidian core. He glanced in satisfaction at what he'd already flaked this morning, an axe head that needed only a haft, half a dozen scrapers, two spearheads, and a dozen arrowheads.

The spearheads would be given to the new people. They would find shafts and make new spears to replace those taken from dead raiders. Piotr's spear-points were of much higher quality, and in any case, people needed to know how to make their own weapons.

Piotr would use the arrowheads himself. A second quiver of arrows would be on the cart when he joined tomorrow's hunt.

* * *

MATT LEANED against one of the partially-trimmed trees that formed the makeshift fence, watching Tex rub down the sweaty stallion. José and Ernesto had completed currying their mounts and now were cutting more of the dried grass.

"We've been lucky, Matt."

"How so, Tex?"

"None of the people we've fought had bows, but you can bet they'll have them by next year. You're using sinew, but there's wild flax around and some other long-fiber plants too. Somebody will figure how to make better strings, if not from flax then something else.

"It's the same thing with horses. I ain't the only one that can ride. Somebody will see us, and as soon as they do they'll start looking for horses themselves. Either that or give up raidin' north. They won't have a chance, afoot and armed with spears, and it won't take 'em long to figure that out. Soon as people know they're around, just send a few patrols south and start lookin' for their boats. Time the raiders get back, the boats'll be burned and there'll be people waitin' in the weeds to plink 'em full of arrows.

"You watch, by next year people will be huntin' buffalo from horseback, raidin' too. You're going to have to get your tribe mounted and they're gonna need to shoot arrows from horseback."

Matt nodded gloomily. "I guess you're right. How long before your horses are ready to be swapped?"

"If you can loan me a few people to cut hay and learn about horses, Ernie and Joe can spend more time ridin' and breakin' horses. I'm already doin' that."

"Ernie and Joe, hmmm?"

"Don't take as long to say. They'll get used to it. Soon as I get 'em used to callin' me Tex instead of Señor Tex."

The two shared a grin. "Well, don't make 'em mad. If they want Ernesto and José, we can call 'em that."

"You're startin' to talk right, Matt. You can almost speak Texan."

Matt shook his head. "It's catchin', but maybe we can teach you to talk English instead. Anyway, we don't have a lot of manpower to spare, but I'll see what I can do to get you some help. You're going to teach them, right?"

"Shore. Can't have people around that can't handle the hosses. You send 'em, I'll school 'em."

"Just don't do it with your fists, Tex. If you insist on fighting, look me up first."

"I'll do that. You plannin' on ridin' too?"

"I don't have a choice, do I?"

"Nope. Soon as you're ridin', Laz and Lee too, I'll take Ernie and Joe over west of here and we'll catch a few more horses. I figure to start a stud farm or maybe a horse ranch, whichever. We can use wild stuff for ridin', but we're gonna need better stock. I figure to use this stallion for breeding at first, but I'll upgrade as soon as I can catch better stuff. Start the first crop of foals off right and you'll have better mounts within five years or so. Give me ten years and I'll have horses for huntin', horses for pullin' wagons. Hell, even plows if that's what you want. You'll need good wagons if you plan to bring stuff back to this town you're gonna build. You'll need timber, buildin' stone, maybe ore if you're gonna be making your own steel. Coal too, if there's any around. You plannin' on using coal or charcoal?"

"Coal if we can find it. We might be able to develop better electrical generating plants sooner without relying on coal as long as people did downtime, but right now we need coal just to get started. We have to make the tools to make the tools."

"Yeah. I expect there'll be people that know how to do things. Be nice to have a real doctor and maybe somebody that knows more about medicine."

"Elizabeth does a lot, but she could do with more and better bandages, medicine, everything. The good part is that she's well matched to what we've got right now. Her medical supplies are what she's made and she knows how they can be used. Most of us are generalists, we can do a lot of different things, but we haven't had the luxury of developing specialists. I guess that will happen in a few generations."

"Likely, Matt. Too much to learn about some things; if you don't spend all your time workin' on what you do, you'll never be as good as the feller that does. Just like rodeoin', the one that does nothin' but rope steers is bound to be better at it than the one that ropes and rides rough stock too. Gonna mean changes, though; right now, everybody can turn to and do whatever needs doin'. I reckon we'll lose something when people start doin' only one kind of work."

"You mentioned starting a horse ranch, Tex. You have a place in mind?"

"I'm gonna look around, but that seaway is plumb interestin'. Feller claimed some land in downtime Texas near the Gulf, and he built a ranch that was probably still goin' a long time after I got picked up by that futurist. Me callin' him Saint Peter worked just as well, far as I'm concerned. But anyway, there was plenty of grass along the southern Gulf downtime, good water too. The country down near the seaway has better grass than what's around here. More rain down there too, I expect.

"I saw tracks while we were lookin' for those boats. I'm thinkin' the buffalo and them mammoths and such from up north are gonna overwinter down here. There are already some big critters in the low places between the ridges. Some might go north in the spring, but I'll bet a lot of 'em just live down there all the time, back in the canyons."

"You're going to have to fight, Tex. You'll be close to where the raiders crossed. Lots of them, not many of you. They'll be coming."

"I reckon. But the feller that started that ranch, he had to fight too. Comanches, Kiowas, a few local Injuns; soon as I get a few people that can ride and shoot, I'll put them raiders out of business. Hosses can do more work than people for some things."

"You're smarter'n you look, Tex."

"You too, Matt. Well, I need to get back to work."

"See you later, Tex."

"Later, Matt."

35

The tribe headed out a week later. Every adult, other than those on security patrol, pulled a cart. The scouts explored ahead, the less experienced patrolled the flanks. After a day of scouting, they replaced someone who'd been pulling a cart. By rotating, they shared the heavier work; several carts carried salt or amphorae. Bedding, clothing, and skins, by comparison, made for a much lighter load.

If they weren't yet the archers that others were, the new adoptees were motivated. They practiced whenever time could be found. *There's nothing like a spell of captivity to inspire enthusiasm for learning to defend yourself,* Lee thought.

Tex had come through; Matt, Lee, and Laz were mounted now, ranging ahead in the morning, then tethering their horses behind a cart in the afternoon.

The system had worked well so far. The animals rested and grazed as they followed behind the slow-moving carts.

Tex had left the group. José and Ernesto had gone with him, as had Callie; Colin and Margrette were unhappy with her decision, but it hadn't been their choice to make. In any case, if they built where Matt intended, she'd be close enough to visit from time to time. The draft mare pulled the cart, loaded with supplies swapped for horses. Tex led, Callie riding at his side, while Ernesto and José followed with the remaining horses.

* * *

THE TRIBE soon settled into traveling, necessary adjustments having been made. A week passed, then another. Scouts had little difficulty killing a buffalo and the tribe stopped for the day as soon as they came up where the carcass lay. Occasionally they bagged a camel or llama, and twice they'd killed wild sheep. The sheep were not like the domesticated animals of downtime; instead, they resembled Rocky Mountain bighorn sheep. This variety might also be ancestral to downtime desert bighorns. Matt wondered if the animals could be domesticated, but that would have to wait.

They needed a place to live, winter quarters if necessary, but a permanent home if possible. Permanent settlements could include pasturage, fenced corrals and barns, all the things necessary to nurture, control and protect livestock. Could young ones be captured? Matt wondered, and schemed as he walked.

Rolling hills and ridges had given way to flat plains covered with short grasses and brush. Trees were smaller and farther apart, indicating less annual rainfall. Occasional knolls popped up for no reason Matt could see; they were just there, most with a cap of limestone. Perhaps the knolls were the remains of what had once been level surface and the area between had eroded away.

Lee talked with Matt as they dismounted and tied their horses behind a cart.

"Mornings are getting cool, Matt. People are wearing their deerskins closed now instead of leaving them open."

"I noticed. I'm guessing we've got a month at most before weather becomes a problem, but I'd rather not push that long. Just as soon as I find a place, that's where we stop."

"People are looking forward to this promised land of yours, Matt."

"Is that what they're calling it?"

"Some are. Most everyone is tired of traveling. They spent last winter in houses. They weren't great, but they were warm and they were ours. They want to spend winter in houses, not temporary shelters."

"Lee, building permanent shelters will be the first thing we do. We've got more help than we had last time. If we can build shelters that share a wall, maybe with a pass-through fireplace, we won't need to burn as much wood to stay warm.

"The bison, what Tex called buffalo, are common. We should be able to kill as much meat before winter as we can process into jerky, and as soon as it freezes we can start hanging quarters of meat. They'll stay frozen until we're ready to use them. For that matter, there are giant sloths and mammoths around. I killed that mammoth as much by luck as skill, but with several of us working together we can bag bigger animals. It will give us a change of diet. Bears too, and those thick bearskins make good sleeping pads. Bearskin rugs beat a cold hard floor any day.

"The carts are loaded with dried berries, nuts, some dried vegetables and pots of honey, enough to see us through the winter. If we're short of anything, it's sleeping robes and rawhides for leather. We'll need boots and heavy clothing, not to mention more horse tack and reatas like the ones Tex uses. We should be able to get all the hides we need, we just need time to make them into leather.

"But I don't expect winter here to be nearly as bad as last winter was. We're quite a bit farther south, farther away from any glaciers that might still be north of here. The seaway isn't far, so that might help keep the worst of the cold away.

"If we find a place we can grow food and defend, someplace with a year-round supply of game, I'm ready to stop. A good water supply is important too. The first place that meets our needs, that's home."

"How far are the mountains, Matt?"

"Well, we're just seeing a smudge on the horizon right now. That might be mountains, and if so I'd guess they're less than a hundred miles ahead. We're making good time, so anywhere from ten days to a month of traveling. A big river or canyon might force us to turn north. We know the sea is south of here, so any canyon or river is likely to get wider and deeper the farther south we go."

"Matt, the horses are standing up well to being ridden. What would you say to Laz and me riding ahead, maybe take two days on horseback out and another two days back? By then we'll have a good idea of what we're facing. If we find anything, we'll cut the trip short. I'm tired of traveling too."

"We all are, Lee. But if you two want to ride ahead, leave tomorrow morning. We'll look for you four days from now. Just be careful of the horses. You're riding better, but you've still got things to learn. So do I; we all need time in the saddle before I'll feel confident. You know what kind of place we're looking for. If you find anything, look around for game, a place we can cut firewood, see if there's limestone for building. By the time we get there, those two engineers will have a building plan that we can adapt."

"OK, Matt. Well, I've got to go pull a cart for a while."

"Talk to you later, Lee."

* * *

"I'll be glad when we can stop, Matt." Lilia stretched and rubbed her lower back.

"Me too. People are getting short-tempered. We can all use a rest.

Once the village is built and we have supplies, we can laze around through the winter. I'd like to try making music again. What are you planning to do?

"Maybe make small clothing. I'll need at least two sets."

"Really? I know Sandra's starting to show, but is there another pregnancy?"

"Me. You're going to be a father."

"Really? Wow...I wasn't expecting this. Wow. You're sure?"

"I'm sure. It's not my first time, you know. I didn't want to tell you until I was sure, but I'm probably about three months along."

"Wow. Lee is going to be a brother. He'll have a sister or brother."

"Half-sister or half-brother, Matt. As soon as we develop paper, we can start recording births. List the name of the mother, and the father if we know who it is."

Matt was surprised, then realized he shouldn't be. Lee was about seventeen or eighteen years old now. The transplants might still be bearing children a century or more on. Assuming the futurists had done the same thing to the women that they'd done to him.

It would require some rethinking. Absent accident or attack, people might live indefinite lives on Darwin's World. *Would the changes breed true*, he wondered? *Or would they revert in a few years as mutations built up*? Time would tell.

Matt raised his head and looked east. Funny...there were no clouds, but that noise sounded like thunder. Well, perhaps something was going on over the horizon.

Sal was inspecting the carts as he did every morning.

"How are things looking, Sal?"

"Not bad, Matt. Wheels are holding up reasonably well, but we may yet have to go back to dragging stuff. Horses can carry a lot more on a travois than a human can. Did you hear that thunder?"

"I heard something, off to the east. But I didn't see a cloud."

Both men looked across the trees. The sky had been clear, but now there was a thin line of condensation.

Sal looked at Matt. "That's a contrail, Matt. Condensation forms after an airplane flies through supersaturated air. I think we heard a sonic boom."

"So much for the futurists leaving us alone."

"You think somebody else might have been here long enough to develop jets or rockets?"

"Maybe, but that's not the impression I got from the futurist. The miners might have brought one, but I doubt they'd have turned it over to transplants. Maybe they're expanding their mining operation? They equipped their security force with modern weapons, or at least a lot more modern than anything we had."

"No way to tell. I guess we'll just keep on going. I got to liking the idea that this was our world to develop in our own way."

"I hope they leave us alone. We'll find someplace soon enough and build a town. Maybe we can start trading with others, barter what we can make for what they can provide."

"I agree. Long as they come peaceful, I'll be glad to trade. Maybe welcome a few more people into the tribe, but I don't know if I ever want to see a city again. Maybe let the tribe grow, but as soon as it gets uncomfortable we split off and start a new tribe somewhere nearby. I guess that's what Tex is already doing. Sooner or later he'll pick up more people."

"Yeah. Well, I guess we just wait and hope for the best. Still, that aircraft worries me."

"Me too. Well, I've still got a few spare wheels and none that need replacing, so we're okay for now. That mix of wax and grease worked. Glad you thought of it."

"See you later, Sal."

Matt went to find Colin. Lee and Lilia would also need to know about the aircraft.

Discussions added nothing new. A single sighting provided too little information. Lilia simply nodded and went back to what she'd been doing. Lee briefed his guards to watch for strangers, but not to over-react unless they proved hostile. Lee departed with Laz the following morning. Futurists or no, Matt needed information about what lay ahead.

Colin made several changes. Whenever possible, he kept the camp smaller when they stopped, the shelters closer together and located under cover of trees. Cookfires were doused as soon as everyone had eaten. Breakfast was cold food now, most often leftovers from supper. If the futurists were looking for them, the tactics might make it diffi-cult to find the tribe, especially from a fast moving and high-flying aircraft.

The carts left little evidence of their passing; people were careful not to follow in the tracks of the cart ahead. Of course, if the futurists had sufficiently advanced technology the efforts might be in vain, but there was no way of telling. Colin and Matt thought the effort worthwhile.

Time passed and Matt relaxed. Perhaps the futurists weren't inter-ested in a small, obscure tribe.

* * *

Two days later a scout returned to the tribe in late afternoon. He brought with him a man wearing an unfamiliar uniform and carrying a heavy rifle slung over his shoulder.

36

"I met this fellow about half a mile back. I figured I should bring him to you."

"Probably a good idea, Dominick. He cause you any trouble?"

"Not so far. He had some questions, but I decided you should be the one to talk to him."

"Good enough. You can head back."

Dominick nodded and turned away.

"So. Who are you and what do you want?"

"You can call me Chief, it's what people call me. I'm Chief of Security for Mine 23. You're Robert?"

"Robert's dead. I'm Matt."

"Sorry to hear that. You're the one Robert hired to bring meat for the mine crew?"

"I did that. Were you there?"

"I was hired afterward, but Robert left records and I've accessed them. A lot of people ended up being fired over that transaction and some others. The manager was passing out steel weapons and tools without permission and he never accounted for the stuff. We can overlook that, except for the rifle. You've got that, and we want it back."

"What makes you think we've got it?"

"There's a tracker in the receiver group. It's short range...only about five kilometers at most...and it's a good thing we found you before the battery went dead. But the rifle's here. Hand it over and you can go on your way."

"I used up the remaining bullets a couple of months ago. I probably should have just dumped it, but there was no way to tell what might happen. Someone else might have had cartridges. If they found the rifle and passed it on to whoever had ammo, that might have caused problems."

"Good thing you kept it. Quite a lot of ammo was unaccounted for after the fight. The ammo might have been fired or simply lost, of course. There's no way to tell. But this is the only rifle not accounted for."

"I'll get it."

"I'll come with you if you don't mind. You said you have no ammo, but I don't know that, do I?"

Matt grinned. "No, you don't. Come ahead."

Chief followed as Matt went to his cart. "You're in charge of this band?"

"I am, duly elected after Robert died. Not that elections mean much on Darwin's World."

"Are you the one that named it? We've started calling it that too. It sounded better than Earth 4428."

"You number the versions you find?"

"We do. Most others either have humans already in place or the planet is dead. Our version, Earth Prime, was incredibly lucky to have evolved as it did. There were late-time meteor strikes in some of the dimensions. In several cases there's no moon; it crashed into Earth and wiped out all life more complex than bacteria. They're evolving, of course, and someday they may become intelligent. But it will take billions of years."

"You can't move ahead in time?"

"I probably shouldn't be telling you all this, but no. We can cross from one dimension to another...that's fairly easy...but going back in time is energy-intensive. It's theoretically possible to move ahead in time, but there's never been enough available energy to give it a real try. At least, that's the conclusion of the mathematicians.

"That's why we need the mine. We mine...well, it's a rare earth element that's no longer available on Earth Prime. We had enough of it on Prime to begin our operation but it will be years before we accumulate enough to routinely travel back in time. Even though we're operating mines in hundreds of different dimensions, there's just not much of the mineral available on any version."

"Interesting. How did the futurists bring people like me forward?"

"We think they didn't. They sent a few people back to your time with medical and dimension-switching equipment and left them there, a one-way trip. The futurists told you about suicide being the major cause of death? We think this is how the ones who went back choose to suicide. They'll work in the past, sending people from your time across to this dimension. The transplanters will die when the nukes fall. As near as we've been able to tell, they set up their facilities at what will be ground zero for one of the nukes. It could work; they send a few from their past across to a different dimension, and people from their own time cross to the same dimension in *your* future and pick up people they want to integrate into downtime society.

"We could be wrong, of course. They may have the technology to get around the limits we face. They could be grabbing you and bringing you forward, but the only way we could duplicate their efforts with our current level of technology is the one-way trip I described. Even then, we couldn't totally rebuild a body and change the genetic code the way they did."

Matt began offloading the things stacked atop the cart. He glanced at Chief and wasn't surprised to notice increased alertness.

"It's right beneath that roll of deerskin. You can pick it up if you want."

"I will, thank you."

Chief reached beneath the roll and pulled the black rifle out. As soon as he had it in his hands, he began muttering into his collar. Matt realized there was a tiny button microphone there, what Matt had assumed was part of the uniform's insignia. Chief ejected the magazine and confirmed that it was empty, then pulled back on the cocking handle. Locking the action open, he peered into the chamber, then reversed the rifle and looked down the bore.

"Empty, right enough. Thank you."

"You're welcome. We'll be stopping in half an hour or so. Want to stay for supper?"

"I don't mind, if you've got enough."

"We'll be having fresh buffalo, most likely. Occasionally it's something else, but there are a lot of buffalo around and they don't spook when one falls."

"Your bows are strong enough to kill a buffalo?"

"Plenty strong enough. I killed a mammoth with mine, although I think it was a lucky hit. The first shot didn't do more than annoy the thing."

"Mind if I look?"

Matt removed his bow and handed it over. Chief held it with his right hand on the grip, three fingers of the left hand on the string. Grunting, he attempted to draw the bow.

"I see what you mean. How many kilos draw weight is that thing?"

"No idea, we've never had the ability to measure it. But this is my third bow, and every one has been stronger than the last. Most of our other bows aren't as strong, but I can handle this one. I'm happy with it."

"Nice work. There are places in Darwin-Europe that have archery, but I think you're the only group in Darwin-North America that has anything like this."

Chief returned the bow and looked ruefully at the angry red mark left on his fingers.

"I suspect you've got some serious calluses on your fingers too."

Matt nodded. "It took a while. I thought of using a glove or archer's ring, but decided that it was more trouble than it was worth. If we need a bow, we don't have time to put on a glove or thumb-ring. Those things are for when you intend to shoot more than a dozen times. If we ever get into a war, I'll be the first to put on a glove.

"Anyway, we're almost there. See that strip of deerskin, hanging from the branch up ahead? That's our supper; the scouts will already have it field-dressed.

"We've had a lot of practice. Colin will soon have the carcass butchered and his wife will have a nice bed of coals ready. Some of the folks will have gathered fresh vegetables along the way, probably enough for a salad. We've got salt but no salad dressing."

"Salt's enough. I've roughed it before."

"Been a soldier long, Chief?"

"I'm not actually a soldier, Matt, I'm a security agent. We don't really need soldiers now, not since the Bad Times."

"Bad Times? Was there a war after my time?"

"When were you harvested?"

"I lived until the early 21st Century. But my soldiering was done in the late 20th Century."

"Well, the United Nations broke down in the mid-21st Century. After that things deteriorated rapidly. Armies were mostly kept home, but there were at least a dozen active terrorist organizations and they attacked pretty much everyone. There was a major terrorist group in North America too. They started launching strikes against targets in the Mideast and South America. Most casualties were civilian, but they did manage to hit some of the villages where the Muslim terrorists were based. Supposedly, the US and Canadian governments couldn't locate them. The historians can't agree, but most don't think the two governments put much effort into countering the Militia. They weren't hitting locals, and they targeted people who *were* attacking North America and Europe. The financing came out of North America, but most attacks were launched from elsewhere.

"Anyway, the NorAm Militia had motivation and money. Some of that came from Israel and probably a lot of the technology did too, even though the Israelis always denied it. Eventually someone had enough of the nonsense, and what should have been a small brushfire conflict went nuclear. Some of the bombs were relatively clean, but not. There are places we still don't go, more than two centuries on. Somewhere between half and two-thirds of humanity didn't survive.

"Nukes weren't the only things that got used. Europe and Asia got hammered, eastern North America too. The damage extended down into Mexico."

"So which part of America did you live in before you took this assignment?"

"America? Place is still a howling wilderness. I live in Australia. Nobody cared enough to bomb us hit us with germs. No one ever explained this to you?"

"No. The man who picked me up told me why he was transplanting me, but that was all. You're not from the same time?"

"No. I suspect he's a descendant of my time. Can't be sure, of course, not unless that new development...."

"What new development?"

"I shouldn't mention it, but it doesn't matter. You can't use the information. There may, and I emphasize may, be a way around that energy requirement I mentioned, the one that keeps us from traveling into the future. One solution to the equations implies that it can be done, though it's not accepted by the scientific mainstream. The main proponent of the theory is considered a crackpot.

"Anyway, if we can do that, we might just go visit the people who transplanted you. They've got a few things we could use. Research nearly stopped during the wars, except for weaponry. And we could solve *their* problem, the one he told you about. All the transplants apparently got the same story, so it might be true. Anyway, our birth rate is high and our people are quite ambitious. It wouldn't take much for us to take over that future civilization. It's what they want anyway, right?"

"Maybe. What happens to us?"

"You have a world that we really don't need. I suspect you'll be left here to make of it what you will. This dimension might even be quarantined; it's happened before. And you've got no place to go back to.

"That manager I mentioned only put the mine here rather than on another timeline because he thought he could use cheap transplant labor. The new management is using people from my own time. We ship our own food here and don't interact with locals."

"What about the animals? Do they bother you?"

"They don't bother us," Chief said. Matt glanced at the heavy rifle over Chief's shoulder. A closer look revealed several small holes on each side of the barrel's end.

Muzzle brakes, he thought. *I wonder what caliber that thing is?*

Matt stood aside with Chief and let Colin and Margrette butcher the carcass. This one was a young male buffalo, heavy with muscle and with a thick layer of fat over the spine. Margrette trimmed most of the fat and laid it aside; it would be boiled down later for making soap. Some would be given to Sal for axle grease.

"Any cuts of meat you prefer?"

"Why don't you pick one for me?"

"Sure. I prefer the backstrap but I try not to always insist on it. I take a turn with the others. The backstraps are big enough to feed half a dozen people, so you can have a cut. Some prefer roasts anyway, and Margrette's good at making those. A couple of people insist that the tongue is best, and there's a school of thought that insists nothing's better than a T-bone steak. And as soon as the arguments die down, we'll have a llama or a camel for supper next time and then it starts up again. Personally, I think the sheep make the best eating, but we don't bag many. Rabbit and squirrel are good, turkey too, but most of the time we don't bother. They're too small and too much work when you've got a whole tribe to feed."

"There was a woman named Margrette who worked at the mine before I got there. Her name was in the records. Is this the same one?"

"She worked there, but I wouldn't ask her about it if I were you. It would be best if no one knew you had anything to do with the mine. All they know so far is that you're from the future."

"Good enough. Just tell people I came to recover the rifle and leave it at that. We never knew exactly what happened, except that all the people on duty were killed. The manager wasn't there, of course. He stayed on Prime and sent someone cross-dimension to oversee the work."

"The management recruited a bunch of people, and the ones that wouldn't work, troublemakers mostly, they kept around and gave them busywork so they wouldn't cause more trouble by raiding. Anyway, some of them began making alcohol and they got drunk. I don't know all the particulars, but Colin ended up forted up in the kitchen with Sal and their families. Robert got them out and they joined us, been here ever since except for Colin's daughter. She's with a man named Tex. He's starting a ranch south of here. We expect to have more horses by next spring if everything works out."

"You have any trouble from people living south of here?"

"Some. Not in the past month though."

Chief looked speculatively at Matt. "We found where someone had chopped heads off after a battle. Would you know anything about that?"

Matt looked at him and remained silent.

"OK, enough said. It wouldn't matter, but if you don't want to talk about it I'll understand. Is this your whole tribe?"

"We've got people out, keeping watch. This is no country to wander around in, thinking you're safe. We always have guards out and there's an exploring party out ahead too. We're looking for a better place to build, someplace we can defend. We've had trouble during the winter with animals, and mammoths came stampeding through camp a while back. They pretty-much wrecked everything."

"I can imagine."

The two men fell silent and watched the cooks work. Just as the men all took part in hunting and security duties, the women took their turn helping with this essential task. Only Colin and Margrette were always present at the fire during mealtimes. A natural division of labor had taken place, with no need for planning.

Thick steaks were soon broiling over the coals. A mug of Margrette's tea, boiled in one of the metal pots they'd brought from the mine, was soon ready for Matt and his guest. Chief saw the metal pot but said nothing.

"Do you expect to come this way again, Chief?"

"I doubt it. Fuel's expensive, and there's no reason to come all the way out here. I'll be busy around the mine for another year and then someone else will take over my job."

"We won't be here. We're moving on. We'll find someplace soon where we can settle down."

"Luck to you. I can't help you, of course."

"I understand. Looks like the food's about ready. There's an extra plate, but you'll need your own knife."

Lee rode into camp with Laz as they were finishing the simple meal.

"Chief, Lee's our chief of scouts. Laz is his assistant."

"Glad to meet you."

"Likewise. You the one in that plane Matt told us about?"

"I was. We were due to make a survey next month, but I had a reason for looking this way. Matt had something that belonged to us."

"They wanted the rifle, Lee. But you and I can talk after I see Chief back to his aircraft."

"OK, Matt. We came back a little early."

"I noticed. But we can talk later. Horses do all right?"

"They did fine. We picketed them near yours. I figured that was all right."

"It's fine, Lee. You can rest and we'll talk when I get back. You ready to go, Chief?"

"Sure am. The jet's not far, maybe a kilometer. We should go now if you want to get back before dark."

"I'd just as soon. I've been out after it got dark, but none of us like it. We do it when we must, but cats hunt at night."

"Let's go, then." Chief looked at a device on his wrist and pointed northwest. "The plane's eight hundred ninety-six meters away."

Matt nodded and trotted away in the direction Chief had indicated. He set a fast pace and waited to see whether the other man could keep up. He could; he was breathing hard, but managed to still be on Matt's heels when they came to a small clearing. The smell of burned fuel indicated the aircraft's presence, but the mottled pattern made it difficult to see.

"Good camouflage."

"I suspect active camo was developed after your time. We use it, even though a few people have lost their planes if the wrist trackers are damaged. We went in later and recovered them, so don't look so hopeful!"

"I doubt I could fly one anyway. Might be fun to try, though."

"Matt, I can't leave you a rifle, but give me a second to talk to my flight crew. I might have a gift. That steak was tasty."

Matt waited. Chief soon returned with a wrapped packet.

"All we could spare, Matt. Thanks for everything."

"You're welcome. Have a nice flight back."

"Take care, Matt. I probably won't see you again, but...well, take care."

Matt nodded and backed away to the side of the clearing. Huge nozzles swung down beneath the craft and a loud whine grew into a muffled scream. A puff of smoke and then a burst of bright flame appeared before the craft rose into the air. High above, the nozzles pivoted to the craft's rear and it accelerated eastward. Moments later it disappeared.

Matt heard the tell-tale boom a minute later. Chief was on his way, and Matt needed to be in camp himself. As he'd told Chief, this world was dangerous.

Lee and Laz materialized from cover after he'd gone about a hundred yards.

"Figured we might tag along. Just in case, you know. That fellow seemed friendly, but there was no reason to take chances."

"Glad to see you. What say we hurry back to camp?"

The three set off, Lee leading, Matt behind him, Laz bringing up the rear. Whatever was in the packet rattled, a metallic sound. Matt wondered what Chief had given him, but he could wait. They'd be back at camp in a few minutes.

37

M att laid the package on the cart that held his few belongings and went back to the kitchen fire. The tribespeople had remained apart while the stranger was there, but now they looked at Matt.

"You've probably figured out that he came from our future. He wanted the rifle and I gave it to him. It's useless to us. The only reason I didn't dump it was to keep it away from someone who might have ammunition. Anyway, it's gone now and good riddance."

Several people around the fire nodded. They gradually dispersed and went about their business.

Lee and Laz added meat to slabs of bread and sat down with Matt. Scouts, for that matter all the tribespeople, ate a lot of food. The work they did used a lot of calories.

"I wanted to tell you what we found, Matt. I think it's just what you're looking for. We can get there in a week or so, pulling the carts, and the only real problem will come after we get to the canyon."

"Canyon, Lee?"

"Canyon or valley, Matt. There's a river at the bottom but the sides are fairly steep. Anyway, buffalo or maybe mammoths have worn a track down the side. Still steep, but it's not as bad following the animal trail as it would be if you tried to take the carts down somewhere else. There's a good ford at the bottom too.

"The walls are rocky, that limestone stuff you showed me. We explored south after we crossed the river and the valley just kept getting wider. It was a mile wide south of the crossing and the western wall is undercut. We found a big place half a day's ride down the canyon. If that's where you decide to build, there's room enough to house everyone. Maybe build homes under the overhang, at least for now. The floor is thirty or forty feet above the bottom. It's not level, but we could probably fix that.

"No mammoths are gonna stampede through there and the high-water mark from the river is only about three feet up the canyon's walls. That's probably because the canyon keeps getting wider as you go south.

"There are springs there, waterfalls too. It's good water. Best of all, the canyon floor has more game than I've ever seen. We saw big herds of buffalo, camels, and horses. There's plenty of grass and water. We didn't see any of the big predators, but I'm sure they're there. There are also mammoths and something else, maybe a ground sloth. It was too far away to tell for sure and we didn't try to get closer.

"The canyon doesn't run north and south; it's more northeast to southwest and it bends around in a few places."

"You think it would be a good spot to settle?"

"It's got food, shelter, water. I don't know if lions or saber-tooths could climb up where we did, but some of the smaller cats could. The jaguars and mountain lions, the cougars, they can climb better than we can.

"We'd have to haul stone up to the cave, but there's plenty of it on the ground. I'm guessing part of the limestone on that cliff just collapsed and fell down. If you want to see it for yourself, we can get there and back in about four days."

"No, I'll take your word for it. I'll bring the tribe on; leave Laz to serve as guide and take Sal and his crew with you. Let me talk to him first, but if he thinks the carts are good for that distance, we can do without him. You'll move slower, but you'll still get there before the rest of us. You could set up a place for us to camp while we're building quarters.

"The only drawback I see is that we're going to want to trade with other towns at some point. Right now, we need a place we can defend and feed our people, but if the canyon walls are that steep people won't come to us. The only way we could trade is if we send traders to them.

"The canyon probably keeps going and drains into the seaway. How far away is the sea?"

Lee thought for a moment and looked at Laz, who shrugged.

"I'm guessing at least twenty miles. It might be more, but you told me once that the river that was here before bent more northward toward the mountains. Maybe the seaway does too. So the sea might be twenty miles away, maybe a little less. That might be a good thing, Matt."

"You're thinking about the slavers? They were sending people across the seaway, so it wouldn't be much of a stretch for them to start raiding us."

"That's it. We've got almost everything we need except mineral deposits, but we're going to be in the slavers' back yard."

"Let's look at the canyon when we get there. Did you go north, or only south from the crossing?"

"We only went south. The land looked better down that way and up north, where it narrowed a little, the high-water mark was farther up the slopes. Flash floods up that way could be a problem. Water from the mountains could wipe out anything we build or plant on the canyon floor."

"Let's think of it as a winter camp for now. If it's as good as you say, we might stay there next year. How wide is the river?"

"Three hundred yards at least. There are small islands and the channels between are deep enough that the horses had to swim."

"If it's deep enough, we can use the river to trade. Boats can carry a lot of cargo and if the river's not too fast, we can move goods upstream too.

"The original cliff dwellers remained hidden and eventually they either died out or were overwhelmed, so I don't think we can afford to remain isolated. We'll need to trade for what we can't make for ourselves."

"We're also too few to do more than make it expensive for the slavers. If we want to stay in this country, we've got to become too strong for them. That means we need to contact others and recruit good people. There are still villages back east of here, probably north and west too. But wherever they are, we need to make peaceful contact and band together to stop the raiding. Of course, they may not be peaceful, so we'll need to stay ready. The next time, our enemies may have bows. Sooner or later they will."

"Horses too, Matt?"

"Sooner or later; bows and horses are a technological advantage on this world. As soon as one group has an advantage, the others will start working on it. We may not be able to keep ahead of them, so we'll have to train more and organize better."

Matt thought for a few moments, then continued.

"We know where the others are in a general sense. That's an advantage. It might last for a year or two before the slaveholders find us. But we can't coexist with people who depend on new captives. Whether they're keeping slaves or serfs doesn't matter. They're always going to look north, so we'll have to fight."

Lee looked at Laz and nodded.

"Can't we go on, Matt? Just stay away from them?"

"That might work for a while, but if the slavers are allowed to grow without opposition, they'll just keep getting stronger every year. If they enslave our youngsters, we'll get weaker every year. Someday we won't be able to defend ourselves. Our best bet is to keep out of sight and make sure that when they *do* find us, we're too tough a nut for them to crack. I want them to fear us for as long as possible, that's why I had the heads cut off.

"It won't work forever, of course. Sooner or later they'll either get brave or desperate, but if we can hold them south of the seaway for ten or twenty years, we'll be well on our way to developing a real civilization. That's what I'm hoping, anyway. Sandra is going to have a baby this winter..." Matt paused; he'd almost revealed a secret that wasn't his to tell..."and there will be others too. We have to think about the children."

Both men nodded soberly.

"I'm going to get some sleep. Let me know if Sal's going. Anyone else?" asked Lee.

"I'll see. Those two engineers might go. I need to talk to them. I know what I want to build, but whether they can help, I don't know."

* * *

COLIN AND MATT watched next morning as Lee led his little cavalcade southwest. Sal, his helpers, and the two engineers walked behind, pulling a cart loaded with tools.

Others would take a turn at noon, and they would in turn be relieved during the afternoon. Lee intended to set a fast pace; there was much to do before the tribe arrived.

Lee was the only one mounted, but other than that an observer would have found it difficult to separate the men into old hands or new arrivals who'd joined the group only a month before. All now wore buckskin clothing and carried ready bows. Every man had a spear and a quiver filled with arrows. If there was a difference, it was in the ease with which the veterans moved. In time, the others would soon develop the same loose, nearly-silent gait.

They made camp just before dark and Lee built a small fire. Gingerly he placed a pottery bowl nearby and men began gnawing on dried buffalo jerky. Sal poured water from a container on the cart and added a mix of herbs that Margrette had provided.

Soon the savory smell of rose hips, mint, and sage rose from the hot water. Each man took a little and added honey to his taste. The last man added more water so that everyone could have as much of the tea as they desired.

Tired men bedded down as soon as Lee extinguished the fire. Breakfast would be cold jerky on slabs of bread, washed down with water. The bread consisted of a mix of ground grain and nuts, a combination Sandra had developed. It was enough.

Lee kept watch until shortly before midnight, then woke Sal. Piotr had attached himself to the party at the last minute; Sal woke him to take the final shift before dawn. The rest were roused before the sun peeked above the horizon.

Half an hour later the march resumed.

Lee bent the course slightly north at noon that day.

"I'm going to hit the canyon a little north of where we were before. That way, we can head south and be sure of finding it instead of having to search back and forth. I expect to spend tonight on top of the canyon rim and reach the undercut cliff by noon tomorrow. I don't want to spend our first night down in the canyon; we'd have to double up or triple-up on guards as soon as it got dark. Not just because of predators; if the big animals move around after dark, they could run right through our camp. We've done that once, rebuilt after a stampede; next time, we might not be lucky."

"I'm on your side, Lee. Better safe than sorry."

"That's my idea, Sal. Anyway, when we get there we can set up camp someplace where we can live until the rest get here. Pick somebody to do the cooking and tend the fire, probably rotate the duty every day. I won't move into the cave until Matt's looked at it, but we might build a rock fence next to the cliff. I'll hunt in the morning, sleep in the afternoon after I get back, and that way I'll be ready to keep watch during the night. With the fence, we won't need other guards. I can keep that up until the tribe gets here."

* * *

"WHAT WAS in that packet the futurist gave you, Matt?"

"I don't know, Colin. I haven't opened it yet."

"Aren't you curious, Matt?"

"I am, and I'm not. It's strange, but I'm wondering if I want to open it."

Colin looked at Matt in surprise. "Why wouldn't you, Matt?"

"I've been thinking, Colin. We're in North America, right?"

"I guess so. It doesn't look like Europe."

"Say it's North America for the sake of argument. What do you know about American history?"

"Not a lot. There were natives, but when Europeans got ashore they pushed the locals out of the way. Somebody was always fighting somebody. If they weren't fighting Europeans they fought each other."

"That's part of it. European attitudes took over. Other things too, things like raising sheep and cattle and donkeys. Those came to Europe from the Middle East. Europe had a kind of wild cow, but it was wiped out when the new breeds took over. My point is that instead of developing their own way of doing things, Europe and the Americas just adopted what people had done elsewhere. I'm not explaining this very well, but I'm thinking that if we start from scratch and build our own civilization we might be able to avoid the mistakes they made on Earth Prime.

"Take my own time. Too many of my people were fat and they had horrible diseases. There were few *real* dangers, so people pretended. Instead of people living longer because they'd eliminated danger, they died of disease.

"We had arguments about death. Should people be kept alive, or should doctors help them die when there was no reason to stay alive? Our *pets* got better treatment most of the time. What I'm wondering is, do we want to build that world over again? Do we want to develop the same kind of civilization, build the same kinds of roads and machines and science, or should we develop our own? I don't know."

Colin nodded. "I never thought of it that way, but you've got a point. Here, it's just a matter of time. One day, we'll be too slow or too unlucky. If a dire wolf or short-faced bear doesn't kill us, somebody with a spear will. I think if someone had told me downtime what this world was like, I'd have been afraid of it. Here, it just is. If you let down your guard you're going to die."

"That's it. I don't know if I want to open that package. That Chief fellow was trying to help, but do we *want* his help? Or should we just muddle along and make our own mistakes? Maybe our science won't kill off most of humanity. Maybe we won't *have* a world that threatens to kill us because it's getting too hot."

The two sat for a long time, that evening. Neither felt like speaking as they thought about what Matt had said.

38

"I suppose I should open the package. It might be something we all need. I don't think I can decide on my own that we shouldn't have it."

"You're right, Matt. Besides, I'm curious."

Matt carefully untied the tape. Inside the canvas, he found a smaller package and a plastic box. The box had an embossed red cross inside a white circle.

"This is an emergency first aid kit. It looks like something aircrews would use if they were forced down a long way from help. This other packet," he unwrapped the second canvas roll, "is an emergency surgery kit. I guess they figured the crew might need more stuff; there's certainly no way they could get help immediately. I got the impression from Chief that the aircraft we saw is the only one on-planet. He said fuel was expensive, so I think there's not a lot of it available.

"That's a small bone saw and a packet of blades for a scalpel. The injectors contain morphine according to the label. I wonder if they have an expiration date?"

"Does morphine lose effectiveness, Matt?"

"No idea, Colin, but I don't see an expiration date. What's in the box?"

"Bandages, surgical tape, what looks like first-aid dressings. This one is a tube for the airway. I wish we'd had this when Robert was wounded!"

"Yeah, I know what you mean. Those sealed packages there, what are they?"

"Both are labeled 'Powder, Antiseptic'. Whatever that means."

"Maybe they're like the sulfa powders of the mid-20th century. Just sprinkle them on a wound. Anyway, this whole package goes to Elizabeth."

"No second thoughts, Matt? About using downtime technology?"

"No. We need this; I'd take a hundred of these if they were offered."

"I agree. Well, I'm off to bed; see you tomorrow morning. We've had a long trip. I am glad it's coming to an end, at least for this year."

"If Lee's description was right, maybe we're done period. I won't mind settling down. Keeping the tribe protected has been wearing. I want a few months of just settling down and relaxing, with nothing to do but keep from starving!"

Colin chuckled. "I sympathize, Matt. Somebody else can do the butchering and cooking too!"

The two men walked off to their beds. Behind them, Margrette and her helpers cleaned pots. Packing them on the carts, they soon were able to seek their own beds. The abandoned coals glowed for a time, then faded.

Soon the only sounds came from the sentries who kept watch through the night.

* * *

Lee paused on a small promontory and looked down the canyon.

The advance party had crossed the river after descending the animal trail Lee and Laz had found. Tramping south, they'd come some ten miles and the undercut canyon wall lay just ahead. The two engineers came up; they wanted their own look at the site.

"Is Matt set on building up in that cave?"

"Why do you ask?"

"It's going to be tough, building up there. We can build walls up there if he's set on the idea, but it would be easier to build houses down here. If we did it right, it would be easy enough to defend. Say we enclose a courtyard and build the houses of rock and adobe. We passed deposits of clay along the river, and I know how people used it to build. They mixed in a little sand with natural fiber, then molded it into huge bricks. They made the bricks for the bottom thick, with thinner bricks higher up. The courtyard is for horses and any other animals we catch. We might build the houses so that people lived on the second floor and the lower floor was storage. Adobe walls are warm in the winter, cool in the summer. We could easily build in defenses while the houses were going up. What do you think, Bill?"

"Build the lower structures first and people could live in those while we build the upper section? We'll need timbers for framing and some kind of hoist."

"Maybe a tripod hoist..."

Lee left the two to discuss what they had in mind. Matt could accept their ideas, or reject them in favor of his own. Meantime, there was a camp to be laid out.

That night they relaxed around a large campfire while enjoying fresh buffalo meat on slabs of bread, the whole washed down with tea. A tall brush fence surrounded the campsite. It might be a little smaller than Matt had in mind, but it wouldn't be much of a chore to enlarge it. In any case, they had made a good start.

A pride of saber-toothed cats looked prone to argue after Lee killed the buffalo, but eventually they'd left, growls showing their displeasure. Well, they'd get over it. Even so, the half-dozen cats had given him a few moments of uneasiness. It might be necessary to thin out their number after the others arrived.

* * *

THE TRIBE FOUND the camp late on the third day. Lee was sleeping, but he'd left instructions to wake him when Matt reached camp. Yawning, he joined Matt and Colin. Sal joined the small party too, as did Bert and Will, the engineers.

"Glad you're here. We wanted to talk to you first, but if you like what we've got in mind we can start building tomorrow."

Matt was clearly tired, but he found a seat near the campfire and accepted a mug of the honeyed tea as they explained their concept.

"Got a question. Suppose you used large blocks of limestone instead of adobe? Maybe use adobe for mortar? Would that work?"

The two looked at each other.

"We'd have to try it first. It might be tough to chip those limestone blocks to size, but if we used mortar, we wouldn't need to smooth the blocks much. Too bad we don't have coal."

"Why coal?"

"We could make cement, use that instead of adobe. It's permanent. Adobe will wash out and have to be repaired or replaced every year or two. We could use charcoal, but coal would be better. You make the raw material by heating limestone to between nine hundred and a thousand degrees."

"Wouldn't it work better if you heated it more? Coal can melt iron and that takes place around eighteen-hundred or nineteen-hundred degrees."

"That won't work. You'll burn the lime. Temperature control is important."

"Well, we've got no shortage of stuff to practice on. I don't know if it's coal, but I spotted a thin black layer back near the crossing. Could you tell if it was coal by looking?"

"Probably. Maybe a day to go back there and look?"

"I'd have to send a couple of guys with you. But maybe in a couple of days, after we get started on building shelters. I want at least basic shelters underway as soon as possible."

"Makes sense. We don't know how much time we have. What do you think about building houses with storage on the ground level and living quarters above?"

"How much time to build these palaces you've got in mind?"

"Not palaces, Matt. I figure we build basic walls around a courtyard. Do you know how many buildings you have in mind?"

"Probably one for each family unit. Colin would get one, I'd want one, probably Piotr and Lee and Laz too. Maybe one for bachelor men and one for bachelor women? Or build a house for everybody and let the people sort out who lives where?"

"That would be best in the long run. Are you looking at winter quarters or a permanent town?"

"How about winter quarters we can develop into permanent houses? Can you do that?"

"Sure. Even if we have to use adobe for mortar, we can do that. We could coat the joints with lime mortar later after we start producing it."

"If you can make Roman-style cement and concrete, we can build anything we want. Aqueducts to bring water into the town, sewers to take waste away, concrete septic tanks and pipes to carry off the waste water...don't smile, sanitation is important. We're going to be exposed to diseases. I'd rather plan now than have to bury people later."

"We don't have time to lay out sewers or septic systems if we're going to get all those houses built before winter, Matt. That's a project for next year."

"OK, but leave room to put them in later. Think about where you'd pick up water for an aqueduct too. Maybe one of the springs up the canyon wall?"

"We could do that. It would keep some enemy from damming up the river if we used that for our water source. Sure, springs could be done. But for now, we'll put in outhouses. They work, not too appealing especially on hot summer days or cold winter evenings, but we could do it."

"Go to it. We also need to begin gathering food, not too many needed for that because the game's so close. Lilia and Margrette will be drying meat for winter, so they'll be busy. But you have Sal's crew for building and I'm sure there will be others. Don't take too many people off the job of building to start experimenting. Just get us something that protects from weather and that we can defend."

"Priorities understood. C'mon, Bert, we've got our marching orders."

The two headed for the cliff side, the location where they intended to build.

* * *

"Lee, I can take security tonight. You've been working pretty hard."

"Not that bad, Matt. I've been using Brownie to haul the cart. All I had to do was go out, find a good stand and take the shot. Most of the time I only needed one. I've broken a couple of arrows, but I've still got most of a quiver in reserve. I brought it on the cart when we went ahead of you and the others."

"In that case, *I'll* take a break. I can take over tomorrow. I'll need you and Brownie to scout farther downstream, see what's down there. Look for human tracks. If someone from across the seaway has been here, we need to know."

"I'll get an early start, Matt. OK if I take Laz with me?"

"Absolutely. I prefer we work in pairs, I'll have Piotr with me tomorrow. Maybe Colin too, he wants a little time away from the kitchen so I'll see if Lilia can take over. Elizabeth's pleased with the new surgical tools and the medical supplies. They're better than anything we had and she's already taught Bella how to use them.

"We'll set them up a clinic building somewhere near the town center. I'd still like to get more information written down. Elizabeth started listing things she believes have medicinal properties on some of the light-colored deerskins as soon as we had extra."

"Matt, we've been collecting buffalo skins. I had them staked out on the hillside just north of the town site. We'll have all the hides we need by the time snow flies."

Matt nodded. "Good start, Lee. As soon as they're scraped and dry, we'll stack them inside the buildings. I don't want to be caught short when the weather turns cold. Whatever we don't use can be stored; eventually we'll turn it into leather or trade it if we can find people who have something we need."

"You're still thinking of the river for trade?"

"I am. Look for rapids or falls, shallow areas too; if there's not much water, we'll have to offload cargo and portage around the low spot. Same thing with a waterfall or rapids. Low water is usually more dangerous than high water. Anyway, you scout downstream and when you get back, I'll take a ride upstream. Or maybe I'll just take Lilia and we can hike up the canyon. It's been a while since we had the chance to do some exploring. We could use some time off too."

"Sure, Matt. I'll talk to Laz and we'll head out before daybreak. I think we'll reach the sea within a day's travel. A day downstream, look around for a while, come straight back. Two days, maybe a little longer."

Matt nodded and Lee walked away.

Lee had grown into a very confident young man, experienced and equipped to survive on this unforgiving world. Laz was almost his equal. The two were truly an asset to the tribe. Matt turned away. He had other arrangements to make.

39

Laz and Lee rode south at daybreak, taking weapons and food for two days.

Will and Bert explained what they had in mind. They seemed to know what they were doing, so Matt, Colin, and Sal listened.

"We're going to need timbers and more adobe eventually, but we've got enough material to get started right here. There's plenty of limestone, and the blocks are small enough to work with. We'll begin with a foundation, dig it in deep enough so it won't heave if there's more frost than we expect. After that, join the foundations together so that the houses form a long outer wall. We'll use large limestone blocks for the foundation and the lower wall, so we may not need to mortar them in place. We don't want adobe or wood to be touching the ground; adobe will soften if there's moisture in contact with it and wood will rot.

"The adobe will be okay to seal the living quarters. If a few breezes get into the storage area it won't be a problem. There are dry-stacked stone structures in Ireland and the American Southwest that used no mortar and they're still standing after hundreds of years. It's more work, selecting just the right stone, but the structure will last just as long.

"We may fill in cracks with concrete mortar s later on, always assuming we can heat limestone to make quicklime. Anyway, we'll build three sides of a square. The houses will face toward the cliff. They'll share sidewalls with the house next door. You can put in pass-through fireplaces for now, but we'll probably close them off as soon as we finish the second floor living quarters. Those will overhang the outside walls by about two feet for defensive purposes. The only openings will face into the square. Using the cliff for part of the wall means we'll need fewer people to defend the wall.

"Once we build the redoubt...that's what we're calling it...into the cliff hollow, we can use ladders for defense. If we ever need to abandon the houses, we go up the ladders and pull them up behind us. As long as we hold the redoubt, we'll have the high ground and it will take an army to break in.

"We'll build granaries up there for storage, maybe even divert one of the springs so the redoubt will have water and a way to dispose of waste. But before they lay siege, any attacker had better bring his lunch. It's not going to be easy to get into the square, and until they do there won't be an entrance to any of the houses. The houses are like a castle in a way, but designed to kill slavers instead of defeating an army. There's no reason for an invasion, so we should be safe for a century."

Bert chimed in, "We figure to use heavy timbers to roof over the storage areas. That will be the floor for the second story living areas and we plan to fortify that too. Loopholes, murder holes in the over-hang, loopholes facing the square in case someone does manage to break in, maybe even Roman-style siege artillery. Ballistae would work."

"Ballistae are big crossbows that throw spears, right?"

"Right, Matt. We wondered if you wanted portable ones too?"

"Portable ones?"

"Sure. Maybe we could take a mammoth or two after winter gets here. Lot of meat on a mammoth. It would be safer killing a buffalo, too. Some of those big bulls go more than a ton. We talked about it and I wouldn't be surprised if they weigh in at three thousand pounds. Not that we've got anything to weigh one, of course."

"Of course." Matt grinned at them. "Keep it in mind. For now, let's get shelters built. I like the ideas you've come up with, if for no other reason than because it's close to what I had in mind. Plan on building hornos for the women; they're Pueblo-style ovens. Sandra and Millie can tell you how they're built if you don't already know. It would be a good idea to get their input anyway, before you build anything. Show them where the houses will go and let them pick locations for the hornos."

"Furnace on the bottom, front load, rear exhaust, oven space on top of the furnace?"

"That's it, but like I said, get their input first. They might want to build them bigger or smaller. And for sure they'll be pissed if you put them somewhere they don't like."

"Can do. We'll talk to Sal and his men. But first, build at least emergency-level shelters and expand those."

"You've got it. I'm taking a day off and Piotr's going with me. We'll bring in a buffalo or two for meat."

"Have fun, Matt. C'mon, Will, we've got work to do. Jawin' ain't gettin' the town built!"

Matt and Piotr walked east until they reached the river. There were a few tracks, none fresh, so the two turned left and went north. Matt was leading his horse, as yet unnamed, hitched to a cart. Piotr followed some twenty-five yards ahead. If the horse was restive, well...she'd soon get used to pulling the cart.

Matt's spear and bow were slung across his back and the quiver hung at his belt. Jerked meat and water were on the cart, but hopefully they'd not be needed. Still, best to be prepared; sooner or later the animals would become alarmed and avoid the place where the noise was coming from.

Matt looked at bends and watched for possible hazards in the river. Only the occasional stump, carried down during past floods, might be a problem. Islands diverted some of the water flow, but that didn't appear to be a problem. So far, the river looked to be a feasible avenue for shipping goods.

They found no game along the river and Matt considered following the animal trail to the top of the canyon. There were certain to be buffalo up there, but climbing the track, then descending with the horse pulling a loaded cart didn't appeal to him. The previous descent had been hard enough; they'd needed restraining ropes to keep the carts from overrunning the people ahead. With only the two of them, one would have to control the horse from the front and that left only one to check the descent. Not to mention that the horse was barely broke and might panic. He decided to continue upstream.

Piotr found tracks two miles north of the ford that led into a branch canyon. A dozen buffalo were grazing along the grassy bottom; the tracks had been made when they left the canyon to drink.

Matt tied the lead rope loosely to a tree near the entrance, leaving slack so the mare could graze. Carrying his bow and quiver, the two walked silently up the canyon. Piotr spotted a location where they could take at least one and possibly two of the buffalo before the animals became alarmed.

Selecting a young bull, Piotr looked at Matt to indicate which target he had in mind. Matt nodded and picked his own target, a cow that appeared to be in good condition. Bow ready, he waited for Piotr to take the first shot. At the twang of his bowstring, Matt released his own arrow. Drawing another, he waited to see if it might be needed.

Piotr's young bull had fallen. Matt's cow had taken a step and raised her head, so he launched his second arrow. Passing just beneath her muzzle, the arrow struck between the forelegs and punched into the animal's chest, slicing through the heart. The cow tiredly slipped to her knees, then rolled over. The other animals grazed away, seemingly unconcerned.

Matt's third arrow, drawn automatically as soon as he'd loosed the second one, was unneeded but he kept it in position for safety while he and Piotr approached the animals.

Field-dressing, skinning, and quartering the carcasses took some three hours. The horse was fractious, either from the smell of blood or from what she could hear and smell off in the dusk, but they finally got the meat loaded, the skins protecting it from dirt and flies. As a result, they reached camp some two hours after sunset.

Lilia took charge of the meat while Matt led his horse to water, then picketed her where she could graze. Piotr parked the empty cart with others along the cliff. Returning, he rejoined Matt. The two ate a simple supper before heading to their beds.

* * *

MATT WATCHED the grazing horse the next morning and noticed how she barely avoided becoming entangled in the picket line. It might be possible to allow her to graze loose later on, but for now she was showing clear signs of wanting the companionship of other horses. She often stood and looked off toward the canyon rim before returning to graze.

He led her to water and picketed her in a new location on fresh grass, then went to have his own breakfast

Finished, Matt helped dig the ditch where the foundation stones would be laid. Other men, supervised and aided by the two engineers, began laying stones even as the digging chore progressed.

There was no sign of Lee or Laz, but Matt thought nothing of it. The two would return when they'd finished surveying the river.

The foundation was complete by the end of the following day and construction of the outer wall had begun. Once the square was fully enclosed except for a gate, the tribe would have a secure encampment behind stout walls.

Lee and Laz had still not returned by evening of the fourth day and Matt was concerned. They should have come back by now. Riding the horses without a break for that long wasn't a good idea, lest they develop sores and possibly even lameness.

Matt brought the subject up to Lilia that afternoon.

"I'm heading south tomorrow. Lee should have been back by now."

"I was planning on going if you hadn't said anything. We can leave tomorrow."

"I was planning on taking Piotr, Lilia."

"Matt, that's my son out there. I'm coming too."

"OK. We'll leave at dawn. It might be well to take Marc too. If they're injured we'll need extra hands to bring them home."

"I'll be ready, Matt."

* * *

MATT LED the small party south the following morning. Lilia followed immediately behind him and Marc brought up the rear with Piotr. All carried arrows ready on bowstrings; if Laz and Lee had run into trouble, it was necessary their rescuers be prepared.

Late that afternoon Piotr, sharp-eyed as always, spotted a large rusty stain on the sand. Calling Matt's attention to it, he took up a guard position with Marc while Matt and Lilia studied the blotch.

"Bloodstain. Two days old, maybe more. Horse tracks, and from the looks of them something happened here. The tracks are confused, but the horses might have been running. What do you think?"

"Lot of blood, Matt. Maybe one of the horses was wounded? The tracks lead off west and the horse was definitely running. There are more stains by the tracks too."

"Let's have a look up that branch. The horse might have gone there."

The four followed the tracks, now spread out. Half a mile ahead they found a dead horse.

"That's Lee's Brownie. Been dead at least two days. Something's been feeding on it."

"Matt, that's a bear track, big one, too. The other tracks are cat. Could be lion, could be saber-tooth. Think they killed Brownie?"

"No." Matt's voice was grim. "Look at the neck, just behind the head."

"Arrow, Matt. That's not one of Lee's and I don't think it's one of Laz's either."

"It's not. It's not one of your arrows, is it Piotr?"

"I never made a nock like that, Matt. Looks crude."

"Crude it might be, but it worked. Somebody else has a bow and arrows, fairly strong one too; that arrow's deep. Let's see if we can get it out."

Fifteen minutes later Matt was examining the arrow.

"Steel arrowhead, locally forged. What do you think?"

"Doesn't look like anything we've made. We had only salvaged steel to work with. This looks different. I think it's locally produced."

"I think you're right, Piotr."

Lilia and Marc had scouted the location and had gone downstream half a mile. Matt looked after them. The two had stopped to examine something on the ground but were now returning.

"What did you find, Lilia?"

"No horse tracks, Matt. No idea what happened to Laz's horse, but I found moccasin tracks from at least a half dozen men. Two were either big men or they were carrying heavy loads. I think the slavers are back, and I think they've got Lee and Laz."

"Let's see where they've gone before we decide what to do."

Two hours later Matt, following the river, left the canyon's mouth. Ahead lay the seaway.

"Look at this."

A shallow trench led from the water up the shore. "Somebody beached a boat here. Tracks all around, more than six men would have left. So somebody was left on guard while a detachment went upriver. At a guess, they found Lee and Laz and shot Lee's horse. They got Laz too, otherwise he'd have come back to warn us. If they killed him we'd have found the body.

"We can only hope they're slaves. It's too late to stop the raiders, but I'm going after them. I won't leave Lee or Laz in their hands."

"Matt, it's going to be dangerous. They've got bows and arrows now, and they've begun smelting iron. Their arrows have metal points."

"Doesn't matter. A flint or obsidian arrowhead can kill a man just as dead. We've used them to kill buffalo, bears too, and anything that kills one of those big bears will kill a slaver. Putting the arrow into him is what counts, not what the arrowhead is made of.

"I figure two weeks at most before I'll be ready. I'll want a small party, no more than four men. We'll go on foot, hide during the day, travel by night. I'm tired of waiting.

"I'm going to take the fight to them."

The adventure continues in Darwin's World Book III, Home.

AN EXCERPT FOLLOWS.

40

"I don't see anyone, Matt. How about we steer for that little cove?" Piotr asked.

"Go ahead. We'll drag the boat up on shore and hide it; if it cracks, it cracks. We can patch it again or just steal another one. We took this one, we can do it again."

"Sounds good, Matt. You want to go in now or wait until dark?"

"We go in now. We're in one of their boats, so if anyone's watching they won't be suspicious. If we waited offshore until dark, they'd wonder why we didn't land."

The boat, driven by the paddles, glided smoothly into the sheltered water of the cove. The beach was a gentle slope, mixed sand, pebbles, and shell. A small overgrown gully offered concealment.

The men dragged the boat into the gully, turned it upside down, then covered it with branches. Moving up the slope, they concealed themselves to watch the beach and wait for dusk.

* * *

PLANNING HAD BEGUN the week before.

Five people, buckskin-clad, gazed south across the seaway. They appeared to be in their early twenties, but looks were deceiving; all had undergone the Futurists treatments before being transplanted. Aging bodies had been rejuvenated, their memories retained and augmented. None showed signs of further aging. Even scars, the result of living in harsh conditions, vanished after a short time.

"We're never going to keep those bastards away if all we do is respond. They've got to learn there are consequences." The speaker was tall, dark-haired, and armed with bow and spear.

"I agree, Matt. But they've got more people. Their weapons are as good as ours, maybe better."

"Even so, if we don't act they'll keep taking people. As for numbers, there are probably more of them but I'm guessing only a few hundred. Otherwise, wouldn't the raids be bigger?"

"What if they're also raiding south, Matt? Or maybe further to the west?" asked Sal.

"They're not capturing many people, less than a hundred slaves during the course of a year. There just aren't many people here. Maybe slavery is only a sideline, a part of what they're doing down there."

"Matt, I'm not sure I understand. I guess if you know, the rest of us can just go along for the time being."

"We have to go soon. They could be taking Laz and Lee farther south right now. It's a hard choice. We can't mount a rescue without hurting our own chances for survival, not yet. We have to finish building winter shelters and gather food. Not much time before the first snow and we're also short of manpower.

Matt's tone was bitter. "They picked the right time, probably why they prefer to raid in late summer and early fall. They're not slaveholders; farmers and miners can't leave slaves unguarded. Besides, who would make sure the crops got tended? The ones that grabbed Lee and Laz are middlemen, captors who sell the ones they catch. Anyway, that's what I think.

"I'll take a small patrol and spend a couple of days sneaking around. With luck, the farms won't be far inland, but I'll go into the interior if I have to. It's too much to hope we'll find Lee and Laz as soon as we get over there."

"You're just looking, Matt?" Piotr asked.

"For now. Think you might be up for a little walk in the woods?"

"Sure, Matt; it beats sitting around and chipping stone. When do you plan to leave?"

"As soon as I've got enough people. Five should be enough, six is too many. If we take more, the odds of being discovered go up. I don't want them to know we're coming."

"I want to go too, Matt." Lilia wiped a tear from her face.

"Not this time. I can be risked, but if you're in danger so is our baby. No, you help Colin. Get the village built and see to stocking it with food. We'll need furs and firewood as well as meat, plus whatever vegetables you can gather."

Lilia reluctantly nodded agreement.

"How are you going to conduct the scout, Matt?" asked Piotr.

"Move after dark, hide during the day. With five people, there's enough for two pairs, one watching while the other sleeps, and I'm the spare. We'll only stay three or four days, a week at most. I'm not intending to fight, not yet; I'd rather get Laz and Lee back first. Then teach the slaveholders they've got something to lose. I'll burn them out, destroy everything I can and hit them where it hurts, in their wallet. If we can free other slaves, great, but the priority is to get our guys back. Chopping out the slavery cancer might have to be left until later."

The others nodded, then left to go about their business. Lilia remained behind.

"What about our people, Matt?"

"I've got you and Colin to look after them, Lilia. The engineers too, they'll be working with Sal and his crew to get shelters built. For that matter, everyone will have to pitch in. With luck, the houses will be up and the walls finished by the time I find Laz and Lee. No idea how long it will take; I can't just amble up to the slavers and ask them nicely to return our people. At the same time, I won't be able to operate after first snow. We'll leave too many tracks. So that gives me a month or two, probably not more than that."

"You're sure you can do this, Matt?"

"I have to try. He's my son even though he had a different father. We fought together, risked our lives for each other. Laz too. I'll bring them out or die in the attempt."

"Don't talk like that, Matt. I depend on you, we all do. You're the heart of the village. The buildings are just buildings, they need people to make them into a town. That means we need you."

Lilia paused for a moment. "It's not easy to say, but if the choice is rescuing Lee or coming back alive, leave him. He might escape anyway. He's very resourceful, in part because you taught him, but I can't lose you. Our child can't lose you. We need you."

"I'll keep it in mind, Lilia."

Matt left to find Marc and Michel.

"I need you two to find that boat, the one we hid after we wiped out that raiding party. I'll get the other guys together and we'll meet you when you get back."

"We should be ready to go as soon as we've got trail rations."

"Thanks, Michel. We'll be waiting when you get back."

* * *

MARC AND MICHEL paddled wearily up the river, late on the afternoon of the second day. They rested, leaning on the thwarts, while Matt, Piotr, and Santiago dragged the boat up on the beach.

"Took longer than we expected, Matt. We found it where we left it, but the bottom had dried out. A long split had opened up. We punched holes and laced the crack together; I sealed it with pine rosin, the ties too. After a while, it stopped leaking. I think it swelled and caused the crack to close up. I tightened the laces before we left this morning, and only a few drops have leaked in since."

"Good work. Get something to eat and rest. We'll be ready to go in another two days, three at the most."

* * *

MATT CALLED the four men together at dawn.

"We'll take our spears, bows, and a dozen arrows. Carry your belt emergency kit. Pack a spare bowstring, two water gourds, and dried meat for four days. Lilia has dried fruit so take some of that too. No sleeping furs, we'll huddle together if we need to. We'll travel after dark so moving will help us stay warm.

"Questions or suggestions?"

"Knives and hatchets too, Matt?" asked Santiago.

"Right, but tie them in place so they don't bang against anything. We'll carry the bows unstrung. If we're hit in the first few minutes, we won't have a chance to use them. Spears work better in close anyway.

"One pair sleeps during the morning, one sleeps in the afternoon, and we stick to the schedule until we get back. We'll probably be short of sleep, but if someone's too sleepy I'll take his place. We should be able to get ashore, sneak and peek, look for a place to land a raiding force. If we do it right, nobody will know we were there. Find out as much as can, then it's back to the beach and head for home. We have to know *where* they are, *how many*, and whether there's a lot of movement. We need to know about roads, obstacles, anything that will hinder us later on.

"Piotr takes over for me if necessary. If we're discovered, evade. If we can't remain together, try to escape in pairs. If you get separated, go back to the beach and wait by the boat. Wait long enough to see if anyone else got away, then move the boat offshore. You can watch for a day or two, see if anyone else gets away, but the priority is to get information back.

"Today, we'll practice setting up a typical hide. I'll show you how to keep watch, then we'll walk through patrolling while it's still daylight. Tonight, we rehearse moving after dark. Collect supplies tomorrow, get a good night's sleep, and cross the seaway the next day.

"Let's get to it."

Two days later, they crossed the seaway.

* * *

THE SLOW MINUTES passed as they crouched in screening brush, only a hundred yards from where they'd concealed the boat. Wavelets lapped on the shore, a light breeze stirred the sparse grass. They waited, silent, listening, as the sun sank behind the western mountains.

Matt decided it was dark enough to move. Motioning to the others, he soundlessly made his way toward the line of trees south of the beach.

The men were all experienced woodsmen; moving silently was an ingrained habit. Matt scouted ahead, setting the pace; Santiago came next, carrying the knotted end of a woven cord. Other knots had been tied, five feet apart. Marc held the first, Michel the second, and Piotr held the coiled end. Santiago had wondered at the extra length. Matt showed how the patrol, despite the darkness, would remain together yet far enough apart to keep from blundering into each other.

"Shouldn't we cut off the excess, Matt?"

"We're looking for information. Not only what to expect on the ground, but enemy forces, weapons, training, how alert they are, things like that. We explore the terrain first, maybe snatch somebody. That's what the extra rope is for. We might even find Laz and Lee."

Walking was easy; the ground was even, only a slight slope leading up from the shore. There were few bushes beneath the trees. Shallow creeks slowed their pace, but otherwise presented few difficulties. Their wet buckskins were uncomfortable, but soon dried.

Matt estimated they'd traveled at least a mile when they came upon a well-traveled path leading south.

* * *

DAYS WERE SHORTER NOW, leaves changing color. Summer had begun to give way to fall. The icecap was gone, the warm, green lowlands home to wildlife. Glaciers plugged the upper valleys between peaks, shaping the mountains. In time they too would vanish, victims of advancing warmth.

The massive glacier had been retreating for centuries. Snow fell from time to time, turned to ice, and joined what was already there; the ice mass complained, cracking and grinding as it pushed down the valley.

A block of ice cracked off, eventually falling onto boulders left by the melting face of the glacier. It became trapped and for a time joined the growing terminal moraine. Meltwater from beneath the glacier backed up behind the ice dam and formed a small lake at the base of the glacier.

Loud noises sounded from deep within the ice. Rumblings were followed by an explosive crack, then another as a fissure opened across the front of the glacier. Alarmed birds flew away. If this one was wider than others, the block of ice larger, such is the way of glaciers. Ice always pushed on until blocks calved off.

Behind the block, freed meltwater swelled the pool. Inquisitive birds looked for food near the edge, but found nothing and soon flew downstream. Small fish swam where the cold meltwater flowed into a small creek. The birds landed and began wading near the banks.

Quiet returned. The meltwater pool behind the ice dam grew larger.

41

"Wait here. I'll take a close look at that trail." Matt whispered. Piotr nodded, then turned back to pass the message along.

Matt returned a few minutes later. Gathering the patrol around him, he whispered, "The only recent tracks go south. They were probably made by raiders; there's nothing else up here. No village, no farms, they only come up here when they're raiding. The tracks weren't new, so there's probably not much traffic. Still, there's a chance someone could spot us. The trail leads where we want to go, so we'll follow it. It's too dangerous to walk on the trail, so we'll stay off to the side. We should be able to see anyone on the trail before they see us. Comments or questions?"

No one spoke, so Matt resumed, "We'll eat now. If you need to crap, do it off to the side and cover it up. Don't make it easy for them to find.

"Michel, you're lead when we move out. Piotr, you're second, I'll be third. Fifteen minutes, people."

* * *

THE HALF-MOON PROVIDED LIGHT; Piotr had no trouble seeing Michel when he stopped suddenly, hand up in warning.

Piotr whispered, "Matt, Michel's found something."

"Wait here. I'll see what's going on."

Matt crept up to where Michel waited.

"What have you got?"

"Looks to me like a skeleton, up ahead of us. I wanted you to know before I went any closer."

"Good call. I'll bring up the others, but we don't want to make a lot of tracks around it."

"Understood, Matt."

The skeleton appeared to be complete. A large ant's nest was nearby; the industrious insects had picked the bones clean. He picked up a femur and hefted it, thinking.

"Piotr, feel the weight. If the bones had been here long, this one would be lighter."

Piotr examined the bone. "You're right, Matt. I figure at least a month but less than a year."

"A month, maybe even two, so it's not Laz or Lee. It wouldn't matter anyway, we keep going."

The others nodded.

Marc whispered, "Should we do anything, maybe bury the bones?"

"We can't," Matt said. "They might find the grave and wonder who dug it.

"Anyway, it's time to swap scouts. Piotr, you're lead, I'll be behind you, Michel's tail-end Charlie."

* * *

THEY CROSSED A STREAM, refilling their water bottles before taking a short break. The trail remained deserted.

Matt, leading again, found a brushy covert where they could wait for darkness. They moved in and made themselves as comfortable as possible. Dawn found three already asleep while the remaining two kept watch.

The watchers woke the sleepers at noon. The men ate jerky and drank from their water bottles. New sentries took over, the others slept. There was no traffic on the trail.

"I think we can use the trail. Nobody's stirring, and even when they do walk the trail, they probably only do it in daylight. Any objections?"

The men remained silent. The decision was made.

The men moved onto the trail at dusk, now able to move faster. They saw only a few small animals, raccoons, opossums, rabbits, squirrels, others Matt couldn't identify. The squirrels vanished with the light; the nocturnal raccoons and opossums occasionally forced the column to halt, seeking concealment in the brush alongside the trail. The moonlight silvered the trail; Matt looked for tracks of people, but also for big cats, wolves, and bears. He found only a few moccasin tracks, all heading south.

The time was perhaps three o'clock in the morning; the moon had not yet set, but dawn would soon make it necessary to hide. Santiago, now leading, stopped and held his clenched fist overhead.

Matt whispered, "Bring up the others and wait here, Piotr. I'll join Santiago; we'll either wave you up or come back."

There was a new tenseness about them when Matt and Santiago rejoined the patrol.

"There's a cleared field and a house up ahead. No lights, they're not stirring yet. The field's not very big. It's basically a cleared area in the forest with a house in the middle. There's something's growing, but it's too dark to tell what it is. We'll bypass it and hide on the far side. I want to get a better look in daylight, but unless we see Laz or Lee, we keep going."

* * *

DAYBREAK FOUND THEM SPREAD OUT, concealed behind brush a few yards past the edge of the field. Two men, armed with bows and spears, carried hoes out to the field. Laying the bows and arrows aside, they began working among the plants. The spears remained slung across their backs.

Minutes later, Matt signaled to Piotr, who passed the signal on. One by one, the men slipped away into the forest.

The team reassembled half a mile from the small farm, once again near the trail.

"Nobody I recognized. How about the rest of you?"

One by one, the patrol members shook their heads.

"There was no overseer and no one was wearing a collar or restraints that I could see. They also had weapons, so they aren't slaves."

"Matt, just because some people keep slaves doesn't mean they all do. According to what I remember from history, only a few could actually afford slaves. Maybe this is one of the poor ones."

"Could be, Piotr. We'll move on a little farther, then lay up for the day; just keep your eyes peeled, we don't want to be spotted now."

The team moved away through the trees. An hour later they found a thick covert.

The rest of the day passed as had the day before. The sentries saw no one.

Moving out at dusk, they headed farther south.

* * *

THE NEXT FARM WAS DIFFERENT. The farmhouse was larger, not unlike the blockhouses they intended to build for Home. The surrounding fields were much wider too.

"There's a light on that second floor, a fireplace or maybe a candle. There aren't any lights on the bottom. If that part even has windows, I don't see them."

"The fields are big enough that they'll need more people to work them. Matt, if they've got slaves, maybe they keep them on the bottom floor. I don't see any stairs, but there's a ladder by the railing up there on the second floor. They probably let it down during the day."

"I expect you're right. Anyway, I want to do the same thing we did last night, lie up on the other side. We'll watch for a while, but we've got to start back tomorrow night. We've got a little information, not much, but the fact that everything is so spread out is important. We can raid one of the farms and be gone before anyone else knows about it."

* * *

THERE WAS no question about what they saw when the sun grew bright the following day.

Two men came out onto a veranda on the second floor. Looking around, they lowered the ladder, then one climbed down. Bracing the ladder, he nodded to the man above. Seven other men filed through the door and awkwardly climbed down the ladder. An eighth man followed, carrying a bow. He had a quiver of arrows at his waist and a spear slung across his back.

"Those are slaves; they're tied to a long strap, just like the captives in that village we raided."

"I don't see much chance of capturing one of those slaves, Matt. You still don't want to raid this place?"

"I've been thinking, Piotr. There's only one man with weapons. Two others are workers, but they're not tied. The rest are linked to that strap. We do almost everything outdoors, so what would anyone else be doing in the house? Wouldn't they be out here working, or at least supervising?"

"Maybe not, Matt. This many people will need someone to feed them. Could be a man, maybe a woman, maybe more than one. There's smoke coming from the chimney, so someone's in there. It will take time to cook the next meal."

"That overseer and those two working by themselves are probably the only free men on the place, Piotr. If we killed them, we could take the others with us. Spread out the way the farms are, it would take time before anyone realized there had been a raid. They'd have to get people together, too, so I figure we'd have half a day before anyone came after us. We'd have to travel fast, but we could do this. There are seven captives, we could take the woman, women, too. The boat can carry sixteen people so we won't have any trouble crossing the seaway.

"This is only the second farm we've seen, the first one that's keeping slaves. We don't know anything about their mines or industry, but that arrowhead tells us they've got them. We haven't seen any sign of organized enemy forces and no one seems to move around at night. The way I see it, our best chance to get information is to rescue the slaves.

"We'll shoot the overseer and the workers, take the slaves with us. I'm sure Colin and Lilia would like to talk to the woman, or women. What the fieldworkers don't know, the women likely will. We don't have enough to feed them, so we'll have to loot the place. The fieldworkers can carry everything we take."

"Sounds good, Matt; how do you want to do this?" Piotr asked.

"You and Santiago hide near the house. You're the stoppers in case the rest of us miss one."

"What if those two guys are trusties or freedmen, Matt? They might be former slaves."

"Can we take the chance, Piotr? If someone gets away, he'll warn the others.

"Matt, I don't see any weapons on those two. Only the overseer is armed. I think that if you take him out, the rest will be easy. We can watch the other pair and if they try to run, Marc and Michel will shoot then. If they head for the house, Santiago and I will ambush them before they can get inside. You plan to burn the house anyway, right?"

"That's what I was thinking, Piotr. We can make it look like this was a slave uprising. Put the bodies inside and burn the place. Even if someone sees the smoke, I doubt they can put out the fire."

"Matt, if the other two are freedmen, would the slaves kill them?"

"Good point, Piotr. No, probably not. The slaves might take them along to keep them from warning others, but they probably wouldn't kill them. If there were more bodies than expected, that might cause suspicion. All right, we'll try to bring them out too.

"Okay, we've got a plan. Piotr, you and Santiago hide by the house, signal us when you're ready. I'll take out the overseer. If the workers run for the woods, Marc and Michel will deal with them. As soon as the overseer is down, go up the ladder. If anyone heads for the house, you shoot them. Make sure the door doesn't get blocked. I'd rather not burn anyone alive, but we can't leave witnesses. Did I miss anything?"

"Hopefully we won't have to kill anyone except the overseer," Piotr said.

Matt nodded, then moved off with Marc and Michel. Piotr and Santiago slipped away, working their way around behind the house. They would approach, using the house for cover.

Their pace was slow. Occasionally they crawled, the rest of the time they crept on their bellies.

Two hours later, they were ready.

* * *

MATT WAS WATCHING for Piotr's signal, so needed only seconds to arrow the overseer where he stood watching the forest. Even as he collapsed, Matt had a new arrow ready on the string.

None of the workers noticed.

Piotr and Santiago slipped to the ladder and climbed, watching the door above.

As they disappeared through the door, someone finally realized the overseer had fallen. The men stood upright and stared at the body.

Matt watched them as he walked over to Marc.

"Keep your eyes peeled, this isn't over yet. You go talk to the two freedmen, if that's what they are. Michel keeps watching the road, backup in case we have a problem. I'll talk to the slaves."

Marc nodded, then walked slowly toward the two freedmen, now standing near the slaves. He held his bow loosely at his side, the arrow in the same hand that held the bow. He did not look threatening, but even so, he could have the arrow ready in seconds.

Matt walked up to the slaves. The attack had gone well.

But it wouldn't be over until they were safely across the seaway.

* * *

WHEN YOU'RE ready to keep reading, Home is available in ebook, print, and audio formats from Amazon.

ABOUT THE AUTHOR

Jack Knapp grew up in Louisiana and joined the Army after graduating from high school. He served three tours in Germany and traveled throughout western Europe before retiring. His current circle of friends and acquaintances, many of them fellow members of Mensa, live on every continent except Antarctica. Jack graduated from the University of Texas at El Paso before beginning his second career, teaching science.

Always an avid reader, he took naturally to writing. He's experimented with ESP (The Wizards Series) and woodcraft/survivalism. The deep woods of Louisiana were his playground, the setting for his Darwin's World Series. He's a knight of the Society for Creative Anachronism, so combat scenes involving swords, spears, and bows and arrows are reality based.

Recent novels examine the challenges humanity will face when we begin to spread out into space. Beginning with a startup company building the first practical spacecraft (The Ship), to growing a business in space while overcoming Earth-based obstacles (NFI: New Frontiers, Inc), to humanity's first contact with a non-human species (NEO: Near Earth Objects and BEMs: Bug Eyed Monsters) the novels are largely based on current events. A fifth novel in the New Frontiers Series, MARS: the Martian Autonomous Republic of Sol, is due out early in 2017.

Jack's boundless imagination is evident in all his books.

How imaginative? You'll have to read his novels to find out!

[f]

Made in United States
North Haven, CT
16 September 2023

41635433R00243